MEAT

DANE COBAIN

Cover Design by Larch Gallagher
Illustrations by Steve Woodcock
Edited by Pam Elise Harris

CONTENTS

BEFORE THE STORM

THE SIGN SAID: WELCOME TO SUNNYVALE.

It was a large sign, the size of a family car, and it was showing its age. The passing vehicles had kicked up the dust from the road, which had reacted with the rain and trickled down its façade in little rivers, leaving a trail of sediment behind. Some of the kids from the village had taken potshots at it with their BB guns, leaving angry welts in the surface of the metal. It was plastered with bird shit and the facility's cartoon mascots – all animals, of course – looked like they were suffocating beneath the weight of it all. Sunnyvale's tagline was right there beneath it: *The Home of Good Food*.

Tom Copeland stared at the sign as it grew larger in the windscreen, floated softly past on the passenger side and then disappeared as the path rolled away beneath them. Calling it a road would have been like comparing a burger van to a McDonald's. At best, it was a narrow dirt track that had been worn into the grass by the passage of vehicles and time. Copeland was glad he was in the back of a Land Rover and not on foot or bouncing up and down in his Vauxhall Corsa.

It had been an unusual day so far. This was his first time visiting the facility, and he was following the strict instructions that John MacDonald had given him when he was offered the job. He'd met the three men he was sharing the Land Rover with in the car park of the Red Lion.

"You'll need to hitch a lift until you're given security clearance," MacDonald had explained. "If you don't have a key card, you can't get in."

The Land Rover hit a bump in the road and the driver, a

dour-faced Scot with a bristly ginger beard, smacked the steering wheel with the palm of his hand and shouted, "Come on, ya bastard."

Copeland turned his face to the window again. He was sitting in the back behind the passenger seat because it was the only seat left when they'd picked him up. There had been no time for introductions. That had come later, once the Land Rover had started to worm its way through the back roads and, eventually, the countryside. Sunnyvale was tucked away in a natural dip in the Chiltern Hills, a good ten miles away from the nearest major town or village. There was plenty of time for them to talk during the commute.

The driver had introduced himself as Big Jim Benton, and Copeland had made an immediate mental note not to mess with the guy. Big Jim had a mess of scars poking out from beneath his fiery beard, deep, sunken eyes and a fat face. He was built like a brick shithouse thanks to twelve years of professional hooliganism and ten years before that of amateur street fights in downtown Leith. His right arm was a mesh of tattoos, and they caught and reflected the sunlight when he hung it out of the window. His hair had started to recede and he had a small mole on the left side of his face. He was a little overweight, but he was far from obese. The excess was from the cheese, the beer and the kebab meat, and it clung mostly to his face, his waist and his stomach. It was the kind of bulk that belonged to professional wrestlers, a slowly cultivated weight that came in handy when he needed to use it. He could turn it into a weapon when he got in tussles with unexpected vandals or trespassers. It's what his job was all about.

The passenger seat was taken up by Big Jim's second-in-command, an Irishman called Darragh O'Rourke. He wasn't as muscular as Big Jim, but he had the look of a wiry street dog with a bruised muzzle. He wore his greasy brown hair down to his shoulders, where it grazed his skin and brought blackheads and spots out in angry welts. He had a disconcerting habit of reaching beneath his Kevlar jacket and scratching at the skin, then bringing his hands back out and investigating his fingernails for blood and pus. He also bit the damn things, which Copeland thought was nothing short of cannibalism.

"Darragh's from Belfast, ye ken," Jim said.

"That's right," the Irishman confirmed. "I came over to Liverpool during the recession and ended up moving here for work."

"Ah worked with Darragh afore Sunnyvale," Jim continued. "Eh's a good lad, ye ken. Eh's goat a dog. Ye'll like tha, Mr. Vet Man."

"Yeah?" Copeland said, raising an eyebrow. He'd never much cared for dogs, but he was socially adjusted enough to know when he was expected to say something more. "What breed?"

"She's a little Jack Russell called Milly," O'Rourke said. "She's got a lot of energy. The missus says it's good practise for when we have kids."

"Take mah advice," Jim grunted. "Git yeself tha snip afore it's too late. Ah cannae stand wee bairns. Ah'd rather stick ma dick in a blender thun huvtae raise some wee shite ah didnae want in tha first place."

"I'll bear that in mind," O'Rourke replied, but he was laughing.

The Land Rover's final passenger sat to Copeland's right, slouching back against the leather seats. He couldn't have been out of his teens. He was an Englishman from Bootle with a thick accent who looked as out of place in his security gear as a bum in a shirt and tie. He had short black hair with zigzags shaved into the back of it, as well as big lips, big ears and a massive nose that looked as though it had been broken a dozen times. The kid's face reminded Copeland of a cross between a cauliflower and a bowling ball.

The young man nodded at him. "First day?" he asked.

Copeland nodded, then flashed a glance at the man's name badge. "Sure is, Chase," he said. "The first day of the rest of my life."

"Yeah," Chase replied. "Something like that. What are you doing here, anyway? You working the line?"

"I'm a veterinarian."

"Jesus," O'Rourke said. "What the shite are you doing at Sunnyvale?"

"What do you think?" Copeland replied.

That killed the conversation, at least until Big Jim hit a button on the radio. He'd matured into adulthood while grunge was on the rise and was still listening to Pearl Jam and Alice in Chains all these years later. Kurt Cobain was dead. Layne Staley was dead. Chris Cornell was dead. And in a lonely hotel room somewhere, Eddie Vedder was shitting himself at the prospect of being next.

As they cruised towards the entrance to the complex, they were listening to L7, an all-female riot grrrl band. Benton was nodding along to the beat, the feminism wasted on a man with a Hibs tattoo and a history of casual domestic violence, but O'Rourke was lying back in his seat with his eyes and his ears closed, and Chase looked like he'd tried to swallow a pickled onion without bothering to chew it.

Tom Copeland looked at himself in the rear-view and took stock of what he saw there. Back in the day, when he'd been running his own practice instead of "working for the man" on a factory farm, he'd shaved every morning and gone to great lengths to make sure that he smelled of expensive cologne. But he'd lost all that when he'd been dumb enough to steal ketamine from storage. His partner had called him out on it and given him two options: either sign over his share in the company or be reported to the police. For Copeland, that was no choice at all.

A shadow passed across his face as he stared at the mirror. It was an ordinary face with a large forehead and a receding hairline. He had short black hair that flicked up from his head because of the way he slept, and he had thin, weedy eyebrows that looked like he waxed them, although he didn't. He also had big, flat ears that hung to the side of his head like two strips of bacon, but his face wasn't fat and neither was his body. He kept himself in shape, but it didn't come easy to him. And he'd let himself go since Linda had left him all alone in the big, empty house that he could no longer afford.

When he thought about stuff, he started squinting, and he saw from the mirror that he was squinting then. He was a good guy. He *knew* he was. But he'd made some bad decisions, and sometimes he felt like an asshole. But he did his best, especially for the animals. His fellow humans chose to be evil and corrupt. The animals had no choice.

Copeland had only stolen the drugs because a very unpleasant man had forced him to do it. He recognised the man by sight – he'd seen him in the practice's waiting room – but he didn't know his name. The name didn't matter too much when he had his metaphorical knife to Copeland's throat and his mouth full of threats against his family. The irony was that when he'd been caught in the act and kicked out of his own veterinary practice, Copeland had lost his family anyway. But at least no one had lost their life.

Copeland looked away from the mirror. A stilted silence hung heavy on the air. He fiddled uncomfortably with his seatbelt and shifted position to try to get comfortable.

"Jim," O'Rourke said. "Be a top man and put something else on."

"Like what?"

"How about some grime?" Chase said.

"Fuck ya grime, ye wee gobshite," Big Jim snapped. He flashed a glance at Copeland in the rear-view. "Chasey boy thinks eh's a rapper, ye ken."

Copeland smiled. "Is that so?"

"Yeah," Chase replied. "Opened for Devilman a couple of months back."

"And how come you're working at Sunnyvale?"

"I've got no choice," Chase said. "I need the money. Used to work as a labourer, and before that I was at a warehouse. Then I saw Sunnyvale was hiring and I thought I'd give it a shot. Besides, women love the uniform."

"Aye," Jim conceded. "That's true. But ah'd appreciate it if ye could keep yer trap shut fae a while. Ah cannae be dein wi yer chat today, ye ken? Ah've goat a hangover. If ah hear another peep, ah'm gonnae drop ye off and let ye walk tae work."

Chase opened his mouth to reply and then thought better off it. Copeland stepped in to fill the silence. "An Englishman, an Irishman and a Scotsman," he said. "What is this, some sort of joke?"

Big Jim fixed him with another penetrating stare in the rear-view, but he said nothing. A hundred yards or so in front of them, two of Jim's men were working a checkpoint. A high chain-link fence stretched to the left and the right of the checkpoint as far as the eye could see, disappearing into the trees and following the curve of the land. The fence was festooned with "danger of death" signs, their black lightning bolt insignias popping out from their bright yellow backgrounds. Other signs, white ones this time, warned of guard dogs patrolling the premises. Curlicues of barbed wire lined the top of the fence. Copeland spotted the feathered remains of a bird – a pigeon, perhaps – caught amongst the metal.

"Welcome to Sunnyvale," O'Rourke murmured.

"Aye," Big Jim added. He glanced at Copeland in the mirror again and caught his eye. "Ah'm guessin' this'll be yer first look at the place. It's a shithole, but it's our shithole."

He idled the car to a stop at the barrier and leaned his head out of the window. "Open the gate, ye whoresons," he shouted. "It's me, Big Jim."

One of the men on the gate shouted an acknowledgement and held his thumb up. The other raised the gate and waved them through. Copeland got a good look at the gatekeepers while Jim was revving the engine and easing the vehicle back into its slow, inexorable crawl towards the complex. They were wearing army greens with Kevlar vests and heavy truncheons on their belts.

Chase caught Copeland's eye and said, "Sunnyvale's got the best security this side of the Mersey. Top lads."

"Why so much security?"

"It's more than my job's worth to tell you that," Chase said. "Especially not with Big Jim at the wheel."

"Aye," Jim said. "Eh'll find oot fae hisself soon enough."

Copeland nodded. "I'm looking forward to it," he said. "I love a challenge."

"Is that why you're here?" O'Rourke asked. "The challenge?"

"Something like that," Copeland said. He sighed. "Ask me about it some other time."

The Land Rover was slowing again, and Copeland peered over O'Rourke's shoulder and out through the windscreen. They were approaching something else, another mess of metal. As the vehicle drove closer, scattering dusty pebbles every which way across the dead ground, the terrain levelled out. At the same time, a wave of brutal fragrance pierced the vehicle and Copeland started coughing.

It was the kind of smell that lingered in the nostrils. There was a certain stickiness to it, like second-hand cigarette smoke. It reminded Copeland of a kid he'd gone to school with who reeked of starch, fat and vinegar because his parents owned a chip shop. Sunnyvale didn't smell like starch or vinegar, but it did smell like fat. It also smelled like sweat and fear, blood and bile. There was a not-so-subtle hint of rotting flesh and a fishy aroma that put Copeland in mind of bad sushi. It also smelled like desperation. It was a depressing smell, and Copeland couldn't help turning his nose up at it.

"That's the famous Sunnyvale stench," Chase said.

"Do people get used to it?"

"Nah," Chase replied. "They just accept it. Ain't no use holding your nose, pal. You've just got to get on with it. It's part of the job. It's what we get paid for."

"Smells like shit," Copeland observed.

O'Rourke laughed from the passenger seat. "Smells like a whole lot more than that," he said. "But Chase is right. That smell won't go away no matter what you do."

"It gets in yer heid," Jim said. This time, he didn't look back at Copeland in the rear-view. His eyes were firmly on the road ahead. They'd reached the second mess of metal, and now they were closer, it was clear what they were looking at.

"Is that another checkpoint?" Copeland asked.

"Aye," Jim replied. "It's like Chase seid. Sunnyvale's goat the best security this side ay the Mersey."

Big Jim reached forward and turned the music off. The atmosphere in the Land Rover had changed, probably because the great facility was looming in front of them on the other side of the formidable fence. It blocked the sun and cast the approach into shadow, reminding Copeland of a

Transylvanian castle in some old vampire movie.

The hairs on the back of his neck stood on end. *It's a far cry from the old practice in Chalfont St. Peter,* he thought. It was followed by a second, more urgent thought, something that came from somewhere deep within him. It was a primal thought, like the urge to eat or drink or ejaculate, and it came on suddenly and without warning.

We're being watched, he thought.

SUNNYVALE CEO JOHN MACDONALD was standing on a cast-iron gantry. When he'd signed off on the final designs for the complex, they'd featured his own little addition. MacDonald had arranged for the workers to build the gantry outside his office, on the top floor of the admin building, so he could step outside and walk around all four corners of the building and up on to the roof.

It made him feel even more powerful than usual. Standing there on a sunny day, as the light dispelled the shadows that seemed to haunt the place, he liked to watch his employees as they scuttled past like little worker ants bringing food back to the hive. Which in a sense was what they were.

At forty-six years old, the CEO of Sunnyvale had seen enough of life to walk with a crippled confidence, like a dog who's been kicked so many times that he knows he can always get back up. He had messy hair and a grey goatee, steely eyes and a good physique, the kind that's been carefully shaped from middle-aged man fat by thrice weekly sessions with a personal trainer. He looked like the businessman that he was. Some of his staff joked that he looked like Richard Branson's younger brother, and the resemblance was definitely there, in the hair and the eyes and the jawline. But as far as John MacDonald knew, they were unrelated.

On that day, he was wearing a sharp Italian suit with a pair of leather shoes. They were impractical when walking around the facility, which is why he only ever wore them in his office, substituting them for a pair of overalls and safety boots when he had to leave his sanctuary. He kept another pair of shoes, some plain black loafers, in the glove compartment of his Bentley Continental, so he could drive home without getting pig shit on the driver-side floor mat.

The car still reeked of Sunnyvale, though. There weren't enough scented trees in the world to hide that smell. *The smell of death.*

It looked like life was moving on as normal, at least for the staff. The animals weren't so lucky, but they were just numbers on a spreadsheet. It was MacDonald's job to boost those numbers and to increase the final figure in the little green cell marked "net profit." But his employees were still scuttling, the machines were still running and the trucks were still making their way slowly to and from the complex. After being waved through Sunnyvale's two layers of security, of course.

MacDonald didn't smoke and he never had, but sometimes he wished that he did so he could lean over the railings and survey his domain while enjoying a Cuban cigar. Instead, he had to make do with a hot cup of coffee, which he cradled delicately as he walked the perimeter. To the north, the lake and the sustainable fishery with its underwater cages and its 28,000 rainbow trout and salmon. To the north-east, the recycling plant and the refuse pit, not quite in the water but pretty close to it. They'd almost been forced to redesign the complex to place the plant outside, but that would have drastically affected security and MacDonald, with the help of the best lawyers that Sunnyvale's money could buy, had successfully challenged the legislators and won the battle to keep the trash inside.

"If we build the plant inside the gates," MacDonald had argued, "then we can control the conditions and leave the lake cleaner than it was when we arrived. If we build the plant outside the gates, it'll push up costs and force us to import water from elsewhere. There'll be more lorries on the road, worse traffic, more pollution, greater costs and less of a profit for the local council."

That final point was the one that hit home, as MacDonald knew it would be, and they'd won the motion by eight votes to five. And no one was any the wiser about the money that had changed hands and bought the decision. Nor did they know the true water quality in the life-giving lake that was nestled amongst the Chilterns like a puddle in the furrow of a field.

MacDonald reached the north-east corner of the building and hit a right. He increased his pace as the wind picked up and blew the stench of dead flesh from the slaughterhouse, an imposing green building built from breeze blocks and corrugated metal. It was the largest slaughterhouse in the country and one of the biggest in Europe. It was the thorn in Sunnyvale's bloody crown. While MacDonald looked at the lifeless building like a father looking at a child, the smell of it made him want to vomit. It seemed to follow him as he walked along the gantry towards the south side of the building.

He paused at the corner and looked out at the livestock shed. The building was even bigger than the slaughterhouse, and if his memory was correct, there were approximately 6,000 cows and 9,000 sheep cooped up beneath the harsh artificial lights, many of them in small cages that stopped them from moving and caused lesions to grow. It was a shame, he knew, but it was necessary. The people needed meat, and they didn't care how they got it.

MacDonald reached the corner of the building and hit another right, heading west across the complex and moving on from the livestock shed. He paused halfway along the gantry and stared at the facility's only entrance, where Big Jim's security team was clustered around a Land Rover. He held a hand over his eyes and squinted in the direction of the gate, but he couldn't make out who the visitors were. He made a mental note to ask Carol to order a pair of binoculars.

Whoever it was at the entrance, they didn't look like trouble. Jim's team was the best private security team that money could buy. MacDonald knew this because he was familiar with the company's finances. He knew exactly how much each of his employees cost on a monthly basis, but Jim's team was worth its weight in gold and they had a big tick next to each of their names to remind everyone how irreplaceable they were. The butchers, the cleaners and the deliverymen were all disposable, but the security? They were as important to Sunnyvale as the machinery.

MacDonald paused for a moment and leant on the safety rail. He watched as the security team waved the Land Rover through. The vehicle trundled along the dusty path and into the car park, which was unusually full for such a boring, normal day. They were taking on supplies, mostly grain, straw and sawdust, and the asphalt was full of the big green lorries that Lehmann's used. The Germans were the only third-party that was allowed access to the site, and even then they were asked firmly but respectfully to stay in the car park and away from the rest of the facility.

MacDonald watched the Land Rover park and recognised Big Jim's fiery mane from a distance as he climbed out of the vehicle. A little more relaxed, he continued his stroll along the gantry to the admin building's south-west corner, where he was afforded a view of what the staff referred to as the chicken shack. Like the slaughterhouse, it was big, green and made from breeze blocks and corrugated iron, but it smelled less like death and more like chicken shit. It was perched over a deep hole in the ground, the site of a former quarry, and used a radical new design to ferry the chicken shit deep beneath the building, where it was stored in a reservoir. Perhaps one day it could be sold as fertiliser, but right then it was just a giant mound of guano.

The chicken shack was split in two, with one half of the building dedicated to the broiler chickens, the rapid turnover birds that were pumped full of hormones and forced to grow at three times their usual rate so they could be served on dinner plates. The other half was for the laying hens, which were cramped into small cages with barely enough room to stretch their wings. All told, the building housed over a hundred thousand birds when it was at maximum capacity, which it usually was. John MacDonald didn't believe in wastage.

The last leg of his walk took him past the pigsty. They were bigger animals and slightly less docile than the cows and the sheep. MacDonald had heard that pigs were as intelligent as dogs, which didn't surprise him. The devious little bastards kept trying to escape, and they posed him more of a problem than the rest of the animals put together. They'd even reduced their stock to just 1,200 pigs, which was down 30% since the big opening, but it made the place more manageable. It also made the place smell slightly less like pig shit, which could only be a good thing.

MacDonald sped up a little as he walked along the rest of the gantry and then re-entered the building. He looked around his office. His mahogany desk was as clean as ever, though his in-tray was starting to grow again, and his dual computer screens took up more space than anything else. His machine was locked and scrolling through the day's news while it idled. He swiped the mouse and tapped a few keys to enter his password, and he'd just settled in to check his emails when the phone on his desk rang.

He put the call on loudspeaker and said, "Yes? What is

it?"

"It's Big Jim, sir," the caller said. He recognised Carol Rawlings' voice instantly. It was husky from too many Rothmans and not enough sleep. "He says your visitor is here."

"Visitor?" MacDonald barked. "What visitor?"

"Tom Copeland," Rawlings said. "The new veterinarian. You asked Big Jim to bring him in."

"Ah, yes," MacDonald said. "I remember now."

"Do you want me to bring him up?"

"No," MacDonald replied. "I'll come down and show him around."

Rawlings let out a delicate little cough, which crackled and sent waves of static through the phone line. "Sir," she said. "You have a call in twenty minutes with–"

"So reschedule it," MacDonald said. "Screw 'em. I'm going to meet Dr. Copeland. Best to start off on the right foot, eh?"

"If you say so, sir."

MacDonald picked up a pen from the pot on his desk and rolled it across the knuckles on his left hand. It was a habit he had when he was deep in thought, and Rawlings had learned to recognise the sound of its shrill click-click as it flitted its way across his knucklebones.

"Can you find some other time for that call, please, Carol?" he asked. "And anything else that might be in my diary. I have a feeling I'm going to need to spend the day with Dr. Copeland."

"Sure."

"Thanks," he said. Then he put the phone down.

Eleven seconds later, he picked it back up and hit the redial. He started speaking as soon as Carol answered, cutting her off at her friendly, professional "hello."

"Carol," he said, "I just had a thought."

"What?" she asked. "What is it?"

"I could murder a cup of coffee and a bacon butty," he said. "Would you mind?"

MacDonald met Copeland in the car park, where Big Jim's security team was still keeping him company. The Scotsman himself had disappeared, as had his second-in-command and his new recruit.

Good, MacDonald thought. *It's as it should be. They have a job to do.*

He tossed his half-empty coffee cup into the cast-iron trash can beside the ashtrays in the smoking area, walked past the benches that he'd reluctantly installed after an employee petition and approached Tom Copeland, who was slouching nonchalantly. MacDonald shook Copeland's hand and introduced himself, then told him to follow him across the gravel towards the admin building.

"I'll get someone to give you the full tour a little later," MacDonald said. "There's, uh, a lot to see."

Copeland nodded at him. "I can't wait," he said. "Nice place you've got here."

MacDonald stared at him for a moment, taking in the lines of his face and the thin bead of sweat that was trickling slowly down his cheek, losing itself in the stubble of his five o'clock shadow. He scrunched up his nose involuntarily against the stench. Some of the workers called it the Sunnyvale Scowl, and it was an automatic self-defence mechanism. It wore off after a couple of hours or so, and every subsequent exposure seemed to lessen its effect. It was the sure sign of someone who was new to the facility.

"Don't worry," MacDonald said. "You'll get used to it."

"What?" Copeland asked.

"The smell."

"Oh no," he said. He looked mortified, like he'd been caught with his trousers down by a film crew. "No, it's not that, it's just–"

"It's always the smell," MacDonald continued. "It hits people when they first come here. Why do you think you were interviewed offsite?"

"I did wonder."

"The truth is, we don't like strangers," MacDonald said. "We're secretive here. We run a tight ship. You'll have to sign a confidentiality agreement before you officially start and receive your gate pass."

"Where do I sign?" Copeland asked.

MacDonald smiled at him and said, "Follow me." He led the way along the asphalt, out of the car park and along the red gravel path towards the admin building. The path was red for two reasons. The first was that it brightened the place up, although it also looked like a river of blood. The second was that the red gravel had been discounted.

MacDonald explained all this and more as he led Copeland along the path towards the admin building. He didn't explain what the gantry was for, even though there was no way for Copeland to miss it, but he did check that no one was walking his route along the top of the building. There were rules against that. It was his place.

But nobody was up there, and he continued to talk shop with Copeland as he led him through the revolving door of the admin building and into the large reception area. In contrast to the rest of the site, which looked and smelled like a pile of shit, the reception was light and airy with working air conditioning and an opulent take on interior décor. It was painted in light blues and yellows with cream upholstery.

"The cleaners have a devil of a job," MacDonald explained. "But white looks so much more impressive, don't you think?"

"I guess."

"Make sure you wipe your feet there," MacDonald said,

gesturing to a rugged black mat which had seen better days. He wiped his own shoes on the surface, waited for Copeland to do the same and then led the way across to reception where little Jill MacDonald, his eighteen-year-old niece, was learning the ropes from Maude Harrison, the chief receptionist who ran the admin building with an iron fist.

Maude was a good-looking woman in her mid-to-late thirties with blonde hair that hung down over her eyes and a welcoming smile that helped her to make friends with barely any effort. Her eyes were sunken slightly with crow's feet from her contagious laughter, which had a habit of passing around the admin building like a Mexican wave. She was a much-loved employee with no enemies, and half of the guys had a crush on her. That's why she took extra care to flash the wedding ring on her left hand when she saw someone's gaze creeping away from her eyes and towards her breasts, which is exactly what happened when Copeland locked eyes with her.

He smiled at her and she looked away.

"Morning, ladies," MacDonald said. Maude was on a call, but MacDonald knew damn well that she'd mastered the art of paying attention to two conversations at once. "I've got a new recruit for you. This is Dr. Copeland."

"Hi," Copeland said, holding out his hand. "Call me Tom." Jill took his hand and shook it limply, like she was grasping the slimy limb of some sea monster.

"Tom needs to sign the NDA," MacDonald explained. "I wondered if you'd be good enough to print a copy and walk him through it. We'll also need to take his photo and print him an ID so he can get past security."

"Great," Jill said. "So... how do I do that?"

MacDonald sighed benignly like the impatient uncle that he was. He was about to answer when Maude held her hand over the speaker of the telephone and said, "The NDA is on the server. I showed you where to find the onboarding kit the other day, remember? As for the ID, get a photo on that phone of yours and we'll sort it out later. I'm sure Mr. MacDonald and Dr. Copeland are very busy."

Maude took her hand away and carried on with her phone call as though nothing had happened, and MacDonald tipped her a friendly wink as his niece tried to find her way around the facility's archaic filesystem. He engaged his new recruit with some of his patented patter to pass the time while the girl found the files and printed off a couple of copies.

"Here you go," she said, handing the sheaf of paper to her uncle. "One for our records and one for, uh…"

"Tom," Copeland reminded her.

MacDonald handed him a copy of the paperwork and asked his niece for a pen. "A black one," he said.

"Is it all here?" Copeland asked.

"It's all there," MacDonald said. "It's pretty standard, but I'll give you some time to read through it before you sign on the dotted line. Better make it today, though, eh? Otherwise we can't process your badge and you'll be stuck carpooling with Big Jim."

"He's not so bad."

"Aye, ye wee laddie," MacDonald said, pulling off a passable impression of the Scotsman's accent. "Yeh've goat tae get used tae his way o' speaking though, ye ken."

Jill laughed, but Maude was clearly less impressed. She glared at the boss as she worked the phone call, and MacDonald gave her another wink. She was the epitome of cantankerousness, but her attitude entertained MacDonald and so she'd been allowed to stay, while just about any other employee would've been given their marching orders if they tried to get wise with the CEO.

"We'd better get your photo," MacDonald said. He

stood aside slightly so that Jill could line up her smartphone and take a mugshot. Jill fired off a couple of photos and then hustled back behind her desk to copy them across to her computer.

"So you're the new veterinarian," Jill said.

Copeland nodded at her and flashed a smile. She was an attractive girl, although perhaps it was just her youth and the way she wore her makeup. Her hair was long, brown and straight, tied in a ponytail that reached halfway down her back. Her eyebrows had been shaped by a professional and her face was plastered with expensive foundation and a little rouge. But she was also still a kid, too happy-go-lucky for a place like Sunnyvale. Even after just a couple of seconds, Copeland could see why her uncle had agreed to employ her.

"Can you teach me?" she asked. "You know, to be a vet?"

"It's not that easy," he replied. "It took me five years of full-time education."

"So teach me the basics," Jill insisted.

"Most of it comes down to cutting their balls off and putting them to sleep when they're riddled with cancer," Copeland said. "But if Mr. MacDonald says it's fine then I'm sure you can help me out on a few of my patrols."

Jill grinned and turned to her uncle. "Can I, Uncle John?" she asked. "I could help with the animals."

"Sure, sure," MacDonald said, waving a hand impatiently. "Just give him a couple of weeks to settle in. We've got a big backlog that he's going to need to get on top of. After that, if you can both fit it in around the rest of your work, go ahead. In the meantime, we're going to need that badge."

"Of course," Jill said, flashing her hands across her keyboard. "Leave it with me and come back in an hour or so, okay?"

"Great," MacDonald replied. "We'll leave you to it. Tom and I are going to take a look at the facilities."

"The facilities?"

"Yeah," MacDonald said. "You want to see where you'll be working, right?"

"Of course," Copeland said. "What about the contracts?"

"You can read them later," MacDonald replied. "Our last veterinarian left us in something of a hurry, so there's plenty for you to do."

"I'll want to inspect the animals at some point to get a feel for what I'm dealing with."

"We can arrange that," MacDonald said. "But first, you're going to need to do a stock check and see if there's anything you need us to order in. It can take some time for supplies to arrive and so that's going to be your top priority."

"Sounds good," Copeland said. He clapped his hands together and flashed the hint of a smile. "Let's do this."

"THIS IS IT," MacDonald said. "What do you think?"

Copeland looked around the room and tried to figure out how best to answer. MacDonald had led him back out of the admin building and along the gravel path to the north.

"This is the storage hall," MacDonald explained, waving his hand towards the building. In normal circumstances, it might have been imposing. Compared to the rest of the facility, it was a stunted dwarf of a thing, although it did shine in the sunlight. The largest part of the building was the silo that stored the grain.

"How tall is that?" Copeland asked.

"Eighty feet above ground and thirty below," MacDonald replied. "It stores enough grain to keep us running for a couple of months. Comes in useful when there's a shortage."

"I can imagine," Copeland said. "Does that happen often?"

"Not really. We run a tight ship."

The front entrance to the storage depot was far less glamorous than the revolving doors of the admin building. It was a simple set of steel doors with a high-tech scanner attached so that employees could gain entry by swiping their ID cards.

"We use layered security," MacDonald explained. "Your card will get you access to the veterinary supplies and the surgery, but if you try to go somewhere off-limits... well, you won't be able to get in, and Big Jim and his team will take you into a little dark room with no windows and ask you a couple of questions."

MacDonald smiled. Copeland wasn't sure how to take it, so he shrugged it off and followed MacDonald into the building. He tried to memorise the route they took, knowing it would eventually be imprinted inside his head and hoping to speed up the process, but it was hopeless. Even though it was one of the smaller buildings, it was still a labyrinth. He tracked a right, two lefts, another right and then a left before giving up. MacDonald must have noticed the look of concern that flashed across his face and disappeared again.

"Don't worry," he said. "There's a rear entrance for the animals, but you'll need security to keep an eye on you when you bring them in. The last thing we need is for an animal to escape."

"Has that happened before?"

"Are you kidding?" MacDonald laughed and paused in front of another door with a reader beneath the handle. He slipped his key card in and waited for the shrill *bip-bip-bip* that meant he'd unlocked it, then lifted the handle and pushed the door open. "It happens all the time. You try keeping the best part of a hundred thousand animals under control. Sometimes I think we should have stuck with the fish."

"Well," Copeland replied, "I'm glad you didn't. If you did, I wouldn't have a job."

"Yeah," MacDonald murmured. His brows were furrowed in concentration as he groped around the inside wall to try to find a light switch. When he found it, he flipped it and something rumbled inside the walls. A second later, a set of harsh panel lights flared into life on the ceiling and MacDonald led Copeland into the surgery.

"Ta-da," he said. "It might not look like much, but welcome to your new home."

Copeland's heart sank. He'd been prepared for this ever since he first saw the job offer. MacDonald ran a tight ship, but he couldn't stop the rumours from getting out. Sunnyvale had a grisly reputation, if only because it was one of the largest facilities in the country, and no self-respecting vet would work there out of choice. Unfortunately for Copeland, he had no self-respect and he had no choice.

The inside of the surgery was bleak and grey, lined with stainless steel surfaces that had seen better days and a variety of industrial machinery. Sunnyvale clearly had the resources they needed to run a top of the line facility, but it had been poorly cared for and Copeland wondered what exactly his predecessor had been doing that left no time for basic maintenance.

"Do you ever get the cleaners in here?" Copeland asked.

"That's it?" MacDonald replied. "I was expecting something a little more... oh, I don't know..."

"No," Copeland said. "It's not that. It's just that I need to work in a sterile environment. This place looks like the back of a kebab van. I mean, look at it."

"Point taken," MacDonald said. He reached down to his belt and unhooked his walkie talkie, then held it up to his mouth and pushed the button. "MacDonald here. I need Fernandez at the surgery. I want this place bleached, disinfected and polished until it shines."

He released the button and there were a few moments of snowy static as the device waited to receive a message from the airwaves. No such message was forthcoming.

MacDonald held the walkie talkie up to his mouth again. "Can anyone fucking hear me?" he asked.

This time, a couple of responses filtered through, including an "aye" from Big Jim and a confirmation from Fernandez on the cleaning team. MacDonald growled something under his breath, but Copeland didn't catch it. Then he clipped the walkie talkie to his belt again.

"Sorry about Jill," he said suddenly, turning around to

look at the veterinarian.

"What?"

"My niece," MacDonald said. "She can be a pain sometimes, but she has a heart of gold. That's why I gave her a job here in the first place. We don't really need her. But she's my niece, you know?"

"I understand."

"I'd appreciate it if you could humour her," MacDonald said. "Keep her busy. Maybe teach her a thing or two."

"I'll try."

"You'd better," MacDonald said. His expression turned sour and he gave Tom Copeland the kind of glare that could curdle milk. He leaned a little closer towards him and added, "I know what happened at your old practice. I know you got caught with your hand in the medicine cupboard. Make sure that doesn't happen here. I'll find out, you know. I always do."

Then he let go of Copeland's arm and turned his back on him, gesturing around the room. "Why don't you take a look around?"

The veterinarian's mouth was hanging wide open, but then he noticed and pulled his jaws shut so fast that his teeth clicked together. He shrugged.

"Don't mind if I do," he said.

Other than the dust and the desperate need for disinfectant, the place was in pretty good shape. The machines were state of the art, way better than anything he'd ever used before, and while its location beside the slaughterhouse was unsettling, it was undoubtedly the best place for it.

Copeland and MacDonald wandered from room to room, assessing the equipment. The vet's new office was on the other side of yet another locked door and while it was a poky little thing with barely enough room to swing a cat, any cat-swinging could take place out in the precinct or in one of the operating rooms. Meanwhile, the tiny office would provide a place to brew a coffee and to catch up with whatever internal emails he'd received.

As though he'd read his mind, MacDonald said, "You won't need to use the computer much. We'll hook you up with a walkie talkie and radio you when you're needed. I'm not going to lie, Tom. We're going to keep you busy."

"I can imagine."

"You used to work at a village practice, correct?"

"Yes indeed," Copeland replied. "A little family affair in Chalfont St. Peter."

"You'll find things are a little different here at Sunnyvale," MacDonald said. "It's not all microchipping puppies and cutting the balls off friendly housecats. Have you ever put your arm inside a cow or treated a chicken that had a little accident with the hot blade beak trimmer?"

"So far, I haven't had the pleasure," Copeland admitted. "But I'm well aware of what I'm getting myself into."

"Hmm," MacDonald said. "I wonder."

There was silence for a moment as Copeland rooted through the storage cupboards and took a mental stock of what they were missing or running short of. He was jotting notes absentmindedly on the back of his unread contract. *Cefpodoxime. Ketamine. Metacam. Noromycin. Thiabendazole.* It looked like the cast of characters from a bad sci-fi novel, and he was only just getting started.

Then MacDonald's radio chirped into life and a crackle of static interrupted the silence. "We've got a K22 at the birthing shed."

The boss picked up the handset and replied, "MacDonald here. Who's this?"

"It's Makon, sir," the voice replied. "From Bovine. You'd better send someone up here, if you've got someone."

"Roger that."

MacDonald dropped the radio back into its holster and then flashed a grin across at Copeland. "You know what that means?" he said. "It's time for your first callout. Do you remember your way back to the admin building?"

"I think so."

"Good," MacDonald said. "I want you to grab what you need and head back, then keep going towards the car park. Cut a left before you get there. I'll have one of my men meet you outside the cow shed."

"Aren't you coming with me?"

"Are you kidding me?" MacDonald laughed. "No, no, I'll head back to the admin building. I don't like to get my hands dirty. Here, take this," he continued, slipping the walkie talkie and its holster from his belt and handing it over like an offering to a gunslinger in an old Western. "I've got a couple more back in my office. Give me a shout once you've finished with the cows and I'll come down to meet you. We'll come back over here, check those contracts and you can sign them when you're ready."

He paused for a moment and then added, like an afterthought, "If you still want to take the job, that is."

***

It was a lonely walk for Tom Copeland, who got lost twice on his way out of the storage hall. He was carrying a leather satchel on his shoulder, which he'd packed with a basic set of emergency medication and which was bouncing uncomfortably to and fro as he walked. It was made even more stressful by the fact that the walkie talkie was still crackling in his hand.

Back outside, he followed the red-gravel path to the south, trying not to gag on the stench that was blowing in from the cesspit. He could hear the sound of an engine from somewhere, a shrill, whiny sound that was too insubstantial to be the drone of a tractor or a combine harvester. The source of the noise became apparent when he rounded the admin building and spotted Big Jim trundling past in some unholy combination of a golf buggy and an off-roader. Even at a distance and with a patina of dust and dirt all over the vehicle, Copeland could make out Sunnyvale's logo on the side of it.

Copeland did as he'd been asked and hit a left before he reached the car park, then followed the path along towards the cow shed. Now that he was closer, he could see that what he'd initially assumed was one building was actually two standing side-by-side, with just a ten-foot gap between them. Close up, it was wide enough to drive a car through. From a distance, the gap was so small that it paled into insignificance.

Will Makon from the Bovine team was a tall, gangly man with curly hair on the top of his head and closely shaved sides that melded in with a wispy little beard. He was wearing a pair of blue overalls that were a size too small for him with mud and muck splattered up the legs. The legs were tucked into a gigantic pair of wellington boots. When the two men stood together, Makon was a full head taller.

"Nice to meetcha, fella," he said.

"Hi," Copeland replied. "Tom Copeland. It looks like I'm going to be your vet for the day."

"I haven't seen you around here before."

"Today's my first day," Copeland said.

"I've not been here long myself," Makon said. "I used to be a boxer, you know."

"I can tell," Copeland said. And it was true. There was something about the kid and the way he held himself. He was skinny but muscular, tall and well-built, and he had the nose and the ears to match.

"Fought a couple of bouts," Makon continued. "Won them, too. Then I was in an accident. Not my fault, of course, but my car was written off and I spent six weeks in the hospital. Came out with a plate in my head and doctor's orders never to box again. Got depressed for a while, you know."

"Well, you would," Copeland said vaguely, wondering why the man was telling him his life story. But then, some people liked to do that. He'd known a lot of them back when he'd co-owned the practice. He was the other way round. He preferred to keep his private life private.

"Still," Makon continued, "I picked myself back up. Found the love of a good woman and all that. Got the job at Sunnyvale. Took up running as well. Now we're getting married and looking at buying a house."

"Good for you," Copeland said, dying a little inside. He'd never liked people. That's why he worked with animals instead. He changed the subject. "So what have you got for me?"

"Come see for yourself." Makon said. "She's this way."

Copeland shifted the bag to his other shoulder and followed Makon through the security door and into the birthing shed. He was ushered into a small entry room with doors to the left and right of it. Makon led the way through the left door and along a short corridor before sliding his key card through a reader and leading Copeland inside.

The vet's involuntary gasp was clearly audible even on top of the noise, which registered at the best part of ninety decibels when the cows were at their loudest. The room was smaller than he'd expected given the building's size from the outside, but it was still packed full of pregnant cows that lay unhappily on the shit-stained floors of their pens or leant against the metal dividers that separated them into little stalls. Seen from a distance, Copeland was hit with an immediate impression of hip bones that poked from their skin like coat hangers through a flimsy shirt. The floor and the walls of the shed were made of concrete, and the cows were lined up in two-by-twelve grids that were separated by waste trenches around the outside and concrete dividers between each group of two dozen cattle. Copeland could see around a half dozen grids, and a little mental arithmetic told him that there were around 150 pregnant cows in the barn, give or take.

The smell in there was unpleasant but not unbearable. The cows were lying on metal grids that were layered over with straw. Their urine drained through the bottom of the grid and into the network of culverts and sluices that literally took the piss. The shit mixed with the straw and formed a faecal mattress that most of the animals were lying in.

Copeland wandered around the perimeter of one of the stalls, taking in the state of the animals. Most of them were heavily pregnant, but there were one or two of them with stomachs that were too distended for a simple pregnancy. Copeland made a tentative diagnosis of malnutrition and trapped gas pending further investigation and moved on.

"So what's the problem?" he asked.

"I'll show you," Makon said. He led Copeland through the concrete labyrinth and deeper into the birthing room. The problem heifer was in the third group of two dozen. By the time they reached it, Copeland had started to get used to the smell, although he'd also started to suffer from the stifling, still air. It wasn't hot in there. If anything, it was cold and calculated, like the inside of a desktop computer after it hasn't been turned on for a couple of hours.

Copeland spotted his patient from a dozen paces away, and he rushed over to it as quickly as he could manage in his smart shoes, which had turned out to be more of a hindrance than a blessing on the factory farm. His destination was one of the thin concrete sluices that carried away the urine. They sank a foot or so into the floor and there was something down there. It moved feebly as it tried to right itself, but the poor little thing was as defenceless as a fly in a spider web. Even if it had been on solid ground, it would have been too young to support itself. It looked like a little red kidney bean.

The calf was a couple of hours old at best and was still covered in the blood and mucus that had eased its fall from its mother's womb. It had placenta plastered to its face and little blind eyes that saw nothing of the horror around it. It was moving its feet like a dog in a daydream, but there was no purchase and the movements were weak and feeble. Too weak and feeble.

Copeland tried to get a better look at it in case there was a breakage or some other injury, but he couldn't see any immediate cause for concern. He leaned down close and scooped the calf out of the concrete channel, then held the tiny creature in his arms as he gave it the once over. "It needs milk," he murmured.

"What?"

Copeland looked up. He'd forgotten that Makon was there, and he wasn't quite sure what the protocol was. Still, he had a job to do. "Which one is the mother?" he asked.

"How should I know?" Makon replied. "Buddy, they don't exactly have names, y'know."

"All right," Copeland replied. "Just give me some space. I'll take it from here."

Makon was only too happy to acquiesce, although he watched warily from a distance as Copeland took his jacket off and wrapped the calf in it. It was barely breathing and visibly shivering, but its vital signs checked out and with a little milk, a warm blanket and some time to recuperate, Copeland thought it'd be just fine.

"Welcome to the world, kid," he murmured.

"So what's the deal?" Makon asked.

"It'll be all right," Copeland said. "It just needs the proper care."

"This ain't a hospital," Makon reminded him. "You make it better and you might save some money, but mark my words. As soon as it's better, it's on his way right back out here to the cattle shed. It'll make a decent bit of veal once it's fattened up a bit."

Copeland hadn't eaten since grabbing a sandwich on his way to the facility, but he'd never felt less hungry.

"It's my job," he said. "I make them healthy, so you can make them into meat."

"Good," Makon replied. "As long as you remember that. Are we done here?"

"Yeah," Copeland said, casting his eyes around the barn. It was a case of picking the right battles, and a whole war could be fought for the cows in this shed alone. But what was the point, after all? They'd only end up in the slaughterhouse.

In Sunnyvale's defence, Copeland had to admit that not all of the animals were suffering. Some of them were just tired and resigned, too lethargic to even flick their tails at the flies that swarmed around their shit. But some were on the other end of the spectrum, suffering from severe mastitis with swollen red teats and crusty sores on their underbellies. It had about as much in common with his old practice as a hospital has in common with a concentration camp.

"So what's next?" Makon asked.

"I'm going to take this little thing off to the surgery and keep an eye on it," Copeland said. "We'll give it some fluids and stick it in the incubator. It should be with its mother, really, but… well, how are we going to tell which one it belongs to?"

"It belongs to the farm," Makon reminded him.

"So it does," Copeland said. "And it's my job to take care of company property."

Copeland nodded at Makon and then turned to the side. He placed the bundle on the floor and rested a foot lightly on it to swaddle the calf in his jacket, then grabbed the walkie talkie from its holster around his waist. He pressed the transmission button.

"Copeland here at the cattle shed," he said. He paused. "Mr. MacDonald, can I meet you outside the admin building? Something's come up. I need to go back to the surgery."

There was silence on the airwaves. Then MacDonald's clipped tones filtered through. His voice was surprisingly clear, as though he was standing there right next to them.

"MacDonald here," he said. "Roger that. Let's sign those papers while we're at it."

COPELAND SIGNED THE PAPERWORK, and MacDonald passed no comment on the calf inside his jacket. He approved a purchase order for a bulk buy of towels on the spot. He didn't offer to buy the vet a new jacket, though.

But Copeland didn't care. Any doubts he'd had about signing the contract had been dispelled by the calf he'd found in the birthing room. After he signed it, he was escorted out of the boss' office and over to his new base of operations.

On the vet's third day at the complex, Copeland, O'Rourke and Big Jim were interrupted on their way into work by a small gaggle of people who had surrounded one of Sunnyvale's import trucks. They were leaning in and pouring water through the gaps in the bars to quench the thirst of the animals that had been travelling for days in cramped conditions as they made their way from the west coast of Portugal to the abattoir at Sunnyvale. Later, they'd be wrapped in cellophane and sold on supermarket shelves.

"What's going on?" Copeland asked.

"It's a vigil," explained Darragh O'Rourke from the passenger seat. "Animal rights protestors. They take footage on their phones and share it online. We've seen this group before. They're the Buckinghamshire Save group, affiliated with Anonymous for the Voiceless and a couple of splinter groups."

"Aye," Jim growled. "Fuckers. We'll be late fae work. It's your fault an aww, Mr. Vet Man. Why am I still giein ye a lift tae work?"

"My car failed its MOT," Copeland said. "The mechanic

said it needs a new engine and that the brakes aren't road legal, but I think he's–"

"Ah doan wanna hear it," Jim said. "Get it fixed or ye'll be walkin'."

Over the next couple of weeks, Copeland learned more and more about the facility, and some of it was the stuff of nightmares. When he went to sleep in his lonely double bed, he saw scenes from the slaughterhouse as he drifted off to Slumberland. They played on his mind when he wandered the aisles of the supermarket. While he didn't stop eating meat, he did start to buy from the local butchers. There was no way in hell he was touching any of the stuff that Sunnyvale produced.

But Copeland was a special case, and most consumers found it hard to tell Sunnyvale meat from anything else. It was wrapped in plastic and shipped off to dozens of different supermarkets as own-brand bacon with Photoshopped images of pasture-fed pigs on the front of it. It never had a problem selling. It was bought by the people who didn't care what they were eating, or who didn't have a choice because it was all they could afford.

He also got to meet some more of Sunnyvale's employees and learned more about the ones he already knew. Will Makon in particular took a shine to him, grabbing hold of his arm every time he saw him and asking some question about the animals. Copeland would answer it, and then Makon would somehow divert the flow of the conversation to start talking about boxing. It was infuriating.

Copeland also got to know a guy called Lee Keyes, a production worker who looked like a junkie Sylvester Stallone. There was something about the face and the haircut, but his cheeks were sucked in and his meat hung tight to the bone. Keyes reminded him of Will Makon, because both men were well-built and they both liked to start conversations with him when he was trying to get something done.

When Copeland first met Lee Keyes, he was laughing and joking with a circle of his colleagues around him. He was recounting the story of some historic sexual exploit and it seemed to be going down well. He was the type to befriend everyone, and Copeland took an instant dislike to him because of it.

Over lunch one day in the canteen, Copeland made friends with Bob Knowles, one of the packers who worked in the chicken barn. He was a gaunt-looking skinhead with a goatee, and Copeland guessed he was in either his late forties or his early fifties. He had the kind of dead brown eyes that looked like autumn leaves in a puddle of slush. His face was wrinkled, making him look perpetually worried.

Knowles was the paranoid sort, a conspiracy nut who was talking about David Icke within five minutes of introducing himself. It only took him so long because he'd started out by talking about his music.

"You play?" Knowles asked.

Copeland shook his head, but that didn't stop him.

"Shame," Knowles continued, oblivious to the fact that he'd already lost his audience, like most musicians. "I live for my music. It's the only thing that gets me through the day."

"Ah," Copeland replied. "Like Big Jim and his whiskey."

"Something like that," Knowles said. "I'm writing a musical. It's based on *Silas Marner*. You know, George Eliot?"

"I never read his stuff."

"*Her* stuff," Knowles corrected him. "She wasn't very good. My musical will be better."

"I'm sure," Copeland said. And that was that. It didn't take long for the conversation to turn to Sunnyvale.

"I'm telling you, man," Knowles said, "Sunnyvale's a great gig, but you've got to turn a blind eye every now and then, if you catch my drift. I wouldn't want to be in your shoes. You're the new vet, right?"

"That's me," Copeland said.

"You know, the guys have started calling you 'Doc' on account of what you did with that cow the other day."

Copeland shrugged. "Just doing my job," he said.

"I don't know about that," Knowles said, leaning in a little closer. Copeland could hear the disturbing sound of mastication as the man chowed down on his chicken sandwich, spraying meat and mayo in the air every time he talked with his mouth open. "Our old vet would've just slipped the thing some barbiturates and put it out of its misery."

"Yeah, well, I'm not the old vet," Copeland reminded him. "I'm the new one."

"For sure," Knowles said. "It makes for a nice change around here. Sunnyvale isn't known for the Dr. Doolittle approach. I'm not sure you know what you let yourself in for."

"I've got a good idea."

By that point, neither of them was eating. Knowles had finished his sandwich and tossed the crusts onto the table, but Copeland had left his own inside his lunchbox. For some reason, he didn't feel much like eating.

"You see the chicken shack yet?"

Copeland shook his head.

"You're in for a treat," Knowles said. "Can't tell you about the beef, the lamb, the fish or the pork, my friend, but I can tell you plenty about chicken shit and bird flu."

"Bird flu?"

Knowles nodded. "Ain't happened here yet, but I'm not saying it never will. Those birds are plenty diseased. You've got to constantly pull out carcasses and chuck 'em in a wheelbarrow. Maybe as many as a couple hundred a day. And it ain't just disease that kills 'em."

"What do you mean?" Copeland asked.

"I don't know if you noticed, but this place ain't exactly conducive to good health. Some of 'em have heart attacks or kidney failure 'cause they grow so fast that their internal organs can't keep up with their muscles and skeletons. It's all the growth hormones and the antibiotics."

"It's only natural to lose a few of the animals along the way," Copeland said.

"Yeah," Knowles said. "But these ain't just a few. I mean, it's inevitable. You keep enough birds in a single place and something's bound to go wrong. At least the broilers get to spread their wings a little, though they say there's less space per chicken than the area of a sheet of paper. The layers are cooped right up in those little boxes of theirs."

"I'm familiar with battery hens."

"Good," Knowles said. "You just be sure and wear some gloves if you go in there."

"You mean you don't?"

Knowles shrugged. "Not always," he said. "Some of the guys get lazy and end up with diaper rash from the heat and the dirt and the shit. Course, half of us end up with rashes anyway. Best way to avoid it is to powder up before you put the gloves on."

"I'll bear that in mind."

"Say," Knowles said, gesturing to the vet's forgotten sandwich. "You gonna eat that?"

Copeland shook his head and slid it across the table.

"Nice one, buddy," Knowles said, grabbing the man's sad sandwich and unwrapping it. "Appreciated."

There was silence for a couple of moments as Knowles unwrapped the sandwich and bit into it. Copeland noticed that some unseen speakers were piping muzak into the room, presumably to boost the morale of the staff when they came in for a bite to eat at the end of a long shift. The room was emptier than it had been when they'd first entered, but there were still half a dozen people dotted across the forty or so chairs that were provided. Most of Sunnyvale's staff ate alone, if they ate at all, and Copeland and Knowles were conspicuous as the only two who were carrying out a conversation. That was why they were both speaking so quietly. It still felt sacrilegious somehow, as though the silence of the cafeteria was sacred. Copeland felt like they'd just started up a rave in a public library.

"Man," Knowles murmured. "This is the real shit, right? Free range?"

Copeland nodded.

"Figures," Knowles said. "You can taste it. The marketing guys would never admit that, though. I tell ya, it ain't a good life for factory fowl. From the second they hatch, they go through hell, if they live that long. If they're breeders, they'll chuck the males in the grinder. You ain't never heard nothing like it. They get thrown in whole as shrieking, clucking, shitting little creatures and come out as bone meal for the pigs and cows."

"Doesn't that pose a disease risk?" Copeland asked.

Knowles shrugged. "Maybe," he said. "Ain't my job to worry about it."

"What exactly *is* your job?" Copeland asked. The man was starting to annoy him a little, although he couldn't say why. It was probably the noise he made while he chowed down on Copeland's sandwich.

"I told ya," Knowles said, "I work with the chickens. Not much for me to actually do, truth be told. The machines look after 'em for the most part. Food comes in on one conveyor belt, eggs go out on another. The shit drops down through the cage and gets carted off to the lagoon."

"The lagoon?"

Knowles nodded. "It's what they call the waste pit. They store the shit there until they can spread it on fields or pay some clean-up crew to come and take it away."

"What happens when it rains?" Copeland asked.

"I guess we just hope that it doesn't," Knowles replied. He shrugged. "Like I said, it ain't my job to worry about it. I just keep an eye on the chickens, but mostly I let the machines do the work. MacDonald's got this place running like an engine. He's thought of everything."

"What do you mean?"

Knowles paused for a moment and looked uneasily around the room. "I probably shouldn't tell you this," he admitted. "But I can't see a reason why not to. Ain't a secret as far as I know. You'll see for yourself if you're around here long enough."

"It'll be fine," Copeland said. "And besides, I need to know what I'm dealing with. I'm not expecting to save the world or anything. My job is based on a single metric: the percentage of animals that make it through to the slaughterhouse."

"Sounds about right," Knowles replied. "The whole place is designed to run like a machine. They don't want the chickens to bend down to reach their food because that would waste energy. And they make sure there's plenty of food in the pens at all times. They do the same with the water lines, only those are up above beak level. The birds've gotta raise their heads to peck at the pin that makes the water go down their throats."

"Why?" Copeland asked. "What's the point?"

"The company wants water in those birds," Knowles said. "Especially those broilers. Makes 'em grow faster. They dope 'em up with arsenic, too. Not enough to poison them or to spoil the meat, mind. Just enough to make 'em drink more. They put salt in the feed, too. They're some thirsty fuckin' chickens."

"What's the obsession with water?"

Knowles shrugged. "Fattens 'em up," he said. "Makes 'em grow quicker. The retailers pay by weight."

"That's not good for their kidneys," Copeland said.

"I'm sure it isn't," Knowles replied, stuffing the last bite of the vet's sandwich into his mouth. "But no one here gives a damn about what's good for a chicken's kidneys. If the answer ain't gravy, they don't wanna know."

The door to the canteen opened and two men walked in. The taller of the two was undeniably Big Jim, the Scottish head of security, but Copeland didn't recognise the smaller one. He was an unremarkable man, and his balding forehead was red and blistered from the sun. His eyes were half open in a stoned leer. When he wasn't talking, his mouth hung slightly open. He wore an ID badge that identified him as Bruce Laing from the sheep shed.

"Wait a minute," Copeland murmured, "I know that guy."

"What guy?"

"That guy," Copeland said, gesturing towards Laing. "He used to be a butcher."

"Yeah," Knowles said. "He used to run his own shop somewhere. But then the recession hit, the market tanked and he ended up at Sunnyvale. He thought he'd be working in the slaughterhouse. Wrong. He's just a glorified shepherd."

Copeland laughed and looked up, making awkward eye contact with Laing from across the room. He wondered whether the guy remembered him. Copeland had bought pork chops and half chickens from him.

"So anyway," Knowles said, clearing his throat and

flashing a nervous look at Tom Copeland. He clearly wanted to change the subject, and Copeland thought he understood why. "You know I told you about my musical? I think I've found someone to play the leading lady. You should hear her sing, she—"

"Alreet, boys," Big Jim interrupted, marching across the room towards them and grinning an unsettling grin. "Havin' yeselves a wee chinwag? You boys goat no work oan?"

Copeland nodded at Jim and then lowered his eyes. He liked the man, but he also feared him. He murmured something about cataloguing a delivery, stood up and walked towards the door.

Knowles got up to follow him out, but Big Jim reached out with a massive hand and pushed him back down into his seat.

"Where ye think yur goin', pal?" Big Jim said. He smiled and for a split second, his fiery beard looked like a living animal, a fox perhaps. He leaned in a little closer and said, "Wir gonnae hae ourselves a bit o' a chat, ye ken."

Copeland closed the door on his way out.

KNOWLES AND COPELAND didn't speak much after that, and they both learned a valuable lesson. Knowles learned when he needed to keep his mouth shut, and Copeland learned that if he wanted to keep his job, his house and his teeth, it was best to keep himself to himself.

And so that's what he did. He busied himself in the newly reinstated Sunnyvale surgery. He was the only one working there. If he needed extra manpower then he had to call for backup from the production workers, so most of the surgery was small scale stuff to keep animals from keeling over. Back in the practice in Chalfont St. Peter, the mantra had been "prevent, intercept, cure." Here at Sunnyvale, the motto was "patch up and hope for the best." If an animal died in his care, he didn't have to deal with distraught old women who loved their cats more than their grandchildren. If an animal died at Sunnyvale, he just had to take it out back and put it in a wheelbarrow. He had no idea who took over from there, but someone did.

John MacDonald, the big boss who signed off his paycheques, didn't like it when animals died on Copeland's shift. It wasn't because of his ethics, though. It was a purely practical decision, driven by the laws of profit and loss, supply and demand. If an animal died before it reached the slaughterhouse, it was considered spoiled product and couldn't be sold to consumers. The rumour was that after heavy processing, it was instead sold as tinned food for cats and dogs. Anything that wasn't even fit for people's pets was recycled and fed to the pigs, thus completing Sunnyvale's twisted circle of life. Copeland didn't know about that – it wasn't his job to know about it – but he did know that MacDonald measured his performance based on the percentage of livestock that survived for long enough to be turned into cheap meat in the slaughterhouse.

The next time Copeland saw Knowles was during a routine visit to the chicken shack. Orders had come down from above to test the birds and then to increase their dose of antibiotics. There were rumours of a new strain of avian flu in South America and Eastern Europe, and senior management didn't want to take any chances. Copeland would have liked to believe that they cared about their animals, but he knew it was because if the birds became infected, they'd have to be slaughtered as a precaution. He was pretty sure that Sunnyvale's insurers – or maybe even the government and, therefore, the taxpayer – would ultimately foot the bill, but it would disrupt their operations and that would be damaging enough.

If it *was* bird flu, the disease had the potential to jump to humans. Copeland filed a report calling for staff to wear face masks at all times, but it was left unread on MacDonald's mahogany desk and by the time that he finally read it, the media panic was over and they were back to worrying about meeting quotas.

But Copeland took to wearing a mask anyway, all over the complex to begin with until he limited it to just his visits to the chicken shed. The birds were doing fine, perhaps as well as could be expected under the conditions they lived in. Copeland had tried to psych himself up so he was ready to deal with the stench of chicken shit, but it was no use. It overwhelmed him every time he went in there. He saw Knowles in the broiler shed, where the birds were allowed to roam slightly more freely. It was an alarming sight, a huge, cavernous room with tens of thousands of birds crowded together in flocks, often pecking at each other or trampling over the smaller birds in random stampedes. When one of the production workers had to make their way from one side of the room to another, the birds parted like the red sea.

Copeland saw Knowles from about twenty feet away and waved at him, but the man ignored him. He called his name, causing a minor avalanche of feathers as the nearby fowl registered their disapproval, but Bob Knowles still didn't acknowledge him. Up close, Copeland could see that the man had a bruised cheek and a black eye. His expression reminded Copeland of a dying dog realising his own mortality.

The vet nudged a nearby worker, a heavyset woman with short, spiky hair and leathery skin. Her name badge identified her as Yvonne Strong.

"What's up with him?" Copeland asked.

The woman laughed. "You'd better be careful who you talk to, pal," she said. "I ain't sayin' nothin'. Big Jim and his boys don't like it."

"I see," Copeland replied. But he didn't. Not really. It was a different world to what he was used to.

"Trust me," she said. "I love this place. I'd die for it if I had to. I even met my husband here. Met him, married him and buried him within five years. The best five years of my life. All thanks to Sunnyvale."

"Are you being sarcastic?" Copeland asked. He was finding it difficult to tell, and Yvonne Strong wasn't making it any easier. And she didn't answer his question, either. She just stared at him from her beady little eyes.

"You look after yourself," Strong said. "And don't go making friends with the wrong people. You don't want to get yourself into trouble. Keep yourself to yourself and above all else, never criticise Sunnyvale. The walls have ears."

"Understood."

Apart from the occasional bird here and there that Copeland condemned to an early death for the greater good of the flock, the chickens in the broiler house weren't too bad. Copeland had no problem with certifying the request for more antibiotics, and he signed and dated a chitty that would put the order into effect once he returned it to the admin building. Unfortunately, at Sunnyvale it was never as easy as simply getting stuff done. Nothing could ever happen without a paper trail.

His next stop that day was the pig shed, which was the building to the north of the chicken shack. The two buildings were a similar size, but while the chicken shack was separated into broilers and layers, the pig shack was just an unending series of metal crates in which the pigs were kept until they were ready for slaughter. The luckier creatures were gathered together in pens, where they were mostly shoulder-to-shoulder but occasionally had a little room to manoeuvre. The downside was that they liked to fight each other, especially when life in the shed got stressful. Many of them had bites and blister marks, chunks out of their tails or blinded eyes from teeth and trotters. Many of the wounds were infected, and Copeland wondered whether they'd need to put more antibiotics in the pig feed, too.

Copeland turned to the man beside him and said, "Show me the crates."

The man nodded and led the way further into the porky labyrinth. His name was Pete Fields and he was the section manager, which was a fancy way of saying he was in charge of the people who worked the floor and precious little else. Fields was a tall, skinny man with short blond hair and a little stubble. He had a ruddy complexion and stoned-looking eyes and wore so much aftershave that even in the middle of the pig sheds, Copeland could still smell it. His company overalls were two sizes too small, making him look like an oversized child on work experience. But his tired face gave his age away, and Copeland guessed he was in his late twenties or early thirties.

Fields talked as he walked, even though Copeland was half a step behind and could barely hear him over the noise of the animals. The veterinarian focussed on a little mole on the back of the section manager's neck. It looked red and inflamed, as though a hairdresser had caught it with their clippers. Pete's hairdo was typical for a man of his age, short and tidy and swept to one side with a little wax or gel. Copeland himself had more of a bird's nest, and he supposed that their hairstyles said a lot about them.

"I used to work the production line," Fields explained. "It's a shitty job, but someone's got to do it. Then I got my promotion, so now it's my job to make sure that everyone else is doing *their* job."

"Yeah," Copeland murmured. "And it's my job to patch up the animals if you and your boys get too rough with the bacon."

But Fields didn't appear to hear him. "The wife wants me to quit, of course," he continued. "We've got a baby on the way, and she wants me to spend more time at home. Says she's worried that the job'll kill me or I'll bring back some disease, can you believe it?"

"Well, I mean–"

"No sir-ee," Fields said. "Call me crazy, but I love my job, Dr. Copeland. And truth be told, I don't even *want* a kid. Never have done. I'll leave her indoors to whelp the little shit while I'm working overtime or blowing off steam at The Two Brewers. You got kids?"

"I used to," Copeland said, thinking back to his former life before the scandal had shut down his business. "I, uh... don't see them anymore."

"Lucky man," Fields replied.

But Copeland didn't think he'd be buying a lottery ticket any time soon.

The gestation crates were on the other side of a concrete partition that sheltered the sows from the rest of the shed. The crates were laid side by side and kept the animals immobile as they carried their young to term. When they came out – if they came out of the crates at all – they had wasted muscles and bones that had broken and fused back together into unnatural shapes. Most of them had sores on their flesh.

"They say pigs are as smart as children," Copeland said. "They're smarter than chimpanzees."

"Yeah?" Fields replied. He had an air of unfeigned indifference, acquired through years of boredom and unpractised neglect. Fields seemed like the kind of guy who'd been forgotten by society. He had the pinched face of an addict, and while Copeland was no expert, he was willing to bet that some sort of narcotic was to blame. He'd seen similar effects in animals.

"I always thought pigs were dirty creatures," Fields said.

Copeland shook his head. "Not true," he replied. "They're cleaner than most. Intelligent, too."

Fields grunted but said nothing. Copeland wandered off to take a closer look at the pigs in the main barn. The sows in the crates had no room to manoeuvre, but the pigs in the pens had a little bit of space if they were willing to fight for it. They were fenced into metal pens with a dozen or more pigs per pen. There was a narrow walkway down the middle so that the staff could walk up and down to feed the animals, and it was down this that Copeland walked as he checked them for any obvious signs of disease.

But for the most part, it was just the usual. The worst thing he saw was the carcass of a dead hog, which wasn't all that surprising at Sunnyvale. Copeland knelt down and took a closer look at it. It had been a couple months short of its slaughter age when it had died, probably as a result of asphyxiation. When the pigs panicked, they pressed their flesh together into a porky flash mob, moving as one against the bars of the cage. For the unlucky hogs that were closest to the metal, it wasn't unusual to be crushed by the sheer weight of pig behind them.

Copeland tutted and Fields walked over to take a look. He covered his mouth and nose with an arm as he leaned in a little closer. The pig had already started to rot and its marimba skeleton was poking out from the shit-stained straw like a Nazi anti-aircraft gun. The enclosure itself was an Auschwitz, but at least Fields and his team tried to keep their charges alive for long enough to reach the gas chamber.

There would be no liberation.

Fields coughed and tried to cover his mouth and nose with his arm and sleeve. Copeland couldn't blame him. He knew from bitter experience that you never got used to the stench of death, and the poor pig before him was in worse shape than most. The vet knew that it would clog up his nostrils and keep springing up on him when he least expected it. He couldn't wait to take a shower.

"You know what's funny about the smell of dead pig?" Copeland asked. Fields shook his head. "It smells the same as a dead human."

That was enough for Fields. His face, which had already turned a sweaty ochre, went green, and he spewed his mum's chili con carne all over his high-vis jacket. Copeland reluctantly patted the man on the back and waited for him to finish. It took him a while, but after the initial flood of vomit had pooled itself into a steaming mess on the floor, he was reduced to dry heaving, coughing and spluttering. By the time his breathing was back to normal, Copeland had another bombshell to drop.

"You're going to have to clean that up," the vet said. "As quickly as you can."

"Why?" Fields asked. "Can't I leave it for maintenance?"

Copeland shook his head. "No chance," he said. "It's a contaminant. We don't want the pigs getting sick."

"You trying to say I'm diseased?"

"Not at all," Copeland said, raising his hands defensively and taking a step backwards. He had a mean right hook and had boxed for the Gerrard's Cross Amateur League, but that had had been at least a dozen years ago. While he could defend himself, if pushed, he didn't want to. Fields kept on approaching him, but he stopped when he was within arm's reach, just close enough to the vet to send a message.

"Then what?" Fields asked. "Why should I bother?"

"Pigs are the middlemen," Copeland said. "They form a bridge between us and the chickens. When the superflu comes, it'll be because the birds got sick, they spread it to the pigs and then the pigs gave it to us."

"That'll never happen."

"Maybe not," Copeland said. "But it's best to not risk it. You still need to clean that up."

"Right," Fields replied. He frowned. "You made many friends here?"

"It's not my job to make friends," Copeland replied. "It's my job to keep the animals alive for long enough to carry them through to the slaughterhouse."

"So you're going to up the antibiotics?"

Copeland sighed. "Looks like I don't have much choice," he said. "I'll come back and check on you in an hour. If the vomit's gone – and the dead pig as well – then I'll sign the document and you can pump them full of Noromycin to your heart's content. Deal?"

Fields chuckled and shook his head. "You're really quite something," he said. "It's a deal."

The two men shook on it, and Copeland retraced his steps towards the exit. As he stepped outside again into the relative fresh air, it felt like he'd released a heavy burden and was watching it float away over the horizon.

His walkie talkie flared into life with a crackle of static and interference. Even through the distortion, he could tell it was Fields.

"Can someone send Fernandez to the pig shed?" Fields said. "There's been an... uh, incident. Tell him he's got a dead pig and a pool of vomit to deal with. Tell him to bring a big-ass mop."

There was a pause. Then it burst back into life again. "Oh yeah," Fields said. "And tell him to get here in a hurry."

A COUPLE OF DAYS LATER, Copeland was alone in the surgery, running a few tests on some samples from the chicken shed. His radio burst into life. It was Pete Fields, the section manager in the pig shed. He sounded excited. Something had caught his attention.

"We've got an injured animal," he was babbling, broadcasting on the special frequency that was saved for the ops team. It was the frequency that Copeland was expected to tune into, so that they didn't pollute the airwaves on the factory floor. It had the additional effect of keeping the worst of the horrors away from the production workers. "It's a pig, a little one. Oh, man, you've gotta come see this."

So Copeland put his samples aside and packed his leather kit bag, which he hoisted on to his shoulder. He reached down to his breast to check that he had his key card, then he dashed out the door and wormed his way through the building and back outside into the living, sweating, breathing stench that hung over Sunnyvale like a stubborn fog.

Big Jim and his team had their buggies and their 4x4s to get around in, but Copeland had to make do with trekking across the facility on foot. He'd put in a couple of requests for a vehicle, arguing that it'd save time and make him more productive, but there just wasn't the budget. John MacDonald had suggested a compromise.

"Get a bike," he'd said. "It's the quickest way."

Copeland already had a bike, but he wouldn't be using it. He hated the things, and he always had. It's hard to look professional on a bicycle, and even harder to use them to transport injured animals, and so the veterinarian opted to travel on foot instead. He'd created a sort of half-run, half-walk that made him look like one of the broilers in the chicken shed as it tried to make a break for freedom, but it was the only thing he could do in the circumstances. If an animal needed to be moved, he had to call for backup from the security team. And if he wanted the security team to actually help him, he needed a damn good reason why they shouldn't put an injured animal out of its misery right there and then.

He made good time and arrived at the piggery in just a couple of minutes, where he was met by Pete Fields and a couple of his production workers, Kim Roach and Keith Gowan.

Copeland only knew who Gowan was because he was growing a moustache and it was the talk of the complex. It looked like a slug had crawled across his face and fused itself to him. It made it difficult to look the man in the eye, but that was unlikely to be a problem when there was a wounded animal to care for. People had started taking bets about when he'd shave the damn thing off or give up and grow a beard instead. With his blond hair and his blue eyes, he looked a little bit Kurt Cobain, but the moustache was more Freddie Mercury. Not that anyone would have told him that. Everyone knew he'd worked in oil and gas before starting at Sunnyvale, and that made him the kind of man not to be messed with. Copeland wasn't intimidated by his reputation, but he didn't want to get on the man's bad side, either.

As for Kim Roach, she was a formidable woman who looked like she'd fallen asleep on a tanning bed. She resembled a transvestite Big Jim, but there was also something unmistakably feminine about the way she walked. She was the other side of the menopause, happily married if the ring on her finger was anything to go by. She didn't give a damn about what she looked like, but the walk came naturally. Something inside of her, the subconscious memory that powered her legs, thought it was 1968 and she was walking down Carnaby Street. But that had been over fifty years earlier, and her face had the lines and the jowls to show for it.

For a moment, Copeland was hit by the familiar fear of the relentless march of time. He wondered what he'd be doing when he was her age. And whether he'd still be living alone, an absent, divorced dad who spent half his time up to his knees in pig shit. He shuddered.

"Take me to the animal," Copeland said. He followed the pig team inside the shed and towards the east wing, where the pens were smaller and more isolated and where they held the newborn pigs until they were ready to go out into general population.

The animal in question was one of the newer arrivals, just a couple of weeks old and still learning its place in the food chain. Pigs were intelligent creatures, but intelligence and experience were two different things. At two weeks old, the Sunnyvale pigs were yet to grasp the true extent of their predicament. They still hadn't developed the jaded acceptance that kept the adult pigs in line.

The pig that Copeland had been called to look at hadn't been as lucky as some of the others. He'd met with the horror and lost his life to it, robbed of the chance to grow up to have its throat slit and its flesh turned into bacon strips. Copeland bent down and peered closely at it. MacDonald had tasked him with identifying a cause of death, and though there was nothing he could do to make it meet its date with the slaughterhouse, the goal was to stop it from happening again.

"Hmm," he said. "How long has it been lying here?"

Fields shrugged and said, "Couple hours, maybe. Wasn't here last time I took a look around. Why?"

Copeland shook his head. "It doesn't make sense," he murmured. He looked at the pig again. "The damn thing's decomposing. It shouldn't be doing that if it only died a couple of hours ago. And look at those bite marks."

Fields looked a little closer and then covered his nose and backed away again. The carcass was starting to smell, and he'd had pulled pork sandwiches for lunch. "Is that what they are?" he asked. "Bite marks?"

"They must be," Copeland said. "But the teeth are too small for a pig to have done it."

"That's good, right?"

Copeland shrugged. "Maybe," he said. "It means we don't have a case of cannibalism on our hands, but we do have something out there that got a little peckish and decided to take a pig down. We're going to need to find out what did it."

Fields shivered. He cast a sidelong look at his two subordinates and then turned back to look at Copeland, who was still on his knees in front of the carcass with his face a little too close to it for comfort.

"It looks almost like the teeth of a rodent," Copeland murmured. "A mouse, perhaps. Or a rat."

"What kind of rat can kill a pig?" Fields asked. It was a rhetorical question, but it got an answer.

"The Rat King," Gowan said. He was a simple man with a calm, dreamy voice, but he'd been working at the complex ever since it had opened and he had a reputation amongst the workers for being like a Sunnyvale Yoda, except with a Coventry accent and no major talents.

Kim Roach burst out laughing, while Copeland acted as though he hadn't heard anything. He'd removed his bag from his shoulder and was rifling through it to find some of the kit that he needed, like his airtight sample tubes, his scalpel and his cotton swabs.

"The Rat King?" Roach said. "Seriously?"

"Sure," Gowan replied. "You've heard the stories."

"Yeah," Roach scoffed. A couple of years at Sunnyvale had taught her to be a sceptic, and she'd never been one for the gossip that passed between the workers or the habits they had of wearing silver crosses beneath their uniforms. "I've heard the stories, all right."

"But you don't believe them."

"Why the hell should I?" she asked. "Where's the evidence?"

"Perhaps you're looking at it," Copeland murmured, but nobody heard him. Meanwhile, the debate was progressing while Pete Fields stood off to one side and massaged his temples. Copeland glanced at him and felt a sudden and unexpected pang of worry. He'd heard things on the grapevine, things a little closer to home than a mythical Rat King, and he wondered how Fields was coping. The rumour was that his wife had walked out on him and that all he had left was his mother, a woman in her early eighties who was on her way out with Alzheimer's. If the rumour mill was right, she was living out her days in a dingy little hospice while her son worked all the overtime he could get to try to pay for it. Of course, it was just a rumour.

Or was it? Copeland guessed that it didn't really matter. Sunnyvale was like another country, some far-off land in which no one ever had to deal with consequences. What happened in Sunnyvale stayed in Sunnyvale, and people's personal lives were irrelevant. It just wasn't talked about, at least not out in the open. Rumours spread, but people rarely confronted them. Work and play didn't mix in a place like Sunnyvale.

Copeland took one last item – a DSLR camera – from his bag and took a few photos of the injured animal. He nudged it with his shoe to roll it over to take a few shots from a different angle, then he nodded at Fields and said, "We're done here." Then he packed his gear up and pushed himself to his feet before slinging the bag over his shoulder.

"Is that it?" Fields asked.

"Pretty much," Copeland replied. "That's my job done, at least for now. I'll look into it and figure out what I can, but you and I both know that at the end of the day, it's just a pig. My job is to keep them alive. I can't do much if they're already dead."

"And if whatever killed it comes back?"

Fields looked stressed, and Copeland supposed that it came with the job. Fields was the line manager, so it was his responsibility to worry about what to do and how to react. Meanwhile, his subordinates were still bickering about whether the Rat King was just a legend or whether it was something much more serious.

Copeland shrugged his shoulders. "That's not my problem," he said. "Just keep your eyes peeled and call Big Jim and his team if you have any problems."

Fields nodded. Then he gestured towards the carcass on the floor and said, "What about that?"

"What about it?" Copeland replied. "I guess you'd better get someone to clean it up and take it over to the incinerator."

Fields sighed and said, "I'll get Fernandez. Again."

***

Janet Peston was having a shitty day.

She was a production worker in Sunnyvale's pig factory, a job that she despised but couldn't turn away from. She'd polished up her CV and spent a good two years looking for something else, but at fifty-four years old and with no skills to speak of, there wasn't much on the market. She was washed up and she knew it.

Peston was five foot three with long, brown hair tied back in a ponytail and tucked beneath a net, and a face with angles so sharp they could cut someone. She had a tongue to match, which was how she'd survived so long in the toxic, misogynistic environment of the factory farm. The boys used to call her "Granny Weatherwax," but she gave as good as she got. She'd been known to beat her chauvinist co-workers across the back of the head with a heavy fist without even taking the cigarette from her mouth. It took a special kind of woman to make it at Sunnyvale. Janet Peston was one of the rare few with the pure pig-headedness that was required to survive and thrive.

The day had started well enough, or as well as a day can start when the alarm goes off at 4:45 AM. Her car was still making the weird rattling noise it had been making, and she was pretty sure it wasn't going to make it through the winter.

The first shitty part of her shitty day took place at a busy intersection when a shitty driver cut her off and flipped her the finger. She flipped the bird straight back at him, and then he spent the next six miles following her and gesturing for her to pull over. But she didn't, and she was only able to shake him off when she arrived at work. Mike Chase was manning the checkpoint, filling the hours by reading dirty magazines.

Janet Peston had never liked him. There was something about the young man that bothered her, and it wasn't just that he looked out of place amongst the more hardened production workers. He had a big, squashed nose and the kind of dull, dark eyes that put Peston on edge. He reminded her of the kids in the hoodies who lived on her estate and who terrorised the OAPs. She knew he was in his twenties and trying to make his way in the world by joining Big Jim's security team, but she would still have crossed the street if she'd seen him walking along outside the workplace. And she was pretty sure that the kid knew it, too.

Chase recognised her car from a distance, presumably because it was the only pea green Fiat Punto that had the bad luck to regularly grace Sunnyvale's car park. But he didn't recognise the blue Ford Mondeo that was riding right up her ass. He radioed through to the main facility to put them on the alert and then hit the switch in the checkpoint hut to lock the barrier in place.

Janet pulled up first, and Chase walked over to meet her. She wound down the driver-side window and stuck her head out. She didn't bother to say hello. "This ass-wipe won't stop following me," she shouted.

"Yeah?" Chase said. "We'll see about that."

The Mondeo pulled up behind her and Chase turned to face it. He unhooked the truncheon from his belt and raced over to the Mondeo, then tapped it against the driver's door. The man took one look at the truncheon and the uniform and put the vehicle in reverse. He swung the vehicle into a three-point turn, but Chase had time to snap off a few quick hits before it hightailed out of there. The truncheon made angry *whump-whump* noises as it smacked off the bodywork, sending chips of blue paint spitting up into the air like the gristle and bone coming out of the chicken shredder.

After that, Chase had opened the barrier and gestured her through. They'd both agreed not to mention it again.

But the shitty day had continued to be shitty. She literally fell in the shit when she was helping Pete Fields to hose the crap out of the sties, and the section manager had burst out laughing. He'd turned his hose on her and sprayed her down right there in the middle of the animals.

"Fuckin' priceless," Fields said. He pulled out his phone and snapped a photo on it. "You wait 'til I share this with the boys."

Janet could have killed him for that. She would have reported him to her line manager if she could have. Unfortunately, he *was* her line manager, and she needed her job. So instead of telling him to go and fuck himself with a branding iron, she kept her mouth shut, picked herself up and carried on with her rounds. In the relative warmth of the sheds, her sodden clothes seemed to steam beneath the artificial lighting.

But Janet's day was about to get even worse.

It was late in the day, near the end of the shift from hell which was starting to seem like it would never end. Some of her colleagues were already in the process of switching over, which is how she found herself alone in a sty with a couple of hundred pigs that were packed tightly together like a gigantic toad in the hole. There was a smell in the air, a smell like sweat and shit and desperation, but that wasn't unusual in the pig pen. The beasts were castrated shortly after birth and had their tails removed not long later. Many of the animals died when staff botched it, and Janet herself had worked the line in the birthing season despite having no formal training. With such a violent start to life, it was unsurprising that the animals were restless and desperate.

They were also angry – and hungry for revenge.

The first she knew of it was a nudge against her lower back while she was checking the feed trays. She turned around to a horrifying sight. Four hundred pairs of eyes were staring at her. The pigs were lined up, standing shoulder to shoulder across the middle of the pen. There was one pig at the front, a big, ugly beast with pockmarked flesh and deep, pungent sores on its snout.

There was a moment of tenseness, of silence. Then the beast charged straight for her. They were separated by barely fifteen feet, but the pig was ungainly and its wasted muscles were unprepared for the sudden burst of activity. Janet got out of the way, but only at the last second. Then she made a dash for the gate, but the other pigs had blocked her escape route and she was forced to circle back around.

The pig went for her again, smashing itself against the metal fence with a sound like two cars running into the side of a lorry. The impact took its toll on the beast's body, but it wasn't over yet. It picked itself up again and ran once more towards her. This time, there was nowhere for Janet to go, and the pig pushed her back against the wall. It opened its mouth, revealing a broken row of rotting teeth that reeked of dead flesh and abscesses.

Then it ran towards her and clamped its jaws around her arm as she held it up to defend herself.

The pain was unbearable, at least to begin with. Then the adrenaline kicked in, and she pushed back at the pig, somehow knocking it on to its side. The other pigs were backing away and there was a path to freedom. She rushed towards it and was just a couple of feet away when the pig crashed into the back of her, bearing her down to the floor. Her injured arm hit the concrete and the open wound filled up with shit and straw.

Then there was a crackling sound and the smell of roasting flesh, followed by the death-bellow of a mortally wounded pig. She'd heard the sound before when she'd worked for a stint in the slaughterhouse. It was the sound the pigs made as their throats were being cut and their blood was spraying out on to the grass.

Then Darragh O'Rourke grabbed her good arm and pulled her over the turnstile and out into the walkway. That left a thick metal guard between her and the livestock. She was safe. For now, at least.

She had a fleeting moment of confusion as she looked up at her saviour and noticed something different. The Irishman had cut all his hair off. Peston processed the information and had just enough time to think that it didn't suit him. She giggled, and the giggle turned into a hiccough.

Then she passed out in the gantry with the sound of death in her ears.

SUNNYVALE'S ANTIBIOTICS PROGRAMME was launched without a hitch, and John MacDonald and his senior management team had supported the launch with a set of aggressive growth KPIs that he expected the facility to meet within eighteen months. But with no extra storage space for the livestock, it would mean cramming bigger birds and cows into the same spaces.

Copeland was concerned, but he wasn't concerned enough to raise the issue. Besides, he'd been busy in Bovine, working from eight in the morning until eight at night without a break in between. There were new animals to be vaccinated, new illnesses to diagnose and new corpses to analyse and then dispose of. It seemed silly to carry out post-mortems on dead dairy cows, but the cows were worth money. It wasn't about diagnosing the cause of death. It was about protecting the farm's investment.

The deployment of the new programme was bolstered by the presence of Jill MacDonald, who'd been allowed out from behind her desk in the admin building to accompany Copeland on his rounds. He'd taught her how to estimate dosages and to measure out feed, and she'd proved to be a particularly quick learner when it came to isolating veins and giving the animals their injections. She wasn't a natural, but she wasn't far off it. Copeland had secretly suspected that she wouldn't last five minutes once confronted with the mud and the shit and the straw inside the meat sheds, but he'd underestimated her.

Weeks passed and the weather grew slowly colder. Life at Sunnyvale was busy but predictable, and if the animals noticed the shifting seasons, they didn't react to it. Copeland supposed that with no access to outside air and sunlight, any one day was as good as another for the denizens of Sunnyvale. The only news of note was the escape of two Tamworth pigs that made a run for it, but they were tracked down three days later on the outskirts of Beaconsfield and returned to the facility under the cover of darkness. MacDonald had been furious at first, but after the pigs were returned and shipped to the slaughterhouse, he started to see the funny side. But Copeland had still heard rumours that Big Jim and his team were doubling down on security. The Scotsman had hosted an all-hands meeting in which he explained it all.

"Ah doan want tae hear o' any more escapes, ye ken," he'd said. "Ah cannae stress how serious ah am."

They were sitting in the open cafeteria on the ground floor of the admin building. The place was packed with a couple of hundred people, and they'd had to clear the tables and chairs away to make space. Big Jim was standing tall at the front of the room and talking without the aid of a microphone, cupping his hands around his mouth instead.

Big Jim shouted for a couple more minutes, battering Sunnyvale's employees around the head with his semi-indecipherable accent until they would have agreed to anything if only he'd "stoap." And then when it seemed like he was going to keep on talking for an eternity, he did just that.

His place was taken by John MacDonald, who looked incongruous in a tweed suit and black wellington boots. John was half a head shorter than Big Jim and a couple of stone lighter, but he held the audience in his hands in his own special way. He talked quietly but with purpose, and the room leaned in closer to hear him.

"Ladies and gentlemen," he said, "I won't keep you

long. Now as you know, we take security and confidentiality very seriously. We have to be extremely careful about who and what we allow in and out of the property. If we're not careful, we'll be knee-deep in protestors or government inspectors, and I think we can all agree that we're better off without. Meanwhile, if our animals escape then it damages our image in the eyes of the general public and could even lead to disease outbreaks. I'd like to remind you that if Sunnyvale gets shut down, we're all out of a job. None of us wants that, so let's tighten up the ship and make sure it doesn't happen."

He paused for a moment and looked around the room. Most of the faces were blank, while one or two looked bored and a few more were concerned. Copeland stared straight back at him, his expression neutral. He hadn't been at the company for long, but he'd been there for long enough to know that this kind of meeting wasn't exactly a regular occurrence.

"From now on," MacDonald continued, "everyone will be searched as they enter and exit the premises. I've given Big Jim and his team the power to stop and search anybody on-site at any time. Vehicles will also be searched prior to entering and exiting the facility. Anyone who disagrees with me can go and find themselves a new job."

It's like a cult, Copeland thought. *The cult of meat. The cult of gristle and bone.* He'd seen a documentary just a couple of nights earlier about Jim Jones and Jonestown, and it seemed to the vet that MacDonald was using the same tactics. He was creating a culture of fear and suspicion in which Big Jim and his heavies had total control over the complex, and all in the name of two escaped pigs who'd made an understandable bid for freedom.

And like the first cultists to arrive in Guyana, Copeland did nothing to stop him.

"I have one more thing to add," MacDonald said. "Big Jim and his team are going to get some backup. Armed guards on both the gates, to be precise. Now, these chaps will be licenced to use live ammunition thanks to a few strings I pulled with our friends in the government. They'll keep us safe. If someone tries to break in – or if an animal tries to break out – then they're authorised to shoot on sight."

Charming, Copeland thought. But he put it to the back of his mind and tried to think about the animals. MacDonald had taken a backseat after the first couple of weeks and Copeland was now working under a man called Bugsy Drew, a tough-talking American with an aquiline face, a lazy Southern accent and a habit of chewing tobacco, which he spat carelessly on the floor as he walked around the complex. Drew was the facility's operations manager, shipped in from a Texan mega dairy on the other side of the Atlantic. He assigned priorities to different areas of the facility when they were most in need of veterinary support, but Copeland was also free to use his own judgement, as he'd done with the newborn calf that he'd nursed back to health before sending it to face its fate in the cow shed.

It was the same shed where Copeland had been spending most of his time, but it was time for a change of scenery. Drew had assigned the vet to the chicken shed again, but this time Copeland was shown to a smaller room that was built into the back of the broiler shed. It looked like a tumour, and it had clearly been bodged together in a hurry. It was the avian equivalent of a shanty town, housing just under a thousand geese in tiny metal cages. It was the closest thing to hell that Copeland had ever seen.

He arrived at feeding time, when the production workers were ramming pipes down the throats of the birds. They were clearly in some discomfort, but that was hardly surprising. One of the workers spotted the look on Copeland's face and grinned at him.

"Three times a day," the worker said. "Up to four pounds of grain and fat."

"Jesus," Copeland replied.

"Jerry Jones," the worker said, holding out his hand. Copeland shook it. "What brings you over here?"

Copeland looked the man up and down. He had long, unruly hair and a brown beard, with a sunken face and a scrawny neck. He looked like a hippie, but Copeland guessed that even if he was, he must have put the peace and love aside when he signed up to work at Sunnyvale. The facility was more death metal than stoner rock, and Copeland identified with neither. He was a Mark Knopfler fan and proud of it.

"You're not related to Jim Jones, are you?" Copeland asked.

"No, sir," Jones replied, but he didn't look offended. He was grinning from behind his beard and Copeland got a glimpse of off-white teeth and a hint of halitosis before he closed his mouth again. "But sometimes I pretend I am. Depends who I'm talking to."

"Remind me not to drink the Kool-Aid."

Jones laughed and flashed his grin again. "It ain't like that," he said. "But if you ever need to know the gossip around here, you let me know. I run the place."

"I'm sure you do," Copeland lied, thinking about John MacDonald and his eccentric and unpredictable approach to management. In a way, that was why he was there in the first place. He had orders. "Listen, I've got a job to do. Production's down and senior management isn't happy. I'm here to figure out why."

"Pfft," Jones replied. It sounded like air escaping from an aerosol can. "You try swelling a liver up to ten times its normal size. We have a few accidents along the way."

"That may be so," Copeland said, "but too many birds are dying before they're ready. I mean, look at them."

He gestured around the shed at the geese in their cages. Many of them could barely stand because their swollen livers poked out of their abdomens. Copeland bashed the bars of a nearby cage and the birds burst into a cacophony of angry noise. They pecked at each other, as best as they could, but the bars of the cages got in the way. Some of the birds tore out their own feathers, but most of them were simply spent, and far too lethargic to move, much less to bathe and groom.

"What's wrong with 'em?" Jones asked.

"They're covered in shit," Copeland said. "And they're full of infections from the metal bars and the conditions they're kept in."

"That's just the way we keep 'em."

"I know," Copeland said. "But perhaps that needs to change. It's not just for the good of the animals, you understand? How many do you feed each day?"

"Five hundred birds, three times a day."

Copeland shook his head. "That's too many," he said. "No wonder the birds are dying. Looks like it's mostly from aspiration pneumonia, which means you're forcing grain into their lungs or they're choking on their own vomit."

"I have a job to do."

"I'm sure you do," Copeland said. "But so do I. I'll have a word with the boss, see if we can make some changes. His numbers just don't add up. We can't keep force-feeding this many birds this quickly without a problem."

"Well, you be sure to tell him that."

It wasn't a task that Copeland looked forward to, but he managed to book a meeting with MacDonald by sweet talking his PA, Carol Rawlings, into finding a slot for him.

Carol had struck up a conversation with the vet over a cup of coffee in the canteen one day, and it turned out that they had a lot in common. Before starting at Sunnyvale, Carol had worked in reception for a vet in Haddenham, and they both had multiple failed marriages to their names. It was a useful friendship to have, and it was how Copeland managed to blag himself a meeting with the big boss on the same day.

Carol Rawlings was a striking woman with strong cheekbones and a sweet smile. She had long brown hair and wore just enough makeup to highlight her natural good looks. She didn't turn heads when she walked along the street, but she did have the kind of warm smile that could get anyone to take a shine to her. She also looked tired, and Copeland said as much as she led him up to MacDonald's office on the top floor of the admin building.

"I haven't been sleeping well," she said. "Problems at home, you know."

"Nothing serious, I hope."

"Well, that depends," Rawlings said. "My partner's sleeping with another woman to get back at me for the affair he thinks I'm having with MacDonald. And my youngest has to go in for some tests with a specialist. He's not developing as quickly as he should be."

"Little Luke?" Copeland had seen the photos on her desk. He wasn't allowed to see his own kids, but he could ask after hers as much as he wanted. "I'm sorry to hear that."

"Yeah," Rawlings said. "Andrew wants me to spend more time at home. Says it's my fault."

"It's not your fault."

"Tell that to Andrew," Rawlings said. "He's always hated that I'm the breadwinner. But he can't hold down a job. I wouldn't work here if I didn't have to. I'd love to spend more time with the kids, but I can't. I just *can't*."

She paused for a moment. They were at the top of the building now, standing in the ante-chamber outside John MacDonald's office. This was where Rawlings was supposed to work, but she spent more time wandering around the complex than she did sitting at her desk and manning the telephone. There were the girls in reception for that.

"Sorry," she said. "You don't need to hear all this. I'm just having one of those days. Now that I think about it, so is MacDonald. You be careful in there."

She smiled sadly at him, knocked on MacDonald's door and then made herself scarce before he could give her more work to do.

John MacDonald opened the door and invited the vet into his office. His hair was a windswept mess, and the bags under his eyes spoke of long, sleepless nights and endless amounts of worry. For a moment, Copeland felt sorry for the man. And he was glad he was just a veterinarian.

MacDonald was sitting in a luxury leather chair behind a large mahogany desk. Two LCD computer screens were on the left of the desk, while the right-hand side was piled high with paperwork. His in-tray had overflowed and turned into a mountain, and at some point there'd been an avalanche. Copeland couldn't stop staring at it, as though he expected it to collapse again at any moment.

"How can I help?" MacDonald asked. He'd always been direct, and most of the time that was for the best. If nothing else, it saved time.

"It's the geese," Copeland replied. "The foie gras. It's a waste, sir. Better to slow down production and to do the job properly."

"Is that so?" MacDonald asked. He paused for a moment. "I'm not sure if I can sanction that."

"But that's insanity," Copeland said. "You'll be selling diseased birds before you know it. Not to mention the wastage. How many birds do we lose unnecessarily every year? A thousand?"

"Maybe more," MacDonald said. "Definitely more, if you count the females."

"The females?"

MacDonald sucked air through his teeth and said, "Perhaps you didn't do your research, Dr. Copeland. Foie gras is made from the livers of male geese. The females go down the chute."

"The chicken chute?"

"Exactly."

Copeland shuddered. He knew the chute that the boss was talking about. He'd seen it in the chicken shed when Bob Knowles was working the line. When the workers were sexing the layer chicks, they had to pick the tiny creatures up one-by-one and to throw the males down the chute. At the bottom of the chute was the grinder, which tore their flesh and bones apart and spat the goop out into buckets of fertiliser or vats of pet food. The worst part about it, in Copeland's mind at least, was that they were still alive when they flew down the chute to meet their maker. Copeland had seen the output. He'd expected it to be a reddish, bloody mess, but it came out the sludgy yellow-brown of fat and bone marrow. The stench had made him vomit, which wasn't unusual.

"Is this all above board?" Copeland asked.

"It is now," MacDonald said. He grinned. "Look, it's a bit of a grey area. Don't ask, don't tell, right? Let's just say that it isn't illegal, not anymore. Not since we left the EU. No new laws have been drafted to say that we can't use crates, so until I hear otherwise, we're going to crank out as much foie gras as we can manage. It's a big earner. You'll just have to make it work."

"I see," Copeland said. He sighed. "Okay, I'll see what

we can do. We can try to treat the symptoms, see if we can catch the infections early."

"There's something else," MacDonald added, leaning in towards the vet and talking in a low undertone as though he thought that the walls could hear. "I've had reports from some of the section heads and the production workers that the animals are acting strange. Nothing concrete, you understand. There's just a feeling in the air. The calm before the storm."

"Yeah," Copeland said. "I know. I've noticed. I've spent my entire life around animals. They know when something's about to happen. You mean they're not normally like this? It's not just that they know they're waiting for death?"

MacDonald shook his head. "They usually only get spooked when they reach the slaughterhouse. This is different. I want you to find out why."

"You do?" Copeland asked. He frowned. "I thought you didn't like people asking questions."

MacDonald laughed. "I don't mind them asking questions," he said. "As long as they're asking the questions for me."

Copeland was about to say something else, but it was clear from the way that the boss was looking at him that the conversation was over. The vet let himself out and headed for the elevator.

COPELAND WAS AT the northern border of the facility, taking a quick look around the fishery. He hadn't spent much time there since joining the company, but that was because the fish were low priority. You could tell where they stood in the pecking order by the way that they were fed with the shit from the chicken coop, but they did at least have one privilege that the other animals weren't afforded. They weren't kicked, hit and yelled at like the sheep, pigs and cows. There was no need for it.

Sunnyvale's fish were raised in the freshwater lake that the facility backed onto, but they were still kept in cages beneath the water. There were rumours that the water had turned bad and that the fish were starting to die off. Copeland had been drafted in to take a look, and he'd been accompanied by Bugsy Drew, the operations manager who was acting as his direct superior. Jill MacDonald was along for the ride too, exempt from her admin duties to provide a helping hand.

They'd taken a short tour of the facility, but there wasn't much to look at. Unlike the livestock, the fish were effectively invisible, living beneath the water in their metal prisons. Their injuries largely consisted of abrasions from the metal and the ensuing infections that turned their piscine skin into hives of pus-filled sores.

"So whaddaya think?" Drew asked. He was standing to the vet's right, and the three of them were perched on a metal gantry similar to the one around the cusp of the admin building. This one wound its way around the walls of a prefabricated building and looked out through a Plexiglas screen on to the water. It was cold out there. Cold, wet and grey.

"Hard to tell," Copeland replied. "It's not really my area. If you can get me some samples of the dead ones then I can try to spot the cause, but it boils down to this. The water is bad. It's over-polluted, probably because it's too close to the trash facility. Not to mention the thousands of pigs, cows, chickens and sheep around here."

"So what should we do?"

"Move the fish farm," Copeland said.

"We can't do that," Drew replied. "I'm not telling MacDonald that he needs to redesign half the damn complex."

"Then let me tell him."

"Not a chance," Drew said. "What are the other options?"

"I could talk to him," Jill began. "He's my uncle, perhaps he'll–"

Drew's radio crackled into life, and he held a hand up to cut her short. The voice on the other end was distorted, but it was also Liverpudlian enough for it to mean that it could only have been Mike Chase, the junior security recruit.

"We've got a fuckin' emergency," Chase shouted. "We need someone in the chicken shed right now. There's been an accident."

Copeland hesitated for a moment. He met Drew's eyes and then looked away. The boss picked up his handset and buzzed it into life.

"Who's on duty?" he asked, referring to Sunnyvale's trained first-aiders. There used to be two or three of them on duty at any time, but thanks to cuts from senior management and a number of recent departures, that was no longer the case. "Anyone?"

There was silence from the walkie talkie. Drew and

Copeland met each other's eyes again.

"I guess it's just me," Copeland said.

Drew nodded at him and picked up the radio. "Roger that," he said. "I've got the vet with me. We'll be right over."

"The vet?" Chase replied. "I ain't talking about a chicken. Steve-o's got his fuckin' hand in the shredder."

"Ten-four," Drew said. "We'll be right there."

Copeland was already a dozen paces ahead of him with his veterinary kit in hand. It wasn't quite a first aid kit but it would have to do, and he had enough opiates and bandages to treat a horse. That would be enough in most cases, but the mention of the shredder didn't sound so good.

As they reached the outside of the fishery, they spotted a buggy heading towards them. It pulled up alongside them, and Big Jim leaned his head out of the door.

"Oi," he bellowed. "Get yer arse in here, Mr. Vet Man."

He didn't need telling twice. There was only room for two in the buggy, so Bugsy and Jill were left behind to hightail along the path towards the chicken shed. Meanwhile, Big Jim drove the cart like a madman, and they pushed its suspension to the limits as they bounced their way along the grassy verges, going from red asphalt to brown mud to red asphalt again. It took them less than two minutes to cross the quarter mile between the fishery and the chicken shed.

They could smell the metallic tang of blood from fifty paces. Steve-o Puck was one of the more popular production workers, and Copeland guessed that if he got out of this latest predicament then his popularity would soar even higher. Everyone would want to pick his brains about the accident, and there'd be a queue to sit beside him in the canteen. But that was *if* he got out of it, and Copeland knew he was the man's only hope.

He rushed over to where Steve-o was standing in the

middle of a spreading pool of blood. He had one hand stuck inside the shredding machine, a big burnished beast of metal and malice. To one side, the conveyor belt trundled on, carrying the chosen chicks to the debeaking machine, where Bob Knowles was picking them up and holding their faces up to the cauteriser. Like in the theatre, the show must go on. Even an injury as severe as Steve-o's wasn't enough to bring production to a halt, although his co-workers were watching eagle-eyed as he howled in pain and tried to free his arm from the contraption.

Copeland patted the man on the shoulder and whispered something into his ear, then leaned in closer and peered into the innards of the machine. It was dark and disturbing, lubricated with blood and gristle. Someone had hit the emergency stop button, but Steve-o's hand was still stuck inside there, wrapped around the metal. Copeland could tell that there was no way to save it. The bones and sinews were stretched out like a spider web.

"Someone call an ambulance," Copeland shouted, glancing around at the gaggle of workers who were watching from a distance.

Somebody did just that, but Copeland tuned out the babble of the one-sided conversation as he turned his attention to the wounded man in front of him. If he didn't act quickly, they might as well be calling for a hearse.

"This is going to hurt," he said. Then he rooted through his bag and pulled out a clean syringe and an ampoule of morphine. He took the ampoule out of its packaging and stashed the trash in his back pocket, then inserted the syringe into the ampoule. He measured out a decent dose and held the syringe up to the light to check it. Then he bore down on the man who was still struggling with the machine. Steve-o was screaming bloody murder, and Copeland had never heard anything quite like it. It was worse, a thousand times worse, than the squeal of a wounded horse. It wasn't just pain. It was also fear, desperation and adrenaline.

"Hold on," Copeland said. "We'll get you out of there. Just hold on for me, okay?"

Steve-o didn't reply, but Copeland couldn't blame him. The man was going into shock, and he'd be going into a whole lot worse if the vet didn't pull his mangled hand out of the machine. Cardiac arrest, most likely. Copeland found a vein and tapped it, then gave the man a shot of the good stuff like a junkie in a bathtub. The drug hit his bloodstream in seconds and he relaxed a little, which was all Copeland needed.

He took another look at the mechanism. The thumb and two fingers on Steve-o's hand were wrapped around the metal, but the loose flaps of skin and the broken bones were holding the hand in place. Blood and plasma were leaking out from the wounds, and it was that which had pooled around his feet. Copeland was surprised that the man was still conscious and knew that he'd have to act fast.

"No time to wait for that ambulance," he murmured.

He glanced around and saw that Drew and Jill had arrived, and Big Jim and Darragh O'Rourke were there too, forming a perimeter in case anyone broke ranks and ran over. The rattle and the din of the chicken shed drowned out the worst of Steve-o's cries, but the heat and the blood and the humidity were too much for Jill MacDonald. She bent over with her hands on her knees and spewed her lunch up on to the floor. Copeland wanted to run over to her, to check she was okay, but he didn't have time.

Copeland pointed his free hand towards Big Jim's walkie talkie and shouted, "Get MacDonald to authorise a chopper. I don't care how you do it. We need an emergency evacuation right now."

Big Jim opened his mouth to argue, but Copeland had

already turned back to the man with his hand in the shredder. Then he reached into his kitbag for his stainless-steel scissors and leaned towards the machine. The tension hung in the air. The smell of it was almost tangible. And then Copeland started cutting at the flesh, and the man screamed and screamed and screamed.

It wasn't the most sterile of operating rooms. There were ten thousand chickens surrounding them, all of them crammed into a filthy shed the size of a football pitch. They lay beak to beak in their own waste, too tired to fight and too scared to sleep, while the unhealthy air hung low in the shed like mustard gas. It was thick with moist faecal dust and ammonia, which filled up the lungs of both the birds and the workers and which made it difficult to breathe in there. Disease was a problem, a serious one, and Copeland tried not to think about the germs and bacteria inside the shredder.

Time seemed to pass in slow motion, but the vet kept swimming against the tide and was able to free the remnants of first one finger and then another, followed at last by the thumb, which was mostly intact. But Steve-o's index and middle fingers were mangled beyond recognition, and Copeland had left a butchered mess behind from where he'd cut around the flesh and bone.

But at least the hand was free, and that was a start. The next step was to bandage the wound and to apply some pressure to stop the blood loss. The bandage wasn't a problem, and the vet roped in O'Rourke, the Irish security guard, to apply the pressure.

"Don't let go," Copeland said. "We're going to have to walk him outside. I just hope MacDonald got hold of a helicopter."

As if in answer, the birds in the chicken shed whipped themselves up into a frenzy as somewhere in the distance, the dull whap-whap of spinning blades sent tiny vibrations through the air to burst upon their eardrums.

And at that exact moment, Steve Puck passed out and became a dead weight in the arms of the vet and the security guard. They dragged him across the floor just as fast as they could carry him, leaving a trail of rust-red marking their route across the chicken shit.

STEVE-O SURVIVED THE EVACUATION and the subsequent medical intervention, although his hand didn't. The surgeons grafted some skin across the remaining part of his thumb, but his hand was left permanently disfigured. He was stuck looking like he was miming a telephone call.

Not that anyone got to see him. MacDonald hosted another company-wide meeting, but the details were sparse. Steve-o had been granted an indefinite period of leave, and the rumour was that he wouldn't be coming back.

You can't really blame him, Copeland thought.

Meanwhile, MacDonald and his senior management team were worried about litigation. It was still unclear how the man's hand had ended up in the shredding machine, but if investigators found that Sunnyvale was at fault, there was a chance that the company could find itself on the receiving end of a lawsuit.

Whether it was an accident or not, Steve-o's brush with the shredding machine had become hot gossip in the canteen and on the production lines. He wasn't a big personality, but he'd been at the company for a long time and he was a familiar face around the complex. The general reaction was one of shock, as well as one of newfound respect for the vet who'd saved his life. Copeland's reputation was beginning to spread, and so was the use of his nickname. People he'd never met before had started to call him Doc. While Copeland feigned indifference, he liked it. His experience so far told him that you were nothing at Sunnyvale until you had a nickname. It was one thing for his friends to call him Doc; it was something else entirely when it was total strangers.

The day after the accident, John MacDonald called Copeland into his office. He opened his door in silence and then gestured for him to sit down on one of the luxurious leather chairs opposite his desk. He'd had them custom-made with Sunnyvale leather.

Copeland felt awkward in the silence, so he broke it by asking, "How can I help?"

"I think you know how you can help," MacDonald replied. He leaned forwards in his chair like a raven about to peck at a worm in the soil. "It's my niece, Tom. Oh, I was happy enough for you to show her a thing or two, but I can't have her seeing things that she shouldn't see."

"It's not my fault that Steve-o lost half of his hand," Copeland said.

"I know, Tom," MacDonald replied. "But I'm not happy that my niece was one of the first on the scene. The poor girl was traumatised."

Privately, Copeland disagreed. Sure, she'd lost the contents of her stomach, but she'd gathered herself quickly enough to become the first person to call the emergency services. But as much as he liked having her around from time to time as he made his lonely rounds, he'd worried about her, too. She had talent, but she was also a dreamer and an idealist. He had no doubt that she could become a veterinarian if she wanted to. But she belonged in a sleepy small-town practice, not in the middle of one of Sunnyvale's cow sheds.

"Then put her back on the admin team," Copeland said.

"That's exactly what I'm going to do," MacDonald replied. "I'm glad we're on the same page. But listen here, Tom. If she disobeys my order and tries to tail you again, I want you to tell me. Her place is in the admin building."

"Where it's safe," Copeland muttered.

MacDonald didn't respond.

Time rolled slowly onwards. Weeks passed, and then a month. Christmas came and went, and the new year started with a cold snap that took its toll on the animals. They were quieter than usual, like they were waiting for something. And the rumours of something in the water or of some strange new disease were starting to take off. Something was wrong, all right. They could smell it in the air.

Copeland, meanwhile, had been busy in the sheep enclosure. In comparison to the number of birds and fish at the facility, the sheep population was tiny, and they were out of sight and mind for most of Sunnyvale's employees. The production workers were poorly trained and unable to keep the animals groomed at the best of times, and they were also understaffed and under pressure.

As a result, most of the animals were bedraggled and matted with shit-stained wool that dragged along the floor or wrapped itself around the rusted bars of their pens. Copeland knew that Sunnyvale's policy was to shear and sell the wool, but they wouldn't be able to give it away in the state it was in. He wondered where they dumped the wool they couldn't sell and guessed it ended up in the cesspit or the recycling plant.

"How are they doing?"

Copeland stirred from his thoughts and looked across at the man beside him. His name was Arnie Lorn, and he worked as a supervisor. Fifteen feet along from him, Bruce Laing was lurking and eavesdropping while trying to look busy with a shovel. It was his turn to clean the worst of the straw and the shit, and he was taking his sweet time to do it.

Laing was the man from the cafeteria who'd told Big Jim about Copeland's off-the-record chat with Bob Knowles, so Copeland trusted him about as much as he'd trust the water in the lake where the fish shat themselves silly and where the run-off from the nearby fields carried Sunnyvale's effluence back towards its makers.

"Hey," Lorn said, "I'm talking to you, Doc. What's the situation?"

"Sorry," Copeland replied, drawing his eyes reluctantly away from Laing and casting them back in the direction of the livestock. "I guess it's not too bad in here. A couple of minor violations, but nothing to be alarmed about. I'll draft up a new policy document and send it over so you can sign it off before you share it with your team."

"Great," Lorn said. He was Essex born and bred, and he still had the accent, which somehow hid the sarcasm and made him sound sincere. "I can't wait."

Copeland looked across at him and tried to figure the man out. Arnie Lorn was a balding chap with a sinister smile, like a less attractive Jason Statham. The name badge on his uniform didn't show his surname, as they usually did. Instead, it just showed his initials: AL. Copeland guessed he was in his late forties or early fifties, but he was still in shape. And despite the man's hollow eyes, he knew he was dealing with someone ambitious. Thomas had a reputation for violence, which was what had led to his promotion from slaughterhouse production worker to sheep supervisor. The word in the complex was that Arnie Lorn had his eyes on Bugsy Drew's job. But then according to the gossip, Bugsy Drew didn't do much of anything to begin with.

Copeland opened his mouth to say something, but he was interrupted by the crackling of the walkie talkie. Lorn was wearing one too, and they caused a disconcerting lag effect that made MacDonald sound like a ghost on the airwaves.

"Copeland," the boss said. "Report to my office when you've got five minutes. I need a word."

From his vantage point in the nearby stall, Laing

snorted. Copeland turned to look at him. "Is something the matter?" he asked.

"Nah," Laing said. "It's nothing. You have fun up there in—"

But he was interrupted mid-flow by an angry lamb, which had charged the man with its head lowered and sent him falling to his knees in the shit and straw. Laing swore and Lorn burst out laughing, but Copeland simply stared. It was unlike the meek animals of Sunnyvale to attack a production worker – at least, it was unusual for them to do it outside of the slaughterhouse. They were desperate, but they were also demoralised. They fought with each other, of course, but the big men in their high-vis overalls and the hands that reeked of death were usually enough to keep the animals in line.

Of course, Neil Gibson helped in the slaughterhouse by terrorising the animals with his heavy fists. He was an imposing guy, a big bald bloke with a barrel chest who reeked of cigarette smoke and cheap kebabs. Arnie Lorn might have been losing his hair, but Neil Gibson had given up hope of ever finding it. Other than the chip on one of his teeth and the anchor on his left arm, his paunch was his most distinctive feature. And he wasn't even a sailor.

But then, Copeland thought, *it takes a certain type of guy to work in a slaughterhouse, and Neil Gibson fits the bill.*

"Copeland?"

"Sorry, sir," the vet replied, scooping the device back up to his mouth and ears. "I'm on my way."

He nodded at Lorn, glared at Laing and then hotfooted his way out of the building. It wasn't a good idea to keep MacDonald waiting.

Copeland had been working at Sunnyvale for the best part of four months and had already passed his probation, which meant that his electronic key card had been upgraded to give him access to the majority of the complex. That also meant that he didn't have to faff around in reception, waiting for someone to escort him upstairs and into MacDonald's office. He could simply ride the lift to the top floor and knock on the boss' door.

MacDonald looked pleased to see him, but it was sometimes difficult to tell. He played poker on Wednesday evenings with Big Jim and a couple of the security guys, and it paid off in the form of an inscrutable face that never betrayed what the brain beneath was thinking.

"Ah, Dr. Copeland," MacDonald said. "Good to see you. How's the investigation going?"

"The what?" Copeland asked, taken momentarily aback. MacDonald gestured for the vet to take a seat on the other side of his luxurious mahogany desk. Copeland sank into the leather like a stone hitting the surface of a pond.

"The investigation into what the hell's wrong with my goddamn animals," MacDonald replied.

"Ah," Copeland said. He thought for a moment. "Well, I'm not sure it's anything specific. They're just under a lot of stress. You can't really blame them."

"They haven't always been like this."

"What do you want me to say?" Copeland replied. "This place is a hotbed of disease. You asked me to find out what's wrong with the animals. I'm telling you that they're overcrowded and undernourished, kept in unsanitary conditions and left to fend for themselves. My job is to treat the very worst of them, the animals that would cost the company money if I failed to treat them. That's like expecting one person to pick up every piece of crap in a busy city. You want to know what's wrong with the animals? Everything, Mr. MacDonald. Everything is wrong with the animals."

Copeland paused for a moment. He realised that he'd

clenched his fists and that his heart was racing. MacDonald was staring at him, and for a moment Copeland thought he was about to be given his marching orders.

That's the last thing I need, he thought. *It was hard enough to get this job. I won't have much luck finding another.*

But then MacDonald smiled, and the tension dissipated. "There's something else at work here," he said. "I'm sure of it. But if you're telling me that there's no single cause then I guess there's not much we can do."

"That's not true," Copeland began. "We could—"

"Why did you join us here at Sunnyvale?" MacDonald asked. The abruptness of the question took Copeland by surprise.

"I, uh…"

"I heard you used to run your own practice."

"Yeah," Copeland replied. "Back in Chalfont St. Peter."

"So how did you end up here?"

Copeland shrugged. "I fell on hard times," he said. "I explained all of this in my interview."

"I wasn't there," MacDonald reminded him. "Perhaps you'd care to tell me what happened."

"I'd rather not."

"Hmm," MacDonald said. "Well, I can't force you."

Copeland stared at him for a moment and there was an uncomfortable silence. He broke it with a heavy sigh.

"Fine," the vet said. "Business was bad. I'm sure you know how it is in a small town. I realised I had two choices. I could either sell up or risk bankruptcy. I wanted to risk it, but my wife convinced me otherwise."

"You're married?" MacDonald asked. He frowned and glanced down at Copeland's hands. He didn't wear a ring.

"It's complicated."

"I see," MacDonald said. Then, all of a sudden, he leaned across the desk. He fixed Copeland with an intense

stare that seemed to look right through him. The harsh
fluorescence of the overhead lighting made him look like a
demon or a praying mantis.

"What is it?" Copeland asked. "What's going on?"

"I know the truth, Dr. Copeland," MacDonald said. "Big
Jim and his team make for pretty good detectives. There
were some accusations. You were caught with your hand in
the drug drawers."

"That was never proven."

"No, it wasn't," MacDonald agreed. "But it was serious
enough that you were at risk of being struck off the register
unless you took a deal."

"The past is the past," Copeland said. He shrugged.
"Sure, I took the deal. If I didn't, my reputation would've
been ruined. What does it matter to you?"

"I just like to know who I'm dealing with," MacDonald
said. "And I like to know my veterinarian most of all. You're
the only man who could make or break the company. I'd like
to keep you on my side."

"Well you don't have to worry about that," Copeland
replied. "It's not like I have anywhere else to be."

"Good," MacDonald said. He leaned back again and his
chiselled face took on a little more of its earlier expression.
"Our last veterinarian wasn't so trustworthy."

"Oh?"

"Indeed," MacDonald said. He paused for a moment as
he turned over his options. "Well, I guess you'll find out
eventually. Our last vet was a chap called Fishbourne. He
was with us for six years."

"He left the place in a state."

"I know," MacDonald said. "But that's not the half of it.
The damn fool was working undercover, leaking footage
online. Luckily for us, someone couldn't keep their mouth
shut, and I found out about it. So we, uh... dealt with him."

"You did, huh?" Copeland looked at the man, who was now leaning back in his flexible chair. He looked like he lived without a care in the world, but Copeland knew better. He knew how much of a toll running the complex must take. He had hundreds of livelihoods to worry about – not to mention the thousands of animals he needed to guide through the slaughterhouse and towards their final resting place on the shelves of supermarkets.

"Well," Copeland said, "I guess we all have our secrets. I'm sure Big Jim is hardly a saint."

MacDonald laughed. "You don't know the half of it," he said. Then his expression turned serious again. "Listen, Tom, I appreciate what you've been doing for the place. I really do. Just make sure that you keep the momentum up and that you don't make the same mistake you made before."

"The drugs," Copeland murmured.

"Exactly," MacDonald said. "You keep an eye on Lee Keyes, you hear? He's a manipulative son-of-a-bitch with a history of substance abuse. If he can get to you, he will."

"If that's the case, why employ him in the first place?"

MacDonald grimaced. "He's a damn good worker," he said. "I might not like the guy, but I've got a business to run. I can't afford to lose either of you, so just play nice, okay?"

"I will if he will."

"I guess that's the best we can hope for," MacDonald said. "Just be careful. Lee Keyes is the kind of guy who'd shoot you in the face and then stab you in the back."

When Copeland left MacDonald's office, he was still trying to figure out what the man meant.

JANET PESTON was the talk of the complex.

Her "accident" in the pig shed had largely gone unnoticed, thanks in part to orders from above to keep it quiet. A half dozen witnesses had seen Darragh O'Rourke carry her out of the shed and into the back of one of the security team's SUVs. But once he'd pulled out of the complex and raced her towards the nearest hospital – which was a good fifteen miles away along the narrow, winding roads of the British countryside – she'd been forgotten.

That's just the way it was at Sunnyvale. The staff didn't make friends with each other. They were passing acquaintances, and nobody bothered to bat an eyelid when a former colleague disappeared. Staff retention had always been a problem for the meat industry.

But then the rumours started, and even when John MacDonald himself issued a company-wide memo, they refused to be extinguished or diluted. According to the gossip, she'd had an accident on a piece of machinery and taken early retirement. According to John MacDonald, she'd simply handed in her notice and moved on to pastures new. Only senior management and those half dozen witnesses knew the real truth.

MacDonald had summoned Copeland to the scene of the accident not long afterwards and ordered him to carry out a post-mortem on the pig's carcass. Right away, Copeland could tell that something had happened, and after he pushed MacDonald for an explanation, he was given one.

"The damn thing went crazy," MacDonald said. "Took a chunk out of Janet Peston before O'Rourke hit it with a taser."

"I see," Copeland said. "So that's why it smells like smoky bacon."

At the time, Copeland's investigation didn't uncover anything. The only unusual thing was that the pig was decomposing before it died. The closest thing that Copeland had heard of was necrotising fasciitis, the so-called "flesh-eating disease." But it was too late for the pig, and the rest of its pen-mates had been slaughtered and burned as a precaution. If the rumours were true, the ashes had been thrown into the lake under cover of darkness.

Then came the rumours about Janet Peston. Copeland had heard from an inside source – Carol Rawlings, MacDonald's PA – that her condition had deteriorated. She'd been signed off sick after the initial bite, but she'd since been shipped to a specialist hospital with some unknown disease that had burned right through her immune system. They'd placed her on a ventilator. And if the latest gossip was true, they'd turned off the life support.

Copeland tried dropping MacDonald a line for some more information, but the big boss refused to comment. He only repeated his earlier instructions.

"I don't care what it takes," MacDonald said. "I need you to find out what's killing my animals."

"They're killing each other," Copeland pointed out.

"Quite." There was no warmth in MacDonald's voice, but there was no emotion there, either. "I need you to find out why. We've been running this operation for years and I've never seen anything like it. I can't have our stock killing itself off. If it doesn't make it to the slaughterhouse, it doesn't make it to the supermarket. Find out what's happening and then find out how we can stop it."

"How do you expect me to figure out what went wrong in the pig shed if you won't give me any information?"

MacDonald, who was sitting on the other side of his expensive mahogany desk, shrugged his shoulders. "Just do your best," he said.

And so that was exactly what Copeland resolved to do. MacDonald had signed off an order of second hand books on rare diseases and Copeland had started reading them in the evenings. It wasn't like there was anything else to occupy his time – at least, not since the practice fell apart and his wife took the kids back to Wales to live with their grandmother. He used to live in an old country house with a big garden. They had foxes in the winter and blackbirds in the summer. Now he lived in a rented flat in High Wycombe. His salary barely covered his rent, his food and his fuel.

He sat in his armchair with a microwave meal – a crappy ASDA lasagne – and dipped his fork into it. It tasted like cardboard at best, but it was cheap and packed with nutrients, or at the very least preservatives. Besides, he wasn't paying much attention to the food.

He was almost entirely focussed on the second-hand textbooks that had arrived in the mail. He was looking for some information on the mysterious disease that seemed to be wrapping its filthy tentacles around the complex.

But so far at least, he'd turned up nothing.

***

The voice seemed to come from nowhere.

"Oi," it said.

Copeland looked cautiously around. He was alone, as far as he knew at least, in the cow shed, treating one of the dairy cows that had broken its leg by kicking out at the milking machine. It was hard to blame the beast for its stupidity. Copeland would have lashed out too, if their roles had been reversed. The damn things sucked so hard at the cows' teats that they left big sores and occasionally pulled the nipples themselves clean off. The result was the same either way – crippling infections, decreased production and a quick visit to the great milking shed in the sky via a steel bolt to the side of the head. Those who were unlucky had their throats slit instead and were left to bleed out there and then in the cow shed before their carcasses were loaded onto a forklift and ferried over to the butchery in the slaughterhouse.

It had looked like no one was there. But then his eyes adjusted and he made out a lone figure in the darkness. *Whatever this is,* he thought, *it can't be good news.*

The figure approached him and as it stepped out into the light, Copeland could see it was Steve Puck, the man who'd caught his hand in the shredding machine. He'd lost a lot of weight since the vet had last seen him. Puck's face was sallow and shadowed. He looked like he'd been to hell and back, which he probably had.

"What's up?" Copeland asked. The uneasiness hit him in the stomach like a punch from a gloved fist, but his face didn't show it. He could've faced down MacDonald in a poker game.

"What's up?" the man repeated. "What the fuck do you think? My hand. It's fucking killing me." He waved the offending appendage in Copeland's face. The vet was actually impressed. The surgeons had done a decent job, although he didn't want to think about how much skin they'd had to graft or where it had come from.

"If you've come here to thank me, don't worry about it," Copeland said.

"You've got to give me something," Steve-o demanded. He bum-rushed Copeland and grabbed him by the lapels of his high-vis jacket with his good hand. He shook him and leaned in so close that Copeland could smell the bacon butty he'd had for breakfast. "Give me drugs, Doc. Take the pain away."

"I can't do that."

"You've got to," Steve-o said. "You're the reason I'm in this mess."

"That's not true," Copeland replied. "I did what I could. I saved your life."

"Exactly. But what if I don't want to live it?"

"I don't think you get much choice."

"Fuck you," Steve-o said. "Give me the damn drugs, Doc. It shouldn't be too much of a problem. I hear that's why you're here in the first place."

"Who told you that?"

"Word travels fast," Steve-o said. He shrugged.

"I should report you."

"So report me," Steve-o said. "What's Old MacDonald going to do?"

"I wasn't talking about John MacDonald," Copeland said. "I was thinking about Bugsy Drew."

"Drew?" Steve-o spat on the floor, a big globule of saliva with a hint of green in it. He nudged at it with the toe of his boot and it left a residue on the leather, as though a snail had crawled across it. "Fuck him. He only got the job in the first place because he blackmailed the boss. He doesn't actually do anything. Everyone knows it."

Copeland looked at the guy in the same way that he looked at homeless men when they asked him for change.

"I'm not going to help you," he said.

"Puh-lease, Doc!"

Copeland scrutinised the man. He had that look in his eyes, a hungry look. Copeland had seen it before in a former colleague, a Oxycontin addict who'd slipped him the odd bribe to turn a blind eye when he raided the medicine store.

They didn't have Oxycontin, but they did have barbiturates and opioids. The bribes kept coming, for a while at least. Then the money dried up and the bribes turned to threats and blackmail. Copeland went from turning a blind eye to acting as a courier, stealing pills and dropping them off at predetermined delivery points every time the addict called him. If he missed a delivery, the fiend would go public and accuse the vet of stealing the supplies. At first, no one had noticed. But then the stock discrepancies had inevitably been spotted and a well-meaning staffer had followed protocol and reported it to the authorities and the practice's board of directors.

That was how Copeland had lost his job, no matter what Old MacDonald said. And it was starting to feel like history was repeating itself.

Still, Steve-o needed help, and Copeland felt some perverse sense of duty to medicate him. He sighed.

"Why did you come back?" he asked.

Steve-o shrugged. "A man needs a job," he said. "And this was the only one on offer. There's not much on the market for a one-handed labourer."

"I see," Copeland said. He sighed again. "What time does your shift finish?"

***

Something was happening beneath Sunnyvale.

It lived in the darkness and fled from the sounds of man and beast. It hid from the machinery and burrowed deeper when it sensed the security team's transportation carts. It fed off the flesh of dead animals wherever it could find them. In a place like Sunnyvale, it wasn't hard to find nourishment.

It had twenty-six eyes and fifty-two paws, hundreds of abscessed teeth and thirteen brains, all determined to do things in their own way. The creature was blind and frightened, but it was also angry, hungry and out for blood. It moved unevenly, scuttling backwards and forwards or sidling sideways like a crab out of water. It burrowed beneath the ground when the option was there. When it wasn't, it moved by night and crawled along air ducts or through water pipes.

And the smell. It was like the smell of rotting hair and animal sweat, like wet dog in a swamp with a touch of pestilence. The animals could smell it coming, and they made damn sure they kept away from it, as much as they could in their cramped cages. The humans could smell it too, but they put it down to the livestock and not the many-eyed creature beneath the complex.

It was moving, seeking nourishment again. By day, it stayed in its nest in the bowels of the recycling plant, but by night it roamed the facility, when the workers were at home and the security guards couldn't see it even with their flashlights. If they did catch a glimpse of the creature, they wrote it off as the hallucination of an over-tired mind.

But the creature beneath Sunnyvale was all too real, and if it was a monster then it was only a product of its environment. It was meat made living, the reincarnation of a million tortured souls into a new breed of creature which spread death and disease wherever it went.

Right then, it was heading for the chicken shed. There was death in the air, the smell of blood wafting deliciously towards it like the aroma of kebab meat to a drunk on a Friday night pub crawl.

It followed its noses, fighting with itself as it went. There was malice to spread – and it was ready to spread it.

***

Sunnyvale was under siege.

The Buckinghamshire Save protestors had arrived just after sunrise, their arms laden with megaphones and pickets with slogans like "Stop the Slaughter" and "No More Factory Farming" alongside others that said "End the Pollution" and "Dirty Water? No Thanks!" They'd arrived in the backs of SUVs and minivans and were picketing the outer perimeter.

They were led by an angry-looking man with a fiery red beard, who was wearing a patchwork jumper, waterproof trousers and a pair of wellington boots. He was wearing a big blue camping rucksack and carrying a megaphone, into which he was leading the chant.

"What do we want?"

"No more CAFOs!"

"When do we want it?"

"Now!"

John MacDonald was watching events unfold from the security of his office at the top of the admin building. He could watch and listen from the facility's perimeter cameras. Perversely, their chant had made him smile. It was an open secret that the industry hated the term "factory farming". They preferred to call their facilities CAFOs, concentrated animal feeding operations. The protestors' use of their preferred term made the chant lose some of its effect.

But they were still a problem, and problems had to be dealt with.

His walkie talkie crackled into life, and Big Jim's gravelly voice filtered through the airwaves. "Ah'm at the gate," he said. "Permishun tae open fire?"

"Permission denied," MacDonald replied, his hand jumping to the walkie talkie with the speed and finesse of a gunslinger.

"What about them rubber bullets ye told us tae stock up

oan?"

"Permission denied," MacDonald repeated. "Jesus, Jim, we'll have a revolt on our hands if you open fire. No, no. For now, I want you to stay in position and keep an eye on what they're doing. Meanwhile, I want the facility on lockdown. No one enters and no one leaves."

"Aye," Jim said. "Ah'll get Chase oan it."

"Mike Chase?" MacDonald asked. "Where's O'Rourke?"

"Beats me," Big Jim replied. "Ah've goat mah hands full, ye ken. Ask him yeself."

MacDonald pushed the trigger of the walkie talkie, but O'Rourke beat him to it.

"I'm in the cow shed," he said. "And if you don't mind, I'm gonna maintain radio silence over here for a minute. We've got a problem on our hands."

"A problem?" MacDonald asked. But there was no reply, and he surmised that Big Jim's deputy had made good on his promise and turned the volume down on his receiver. It was one of the few drawbacks of the old technology. The walkie talkies were army surplus units, which meant they had a decent range and were built to last. They also worked, which was more than could be said for mobile phones. The rolling Chiltern Hills that surrounded them made it almost impossible to get a signal.

"Ah'm at the gate, bossman," Big Jim said. "There's a fucken ton of 'em. Must be fifty at least, mebbe more."

"As long as they stay outside the fence, we're fine," MacDonald snapped. The static buzz of the walkie talkie was starting to give him a headache.

And he was running out of options.

AT THE FRONT OF THE COMPLEX, the protest continued. Objects were being thrown, chants were being chanted and it was starting to get a little messy.

The man with the fiery beard was called Harry Yorke, and he was there with his wife Janet and their two kids, Jack and Alisha. They were that kind of family. They lived together, they ate together and they protested together. Yorke was leading the protest, but he hadn't arranged it. They were as left-wing as they came, a splinter cell of the Animal Liberation Front which had kept its distributed leadership and adapted it for the new millennium. They had no leader. They didn't need one.

But thirty-eight-year-old Harry Yorke was the chief spokesperson for the day, and if he was arrested then someone else would take over, followed by someone else and then someone else. It was just the way they worked.

Janet Yorke was thirty-two-years-old, a retail assistant by day when she wasn't calling in sick to accompany her husband on his protests. She had long, black hair and a slim figure, an unexpected by-product of her vegan diet, but she still looked as though she belonged indoors and not out in a muddy field trying to lead her kids through a protest against the meat industry.

Jack Yorke, her eight-year-old son, didn't want to be there. He had a sulk on, and the expression on his face could have peeled paint from the wall. He was quite clearly making the best of a bad job, dragging his heels along the floor while his mother tugged at his arm and tip-tapping away at a game on his smartphone.

Jack's sister, eleven-year-old Alisha, was much more into it, but then she was a wannabe vet like Jill MacDonald. She had a thin face and a long ponytail, and she was wearing one of her dad's old bomber jackets to keep herself warm. She was holding a placard that said "down with this sort of thing" and looking for all the world like an extra from a Monty Python sketch. Her father had told her that she could lead the chants with the megaphone if she behaved herself. She was trying to make good on that promise.

Harry Yorke, the closest thing the group had to a lead protestor, was a great, hulking man with a big beer belly and a bushy beard. He was wearing a balaclava on his head just in case he needed it, but the Sunnyvale protest was a far cry from the marches of his youth in the 1990s when he'd clashed with cops over nuclear disarmament. He was glad of it, too. There was no place for kids at those protests, where gas canisters flew through the air and policemen on horseback ushered rioters and peaceful protestors alike into confined spaces, cutting off their access to food and water in an attempt to shut them down.

He missed those days, and he missed the covert operations where he'd worked to free trapped animals from laboratories. But he had a police record longer than those of most career criminals, and Janet had begged him to change his ways after the kids were born. And to his credit, he had. But it was a little like quitting smoking. He had to constantly work at it if he wanted to defeat the cravings.

"Are we nearly done yet?"

The voice belonged to his son, Jack Yorke, and Harry turned to look at him with a vacant expression on his face, as though he'd forgotten the boy was even there.

"Soon," Harry said.

"I don't care about the animals," he said. "I just want to go and play football. All my friends think I'm a loser."

"Shush now," Harry said, turning his back on his son so he could take in the rest of the protestors. There weren't many of them – far fewer than he would have liked – but they would have to do. He wondered vaguely if there'd be any trouble.

Yorke could see Big Jim and his men on the other side of the perimeter fence, staring them down from a distance with their hands hanging menacingly at their sides, where they held their truncheons, their pepper spray and their tasers. A few of the men, Big Jim included, were carrying firearms. But Yorke didn't know who they were, and he didn't know whether they were licenced to carry those weapons or not. If not... well, it wouldn't be the first violation that the facility was responsible for.

Yorke held the megaphone up to his lips and prepared to lead another chant, but just as he was about to shout, he lowered it again.

A car was approaching, a plain black Mercedes with tinted windows and too much chrome across the grille and bonnet. It looked like a custom job, but it also screamed government. Some of the protestors had seen the same cars following them at a surreptitious distance as they went about their business.

Someone threw an egg at the car, and the sound it made as it whizzed through the air reminded Yorke of the tear gas canisters that the cops had launched at a protest up in Wakefield. It splattered against the car's impeccable paint job and flew on to the windscreen. The driver of the car flicked the windscreen wipers into life and smeared the goop across the glass, but he drove on as though he hadn't even noticed.

"Don't worry," someone shouted. "They're free range."

Someone else laughed, but the mood was turning sour and tension was in the air. It was something instinctively felt, just a little less perceptible than the crackle of electricity from beneath a pylon. The animals knew it was there, though. And so did most of the humans.

The protestors rushed forwards as the car approached the clearance gate. The driver flashed a DAERA ID badge and was waved through immediately, but the protestors were hot on the vehicle's tail. They tried to rush the gate as it was lowering, Sunnyvale's security team stepped up to bridge the gap, the protestors refused to back down, and then a fist swung from somewhere and caught one of Big Jim's men on the back of the head. Even amongst the confusion, it seemed like a clear signal, like a handkerchief dropping at the start of a duel, and violence broke out like a flu epidemic. Within seconds, one of the protestors had gone down and another had almost broken his wrist trying to hit Big Jim with a rugby tackle. The stoic Scotsman had stayed upright and clipped the man in the side of the head with a knee before tossing him aside and pulling his baton from his belt.

Harry Yorke was right there at the front with his fists flying, though his wife and daughter had the sense to hang back. He wouldn't be seeing them again for some time. He was standing shoulder to shoulder with a dozen of his best men, but Big Jim and his guards were coming right at them from the opposite direction with the unstoppable force of a battering ram.

They ran towards the protestors with their batons raised. The two groups clashed and broke apart like waves on the rocks as the car rolled forwards towards the complex and its second checkpoint. To the occupant, the melee in the vehicle's rear-view mirror was par for the course, and it played out like a TV movie on a home cinema screen. But to the participants, it was violently, brutally real.

The protestors surged forward again and were held at

bay, just about, but one of Jim's men was taken down and another caught a nasty right hook to the face. Big Jim had discarded his truncheon and was swinging his gigantic, ham-like fists through the air at anything that moved. His fierce eyes were glowing with a red-hot heat, and he was roaring like a wounded animal. There was no finesse there, just sheer rage and aggression. His right hand was wrapped around a pair of brass knuckles. His job was all but forgotten. All that mattered was the melee.

But they were losing ground, and they knew it. The protestors were more determined, driven by their morals and their beliefs. Jim's lads were driven by their paycheques, and they knew that their salary wouldn't mean much if they weren't alive to spend it.

Mike Chase, the junior security guard, was standing beside and a step behind his boss, who was taking advantage of a brief respite to catch his breath. They'd been battling for just a couple of minutes, but Big Jim was a twenty-a-day man and he wasn't as young as he used to be. He had his hands on his knees, and he was wheezing. As Chase leaned over towards him, he spat a great grey hack of phlegm into the grass.

"There are too many of them," Chase said. His face was twitching from the adrenaline and an angry red welt had appeared below his left eye. He looked like he'd seen things, like his mind had switched itself off and gone on holiday. Jim couldn't blame the kid. He was all talk and no substance. He was a wannabe rapper, not a heavy in a private militia. But he'd have to do.

"Ah've goat a plan," Big Jim replied. He looked mean, meaner than usual, but he also looked determined. "Go and get the splasher. And hurry tae fook. We've no goat much time."

"You sure, Boss?" Chase asked. The splasher was their

nickname for the brand-new water cannon, and so far they'd not had cause to use it. They'd trained with it, but that wasn't the same as pointing it at a group of people and opening fire.

"Aye," Jim said. "It's jest water, ye ken. An' if yon liberal snowflakes press charges, ah'll 'ave 'em fae tresspassin'."

"But they're on public property," Chase reminded him.

"No fae long, lad." Big Jim cupped his hands to his mouth and bellowed an order to his heavies, big northern men with Celtic and Viking blood. Some of them shaved their hair off and some of them couldn't grow any to begin with. Either way, all of them were skinheads, though they were hiding their scalps beneath balaclavas that made them look like the Provisional IRA.

"All right, people!" Jim shouted. "Fall back tae the second gate, ye sons o' whores."

Chase made a break for one of the vehicles, the little golf buggies with the Sunnyvale decal that the security team used to get around the facility. The keys were still in the ignition, so he gunned the engine and turned the buggy around. The splasher was hooked up to one of their SUVs, which were in a parallel line in the car park like a mouthful of rotten teeth. The keys were in the security suite of the admin building. He'd need to put his foot down to get there and back before the action was over and a winner was decided, for better or for worse.

The protestors were still close, and they'd already backed Jim and his men over the checkpoint and into no man's land. Now, with the security men retreating, they pushed further. It had only taken a couple of minutes, but it had the feel of a great victory at an epic battle.

And now they were through the first gate and chasing Big Jim and his men towards the second gate and the true entrance to the complex.

***

"Motherfucking fuck."

Harry Yorke was turning the sky blue with his curses, but only a half dozen of his fellow protestors could hear them. Most of them had fallen back the moment Mike Chase emerged with the splasher. It took two men to operate, but reinforcements had arrived, and the tide of the clash had turned just as soon as the water started flowing. It came out at a high pressure and hit like a string of paintballs. At short distances it could break a man's arm or send them tumbling to the floor in a flail of limbs. Worse, for the protestors at least, it turned their solid footing into an uneven quagmire. Big Jim and his men had the advantage of solid ground. Harry Yorke and his ragtag band of protestors were on the grass and the mud – and the grass and the mud had already been heavily sprayed with the liquid fertiliser from the facility's recycling plant.

"Jesus fucking Christ!" Yorke bellowed. He glanced over to his right, where second-in-command Rob Roland was growling at Big Jim and his team like an angry cave bear. His shirt had been torn and hung loose on his muscular frame, and his hairy chest was matted and tangled like the fur of a Sunnyvale sheep. "Rob, get over here!"

"Huh?"

"Get over here!" he repeated. Even with the number of protestors on the decline, there were still thirty men in the melee and it wasn't easy to push through them. But Rob Roland had big shoulders and bigger muscles, and he carved his way through the pack like a drop of boiling water on a tub of butter.

Rob Roland was getting old, though. While he kept himself in good shape by spending most of his evenings at the local gym, he couldn't do anything about the relentless march of time. He was getting on for sixty, and while he dyed his hair to hide the grey, there wasn't enough of the stuff left for him to fool anyone. He looked like a retired accountant, which was exactly what he was. He was just a retired accountant who refused to go gentle into that good night.

Rob Roland dodged a jet of high-powered water and made eye contact with Harry Yorke, who was gesturing frantically towards him. "What is it?" he shouted.

"Change of plan," Yorke replied. "If they're going to play dirty, so will we."

"What do you mean?"

"I need you to distract them," Yorke said. "Keep fighting. Push them back to the gate if you can."

"What are you going to do?" Roland asked.

"There's no time," Yorke replied. "Just do it. Hurry!"

Roland did as he was told, and while the protestors pushed forward, Harry Yorke covered their approach by tossing a hand-made smoke grenade. He'd learned to make the things from *The Anarchist's Cookbook*, and they did the job. He'd worked a little magic to turn the smoke a deep, crimson red, and the result was a huge cloud that looked like a bloody nuke had gone off in the no man's land between Sunnyvale's inner and outer perimeters.

Roland organised the ragtag bunch of remaining protestors into a wedge and they drove forward, pushing Jim's men aside and heading straight for the second checkpoint and Sunnyvale's car park. There was a hum of water in the air as the splasher kept on splashing, but the smoke was too thick and there was nothing for Jim's men to aim for.

Rocks were flying and so were curses, and then a shrill whistle pierced the air as a canister of CS gas flew through it and landed right in the middle of the combat. It was chaos and nobody knew who'd fired it. It almost didn't matter.

While all this was happening, Harry Yorke was making a beeline for the fence, using the smoke to cover himself. It was starting to thin out, but Yorke had reached the finish line and found himself up against the mesh. From there, it was just a case of slipping the wire cutters from his utility belt and making himself a door.

It didn't take him long – but then, it wasn't his first time.

This has always been the plan, and Sunnyvale's staff had fallen for it hook, line and sinker. They'd taken the bait.

Now he was inside the complex at its south-eastern corner. Unfortunately for Sunnyvale, that also meant he was right next to their communications shed. It was barely a hundred and fifty feet away.

He pulled his hood low over his eyes and ran towards it.

THERE WERE THREE PEOPLE in the south-east corner of the chicken shed, and none of them were having a good time.

The first was Yvonne Strong, the heavy-set, leather-faced production worker who'd once told Copeland that the walls had ears. She was tall, especially for a woman her age. Her back had been broken by neither the hard work nor the passing of time and the harsh treatment of an uncaring society. Yvonne Strong wasn't the type to let that affect her. She was a friendly woman, full of life and vivacity, a pleasure to be around. The only reason that none of her colleagues made a pass at her was that they remembered her husband, who'd worked alongside them. But he was long gone by then, driving forklifts in a warehouse in Amersham. Yvonne Strong had stayed behind.

She was joined by Bob Knowles, who'd been subdued since his "little chat" with Big Jim and his men, as well as a Yorkshireman called Hamish Gray who'd switched roles to take over from Steve-o after the incident with the shredding machine. Hamish was an older gentleman, much older than Steve-o, easily in his sixties with thinning hair on the top of his skull and a salt and pepper beard. His nose was huge, but his eyes were small and sunk into his skull. He looked beaten down by life, a half-dead manual labourer who'd been kept on for too long.

Copeland had heard of him. He was one of the "legends", the elite group of employees who'd been with the company since the start. The vet could tell just by looking at him. The old-timers all had a certain look in their eyes.

They'd *seen* things.

They were watching the animals and putting some money down. There was precious little to do at Sunnyvale, and so casual gambling on the animals was as common as one of the admin girls checking her Facebook page when the boss wasn't looking.

In the chicken shed, they were betting on the outcome of one of the ever-increasing fights amongst the animals. They didn't have names – it wasn't that kind of place – but they picked up nicknames during the battles. Right then, it was Big Wing versus Fat Chick.

But that night, something was different. They were used to two birds fighting each other because, like on a night out with Big Jim in Glasgow, a fight was inevitable. They just weren't used to *all of them* fighting.

The noise was almost unbearable, like a harpy clawing at their eardrums. It looked like a pillow fight, except the pillows were sick chickens and the feathers that flew through the air were yanked from their steroid-filled breasts. One chicken grabbed another and broke its neck with a sickening crack that seemed to echo through the complex, and then the other birds rushed towards it and tore the thing to pieces.

The three production workers watched on in disbelief. "I've never seen nothin' like it," Strong said. "What about you?"

Bob Knowles shook his head and Hamish shrugged his shoulders and said, "Nowt."

"Shit," she murmured. "Reckon we should call Copeland?"

"Fuck Copeland," Knowles replied. "That motherfucker's nothing but trouble. We can deal with this ourselves."

"Yeah?" Hamish said. "How?"

"We draw straws," Knowles said.

And so they did. They were surrounded by the stuff. It littered the floor like confetti after a wedding. Yvonne Strong picked up a couple of stalks and trimmed one of them down, then hid the three of them inside a closed fist. She held the fist out to the two boys.

Knowles picked first, and he breathed a sigh of relief when he pulled at it to find a long stalk at the end of the head. Hamish drew second and pulled out a short straw. Then Strong opened up her own hand to reveal another long straw.

"Tough luck," she said.

Hamish groaned and spat on the floor. "Fuck this," he said. "I never wanted this job in the first place. I ought to be retired by now, living out my days in the Yorkshire Dales."

"Someone's got to do it," Knowles said.

"But why does it have to be me?" Hamish replied. "I'm an old man, older than you at least. And I've got a hangover. I've not got a hope. No mortgage, no pension. After the wife died, I lost the house. Now I'm living in a little bedsit."

"You picked the short straw," Yvonne Strong said. "Sorry, old man. We didn't ask for your life story."

He continued to grumble under his breath. But he also did what was expected of him.

The birds were still fighting, and the hail of feathers had been joined by a rain of blood and faecal matter. Some of the birds were already dead on the floor, while others were still letting fly with their beaks and claws. Hamish picked up a metal shovel that was leaning against the fence, unlatched the door to the production floor and walked in amongst the chickens.

There must have been a thousand of them there in just that small section of the massive complex, but a thousand was more than enough. Hamish walked cautiously forwards with the shovel in his hands and smacked it against the floor. It clanged, and the clang echoed until the howl of metal against metal reverberated around the room and drowned the chickens out.

They turned to look at him. Then they attacked.

They started by moving closer, hemming him in with a vicious circle of broken beaks from the trimming machine. It was designed to stop them from hurting each other, but the trimming machine wasn't always accurate. Often, if they were lucky enough to survive the process, they were left with a sharp spike instead of something that looked like a beak. And that was bad news for Hamish when they flooded towards him.

They flew at his feet and legs. They flew at his groin and his chest. Some of them even caught some air time and went for his face, scrabbling madly at his eyes. He managed a swing or two with his shovel, catching one bird a glancing blow and sending another flying through the air, and then his own momentum took him down to the floor and they surrounded him like hyenas at the scene of a fresh kill.

Hamish was in a frenzy. He couldn't hear his colleagues shouting for help or the crackle of their radios, but he *could* hear the clucking of a thousand angry birds as they smelled his blood. Then it went dark as they ripped out his eyeballs, but the sounds just got worse along with the pain, which felt like red hot fire all over him. The birds had even torn off his clothing, and it was just his feet in their protective leather boots that remained unscathed.

He was shouting, crying out again, and then that was silenced too as a particularly large bird caught his tongue and ripped it from his mouth like it was pulling a worm from the ground.

That was when he passed out. He never woke up again.

***

Inspector Diane Hyde was in over her head.

Not that anyone would have known it from looking at her. She was a stern, imposing woman with long, curly hair that took half an hour every morning to look effortless. Her hazel eyes had a hint of steel to them, and the way her jaw was set made it look like she'd never smiled. But that wasn't why she set her jaw like that. She just wanted to keep her mouth as firmly shut as possible so that she didn't inhale too much of the toxic air of the complex. Not that breathing through her nose made it any easier. The stench was almost overwhelming.

As a second generation British Asian with two kids and a mortgage, she also had imposter syndrome. It didn't help that her husband, an Essex boy with Celtic blood, thought it was a woman's job to raise the kids and lay the table. But Harry Hyde was an odd job man, a casual labourer. While he'd wasted his weekdays looking forward to the pub on Friday night, she'd been busy climbing the career ladder. It was a point of contention between the two of them, the nucleus of a war of words that had been fought and won over the last two years.

Her visit to Sunnyvale was set to be her last major inspection before she retired from the role and switched to a part-time desk job. And although she'd initially resisted the idea, she had to admit that she was secretly looking forward to it. It was easier to read about cruelty than to see it.

Hyde worked for Environmental Health as part of a national team that covered the whole of the UK. She'd seen factory farms before, but she hadn't been to Sunnyvale. For a start, it was the largest facility that she'd ever seen, although she'd heard of even bigger ones across the pond in the States. Then there was the protest at the gates, the arrival of which was too well-timed to be a coincidence. Somebody knew they were going to be there, and they'd arranged a little welcome party. She suspected that it was whoever had tipped off her team in the first place.

But they needn't have bothered. Sunnyvale was quite clearly in breach of a number of policies, even though it no longer fell under EU jurisdiction. She'd already seen her fair share of neglect in the fishery, and from there they'd moved on to the slaughterhouse, which had been an eye opener. The line had been moving and so she was able to see first-hand how the birds were taken to meet their maker.

The majority of the process was automated. The chickens were crated and brought in from the shed, and then the production workers were tasked with unpacking them and shackling them by their feet from the production line. From there, they were electrocuted and then dragged past a series of rotating disks which cut their throats, although the birds were different shapes and sizes and so some survived without a scratch while others were decapitated. Then they were dunked into a vat of scalding water. Those that survived the electricity and the buzzsaws were drowned or cooked alive.

But like it or not, they were within the permissible threshold for accidents and non-compliance. Just.

She thought back to the briefing notes that she'd been given by her dour-faced superior, a member of the old boys' club who clearly hadn't bought into equality in the workplace. He'd given her the Sunnyvale job because no one else wanted to do it. And like a fool, she'd taken it on because she wanted to show she was up to anything they could throw at her.

The notes also covered the complex's history, and it was a bloody history indeed. Sunnyvale wouldn't have been possible even five years earlier, but it had sprung up almost overnight to take advantage of loopholes in the law after the country's withdrawal from the European Union. According to the rumour mill, it was financed by the Americans and backed by Chinese venture capital, but as a privately owned company, they were under no obligation to reveal where their money was coming from. The facility was a product of the times, its growth spurred by the falling value of the pound and the rising price of imported meat. The general public wanted cheap sausages and chicken nuggets, and the powers-that-be needed some way to deliver them.

And so Sunnyvale was born. The mega-farm sprung up almost overnight after its applications were approved, and just four years down the line they were still new enough to draw constant criticism. It was the divisive issue of the day. People talked about it over the breakfast table, especially if they lived in the Chilterns where the facility was tucked away, and bloggers blogged about it on both sides of the argument. *It creates jobs. It poisons the environment. It provides cheap food. It causes unnecessary suffering for animals.* Hyde had read all of the arguments, but she'd reserved her judgement until she'd had a chance to see the place from the inside.

This was her chance, and so far, the staff had been courteous, almost welcoming. But then she heard the crackle of a radio and her guide, a man called Carl Taylor from Big Jim's security team, asked her to stop for a second. Taylor was a Kanye West lookalike right down to the goatee and the cropped black hair, but that wasn't what people knew him for. He was a serious guy with a serious job and an almost military efficiency. He also had no sense of humour.

He stepped to one side and spoke a few words into the radio, then said "stay here" before breaking off in a sprint towards the chicken shed.

And because it was her job to investigate any area of the facility that she needed to, she decided to follow him to see what the fuss was about.

She followed Taylor at a distance, almost losing him completely when he flashed his ID badge at the door to gain entry. She had to leap towards it and wedge her fingers in the gap to stop it from closing. It hurt like hell, but while she felt the pain, she hardly registered it. She was on a mission.

Taylor hit a right and two lefts, and Hyde followed his footsteps as cautiously as she could. Nothing could have prepared her for what she was about to see.

The corridor opened up and she found herself at the end of a long, metal gantry which overlooked massive bird pens to either side. The birds were going crazy, squawking their overworked hearts out, fighting to the death with the limited tooth and nail that was available to them and just generally causing a ruckus. She'd never seen anything like it, but she knew that it wasn't normal.

And then she saw the human commotion halfway down the gantry, where Taylor had joined a hysterical Bob Knowles and Yvonne Strong. All three of them were shouting at the same time and Hyde could only make out the highlights: words like "Hamish," "chickens" and "dead." She edged cautiously forwards, mindful of the thousands of birds all around her and the hellish din that turned the air black with sound.

She got a little closer, and she saw the cause of the commotion. She wanted to turn around and get the hell out of there, but her legs and her head wouldn't let her. She just couldn't turn away. But the bloody carcass of former production worker Hamish Gray, his ribs already exposed and poking through his luminescent Sunnyvale outfit, demanded attention. It was all she could see – that and the hive of delirious animals around it. Hyde pulled out her smartphone and flicked the camera open, then began to snap a couple of photographs. The flash lit up the room, and then there was a hand on her arm and Carl Taylor was dragging her away from the scene and out of the building.

"I said 'stay here'," he growled, pushing her through the door and making sure that he locked it behind him.

Hyde fell to her knees and vomited all over the grass. She spewed and spewed until there was nothing left inside her, and then she fell backwards and just lay there on her back, staring at the clouds as they danced past like sheep in the sky.

Then she pulled herself up onto shaky legs and tried to call her superiors, thanking any god that would have her that Carl Taylor hadn't had the sense to take her phone away, but there was no signal at Sunnyvale and no way out if the protestors were still swarming the gate. She needed a landline.

Which meant that she needed to blag her way into the admin building.

Jill MacDonald was manning reception alone. She was wearing a pretty blue dress that she'd been given for her sixteenth birthday and her face was flushed red, like she'd just ran to the shops and back for a pint of milk. She looked like she was in way over her head, which was good news for Inspector Hyde. Jill MacDonald hadn't been fully trained on Sunnyvale's secretive approach to public relations, so she made a fateful mistake. She tried to be helpful.

"How can I help?" she asked.

"I need to speak to your CEO," Hyde replied.

"John MacDonald?" Jill replied. "He's my uncle. But I'm afraid you'll have to"

"It's urgent," Hyde insisted. "Please. Tell him it's a matter of life and death. Tell him it's Diane Hyde from Environmental Health. And let me borrow that phone while you're at it."

Hyde didn't wait for an answer and moved around to

the other side of the reception desk, where two more landlines were perched in front of two password-protected computer terminals.

"You have to press nine if you want to dial out," Jill whispered, before reaching over to her own handset and putting a call in to her uncle.

"Thanks," Hyde replied. She keyed in a few digits and called headquarters. She didn't say much because she didn't have to. She just identified herself and spoke a few carefully coded words that would make sense to her superiors but not to the teenage receptionist beside her. Then she put the phone down.

Jill MacDonald put the phone down too. She looked troubled. "Uncle John says he'll speak to you now. I'm to take you right up to him."

"Good," Hyde said. "Then let's go."

JOHN MACDONALD WASN'T HAPPY.

"Let me get this straight," he said. "You want me to close the facility?"

"That's correct," Hyde replied. She was standing in MacDonald's office and looking down at the man from the other side of his mahogany desk. Sunnyvale's CEO looked at ease, leaning back in his chair with his feet up in front of him. "For now, at least."

MacDonald shook his head. "No," he said. "I can't do that."

"I'm afraid you don't have much choice," Hyde replied. "There's something wrong at this facility. A worker has been killed in the chicken shed, for god's sake. We need to close the doors, quarantine the staff and carry out a full investigation."

"Woah, woah, woah," MacDonald said. "Slow down. Quarantine?"

Hyde nodded. "I'm afraid so. At least until we can make sure there's no chance of an outbreak."

"An outbreak of what?"

"Who knows?" Hyde said. "We'll have to wait until we get some results from the lab."

"How long will that take?"

Hyde shrugged. "It'll take as long as it takes."

"No," MacDonald said. He shook his head and then fixed her with a solid stare. "I can't sanction that. You have no idea how much that would cost us."

"You don't have a choice," Hyde replied. "I've already called it in. You have to understand, the government doesn't mess around. You're only able to operate because they allow you to. And right now, we have an incident on our hands. The army are on their way."

"The army?"

"A special unit to combat disease outbreaks, established in the wake of the coronavirus. They have the authority here. They'll keep things under control."

"Under control?"

Hyde nodded. "Like I said, this is a quarantine situation. No one comes in and no one goes out. Not until we're sure it's safe."

"This is ridiculous," MacDonald said. He slammed his fist on the table and then rose ungracefully to his feet. "Get out of my office."

"That won't change anything," Hyde replied, but she made for the door anyway. Then the lights went out and the computer powered down. A shrill whining noise came through from the walls as the air conditioning unit shuddered to a stop. The daylight was still filtering in from outside so they were hardly plunged into darkness, but the sudden absence of noise and light was still noticeable.

"What happened?" Hyde asked.

MacDonald said nothing, spinning around on the spot and marching towards the door to the gantry. Hyde followed closely on his heels, and they soon found themselves outside and looking to the north. The lights were out in the buildings and there was an eerie silence in the air. It was as though time had stopped and everything was in a state of suspended animation.

MacDonald walked west and then south along the gantry before looping back to the east towards the entrance to the facility. Hyde followed him. If MacDonald noticed her presence or took exception to it, he didn't mention it. Along the route, they looked out over the buildings, but the lights and the power showed no sign of coming back on. When they looked at the car park, they could see that Big Jim's men had successfully repelled the protestors, who were fleeing south. In the other direction, a steady stream of armoured cars was approaching the facility.

Then the hum of stressed sheep and angry cows gave way to a deep, thumping *whump-whump* sound. MacDonald and Hyde turned as one to the east, where they saw a steady stream of army-issue Chinooks from the nearby RAF base. There must have been a dozen of the things.

"You see?" Hyde said. "It's too late. You're not in charge anymore."

***

Harry Yorke was in the communications shed.

The inauspicious building was the size of a large garage, which was small by Sunnyvale's standards. Tucked up beside one of the buildings like an afterthought, it was almost invisible from land and air, and most of the facility's employees hadn't even noticed it. Yorke only knew it was there because he'd seen the maps.

He looked at the mess he'd made of the wiring in front of him. Yorke was no electrician, but he knew enough not to kill himself. After he'd figured out how to pull the manual override to take the power supply offline, he'd attacked the wiring with his bolt cutters and then used the tool like a club to smash up circuit boards and transistors left, right and centre.

Sunnyvale's communications shed held everything that the facility needed from the outside world. It housed the fibre optic broadband cables and the power lines from the electric company. It also housed the telephone lines and sat on top of the facility's water pipe. It was an important part of Sunnyvale's infrastructure, and he was beating the shit out of it with the same pair of cutters he'd used to breach the fence and break into the facility to begin with.

But that wasn't enough. He wanted to do more, to take the facility offline for as long as possible. For good, even. He didn't care about the consequences. He'd forgotten about his family, as he'd known he would. He was ready to become a martyr for the cause, to give his freedom for the freedom of the animals.

So he dipped back into his bag and pulled out the fire-lighters and the fuel that he'd brought with him. He built the foundations of a small fire in one of the corners, where the communications shed was more wood and less metal. He poured the majority of the fuel in the corner and then used the last few drops to lay a trail towards the entrance.

Then he pulled a packet of cigarettes from an inside pocket and popped one in his mouth. He removed a monogrammed Zippo lighter from the packet and lit the flame. He knelt down and applied it to the trail of fuel, then watched as the flame took and rushed towards the wall. He stood up again and used the Zippo to light his cigarette. Then he inhaled deeply and walked slowly, calmly towards the door. His job was done.

Or at least, phase one of his job was done. For phase two, he had to make a getaway, so he leant cautiously out to check the coast was clear before racing towards the fence. He'd hardly gone a dozen steps before the first flames went up. He'd covered a dozen more steps before somebody shouted something. And he was two thirds of the way back to the hole he'd cut in the fence when someone rugby tackled him and bore him to the ground.

"You're in trouble now, Sonny Jim," they said.

***

Greg Hamze looked like an Aryan white van man. His short blond hair was longer on his head than on his face, but only just. He had the kind of scraggly little beard that said more about its owner's insecurity than his masculinity, and a little mole poked out of the stubble on the left side of his face. He had blue eyes, of course, and hardly any eyebrows. Even though he'd caught Harry Yorke in the act, he was still smiling.

Hamze reached down to his belt to unclip his walkie talkie, then clicked the button and held it up to his mouth. "Hamze here," he said, "down by the comms shed. I've apprehended an intruder, requesting backup."

He glanced back at the communications building, which was already burning and sparking like an explosion in a fireworks factory. "Oh yeah," he added. "You'd better get a fire crew over here, too. Quickly."

He didn't wait for an answer. Instead, he clipped the walkie talkie back to his belt and then hauled Yorke to his feet with his hands behind his back. He cuffed the man with his Sunnyvale-issue handcuffs and then dragged him towards the admin building.

"Are there more of you?" Hamze asked.

"Fuck you," Yorke replied, twisting his head and trying to spit at the man. He managed to get a glob of it on Hamze's shoe, but he earned himself a clout round the back of the head for his troubles.

"What else did you sabotage?"

"Fuck you," Yorke repeated, although this time he kept his saliva.

"Suit yourself," Hamze replied. "We'll figure it out soon enough. And in the meantime, we'll stick you in the back of Big Bertha and leave you to stew it out."

Big Bertha turned out to be one of Jim's team's heavy-duty transportation vans. It had been built to carry cattle and repurposed for use as a holding cell on the rare occasions that it was needed. It was parked round the side of the admin building in the security team's not-so-secret compound. It took Hamze the best part of ten minutes to take the man to the van and to lock him inside it. Then he radioed Big Jim and asked him what to do next.

It took the security chief a couple of moments to reply. When he did, it was short and to the point.

"I think ye should come to the gate," Jim said. "We got us a *situation*, ye ken."

***

It was all hands on deck at Sunnyvale. Every member of staff that was on shift had been summoned to the car park, which was the facility's designated meeting point. And almost every member of staff had responded to it. It wasn't like they could get much done with the power out, and it was hard to ignore the smell of the burning communications shed.

The army had arrived at the facility before anyone even knew what was happening. They'd arrived in waves, starting with the first responders in their helicopters and followed by more military in the back of a van. The representatives from Environmental Health arrived last because they had farther to travel, but everyone knew that the military was running the show. These weren't just any soldiers. These were specially trained biological warfare troops wearing big white suits and holding automatic weaponry. They meant business.

The protestors were nowhere to be seen. MacDonald assumed that they'd dispersed and disappeared at the first sign of trouble, although it was possible that the soldiers themselves had taken them away, perhaps to ask further questions or to put them under quarantine. But he didn't give a damn about the protestors. Not anymore.

He looked at his employees. There were around eighty or so, give or take, and the majority of them were wearing the company's high visibility safety jackets or the official overalls that were handed out to production workers on their first day. Half of them were looking straight back at him, in search of some sort of answer. The other half were looking at the army in shock and disbelief.

MacDonald realised it was time for him to say something. He had to take charge of the situation and to reassert himself as the boss. So he moved to the front of the group, cupped his hands around his mouth and shouted for silence. It took a moment or two for the hubbub to die down. It was a hostile crowd, worse even than when he delivered his annual reports to the facility's board of directors.

"What the fuck's going on?" someone shouted. Somebody else jeered and the atmosphere threatened to turn ugly. Big Jim stepped up and stood at MacDonald's side, scowling out at his co-workers with one hand on his truncheon. He didn't need to say anything to get the message across.

"I'm trying to find that out," MacDonald said. He cast his eyes across the crowd, making a mental note of who was there and who wasn't, as well as who looked like they were going to cause trouble.

"When can we go home?" someone else asked. This was greeted by an angry murmur.

"Soon," MacDonald replied. "I'm sure this is all a misunderstanding. I'm going to talk to the soldiers out there to see if we can figure out what's wrong."

"What happened to the comms building?"

MacDonald was pretty sure that this came from one of the production workers, but as to which one… well, that was anyone's guess.

"Someone set fire to it," MacDonald replied, matter-of-factly. "One of the protestors. But Big Jim's men have caught the culprit, and he's currently sitting in the back of Big Bertha."

More questions followed, and MacDonald did his best to answer them. His people were cold and frightened, but he could hardly blame them. Winter was well underway and spring was around the corner, but while nobody was due to knock off for a couple of hours, the heating was out and nobody had any work to do. And MacDonald knew better than anyone else that the devil found work for idle hands.

MacDonald called the questions to a halt and held a hand up. "I'm going to go and talk to them," he said. "Jim, I want you to come with me. You know, in case it turns nasty."

"Ah've goat yer back, Boss."

"Good," MacDonald said. "Then let's go."

He turned his back on his employees and walked across the car park towards the checkpoint. He wasn't sure what they were going to do while they waited for him, and he didn't much care. It wasn't like they could go anywhere. Big Jim followed a couple of steps behind him.

They crossed the car park without a problem, but when they were twenty yards or so away from the soldiers and the checkpoint, weapons were lowered, a warning shot was fired and an amplified voice boomed its way across no man's land.

"Halt," it said. "This is Lieutenant Colonel Ben Runciman speaking. This is a quarantine situation. Nobody leaves and nobody enters."

"I just want to talk," MacDonald shouted.

"So talk," Runciman replied. "Just keep your distance."

"Why are you keeping us here?"

There was a pause. MacDonald suspected that orders were being passed backwards and forwards and someone important was being forced to make a decision. He knew that feeling well enough.

"We think there's been some sort of outbreak," Runciman replied. "No cause for alarm, I'm sure, but I'll need you to keep your people back from the perimeter."

"For how long?"

"We don't know," Runciman said. "As long as it takes. We need to run a few tests."

John MacDonald liked to know who he was talking to, but Runciman was at such a distance that he could only just make him out. He was bald, though. He could see that. The light was shining off the top of his head and he looked a little like a storefront mannequin. He could have been fifty-five. He could also have been twenty-two. And he was wearing some sort of uniform.

MacDonald thought for a moment. Then he arrived at a decision. "You can't do this," he shouted. He took a couple of defiant steps towards them. "This is illegal."

"It's not," Runciman said. "Please, don't come any closer."

"Fuck that," MacDonald shouted. He carried on walking towards the perimeter. He was only fifteen yards away now and closing. Big Jim had stayed behind, eyeing his boss warily and watching the soldiers on the other side of the checkpoint.

"I'm not going to warn you again," Runciman said. His voice drifted on the wind, even and reasonable, but there was no mistaking the underlying threat. MacDonald carried on walking.

Then two shots rang out and hit him in the leg and the shoulder. He fell to the ground like a stolen TV from the back of a moving van.

BIG JIM WATCHED his boss get shot from a distance. He started to run towards him before the body hit the ground, then realised that if he wasn't careful, he'd be the next one in a body bag.

So instead, he held his heavy hands in the air and shouted, "Ah'm comin' ower. Ah'm gonnae check him and take him back tae Sunnyvale."

There was silence for a moment. Then Lieutenant Colonel Runciman picked up the megaphone again and asked, "Is he okay?"

Big Jim shrugged his great shoulders and walked slowly towards MacDonald, his hands still held above his head and his pace slow and measured.

"Gimme a couple minutes," he shouted. "Ah'll check fae a pulse, ye ken."

"I warned him," Runciman said. "This is an issue of national security. No one goes in and no one comes out."

"Aye," Big Jim shouted. "Ye seid. And by whae's order?"

There was a shriek of feedback on the other end of the checkpoint as the megaphone passed hands. The next person to speak had a cultured, BBC British accent, which sounded somehow wrong coming out of a megaphone.

"It's by my order," it said.

"Aye?" Jim shouted. "And who the fuck are you?"

"I'm the Home Secretary," the man said. Jim didn't recognise the voice.

When he reached John MacDonald, the first thing he noticed was the lack of blood. Then he had the fright of his life as MacDonald groaned and started to sit upright.

"Christ," Jim said. "Ah thought you were deid!"

"Non-lethal rounds," MacDonald replied, weakly. He was shaking and his crazy eyes were rolling around in their sockets. "Jesus. Help me up."

Big Jim did as he was told, pulling his boss to his feet with a powerful arm. He hauled the man away from the checkpoint and dragged him back towards the facility.

"A wise decision," Runciman boomed. "Next time, we'll fire live rounds."

"Who's that shite-heid of a wankstain think he is?" Big Jim murmured.

"The Home Secretary, apparently," MacDonald replied. "Shit, Jim, we're in trouble."

"Aye."

"You've got my back, right?"

"Aye."

MacDonald sighed. "Shit," he repeated. "I guess we'd better go and talk to the staff again."

Sunnyvale's employees were where he'd left them. They'd been watching from a distance and seemed surprised to see him up and about after they thought they'd seen him take a bullet and eat the dirt. But then he started shouting orders and it was business as usual.

"All right, folks," he shouted. "Gather round and listen up. Everything's going to be A-okay. We're still figuring out the situation as we go along, but I want us to assume the worst and prepare to bed in here for a few days. We'll house everyone overnight in the managerial suite if it comes to it. Has anyone seen Bugsy Drew?"

"Here," Drew replied. The operations manager had been lurking near the back of the pack beside Tom Copeland and Hector Fernandez from the cleaning crew. "What's up?"

"I want you to form a team and see what you can do

with the communications shed," MacDonald said. "Maybe there's something left that we can salvage. What about the generators, can we get some power running?"

"We can try," he said, but he didn't look hopeful.

"Do it," MacDonald said. He turned to look at Big Jim, who was still standing to his left and slightly behind him. "Jim, I want you to step up security. If we're going to have people staying in the admin building, we need to make sure certain areas stay off limits. I think you know what I mean."

"Aye," Jim said. "And ah've goat a few questions for a certain wee bellend in Big Bertha."

"Excuse me," someone shouted. This voice was female and belonged to one of the production workers.

"Yes?" MacDonald said.

"Well, I mean, how will we live?"

"We'll take one breath after another," MacDonald replied. "Any other questions?"

"What about food and water?"

MacDonald laughed, which was probably a misjudgement considering the crowd and the situation. "What about it?" he replied. "We're on a farm, for Christ's sake. We have all of the food we need here. My main concern is the electricity. We need to get that back online ASAP. Otherwise we're going to have to go old school and feed the damn animals by hand."

***

But the animals had something else in mind.

There was a madness in the air, in the water and under the ground. It spread from bird to beast, bringing pain and misery and misfortune. The infected animals came up in painful-looking hives and their brains swelled up and pressed against their skulls. The ones with the worst infections were slowing to a stop with their brains trickling out through their noses like a pre-mortem mummification. But most of them were just hungry, and they took that hunger out on whatever meat they could reach, even if they could only reach each other.

The beasts were dumb to begin with, but the disease didn't help. As their brains shut down and were slowly overtaken by the infection, they were less and less bovine, less and less avian, less and less animal and more and more a symptom. They lost the ability to feel pain, which had made their lives miserable before the infection when every day had brought more abuse at the hands of Sunnyvale and its less-than-ethical production workers.

The disease had started in the chicken shed, where it had festered for a while as it gathered momentum and developed a resistance to the antibiotics that were forced down their throats with the gruel they were fed. From the chickens, it spread to the sheep and the cows, whose food was occasionally mixed in with the chicken shit to make it last longer and to feed more mouths. The bigger creatures had been resistant at first, but resistance only got them so far and once the disease made the jump from one species to another, it had worked its way rapidly through the rest of the livestock. It had spread to the invertebrates in the soil, as well as the scavenging birds that circled the facility from the air, occasionally swooping down to pluck the eye from a carcass in the perpetual trash piles that were waiting to be processed outside the recycling plant.

Somewhere beneath the complex, in the tunnels, the madness was manifest. It colonised the ventilation shafts and underground pipes with the discarded bones it coughed up and the young that it left behind through its unholy reproduction. But unlike the rest of the beasts at Sunnyvale, it didn't think about sex. It thought about the hunt and it thought about food, but it didn't think about reproduction. It didn't need to.

The creature had a hive mind and it made its decisions by committee. Its different minds pulled its different legs in different directions, which led to it scuttling up and down and around and around at random. But if someone – or something – was unlucky enough to get in its way, there would be trouble.

In the chicken shed, the birds were squawking up a storm and trying to beat their stubby little wings against the ground to get into the air. But their wings had been clipped when they were little chicks and the best they could manage was a couple of feet before they came crashing back down in a hail of teeth and feathers. They fought each other, they fought the bars and they fought the machinery. They fought for their freedom. After the weaker birds had met their end at the hands of their brethren, who pecked at them with their clipped beaks and bludgeoned them to death by throwing them against the bars, the stronger birds banded together. Like the thing beneath the complex, their many minds merged into one, and there was only the need to feed.

In the sheep shed, the ewes lowered their heads and battered them against each other like rams in heat. Like humans and dolphins, they were hunting for sport, their herbivorous nature forgotten as the blood rush took hold and the virus claimed their minds. The sheep were stronger than the chickens, with more muscle power and more momentum when they charged the metal bars that held them in their pen. Their muscles were weak and underused, but as they battered again and again at the metal, they started to remember some primitive shared consciousness that told them, "You belong outside. You belong outside. You belong outside." One of the ewes had her head caved in like a watermelon being smashed with a mallet as she found herself caught between the bars and the hooves of one of her sisters, but it was over so quickly that she felt nothing. It was a small mercy in a sea of insanity as the creatures fought to escape the shed, but the bars were bending, bending and about to break.

The cows were slower and more methodical, but the bloodlust was there in their eyes, many of which had turned a milky white as though the cattle were seeing through the shit-stained walls of Sunnyvale's bovine concentration camp and out into another world. Unlike the chickens and the sheep, which were fighting against each other in an all-out free-for-all, the cows were keeping their distance from each other, turning their heads instead towards the smell of the massing humans to the north-west in the admin building. Then one of the cows scraped its hoof back against the metal grates that they were forced to sleep on and charged into the wall. It bounced back and hit the floor in a disgusting *whumph* of broken bones and ruptured organs, then screamed like a sow in the slaughterhouse as it tried to pull itself to its feet. But it was too late, and it went back down again as the nearby cows raced towards it and started chomping on the broken flesh as though the animal was a bale of hay. It took a long time for it to die.

In the fishery, hordes of carp, salmon and trout turned cannibalistic, gumming and biting at each other with their tiny teeth in an orgy of pain and death so great that their numbers were reduced to 5% in just a couple of minutes. The shit-brown water in the lake turned a bloody hue along the shoreline as the disease spread outside the confines of Sunnyvale's security fence and out into the open water.

In the slaughterhouse, it was eerily quiet. The machinery lay abandoned, the mechanical casualties of the power cut. They'd been processing the spent layer hens, putting them out of their misery by slitting their throats and hanging them upside down by their feet from the production line, when Harry Yorke had set fire to the communications shed. Bill Long and Neil Gibson were working the line at the time, and they'd dispatched the rest of the birds by hand and chucked their bodies on the pile before heading to the main gate to see what was happening. There was nothing left alive in the slaughterhouse. For the time being, at least.

It was the pigs who led the escape attempt. They were hungry, always hungry, and they were smarter than the other animals before the virus took over and turned that intelligence into something different, something twisted. As smart and ferocious as a pack of dogs, the pigs wasted no time trying to attack each other. They also didn't waste energy smashing into the wall at random. Instead, they lined up like soldiers at an inspection and waited for commands.

The many-tailed, many-headed thing burrowed up from beneath the metal bars of their cage and stood in front of them. It looked at them and considered them with its many brains. It made a noise, a horrific noise like a cat whose tail has been stepped on bellowing its cry through a set of bagpipes, and then the air ran out and the noise died down.

Then the pigs charged as one at the walls of their pen and smashed their way through to the other side. In some places, the bars simply bent and the pigs pushed through. In others, the cast iron bars shattered completely, made brittle by the passage of time, the changing temperatures and the wear and tear that comes from housing too many pigs in too small a space. With the bars out of the way, the walls were flimsy things constructed more to keep the wind out than to keep the animals in. No one ever thought that the iron railings would fail.

But they were wrong. And with the pigs streaming through the gaps in the wall and out into the complex, Sunnyvale – and the Environmental Health team – had a problem.

The outbreak had begun.

OUTBREAK

THE STAFF AT SUNNYVALE were still out in the car park, staring at their scattered leadership with varying degrees of curiosity, amusement and terror. MacDonald had issued his orders and then stood off to the side, staring into the distance while Big Jim made things happen. There was a sense of a changing allegiance, a shift in power from the head of the facility to the head of security. Which was why when the outbreak began, it was Jim who heard the news first.

It was Hector Fernandez – the cleaner – who told him. He'd spotted a cloud of dust to the north-west on the other side of the admin building and tugged Jim's arm to get his attention.

"Hey, Jim," he said, "you've gotta see this."

"What?" Jim growled. Then, he turned his head to look where Fernandez was pointing, and he got the message immediately. "Fuck's sake. Ah've goat no time for this an' aw, ye ken. Not a fucken escape. Tell me ah'm no fucken seein' this shite."

"It looks like a lot of them," Fernandez said, doubtfully. His eyes were widening by the second as he saw the scope of the escape. The dust that the animals were throwing up from the arid ground reminded him of a stampede in an old western. "Maybe we should go inside."

"Aye," Jim said, rubbing his fiery chin thoughtfully as he gauged the situation. There were maybe a hundred people there, and there was a pretty long way to go to the admin building. He cupped his hands around his mouth and shouted, "Awrite ye divvies, let's get tae the admin building afore we get squashed by yon animals."

Most people hadn't spotted the outbreak, but it didn't take them long to turn to it after they followed Big Jim's ferocious stare to the north-west. The animals were closer and easier to make out, and there was no mistaking that it was the pigs and not the sheep, the cows or the chickens. They were coming all right, and they were coming with a lick of speed.

And so they panicked, as people do, and it was through force of will alone that Big Jim was able to corral them into running in the right direction. The natural instinct was to flee, to turn and run towards the barrier and away from the complex, but that would only lead to a lungful of lead, although that didn't stop people from trying. Big Jim was too busy making his voice heard over the screams to hear the gunshots, but John MacDonald heard them and it brought him back to reality.

He turned tail and ran towards the admin building with the rest of his employees, while Big Jim gestured to some of his men and hopped in the back of a security buggy. There were a half dozen of them, a half dozen warriors who raced ahead of the employees to head the pigs off at the pass. They parked their buggies in a line and crouched behind them, staring at the pigs as they raced towards them. Closer now, *too* close, they had a better idea of their numbers. There were a lot of them, maybe as many as forty or fifty, and those were just the ones at the front. There were more behind them, the laggards. In the distance, they could see the walls of the pig shed buckling still further.

"Draw yer weapons!" Jim shouted.

His team didn't need telling twice. Thanks to the order passed down from John MacDonald, several of them were carrying firearms, although Mike Chase and new recruit Jack Dunlop had yet to acquire a licence. The guns wouldn't do much damage either way because they were loaded with non-lethal ammunition. They weren't carrying them to police the animals. They were carrying them to police the people.

"Open fire, ya bastards."

And so they opened fire, and the pigs found themselves being pummelled by plastic that struck them like angry bee stings all over their bodies. One or two of them went down in a tangle of angry limbs, but the rest of them barely broke their stride. They were a couple of hundred yards away and counting.

"Keep fucken shootin."

"Boss, I—"

"Ah'm a wee bit busy, ye ken."

"It's not working," Chase said. "Holy fucking shit, we're going to die. We're going to die, Jim."

"Ah seid, git tae fuck.'"

The pigs had crossed a quarter of the distance and were closer, close enough for the security team to smell the stench of unwashed flesh. Behind them, the first of the employees were entering the admin building and the rest of them weren't far behind.

"Jim," Chase repeated, "we've got to get out of here. We can't win this."

"Then we'll buy some time."

One hundred and twenty yards. One hundred and fifteen. One hundred and ten.

"Fuck this," Chase said. He spat on the ground and then legged it towards the admin building. Jack Dunlop followed shortly afterwards, and then Greg Hamze and Carl Taylor stopped firing and turned tail, too. The pigs were fifty yards away and so was the admin building.

"He's right." That was from Darragh O'Rourke, Big Jim's second-in-command and the only member of

Sunnyvale's security team who was still holding the line. He was reloading his weapon while Jim popped off some shots at the oncoming bacon.

Jim turned to look at him. He looked back at the pigs. Forty yards and counting.

"Fuck this shite," he murmured. He glanced across at O'Rourke and shouted, "Run!" The Irishman didn't need telling twice. In fact, he was already a couple of steps ahead of him.

Big Jim left the engine running as he jumped from the cabin and landed on the grass. The pigs were thirty-five yards away when he started running. He was just over halfway back to the admin building when they hit the line of buggies.

The sound was awful, the high, whining sound of broken bones and metal, pigs screaming and engines roaring and then a heavy *whump* as Big Jim's vehicle was tossed through the air like a child's go-kart, carving a deep divot in the earth before bouncing again and coming to a rest beneath a tree.

And just like that, the pigs were through, and he was fifteen yards from the admin building and counting. He wasn't alone.

Most of Sunnyvale's staff had made it inside the building. They'd poured in through the revolving doors and into the lobby and were watching nervously through the plate-glass windows. But two or three of them were lagging behind, and one of them tripped and hit the floor. Another of them, Pete Fields from the pig team, doubled back to drag the fallen man up and to push him forwards.

The pigs were close. Jim could smell the blood. He was ten yards away from the door and there was only him and Pete Fields left. They were five yards away. Then they were one yard away, and Jim leaned in with a shoulder and

barged Fields out of the way so he could run in front of him
and into the revolving doors. It swung around and took Jim
across the threshold and into the building. Fields tried to
follow him in, to dash through into the revolving door, and
he made it – just.

But his coat was stuck in the door, and the machinery
ground to a halt and the door stopped spinning. He looked
across at Big Jim, who was watching helplessly from the
precinct. Then the world exploded in a hail of glass and
angry pork as the pigs smashed into the building's façade.

The shock rippled through the walls and the people in
the lobby started screaming before the glass had time to hit
the floor. Big Jim cupped his hands around his mouth and
bellowed, "Get tae the second floor!" The pigs hit the
building again.

There was a scream and the disgusting wet slap of a
bloody hand on the broken glass. Then the pigs were inside
the remnants of the revolving door, crowding around Pete
Fields like mourners at a funeral before rushing in and
taking angry bites out of his forearms as he flung them up to
protect his face. Fields screamed again and tried to strike out
at them, to blind their eyes with his fingers or to push them
away so he could escape somehow, but there were too many
of them, they were too strong, and they were biting him.
This time they hit an artery and blood started to flow from
the wound, not spurting out like it did in the movies but
pouring down his torso with every heartbeat.

Somebody screamed and Big Jim turned away from the
dead man walking. The crowd had started to dissipate as
they raced up the stairs, and the scream had come from little
Jill MacDonald as poor Pete Fields gave up the fight and
sank beneath the weight of the pigs.

"Upstairs!" Jim bellowed. He followed closely on their
tails, pausing at the cusp of the stairs to look back down into

the precinct. What had once been an open plan reception area with an accompanying coffee stall and great glass windows now looked like the aftermath of a terror attack. He looked down at the pigs at the entrance, which were still devouring the corpse of Pete Fields while treading restlessly backwards and forwards on the shattered glass. Then, almost as one, they looked up at him. His eyes met theirs, and he felt a bead of sweat roll down the side of his head and into the thick stubble of his ginger beard. He tasted it on his lips.

And then the pigs started to push forwards again and the sound of tortured glass as it stretched and strained was enough to spur him on and up the stairs to the second floor.

***

The admin building was in uproar. As Big Jim rounded the stairs, his first impression was that of a refugee camp instead of that of an office. He started to mentally count heads to see if they were missing anyone and then quickly gave up when he realised the enormity of the task. And besides, there were other priorities.

"Ah need some fucken help, ye scallies!" he shouted. When Big Jim shouted, he *really* shouted, and he managed to make himself heard above the sound of chaos and the cries and moans of the injured. It was enough, and a dozen of Sunnyvale's finest stepped forward to help him.

"No time tae explain," he bellowed. "Just help me tae block the fucken stairs."

Big Jim believed in leading by example. He dragged a shell-shocked Bruce Laing by the arm and pointed to the top of a filing cabinet while simultaneously gripping its bottom. Together, they lifted the thing up and staggered across the carpet towards the stairwell. They heaved and then pushed their backs into it at the same time, launching the metal drawers through the air and down into the stairwell.

It formed a barrier of sorts, but it wasn't enough. It also wouldn't withstand much of a battering, but there was still time to reinforce it and now Jim's team of volunteers had sprung into action, too. They tossed chairs down the stairs and followed them up with desktop computers and monitors, cupboards, cabinets and whatever else they could get their hands on.

From downstairs, there was the sound of breaking glass again as the pigs surged forwards and smashed through into the precinct. Then there was a rush of sweaty, fetid air as the hogs charged the stairs and tried to climb them. Their trotters were covered in mud and blood and the stairs were slippery at the best of times, but a few of them made it halfway to the top on momentum alone. At the halfway point, the stairs turned around and continued up, and it was here that the office equipment had been piled into a makeshift barricade.

The pigs were exhausted, but they were driven on by the bloodlust and those that had made it to the halfway point prepared for one last charge. On the other side, Big Jim was bellowing orders and the Sunnyvale team was doing everything it could to plug the hole and complete the barricade. It was a race against time again.

This time, luck favoured Big Jim and his team, and through brute force and sheer determination, they upended a table and dragged it over to bridge the gap. Jim leaned his weight against it, and not a moment too soon. The pigs hit the barricade from the other side and knocked him backwards, but the barricade held. Jim roared something unintelligible while more detritus from the office was carried towards him. The gap had been closed, but the pigs still knew they were there. They could smell their flesh. It smelled like bacon.

It took an eternity to build the barricade until the stairwell was filled to the brim. Some of the heavier equipment, like the Kyocera printer and the sofa from the break room, had been dragged across the floor, gouging a deep welt into the carpet. The groove cut all the way down to the floorboards beneath, but the big machines weighed the makeshift barricade down and the pigs were defeated. They continued to nudge at it, but they couldn't break through and they slowly started to lose interest.

The sounds started to die down. Before too long, an unearthly silence had descended upon the room. It was the kind of silence that belonged on a battlefield. Jim looked around the shell of the room and was shocked by the difference. The finance team's banks of desks and machines had all but disappeared. It was strange to see it like that. The chaos had filled the air with eddies of fine, white plaster, and it clung to people's clothes and caked their hair. Everyone wore the same look of muted shock.

Then the spell broke and someone started to cry. It spread from one person to another like a yawn and before long, the room was in uproar again. Everyone was trying to make their voice heard, and Big Jim winced as the barricade started to jiggle again. The noise was bringing the pigs back, and while he thought that the barricade would hold, he didn't want to chance it.

So he cupped his hands around his mouth and shouted, "Quiet!" Big Jim had a big voice to match his build and it had the effect he was hoping for. The voices died down – not into silence, but enough for him to make himself heard.

"We've goat tae be quiet, ye ken," Jim said. "The animals. They can hear us."

He held a finger to his lips and that simple gesture did more to silence them than his shout had. That had caught their attention, but the finger to the lips was what shut down the hubbub and gave him the floor.

"Good," Jim said. "Now whae's seen the bossman?"

John MacDonald was nowhere to be seen. It made them all nervous. He was the company's figurehead, after all. He was the guy they turned to at times of trouble, and if this didn't count as trouble then nothing did.

Nobody seemed to have any idea, but that was hardly surprising. Their lives had been thrown into chaos and the man that they blamed for getting them there had disappeared. But then Tom Copeland stepped forward and said, "I think I've got an idea."

The vet's idea was to travel up to the top floor, out through the door in MacDonald's office and on to the gantry. The idea made sense because everyone knew it was where the boss went if he wanted to clear his mind. But Jim was still nervous because he didn't want Sunnyvale's staff lurking by the barricade and thinking too long and hard about the animals. They were trapped in there, locked up inside the admin building like the animals they played host to, and when they realised they wouldn't be going home that night, there would be problems.

But those problems would have to wait until later.

Jim nodded at O'Rourke, who was visibly shaken but still very much aware of his job and his responsibilities, and then he told the man to keep things under control and to give him a shout on the walkie talkie if the situation changed. Then he led the way away from the pigs and towards the sky, up the other side of the staircase and through John MacDonald's executive suite on the top floor.

He wasn't in there, but they were ready for that. They also knew exactly where he'd gone because he'd left the door open and the smell of Sunnyvale was seeping in through the doorway. It was sharp and vinegary, a sweaty sort of smell that mixed with the metallic stench of blood and bile. Big Jim and Tom Copeland tensed themselves and walked out of the door and onto the gantry.

JOHN MACDONALD was having a bad day.

His ribs still ached from the rubber bullet, and he suspected he'd cracked at least one of them. But that would have to wait. He needed space. Space to think and to re-evaluate.

He'd already walked round the perimeter once and he'd been deeply disturbed by what he saw. To the north, the blood red lake was lit up by the sun. It wasn't big enough to be affected by the pull of the moon, but nevertheless the water was disturbed and small waves chopped across its surface.

The pigs had initially gathered on the west side of the building, but they'd already started to spread. MacDonald guessed that the admin building would be surrounded within the hour. Not that it mattered much. They were safer inside than out.

When Big Jim and Tom Copeland caught up with him, he was sitting on the gantry with his legs dangling out into the open air. He had his eyes closed and was breathing deeply, working through some of the exercises he'd been given by an executive coach some time back. They were supposed to help him to deal with stress and to focus his thoughts. But they didn't work.

Big Jim approached him slowly from behind and reached down to put his hands on his boss' shoulders. The gesture was supposed to reassure him, but it also served a second purpose. If he showed any signs of leaning forward or falling from the gantry, Jim could grab him with a pincer grip and drag him back on to relatively solid ground.

"You okay, Boss?" Jim asked.

"Hmmm?" MacDonald murmured. He opened his eyes and stared into the distance. He saw freedom, but it was out of reach. It was the same kind of freedom that a prisoner sees when he looks out the window of his jail cell.

"We were worried," Copeland said. He was hanging back a little because he didn't like heights, but his eyes were darting around as he fought that fear and caved into the urge to understand what was happening. It was pure mayhem out there.

"Don't worry about me," MacDonald said. "You should worry about yourselves. We're in trouble here. What are we going to do?"

"You're in charge," Copeland reminded him. "It's up to you."

"I'm not in charge anymore," MacDonald replied. "No one is. Gentlemen, let's face it. We're fucked. You saw what happened to Pete Fields. The animals are unhappy. They're rising up against us."

"Are they bollocks," Big Jim said. "Those wee beasties cannae think."

"Mmm," MacDonald murmured. "I wonder."

He paused for a moment and silence settled down like a plane descending onto a runway. Then there was a horrific sound like someone taking a bite from an apple and one of the pigs on the ground below fell to its side. Another pig had crept up behind it and clamped its teeth around a hind leg. The two beasts came together in a crunch of flesh.

"My god," Copeland said.

"Aye," Big Jim added. "There's some horrible shite down there, ye ken. Better stay put."

"Even if we could get outside," MacDonald said, "we can't leave the complex while the feds are on our doorstep with their rubber bullets."

As if on cue, there was the sound of automatic gunfire to the south. Copeland went pale, but MacDonald jumped to his feet like a man possessed and starting running down the gantry. The vet and the security guard followed him as best as they could, but MacDonald was in a frenzy. Big Jim and Tom Copeland didn't want to risk a fall, especially with the animals down there at the bottom. If the impact didn't kill them, the pigs would.

The gunfire had stopped by the time they'd covered half of the side of the building, but it started back up again as they rounded the corner. Twenty yards further along the gantry, there was a break in the trees on the perimeter and the three of them could see what was happening.

It was horrible.

Some of the pigs had broken away from the main group and mounted a charge at the fence. The army had opened fire, first with their rubber bullets and then with the real deal, and Sunnyvale's car park looked like the beaches of Dunkirk in 1940. Bits of blood and gore were plastered across the vehicles, and the vehicles themselves were riddled with bullet holes and leaking fuel. A stray spark from somewhere had started a fire that was refusing to go out, and a half dozen vehicles, including Copeland's own Nissan Micra, were blazing like bonfires in the darkness. The air was thick with the sick smell of petroleum and burnt bacon. Copeland dropped to his knees and nearly vomited, but it rose up his throat and then died back down again. He spat on the gantry and watched his saliva slip between the gaps in the walkway and down to the ground below. Then he was hit by another wave of nausea and he forced himself to stand up straight and to hold on to the railing.

"Fuckin radge pigs've goat a death wish, ye ken," Jim murmured.

The animals just kept on coming in an endless flood of

flesh. The three men watched as they mounted another charge at the security fence. This time, the pigs broke through and out to the other side, and the men on the gantry watched from their vantage point as the army fell back. Not everyone made it, and a couple of them fell to the rushing pigs. Big Jim, Tom Copeland and John MacDonald were too far away to see what was happening, but they had a pretty good idea. Meanwhile, as the infantry fell back, the animals charged on across the field towards the second boundary. As they watched from the gantry, the army held their line as the dead and dying animals filled up the no man's land between the two fences.

"They're fighting back," MacDonald said.

"Who?" Copeland asked.

"The animals," the boss replied. He spoke in a tone of hushed awe as though he was watching a religious awakening on.

"What's wrong with 'em?" Jim asked.

"I have no idea," Copeland replied.

"Well find oot, ya fuckin wankstain," Jim growled. "Ah thought ye were supposed tae be a fucken expert."

"I am an expert," Copeland said. "But this is like nothing I've ever seen before."

"What's causing it?" MacDonald asked. He seemed a little more lucid, a little more in the now than he had been when they'd first walked onto the gantry and found him there with his legs dangling out over the void.

Copeland shrugged. "Beats me," he said. "A virus, perhaps. Some sort of disease outbreak."

"What if it *is* a disease?" MacDonald asked. "Is it contagious?"

"I hope not," Copeland said. "But I guess that's why we're under quarantine. They're going to watch and wait. They're going to leave us in here so they can see what happens."

MacDonald frowned. He stared moodily out at no man's land, where the action had slowed to a stop. The pigs were dead – not all of them, perhaps, but those that had chased the soldiers – and the army's guns had fallen silent. They'd abandoned their line at the facility's front entrance, though. Even with his naked eyes and his hand holding back the glare from the autumn sun, John MacDonald could see what was going on. They'd established a second, more secure perimeter around Sunnyvale's outer fence. That way, if anyone or anything tried to make a break for it, they'd find themselves full of bullets before they even made it halfway.

"If we're stuck in here," MacDonald said, "then we need to prepare for a siege. We need to stock up on food and water and wait it out in the admin building. And we should build a better barricade."

"What if we catch yon virus?" Big Jim asked. "Ah cannae be doin' wi' mad pig disease."

"That'll fall to Copeland," MacDonald replied. "The boys call him 'Doc,' right? Maybe it's time for him to earn that nickname."

Copeland shook his head. "I'm not qualified. If I tried to treat someone, I'd be breaking the law."

MacDonald laughed. It was a bitter, raspy laugh that floated off on the wind and blended with the squeals of the pigs beneath them.

"What law?" he asked. "We're on our own in here."

But Copeland shook his head again. "Everything's back in the clinic," he said. "And there's no way I'm going out there."

"We need to form a committee," MacDonald said. "I'll chair it, of course. But we need to keep people on our side, and the best way to do that is to make them feel like they have a say. We need to re-establish communications with the outside world, too. I want to know what's happening."

"Don't we all," Copeland murmured.

"And Pete Fields?" Jim asked. "People are gonnae talk, ye ken. What should we say?"

MacDonald shrugged. "Say that he wasn't quick enough," he said. "It's harsh, but it's true. I'm not going to pretend it's all sunshine and rainbows when we're surrounded by a thousand angry pigs."

"Eighteen thousand," Copeland said. "Give or take a couple thousand. Let's just hope they're all we have to worry about."

"What do you mean?" MacDonald asked.

Copeland shuddered and thought about the other sheds and the cows, the sheep and even the chickens. One bird might not do much damage, but if all 160,000 of them broke out then there'd be hell to pay.

But first, they had a committee to form. It was time for John MacDonald to face his employees.

***

Harry Yorke was having a bad day, too.

He was standing in the back of Big Bertha, peeking through the reinforced windows in the rear of the vehicle. It had been parked facing north towards the admin building, which meant that the rear windows faced south, towards the checkpoints and the bloodied battlefield that now lay strewn with dead pork and people. It was a horrific view, but it held a sort of grim fascination that made it difficult to turn away.

Besides, it was all he had to look at.

So far, he'd been lucky. The pigs had passed him by on their mad rush for the soldiers, but that didn't change the fact that he was trapped inside Big Bertha with no food, no water and no idea what was happening. For all he knew, they were going to leave him there to die. Maybe they'd forgotten about him altogether. It didn't make much of a difference. Either way, he needed to get out of there.

He needed a plan.

He started by scouting out the back of Big Bertha, but the vehicle had been built with security in mind. He was alone in the back with just a metal bench to sit on, and the rear doors were locked from the outside. It was dark in there, and the only light was what filtered in through the narrow windows. Big Jim's team had taken his gear and searched him before they'd locked him up in there, which meant that he didn't even have his lucky lighter. He resorted to tracing the lining of the walls, the floors and the ceiling with a fingertip, but it all seemed pretty solid.

He hadn't tried kicking the door yet. He didn't want to attract any attention.

Yorke could see them out there, the bacon on legs with gangrenous teeth, prowling across the grass in packs. They seemed to have calmed down, at least after their initial bloodlust, and they were no longer fighting amongst themselves. They were no longer trying to escape from the complex, either. They seemed perfectly happy to wander around, watching and waiting.

He didn't like to think about what they were waiting for.

Besides, Harry Yorke had other things on his mind. He was hungry and he was thirsty. He also badly needed to take a leak. He held it in for as long as he could, but he couldn't hold it forever and it wasn't like someone was about to pick him up to escort him to the little boy's room. So he took himself into a corner, as far away as possible from the metal bench, and did his business.

He was halfway through when the first pig hit Big Bertha, sending him tumbling down to the floor where he found himself on his hands and knees in his own piss, his dick still spraying right up to the point at which he smacked his balls off the corner of the bench. The pigs rammed him again, and then again.

Big Bertha rocked on its axles, swinging from side to side and picking up a little momentum. Yorke's piss had been forgotten, and it sloshed around and started to trickle out through the tiny gaps here and there in the welding. It dripped to the ground outside and the stench of it attacked the pigs' noses and pushed them to redouble their attack. Big Bertha rocked again in a great arc and then two wheels left the ground and it flipped onto its side.

Harry Yorke tumbled through the air and then hit his head on the metal bench. He reached up to his scalp and brought his hand away again, feeling something moist coating his fingertips, but he couldn't be sure whether it was blood or piss. He wondered if it mattered.

He felt suddenly sick. When he tried to hold his head up, the nausea got worse. His head lit up with a blinding pain like the worst migraine he'd ever felt, and he clutched a palm to his eye as it washed over him. Then he fell to the floor.

He lay there for a moment, dazed and disoriented. His mind went out to his wife and his kids, wherever the hell they were. He hoped they were okay. He hoped they'd got away. He hoped they were safe.

The last thing he remembered seeing was the evil red eyes of a dozen pigs on the other side of the reinforced windows. He wondered exactly how reinforced those windows were. He looked at the eyes again. They weren't moving and they weren't attacking – they were just staring at him. Watching. Waiting.

Then the darkness overtook him and he slipped into unconsciousness.

***

Lieutenant Colonel Ben Runciman was troubled, and that was unusual. He wasn't a big thinker – he didn't have to be; he left that to his superiors – and he was better suited to handling the little details. He was good at implementation. That's how he'd got as far as he'd got.

He looked at his foam-covered face, which stared back out at him from the mirror as he caressed his cheeks with his razorblade. His hands were shaking, which was unusual, but he retained enough of a hold on himself to be able to steady them as the razor drifted across his five o'clock shadow. Even with the world going to hell in a handbasket, he had to look presentable. It was his duty, just like it was his duty to man the temporary perimeter fence.

He had a feeling that they'd be there for some time, so he'd packed a few essentials, primarily consisting of a couple of non-fiction leadership books and his shaving kit. He also had a small leather photo album that he kept under his pillow. The images of his wife and his daughters gave him strength when he was forced to make tough decisions, which seemed to be happening more often than not of late.

There was a knock at the door of the high-tech campervan that he was using as a base of operations. He shouted something unintelligible at the door and splashed a little water across his face as it opened. Then he spat into the basin and turned around.

"Yes?"

"Sorry to bother you, sir," the visitor began, the words babbling out of her as they usually did. She was Diane Hyde's supervisor, a well-built woman in her early fifties with a volcanic personality and a sort of steely charm.

"Who are you?"

"My name is Dena Lymbery," she said. "I'm with

Environmental Health."

"I should have known," the soldier said, chuckling bitterly to himself. "What do you want?"

"Pardon me if I'm overstepping the line," Lymbery replied, not looking at all apologetic. "But there are people in there, Lieutenant Colonel. You have a duty to get them out."

"On the contrary," Runciman replied. "My priority here is to maintain the quarantine. We're still running tests on the samples that we've received from the infected animals. Until we know what we're dealing with, no one enters and no one leaves. We can't risk the outbreak spreading."

"And how long will that take?"

"I have no idea," Runciman said. "That's not my concern, but I promise I'll update you and your people once I have some news."

"And what about the people who are holed up inside there?"

"What about them?"

"Have your men tried to make contact?"

"We're working on it," Runciman said. "Listen, lady, I appreciate you have a job to do, but so do I. What do you want from me?"

"I want you to *do* something," Lymbery replied. "Anything."

"My hands are tied."

"You could at least try to deliver some food, maybe even some medical supplies."

Lieutenant Colonel Runciman paused for a moment, then patted at his pockets for a packet of cigarettes, which wasn't forthcoming. He sighed and turned to look the woman dead in the eye.

"I'll think about it," he said. "Now get the hell out of my sight while I get my shit together. Go and do whatever it is that you're supposed to be doing here."

***

By that evening, the decision was out of Runciman's hands. Someone, and Runciman suspected it was Dena Lymbery from the environmental health department, had talked to the press. The spin doctors were saying that there were survivors inside the complex and that the army was just leaving them to die.

It was a public relations nightmare, and it fostered an atmosphere that Runciman was unfamiliar with. His team had been in the news before, of course, but usually only after its mission was completed, and always in a positive light. Now he was facing pressure from his superiors to mount a rescue mission, against his better judgement.

And so, as the sun set on the besieged facility, Lieutenant Colonel Ben Runciman found himself briefing a team of six elites on an exploratory foray into the facility. They were six good, strong soldiers, with a background in counterterrorism and, more importantly, a thorough understanding of biological warfare. By penetrating the quarantine zone, his men would be putting themselves at risk, despite the protective suits that they'd be wearing. And even if they made it out of Sunnyvale with the besieged employees, they'd all be placed immediately under a second quarantine outside of the facility's gates. Privately, Runciman thought the plan pointless because freeing the workers from the complex would still leave them under quarantine in his own camp. But he had his orders.

He checked his watch and saw that the hands had moved inexorably on. It was time to get the briefing started.

***

His men rolled out just before dawn, on the premise that it was the least likely time for the animals to be awake and roaming the grounds. They were ferried away from base camp in the back of a transport and then directed to a couple of boats on the shores of a lake. They'd looped around the facility to the east and approached it from the north. Their destination lay to the south, on the other side of the lake.

They were also armed to the teeth, with orders to shoot animals on sight. This first, exploratory mission was simple: to deliver supplies and communication devices to the survivors inside the admin building.

Lieutenant Colonel Ben Runciman would have loved to have been with them, but his orders were to hold back and to coordinate the mission. And so he listened as updates trickled through, blow-by-blow, on the radios, while a night vision video feed from his soldiers' headcams streamed on the two high-definition LCD screens on the walls of his mobile office.

Ready?

Affirmative.

Let's go.

A silence descended, as expected, and Runciman switched his focus to the grainy video feeds. So far, there wasn't much for him to see, and their flashlights were only lighting the way a dozen feet in front of each of the vessels. They weren't silent, but they were pretty quiet – quiet enough, they hoped.

Eight hundred metres to go until we hit the shore.

Roger that.

Another silence, and Runciman sat back, then immediately sat forward as he spotted something on the night vision scope. A split second later, the radio crackled into life.

Six hundred met–

What the hell?

Looks like we've got company.

The water around the boats was alive, turgid, throbbing with life that sent the infra-red scanners into overdrive. The water glowed brighter than the six men in the two boats.

Five hundred metres.

The fucking fish are pitching a fit.

I don't like this at all.

Both of the boats were rocking now. When the moon peeked out from behind a cloud, it illuminated bloody red swathes of water on both sides of the boats.

Four hundred metres.

I can't see shit. I'm steering blind!

Runciman mopped the sweat from his brow and inched closer to the bank of screens. Both boats were listing dangerously in the water, and the glow from the night vision scope bathed everything in light.

Three hundred metres.

Then, disaster. The boat at the front hit a particularly heavy swell and started to bank on its side. One of the soldiers fell overboard, and the heat from his body was immediately swallowed up by the unnatural heat from the water. Runciman had an awful vision of the man being swallowed up by lava, but lava didn't move like whatever he was looking at.

One hundred and fifty metres.

This was from the boat at the rear, which had continued to fight the tide of light on the cameras and which was still surging towards the shore. The second boat had stalled and then frozen in the water. As Runciman turned to look at the feeds from his soldiers' headcams, a mighty lurch sent them tumbling towards each other and over the sides of the boat. They hit the water at the same time, the night vision feeds instantly cutting out as they were overwhelmed by the warmth of whatever it was that was beneath the waves. Runciman didn't see what happened to the boat.

Seventy-five metres.

What the fuck is going on?

Too late to turn back now, boys!

The remaining boat was slowing, slowing, and it was rocking from side to side like a bull at a rodeo. But the soldiers held on, even as the boat's engine started to whine and to cut out entirely. Through the night vision feed, Runciman could finally see a patch of darkness, the cold, hard shoreline pitching up in front of them.

Twenty metres.

But would the boat make it? Runciman wasn't so sure, until some last god-like rush of kinetic energy from the vessel's battered engine thrust it across the finish line and on to the shore, where it came to a stop in the mud.

We made it.

What the fuck just happened?

No time for that, let's establish–

No time for that, either. Eyes at four o'clock. There's something–

It's a monstrosity!

We've got to – ungh!

This was followed by a volley of gunfire, but it was too little too late. Two of the soldiers were already down, the feeds from their cameras facing the sky and the soil like some twisted attempt at an eye roll. The last of the soldiers, a man Runciman had served with on the other side of the world, was turning his head rapidly from left to right. On the feed, Runciman could see what he was looking at. It was a huge red cloud in the darkness of the night, a massive cow – a bull – that was running straight towards him.

Lieutenant Colonel Ben Runciman didn't see when the camera cut out. He was busy tumbling backwards out of his chair.

THE SUNNYVALE SURVIVORS, as they'd voted to call
themselves, had been called to order slowly but surely as the
call-to-arms passed around by word of mouth. Big Jim's
warning about staying silent hadn't gone unnoticed, and
they'd gathered in John MacDonald's expansive office on the
top floor in a state of relative calm.

It was standing room only, except for John MacDonald
who was sitting behind his mahogany desk with his arms
resting on the wood before him. He was flanked by Big Jim
and his security team, who were making no secret of the fact
that they were armed with batons and stun guns. Jim was
still holding the pistol he'd used to shoot at the pigs before
Pete Fields was killed. The safety was on and he held it
lazily, the barrel pointing at the floor beside his feet, but it
was loaded. There was no doubt about that.

MacDonald was leading the meeting from his seat,
trying his best to make it seem like business as usual despite
the fact that Pete Fields was lying dead downstairs with his
body torn to pieces by the pigs he was supposed to
supervise.

"Now then," MacDonald was saying. "The first order of
business."

"The first order of business is how the fuck we're going
to get out of here," someone said. They didn't shout it, but
their voice carried clearly across the silence, and Big Jim
made a note to have a little word with Lee Keyes, who he
suspected of being the perpetrator. But if MacDonald had
heard him, he didn't acknowledge it.

"We need to take a roll call," MacDonald said. He

drummed his fingers on a printed document that was lying on the desk in front of him. "I have here a list of all employees who were on duty when the quarantine began. I'd like you all to be silent as we run through the names and to respond with 'here' if you're present."

He glared out at the assembled employees as though expecting one of them to crack a joke or to say something. But nobody would have dared, and not just because they didn't want to piss him off. He knew how they felt because he felt it, too. A lot of people were unaccounted for. The animals had taken their toll.

They started with the admin team.

Lois Best? *No response.*

Richard Carroll? *No response.*

Bugsy Drew? *Here.*

Charlene Folma? *No response.*

Maude Harrison? *Here.*

Zona Jones? *No response.*

Jill MacDonald? *Here.*

John MacDonald? *Here.*

Harry Peterson? *No response.*

Carol Rawlings? *Here.*

Sarah Sinclair? *No response.*

John MacDonald paused for a moment and figured out the survival rate of the admin team. It wasn't looking good. MacDonald made it slightly over 45 percent, and these were the people who called the admin building home in the first place. The problem was that the quarantine had descended while people were on their lunch break, and many of them had taken that opportunity to check how the protest was developing. It had been a fateful – and fatal – decision.

Next up on the list was the avian team.

Jamie Fletcher? *No response.*

Hamish Gray? *No response.*

Alex Ingram? *No response.*
Jerry Jones? *Here.*
Jonathan Kennedy? *No response.*
Logan Kelly? *No response.*
Bob Knowles? *Here.*
Anthony Mann? *No response.*
Evan Marshall? *No response.*
Christopher Payne? *No response.*
Archie Pearson? *No response.*
Samuel Powell? *No response.*
Steve-O Puck? *Here.*
Joel Sheppard? *No response.*
Yvonne Strong? *Here.*

Perhaps unsurprisingly, the survival rate had dropped to a third. And when John MacDonald progressed to the cow team, it only got worse. Will Makon was the sole survivor. Then they moved on to the pig team, followed by the sheep team, which fared even worse at a 20 percent survival rate. Bruce Laing, Lee Keyes and their supervisor, Arnie Lorn, were the only survivors. As for the slaughterhouse, only two men remained, Bill Long and Neil Gibson. But there were only five of them on duty to begin with.

"What about the guys from the fishery?"

John MacDonald couldn't tell who'd asked it, but it didn't really matter. He squinted into the crowd and shrugged, then read out a list of names into the silence.

Alexander Barrett? *No response.*
Louie Burgess? *No response.*
Jacob Hammond? *No response.*
John Hanson? *No response.*
Reece Hill? *No response.*
Jamie Howard? *No response.*
Harry Joyce? *No response.*

Joe Lloyd? *No response.*

Josh Morley? *No response.*

Nathan Palmer? *No response.*

Isaac Sharp? *No response.*

Taylor Smart? *No response.*

"Jesus fucking Christ," MacDonald said when he finished reading the names from the sheets of paper. "I think we should have a minute of silence."

And so they did, although they didn't time it. MacDonald tried to tell himself that some of the staff from the fishery had survived, that they'd somehow escaped the complex and made their way to freedom. He'd be lying to himself if he claimed it was due to any deep-seated concern about their safety. Employees were replaceable, and he wouldn't have remembered their names without the sheet of paper in front of him. The problem was that he had a duty of care, and a lot of his employees were unaccounted for. Too many of them. He'd never get a job again.

"Okay," he said, when he felt as though they'd maintained the silence for long enough. "The leaves us with the security team."

Big Jim went visibly pale, and John MacDonald wasn't surprised. He was tough on his team, but he was also something of a father figure. He loved them in his way, not like a biological parent but like a foster parent. It was something more than just a manager taking his underlings under his wing. It was the kind of brotherly camaraderie that's usually saved for members of the armed forces.

John MacDonald began reading out the names, and every *no response* was met by a growl of pain or by a rapid torrent of Scottish curse words.

Robert Bates? *No response.*

James Benton? *You know ah'm fucken here.*

Mike Chase? *Here.*

Jack Dunlop? *Here.*
Greg Hamze? *No response.*
Andrew Gardiner? *No response.*
Corey Kennedy? *No response.*
Darragh O'Rourke? *Here.*
Stan Samson? *No response.*
Luke Schofield? *No response.*
Carl Taylor? *Here.*

John MacDonald made that less than 50 percent. And that was from Sunnyvale's highly trained but slightly out of shape security team. It was no surprise that nobody from the fishery made it all the way down from the north of the complex to the relative safety of the admin building.

MacDonald shook his head to try to clear it. He looked down at the list of names in front of him, but before he had a chance to say anything, he was interrupted by an unexpected question from an even more unexpected source.

"What about the environmental health inspector?" This came from Jill MacDonald, who cringed back a little when her uncle turned to look at her. He smiled at her, but it was an icy smile.

"Diane Hyde?" MacDonald asked. He shrugged. "Who cares? It's her fault we're in this mess in the first place. Maybe she got away, and maybe she didn't. I rather think she didn't, don't you? I don't fancy her chances of breaking through the quarantine. No, no. Diane Hyde is dead, and if she isn't dead now, she will be soon. Do you have any idea how many animals are out there?"

"Why don't you tell us, Boss?"

MacDonald turned sharply around to look at Lee Keyes, the perpetual dissenter. He frowned at him.

"We've got not far off a million animals here if you count the fishery," MacDonald said. "Four hundred and eighty thousand fish in the lake alone. As for the chickens, we've got ninety thousand broilers and seventy thousand layers, plus eighteen thousand geese and twenty-four thousand turkeys. Then we've got nine thousand dairy cows and nine thousand meat cows, plus two thousand calves for veal. Then there are eighteen thousand pigs and nine thousand sheep. That enough for you?"

Lee Keyes whistled softly but said nothing. John MacDonald looked around the room and could tell what the people were thinking. They were doing the maths in their head. The only reason that MacDonald didn't need to bother was because he had shareholders to report back to. It was his business to know exactly how many animals were on the premises at any given time.

But he'd never expected that information to come in useful in a life and death situation like this. He sighed and rubbed his eyes with the back of his hand. Then he looked around the room again.

"Seems to me," MacDonald said, "that the first thing to do is to catalogue the known threats and to figure out how best to protect ourselves. Threat number one, of course, is the animals. Fortunately, I believe we've dealt with the problem, at least for now, with the barricade."

"For as long as it holds," Copeland murmured.

"Unfortunately for us," MacDonald continued, "the animals aren't the only threat. We need supplies. Food and water. We may be here for a while."

"May I make a suggestion?" Copeland asked. MacDonald nodded and the vet stepped forwards, pushing his way to the front of the crowd. "I think we need to make an inventory of what we have here in the admin building. The ground floor's out of bounds, of course, but there's the staff kitchen on the first floor and the vending machines by the lift."

"We should barricade the lift an' aw," Jim said. "In case

the power comes back, ye ken."

"Can pigs use lifts?"

"Ah dinnae ken," Jim replied. "But a'hm no taking chances."

"Then make it happen," MacDonald replied. "Can I trust you and O'Rourke with it?"

"Aye, ye can count on us."

"While Jim's doing that," Copeland said, holding a hand up for silence and jumping into the conversation before the crowd had time to grow restless, "I'd like to make another suggestion."

"Go ahead."

"I think we should send a scouting party around the bathrooms," Copeland said. "This might sound grim, but it's better to be safe than sorry. I think we should syphon out the water. We might need it. We can refill the empties from the drinking fountain. We'll need to look around for any other canisters as well. And it goes without saying that we'll need to keep it clean and sanitary, as much as we can with pigs running around downstairs."

"Clean animals, pigs," MacDonald murmured. "Despite their reputation."

"What's that?"

"Nothing." MacDonald looked around the room. He couldn't see everyone from his seat, but he could see the shapes of enough people to have a good idea of how many were there. And how restless they were. He sighed.

"What about the bull?" someone shouted.

"Fuck the bull," Big Jim replied. His heavy hand went automatically to his belt and patted the truncheon.

"Perhaps there are other survivors," someone shouted. "We should look for them."

MacDonald's head snapped round and he locked eyes with Lee Keyes, who'd broken the uncomfortable silence again to make his voice heard.

"If you want to go and look for them, feel free," MacDonald said. "But right now, I'd rather focus on the people in this room."

"Doesn't matter anyway," Keyes murmured. "We're all fucked. We're going to die in here."

"Shut ya fucken pie hole," Jim bellowed. Keyes was pushing forwards, struggling against the crowd as though he planned to swim upstream to John MacDonald and to take him out with a fist to the face. Jim grinned recklessly and raised his pistol. He pointed it at Keyes so that the barrel was aimed right between his eyes. "Feelin' lucky, ya daft cunt?"

Keyes shook his head and took a step backwards, muttering something under his breath. Jim watched him go and then holstered his weapon once he was satisfied that the man meant no mischief.

He leaned in close to MacDonald, who was still sitting calmly behind his mahogany desk.

"You want tae keep an eye on that yin," Jim whispered. "He's lookin fae some trouble, ye ken."

"I couldn't agree more," MacDonald replied. "We need a strategy. We need to keep people busy. Any ideas?"

Big Jim shook his head, and it looked like that was the end of the conversation. Then MacDonald smiled, cautiously at first before it spread across his face like a bad rash.

"It's a good job I'm the brains of the outfit," MacDonald said. "I've got an idea. Here's what I want you to do..."

***

MacDonald's idea turned out to be controversial. After the meeting died a death and the first disgruntled murmurs of a riot were in the air, Big Jim and his team were tasked with shepherding the Sunnyvale Survivors out of the boss' office and finding a place for people to call their own.

The first floor was off limits, of course. Even if anyone had been brave enough to set up camp down there, the pigs were still rooting around on the ground floor, dragging their weary trotters through drifts of shattered glass and the sticky puddles that Pete Fields had left behind. Big Jim had his team working shifts with two men on guard at all times on the bottom floor in case there was a breach and the pigs made it through.

But there was more work to be done. Carol Rawlings was heading a team that was helping to scout for supplies. Another team was working through the second and third floors, dragging the desks around and manipulating the partitions to create rooms within rooms. It wasn't perfect, and it was going to get pretty cosy at night when the Sunnyvale Survivors were sleeping top and tail, but it would have to do.

As for what would come next, John MacDonald was out of ideas. That's why he delegated the task of keeping people busy to Tom Copeland, who'd formed an alliance with the boss' niece and formed a number of smaller, more nimble teams with the majority of the remaining staffers. Their jobs were to find containers to collect rainwater or to hunt around the office for potential weaponry. They even had two of the juniors making spears by lashing scalpels from the art department to whatever they could find. They weren't the most effective weapons, but if it came down to it, it was better to have a scalpel on a stick than to go up against the pigs' evil teeth with fists and feet.

Big Jim Benton, meanwhile, was in John MacDonald's office, chairing an off-the-record meeting that could spell the difference between life and death, especially if they were trapped inside the admin building for a prolonged period of time with no food, no electricity and no running water. If they didn't die of thirst or starvation, a disease would kill them. They needed to gather more food and medical supplies, and the only way to do that was to form an assault team which would leave the relative safety of the admin building and try to make it to the veterinary surgery and back.

And while all this was happening, the sun was going down. It hung bloody red in the sky like a smear against the clouds, and the shrieking birds in the chicken shed sang an unpleasant cacophony as the moon came out to play. They were joined by the bleating of the sheep and the mooing of the cows, both of which were distant, eerie noises that floated out through the cracks of their sheds. But the pigs, for some mysterious reason of their own, stayed silent.

The Sunnyvale Survivors slept uneasily that evening. With the power out, the building felt quiet and unlived in, a shell of its former self. The strange surroundings, which seemed so normal in the daytime, stopped them from settling in and making themselves at home. When the darkness closed in, they found themselves staring right into the void.

"No light," MacDonald had said. "No light and no fire. Nothing that could call attention to us. The last thing we need is a bunch of bloody pigs bashing the building down."

The survivors weren't happy, but they seemed to see the sense of it. Still, as the evening turned into night and they found themselves playing bingo with Jill MacDonald to take their mind off things, they started to wonder what the morning would bring.

***

Meanwhile, deep beneath the facility, the thing with the

many minds and the many legs crawled slowly to the surface. It came up through a ventilation shaft beside the burnt-out wreck of the former communications hut and started to patrol the facility. It explored the land. *Its* land, the land that had created and sustained it.

The pigs left it alone. They knew it was something not to be touched, a *bad thing* that would mean death or something worse. It wasn't a case of the risk of hunger versus the risk of disease. It was a case of self-preservation.

And as the night wore on, it walked in meandering concentric circles. They brought it closer and closer to the admin building.

DAWN BROKE SLOWLY the following morning. As the sun rose, so did the Sunnyvale Survivors. Not one of them had slept well, and there were at least a dozen who hadn't slept at all.

"It's like being in a nightmare," Will Makon grumbled. The production worker from the cow shed had never been a morning person, and there wasn't even any hot water for a cup of coffee. "One you can't wake up from."

MacDonald didn't have an answer for him. And besides, his mind was preoccupied elsewhere.

It began just after 6 AM, when the sun was still low in the sky and casting grey light across the facility. The animals had been loud at night to begin with, but they'd started to settle down as time wore on. When the sun rose, the facility felt almost peaceful. There was a tangible, heavy atmosphere. It felt like something was waiting.

There were six men on the so-called assault team. Big Jim had volunteered to lead it, not because he wanted to but because he had to. The burly Scotsman needed to stay in control, and the only way to do that was to head the team and shoulder the burden of the mission and its success or failure. Jim was joined by Keith Gowan, a production worker from the pig shed who seemed unfazed by the death of his line manager, as well as Bruce Laing from the sheep shed and Neil Gibson from the slaughterhouse, who'd both volunteered. The team was rounded off by Greg Hamze and Jack Dunlop from the security team, who'd drawn the short straws. Darragh O'Rourke had volunteered, but Big Jim had told him to stand down.

"We cannae risk it," Jim had said. "Ye've goat tae stay here and look after the rest of 'em, ye ken. Ye're in charge now."

And so the six of them met in MacDonald's office, which was being used as their headquarters. The boss had stayed up all night, pacing the room in the darkness and occasionally pausing to lean down on his mahogany desk. According to the rumour mill, he was starting to go crazy.

"Are you ready?" MacDonald asked. He was looking sternly at his troops and hoping to high hell that they were making the right decision. Big Jim nodded at him. "Good. Then let's begin."

They started by edging out onto the gantry. It gave them the high ground and allowed them to check whether the beasts were waiting for them before they lowered themselves to the floor. With the stairs blocked and the lift out of commission, there was no chance of them taking the easy way. Dropping down from the roof was hardly ideal, especially when the only rope they had was a relic of a simpler time, a time when it had occasionally been used on the animals. It was frayed but it was heavy, and it was enough to allow them to climb down to the ground. They hoped.

They found a spot halfway along the north end of the gantry where they could lower the rope and drop down between a couple of air vents. It offered them a little protection from the elements and the bottom was clear, for now at least. There were pigs and they could see them, but they were further north towards the fishery. They'd gathered along the shore of the lake because it was the only place to drink from. They'd be getting hungry, though. With the electricity off and their shed smashed to pieces, they had no access to the automated feeding machines.

Big Jim went first as the leader of the expedition. He shot

down the rope like a fireman sliding down a pole, but he'd been prepared for the friction and wrapped both of his hands with scraps of an old tea towel. He landed heavily on the floor and dropped and rolled, then pulled himself to his feet and backed against the wall. He drew his weapon, one of the few that fired live ammunition, and looked cautiously around. There was still no sign of any of the livestock, so he looked up to the top of the rope and gestured for the rest of them to follow.

Greg Hamze followed next, and then came Neil Gibson and Bruce Laing. Keith Gowan and Jack Dunlop came last. They climbed down one by one, inching their way to the bottom at a snail's pace. Big Jim was growing impatient, but when the last pair of boots hit the ground there was still no sign of movement.

Without saying a word, Jim turned to his right and led the way north-east, hugging the wall of the admin building and moving as quietly – and as quickly – as possible. The rest of them followed in single file, twitching nervously at every sound, every snatch of birdsong or every twig that crunched beneath their feet.

They made it to the edge of the building without a problem, but the next stage was much more dangerous. They had to run across the open grass towards the north, but that brought them closer to the waterfront where the pigs were gathered. They took the run in single file, their heads held low and their footsteps steady as they smashed their boots into the mud.

They hit their first problem when they reached the entrance to the storage building. They needed to get inside to access the supplies, but with the power out, there was no chance of using a key card. The six of them stood nervously outside the door. In the distance, the pigs were moving. They weren't coming towards them, but they *were* pacing the shores of the lake or walking around in restless circles.

Luckily, Big Jim came to the rescue. "Watch me now, boys," he said. "All ye need is the right tool, ye ken? Wi' the power out, it's just a standard latch lock. Ye've just goat to jimmy it."

He was carrying the perfect tool for the job, a long, thin file from some old tool cupboard. Sunnyvale had been a farm for the best part of two centuries. The latest iteration was just a different type of farm, the next generation. But nothing can run so far that the past can't catch up with it.

Big Jim slipped the file into the lock and popped the door open. He grinned. "A little trick ah learned back in Scotland, ye ken. I dunnae make it a habit."

They followed him inside and pulled the door to. Jack Dunlop was still at the rear. He grabbed a fire extinguisher from the wall and used it to wedge the door open. He didn't want to get trapped inside and to die in there.

Big Jim had to force another two or three doors as they wound their way through the hallways. For the most part, there was no natural light, and they had to light the way with torches. With the power out, John MacDonald had passed what he called an executive order and all of the phones had been handed in to him and locked in one of the drawers of his mahogany desk. The plan was to conserve the batteries as much as possible and to keep on checking them in case one of them managed to break its way out of the infamous Sunnyvale blackspot and to find a signal. Whenever the foraging party stepped into the rosy glow of a window or a skylight, the effect was disconcerting. It was only the early morning, but it felt like the middle of the night as they wandered through the labyrinth.

The mission was going well. It was a shame that they couldn't radio MacDonald, who was presumably biting his fingernails at his mahogany desk, but they'd agreed in advance to maintain radio silence for fear that the unnecessary noise might summon the animals. It took them just over ten minutes to reach Copeland's office, a journey that would normally take just two or three, but they thought they'd made good time.

"Right," Jim said. "Ye ken what tae look for."

And they did. Copeland had stayed up late the night before, writing out lists and instructions and briefing the men on what they needed. Ketamine for anaesthesia. Morphine and co-codamol for pain relief. Penicillins, cephalosporins, macrolides and fluoroquinolones to treat infections. Antihistamines and anti-inflammatories for allergic reactions. Anything he could think of that they could conceivably need. But he'd had to keep the list short, too. He'd had to draw maps from memory showing them where to look, and he'd had to distribute the work amongst the six of them while making sure their search was as efficient as possible.

They hunted down as much medication as they could, with Big Jim going shoulder-to-shoulder with his men as he timed their search on a stopwatch. When they hit ten minutes, he called time. His men were carrying rucksacks and canvas bags, whatever they'd been able to find around the office. The meds filled them up to just under a third of capacity, but they had another stop to make.

The storage facility was also home to the grain warehouse, a huge, cavernous room full of feed that was usually destined for the stomachs of the animals. It didn't taste great, but it was genetically engineered for nourishment and it certainly fattened the meat up. They scooped up as much of the stuff as they could carry until their bags were weighed down, and then they took what they had and retraced their steps back out of the storage building and into the sunlight.

It took a moment or two for their eyes to adjust to the brightness, even though they hadn't been inside for long and the low sun was yet to rise to its full glory. The air was still and chilled to the bone if they stood around for too long. The absence of wind floated an eerie silence around the facility, broken only by the occasional grunts and shrieks of the pigs as they browsed the shore.

"Let's gae back to Old MacDonald," Jim said.

The men didn't need telling twice. It was going well, too well, and their luck held out as they scuttled back to the south-west, retracing their steps but with heavier bags and elevated heart rates. Gowan's bag split halfway back and began to leave a trail of grain behind them, but they didn't have time to find a fix. He ended up clutching it to his chest like a mother with a newborn baby.

They made it back to their entry point without a hitch, and John MacDonald was waiting right there for them. He'd recruited a dozen of the early risers to sit up there on the gantry with him, keeping watch for the return of the scout party. They saw them when they were just little ants creeping out from the side of the storage depot and were ready when they reached the side of the building.

They raised the bags up first on the basis that they needed people on the bottom to tie the bags to the rope. They did three bags at a time and made short work of it, but then their luck ran out.

The first they heard of it was the big bang from the south-east. It sounded like a bomb had gone off, and the men on the ground instinctively shrank back and tried to shield themselves against the wall. But the people on the roof had a better view, and young Jill MacDonald was the first one to sound the alarm.

"Cows!" she shouted.

John MacDonald raced along the gantry to see what she

was looking at, then cursed under his breath as he spotted the tell-tale dust cloud. If it wasn't the cows, it was the pigs, but either would be dangerous in close quarters. Especially with the strange Sunnyvale bloodlust that had taken the animals and turned them against their masters.

MacDonald put his fingers in his mouth and whistled, a high, piercing whistle that carried all over the complex. There was no point trying to be quiet, not now. The pigs might have heard, but the pigs weren't the most pressing concern.

The men on the ground knew what the whistle meant. They'd been hoping no one would use it.

Their frenetic pace doubled, and Big Jim's team took to the rope two at a time, hauling themselves up at the same time that the team on the roof pulled at it like some post-apocalyptic tug of war. Jack Dunlop and Neil Gibson went up first, and when they reached the top a great cheer erupted from the roof team. But not everyone was happy. John and Jill MacDonald were staring fixedly at the oncoming cows, which were now close enough to make out. They could see the patterns on their hides and the slightest hint of the tell-tale scarring that the branding irons left behind.

"Hurry up!" MacDonald bellowed. "They're coming."

Bruce Laing and Keith Gowan were the next two to take to the rope. Big Jim looked tense but not nervous, and he insisted on staying to the end like a captain going down with his ship. Laing and Gowan reached the rooftop without a hitch, and the rope was lowered again to the last two men on the ground. The cows were getting even closer. They could smell them.

Greg Hamze shifted his bulky frame on to the rope and started to climb it, putting one hand over another and hauling himself up like his life depended on it, which it did.

Big Jim climbed on next, an equally heavy man with equally strong forearms and no desire to get left behind. But Hamze was making faster progress, and he was almost at the top when the accident happened.

The rope had taken all the weight it would take. It stretched like a bungee cord morphing into melted cheese and then snapped with a crack like a gunshot or a whip breaking the sound barrier. Big Jim and Greg Hamze tumbled to the ground.

Jim only fell fifteen feet, and he hit the ground rolling and somehow came out standing up. He didn't know how he did it, but it saved his life. Hamze wasn't so lucky. He fell the best part of forty feet and though he landed on the grass, it did little to cushion his fall. But it didn't kill him.

Big Jim could hear Hamze crying out in pain. He could see a shard of snapped bone sticking out of his leg and through his uniform. His eyes rolled back in his head and he started to choke on his own saliva. In the distance, less than eighty feet away, the cows were getting closer. The survivors on the roof were crying out. Big Jim made eye contact with MacDonald on the gantry and they locked on to each other for the briefest of moments. Then the spell was broken and they both looked away.

Big Jim turned and ran to the south, away from the pigs to the north and the cows that were closing in from the east. He hugged the contours of the building and tried to block out the screams of pain and the dreadful crunch of broken bones as the creatures bore down on his subordinate.

***

MacDonald ordered the four men from the expedition to keep their mouths shut about what had happened, so naturally the news spread throughout the survivors like a virus. By lunchtime, there was a general undercurrent of fear and anticipation. The people were waiting, but they were growing impatient. And there was no Big Jim there to keep the peace with his heavy fists and his firearm.

Darragh O'Rourke had stepped up to take the place of his boss as the de facto head of security, but MacDonald insisted that his most important role would be to tally up their haul from the veterinary clinic and the grain silo and to make a full list of what they had.

"We'll add it to the rest of our resources," MacDonald said. "Get a real idea of what we're up against here. We might have to start rationing if we're low on food, which I suspect we are."

"Can't we send out another team?" O'Rourke asked.

MacDonald shook his head. "It's not like they're just popping down the shops for a pint of milk," he said. "Did you see what happened to Greg Hamze?"

"No," O'Rourke admitted.

"Well, I did," MacDonald replied. "And I don't want it to happen again. Not if I can help it."

"So what do we do?"

"We wait," MacDonald said. "It's all we can do. It's too dangerous out there. No, no, we'll stick to the plan and barricade ourselves in here for as long as we can hold out. Help is bound to arrive eventually. They can't quarantine us forever."

O'Rourke wasn't so sure and it was written all over his face, but he also had a job to do. With Big Jim gone, he was the new head of security. A hell of a job to have when the world was falling apart and the food chain had been snapped in half and welded back together the wrong way round. MacDonald saw the fear in his eyes, but he also didn't have time for it, so he dismissed the man with a brisk wave of his hand and set about building a team to look after food and supplies. In particular, he needed a cook. He needed several of them.

The sun was rising high in the sky and noon had come and gone. Many of the survivors hadn't had anything to eat for over twenty-four hours, and MacDonald knew from bitter experience how starvation could sap a man's morale and turn even a loyal employee into a dissident. Boredom was another factor. He thought about Frank Herbert and the battered copy of *Dune* which had captured his imagination as a child. *Fear is the mind-killer*, he thought. *But hunger and boredom can kill the soul.*

His plan to fight the boredom began just after 2 PM. He'd already tasked the admin girls with hunting down as much cooking equipment as possible, and they hadn't let him down. The power was still down and so the microwave was out of the question, but they'd raided the cutlery drawers and found a bunch of paper plates and plastic sporks that were left over from some Christmas party half a lifetime ago. They'd also dug up an old metal cauldron from a Halloween party. MacDonald vaguely remembered it. They'd held it at an old manor house and filled the cauldron with punch. At the time, MacDonald had tried to veto it as a waste of company funds, and when the party was over, he'd insisted on keeping the thing.

It was a decision which might have saved their lives.

Now, with the sun high in the sky and half the daylight already gone, it was crunch time. Jill MacDonald and Tom Copeland had spent several hours seeking applicants for their newfound head cook position, and they'd narrowed it down to three people who'd been able to offer up some sort of evidence to back up their claims. Maude Harrison, the receptionist, had spent two summers working in the kitchen of a Beefeater just north of Coventry, and Bill Long used to run a kebab van in High Wycombe. Will Makon had no actual experience, but he'd been on an episode of *Come Dine with Me* and ranked runner-up, so he'd have to do.

The three of them were summoned to see John MacDonald, who listened to their stories and nodded his approval, and then they were led out through the fire exit and on to the gantry that circled the admin building.

"Don't look down," MacDonald said. And so, of course, they did. Will Makon lost his lunch from the day before. The vomit dribbled down the support struts and started dripping to the floor. Far below, four dozen cows were chewing on the crushed and leaking body of Greg Hamze, who'd lost his eyes to the crows and whose mouth was wide open, his teeth bared like fangs in an invisible scream. It looked like he was shouting into the void, like he was not going gently into that good night.

The volunteers were led up one last flight of steps and onto the roof, where a small wall gave them some respite against the winds, which were blowing down through the Chiltern Hills and sweeping across the top of the complex. The ingredients they'd been given were simple, just grain, corn, soy, water and what little seasonings and supplementary items they'd been able to find in the building.

Luckily, Maude Harrison was also a health freak, and she quickly took charge of the situation. "Bring me some wheat grain," she said. "Weigh it out as best as you can. We need two and a half parts water for every one part of wheat grain. Start filling those pint glasses with water and grain, it'll give us a good enough approximation. Quickly now."

The two men just looked at her, dumbfounded. They'd never crossed paths with her before and hadn't yet heard that she wasn't a woman to mess with. She had no patience for it, just like John MacDonald.

"Do as she says," MacDonald ordered. "Finally,

someone's taking the initiative."

They watched in silence as Harrison continued to lead the team. They heated the cauldron on a small fire that they built on the rooftop, laying a foundation on a pile of loose bricks that the builders had left behind and quickly forgotten. They burned paper and wood from the furniture. It reeked, but it was a small price to pay for hot water. Before long, the cauldron was bubbling away and the Sunnyvale chefs were pouring grain into the water.

"You know," Bill Long murmured, "we could also make whiskey if we wait around for long enough. I wonder how long we'll be stuck here for, anyway."

"Not long, I hope," Harrison replied. "This stuff will fill you up, but it tastes like... well, like nothing. People aren't going to be happy."

And she was right. The stuff that came out of the cauldron was barely edible at all. It was basically just porridge, but not the kind of porridge that they were used to from the supermarket. It was more like a thick, viscous gruel, the kind of porridge that would have been served in a county jail in the 1800s but with an extra serving of the antibiotics that were pumped into the animals to enhance their growth.

The arguments started as soon as they started to serve it out by doling the thick, grey gloop onto paper plates with a wooden spoon. They had to eat it with the plastic sporks, and Darragh O'Rourke and the remnants of the security team gathered up the used cutlery at the end. Every spork had to be accounted for. They had limited resources.

And the dissenting voices only grew louder after people swallowed the first couple of mouthfuls and realised it wasn't going to get any better. It was Lee Keyes from the sheep team who was the most obnoxious, of course.

"You seriously expect us to eat this shit?" he was asking.

"I've seen what happens to the animals after a steady diet of this stuff and if you think I'm going to let that happen to me, you can think again."

John MacDonald overheard this and he wasn't happy. He stared at the man as though willing him to self-combust and Keyes took an involuntary step backwards, nudging into someone else and sending their porridge scattering down on to the floor.

"Take it or leave it," MacDonald said, softly. His voice was quiet, but the whole room was watching in silence and the only other noise was the distant braying of the animals. His words floated on the air like blow darts. "It's all we've got."

"It's not good enough," Keyes replied.

MacDonald exploded. "It's not good enough?" he bellowed. "Well you're shit out of luck, buddy, because it's all we damn well have. You don't want to eat it? Feel free to starve."

"There must be something better."

"People died for this!" MacDonald shouted. "You understand? The food you're complaining about was bought with blood and bone."

Another angry murmur passed through the crowd, and MacDonald could feel the tide of popularity pass once more back over to him. He took another deep breath and rolled the dice again.

"Listen," he said. "I won't lie to you guys. This is a life and death situation. Sure, the food tastes like shit. Sorry, Maude, but that's a fact. Unfortunately, it's also all we have. If we're going to stay alive in here, we're going to need to eat. And if we're going to eat, we have to eat this. That's all there is to it. Any questions?"

He was pleasantly surprised to find that there weren't.

MacDonald cast one last look around the desperate,

shell-shocked faces of the Sunnyvale Survivors and then handed back over to Darragh O'Rourke. He took a bowl of the porridge on his way out and then climbed the stairs to eat the gruel at his mahogany desk.

LATER ON that evening, MacDonald was sitting alone on the roof, watching the pigs and the cows wander the grounds by the light of the moon and the stars. They seemed to be getting closer, although it was hard to tell due to their numbers. They orbited the admin building like a thousand moons, always keeping their distance as though they were trying to tempt people out to take their chances. Nobody seemed keen to take the risk.

MacDonald reached into his pocket and pulled out a pack of Pall Mall cigarettes that he kept in his desk with a book of matches in case he ever needed one. He'd kept them there for several years without touching them, but since the outbreak had started, he'd found himself craving them more and more like a lonely man missing the voices of old friends. He was down to his last one.

He put the cigarette to his mouth and struck the match, then cursed as the cold wind blew it out. He turned his back to the wind and hunched over the matchbox, then tried again. The second time, he lit it, and he took a deep, unsatisfying drag from its time-yellowed filter. It tasted flat and stale, but it also tasted like a cup of water to a thirsty man, metallic and impure perhaps but somehow still refreshing.

His nerves were shot and he was on edge, but so were everyone else's. He smoked on in silence and tried not to think about what might happen next.

Downstairs, on the second floor of the admin building, the Sunnyvale Survivors were in low spirits. The food had filled the holes in their stomachs, but it did nothing to plug the invisible wounds through which their morale leaked like fuel from an overturned tanker. They were starting to smell, but they couldn't afford to waste water washing. They were also starting to realise that they might be spending a long time at Sunnyvale.

And as they prepared to get ready for sleep, something moved beneath the facility.

There were rumours about it, too. They were old, half-forgotten rumours that had been born with the facility and which only stuck around thanks to the old-timers.

They called it the Rat King.

"Some of the lads say it's nature's revenge for the way we wronged her," Bill Long was saying. He was sitting in the middle of a semi-circle as the other survivors sat around him and tried to make out his face in the darkness.

"But what is it?"

"They used to say it was thirteen rats," Long replied, his voice taking on a dreamlike quality as he thought back to his first tentative days at the facility, back before Big Jim had joined the security team and risen through the ranks and before John MacDonald had been offered the CEO spot. "A baker's dozen, you understand. With their tails tied together so they're forced to think and move as one."

There was a visible shudder amongst the listeners, measurable only in the shifting quality of the shadows. Long paused for a moment and hacked up a little phlegm before continuing. He was missing his medication and the dust and the muck made it hard for him to breathe.

"It's all a lot of nonsense, of course," he said. "Just rumours passed from man to man at the end of a long shift. But still. It makes you think."

The listeners nodded and agreed that yes, it did make them think. It made them think dark, dark thoughts. It made them think about their families and how they might never see them again. It made them think about how they might die beneath the hooves of a Sunnyvale cow or starve to death on the second floor of the admin building. It made them think about a lot of things that they would have preferred not to think about.

On the third floor, Tom Copeland was treating Yvonne Strong, who'd somehow popped her shoulder out of its socket by getting overexcited trying to smash furniture into its constituent planks so they could burn it beneath the cauldron. Copeland popped it back into place while she bit on a wooden spoon. It cut the noise down a little, but her scream still drifted out across the complex like the cries of the animals that were milling around outside.

At first, Copeland had protested. "I'm a vet, not a doctor," he'd argued. "I could make it worse. Damn it, I could kill her."

MacDonald had worried that he'd have to apply a little pressure, but he'd reckoned without an injured Yvonne Strong, who'd grabbed Copeland by the throat with her good arm and said, "Fix me." He'd fixed her up after that all right, although he continued to grumble about it.

Copeland offered to give her some of the painkillers that Big Jim's team had brought back, but Strong had lived up to her name and refused them.

"I could never stand opiates," she said. "I've got enough problems as it is without picking up an addiction. And besides. We should save them. Someone else might need them."

The veterinarian shrugged. It made no difference to him, but he did hold a certain respect for her. It wasn't the choice he might have made in her place, but it was still a brave choice nonetheless. He told her to take it easy and to rest the shoulder, knowing full well that if MacDonald ordered her to do something, she'd have to do it. He resolved to have a word with the boss about leaving her name out of the rota for a couple of days.

When they bedded down later that night, the mood was much lower than it had been the night before and the naysayers were saying their nays more vocally. As usual, it was Lee Keyes at the centre of it.

"We can't trust John MacDonald," Keyes was saying. "The man's a fucking sociopath. He always has been. And now you expect me to trust him with my life? I don't know, guys. You can drink the Kool Aid, but I'm not touching the stuff. I'm my own man, and I'll make my own decisions."

By this point, John MacDonald had come down from the gantry and had settled in amongst the rest of the survivors. It wasn't quite a social call because he was more interested in just sitting back and listening to the chatter that passed from person to person, but he piped up every now and then when challenged. Mostly, though, he just listened to his people and tried to figure out how he could turn their complaints to his advantage. He heard Lee Keyes, and he had a sneaky suspicion that Keyes knew it. But he also didn't want to confront him. It would legitimise his complaints.

Most of the talk centred around a single question: "What's going to happen?" It was a question that had been on MacDonald's mind as well, but he was yet to find an answer. Or rather, he had too many answers to choose from and he couldn't be sure which one was correct. Worse, as if his own theories weren't enough, there were plenty more to be considered. There were a dozen theories for every man and woman in the building, some of them more optimistic than others.

"Don't sweat it," Bugsy Drew had said. The operations manager was having the time of his life in post-pandemic Sunnyvale. He was enjoying a well-earned break now that he didn't have any work to do. Not that he was known for doing much in the first place. "They'll have us out of here in no time. You'll see."

Lee Keyes wasn't so sure, and his single voice of dissent had been joined by that of two others, Jerry Jones from the foie gras team and Kim Roach from pigs. Roach wasn't much of a looker to begin with, but the long period of confinement and the lack of running water had taken its toll. The skin on her face looked gaunt and grey. She didn't look healthy at all.

"I saw a documentary on this," Jones said. "It's the government, all right. A conspiracy. You mark my words. They're probably testing some new biological weapon. Trust me. We're the guinea pigs."

"Rubbish," Kim Roach replied, her voice cracking from too many Richmond Super Kings. "It's the fuckin' zombie apocalypse. I've seen the movies."

Lee Keyes shook his head, the darkness casting a dark shadow over his face. He was smiling, quite clearly enjoying himself. All eyes were on him.

"This is all John MacDonald's fault," he said, slowly. "He's supposed to be the boss. How could he let this happen?"

MacDonald didn't know if Keyes knew he was there or not, but he wasn't about to let it slide. The stakes were too high. He climbed to his feet and walked over to where they were sitting. Their hangdog expressions when they looked up at him reminded him of a gaggle of giggling schoolgirls trying to summon spirits from a Ouija board.

"I'm only going to say this once," MacDonald said. His voice was quiet and as sharp as a knife's edge. It felt thawed and ready to freeze in the cold, unheated air of the admin building. "None of this is my fault."

"Pshhh," Keyes murmured.

"I didn't ask for this," MacDonald said. His keen eyes seemed to look into the minds of the people that were sitting in the ragged semi-circle before him. "You'd do well to remember that. I'm trapped here just as much as you are. We're all victims here."

"If we're victims," Keyes asked, "then who in the hell is the perpetrator?"

MacDonald frowned for a moment and thought it over. "That," he said, after a moment, "is exactly what I intend to find out."

***

When the sun rose the following day, MacDonald called for a strategy meeting around his mahogany desk and summoned a half dozen of his most trusted employees to consult with him.

"What's up, Boss?" That came from Darragh O'Rourke, who was leaning back against the wall and picking at his teeth with the blade of a pocket knife.

"I've got a job for you," he said. "For all of you. We need to get in touch with the outside world. See if we can't find out what's happening."

"How?" Copeland asked. The vet looked tired, and his face was cast into shadow by the beginnings of a beard. "The phones are out. So is the electricity."

"I know," MacDonald replied. "We need a radio."

"There's a radio in Big Bertha," O'Rourke said. "But I don't think much of our chances of getting it. No one will go back out there."

"We might not have much choice."

"Yeah?" O'Rourke said. "Are you gonna go?"

"No, I'm not," MacDonald replied. "You are."

"Fuck that."

"Well," MacDonald said, "I guess we'll have to figure that out. If only Big Jim was here. He'd know what to do."

Nobody spoke for a moment. It was a sign of the esteem that they held him in that no one needed to say anything.

"Okay," MacDonald said. "Well, if we can't get the radio, I guess it's plan B. We need a lie."

"What do you mean?" Copeland asked.

"A lie," MacDonald repeated. "If we want to maintain control, we need a lie to give the people hope and to keep them in line. It's an old management trick. We have to tell them that everything's going to be okay. We'll say we made contact with the outside and that they gave us an update."

Copeland shook his head. "They're not going to buy it," he said.

"They'll *have* to buy it," MacDonald said. "If they don't, there'll be no stability. And if there's no stability, we're all going to die here. That's why I'm not going to tell them. You are."

"I am?" Copeland asked. He didn't look too happy about it.

"Our fate is in your hands, Dr. Copeland," MacDonald said. "And there's something else, something we all need to think about."

"What's that then?" This came from O'Rourke, who was standing awkwardly off to one side and squinting as the sun filtered past them and into his eyes.

"It's the animals," Copeland said. "Right?"

"Right," MacDonald said. "If the power's out, so are the food and water systems."

"The animals have been drinking from the lake," Copeland reminded him. "But as for food, I guess they're in as much of a bind as we are."

"If they're hungry, they're going to get more desperate and aggressive," MacDonald said. "We have to be on our guard. They can smell us in here."

"They've turned into cannibals," Copeland added. "Perhaps they'll turn on each other before they turn on us."

"We can only hope," MacDonald said. "But it looks to me like they're eating whatever the hell they can get their vicious little teeth into. I think–"

Their conversation was interrupted by a deep, languorous boom that echoed across the complex, followed by another and then another. The war council dashed to the fire exit and ran out on to the gantry, banging shoulders against each other in their hurry to find out what the noise was. It came from the south-east and they had to make their way onto the roof and across the asphalt to see what it was, although they all already knew before they got there. The visual just confirmed it.

The cows and the pigs had banded together into an unholy alliance of angry flesh that was battering itself against the walls of the sheep shed. The building backed onto the cow shed, and so its aluminium walls were already weakened. The pigs and the cows were determined. They were a horde of creatures moving with a single mind, a little bit like Bill Long's Rat King.

And then the walls gave in and the sheep poured out and the roof collapsed inwards and sent a cloud of dust and muck floating into the air like the aftermath of an atomic bomb in the desert. And when the sheep were free, they joined the pigs and the cows and started racing around the admin building in a circle, like a never-ending stampede on the savannah.

MacDonald swore and turned his back on them. "Come on," he said. "We're going back inside. Gather the survivors and call an all-hands meeting."

"Are you sure, Boss?" O'Rourke asked. "Is that a good idea?"

"It's the only idea we've got," MacDonald said. "Just do it."

It didn't take long for people to gather. There was precious little entertainment on offer and every new announcement could be a matter of life and death. When MacDonald called for a meeting, they wanted to know what he had to say. It might just be important.

He started by telling them that the sheep had made their escape and that they'd joined the pigs and the cows in the no man's land outside the admin building. This announcement was met by audible gasps of disbelief and an unhappy murmuring, and little Jill MacDonald passed out and had to be caught by one of the lads from the slaughterhouse.

MacDonald held his hands up in a conciliatory gesture and said, "I know, I know. Unfortunately, at this point in time, there's not much we can do about it. Our first priority is our survival. We need to focus on rationing, sanitation and all the other stuff that will keep us alive in here. We also need to strengthen the barricade and double the guard. All we need is a single breach and we're done for."

This was greeted by a fresh round of angry murmuring, much of it coming from the security team and the temporary recruits that they'd added to swell their numbers. They were sick of standing guard, a job that seemed redundant thanks to the barricade and the apparent lack of interest from the animals, but MacDonald was having none of it.

"We just need to hole up in here a little longer," he said.

"What happened to the goddamn army?" someone shouted. MacDonald didn't even need to look to know it was Lee Keyes, lurking off to one side with his band of cronies. "They should be busting in here to get us out."

"Ah," MacDonald said, forcing a reluctant smile onto his lips and turning to face the man. "I'm glad you asked that." He forced himself to count to three before he continued.

"Listen, I've got bad news for you. We're on our own over here. It's an issue of national security. No one comes in and no one goes out. It's to stop the spread of the infection."

"Bullshit."

MacDonald glared at the man before turning to Copeland and nodding at him. "Do you want to take this?" he asked.

Copeland swallowed and climbed nervously to his feet. He'd been sitting in one of the chairs with Darragh O'Rourke and a couple of others from MacDonald's inner circle.

"It's true," Copeland said, looking around the room while trying to avoid the eyes of the onlookers. "We've had contact from the outside. On one of the radios."

The crowd erupted in a cheer and launched into a spontaneous round of applause, but MacDonald held up his hands for silence.

"Quiet!" he snapped. "Remember, if those damned dirty beasts hear too much noise, they'll come for us."

That did it. Even Lee Keyes saw the wisdom in his words and stayed silent. MacDonald glowered around the room and then gestured for Copeland to continue.

"Here's how it is," Copeland said, getting into the swing of things and embracing the lie. "We're under quarantine. We know we're under quarantine. The army and the environmental health teams are here to make sure that whatever's wrong with those animals doesn't spread outside the complex, which is why they've surrounded the perimeter. No one comes in and no one goes out. For now, at least."

Copeland paused and risked a glance at MacDonald, who was watching his performance with a hint of approval hidden behind the set of his jaw. He swallowed again and turned back to look at his colleagues, people he'd known and worked with and who he was now lying to for what John MacDonald referred to as "the greater good", whatever that was.

Then he had a brainwave.

"The good news is that the boffins in their laboratories have come up with a vaccine, a little something to make sure that we don't catch whatever the animals have. Not that it's likely, you understand, but it's better to be safe than sorry." Over to his right, MacDonald was glaring at him. This wasn't part of the script.

"We're still waiting on the delivery of those vaccinations," Copeland said. "They're going to deliver them by drone, and I'll devise an inoculation schedule when we're ready. Until then, I'd advise you to keep your heads down and to stay the hell away from the animals, although I'm sure no one needs a reminder."

Copeland handed over to MacDonald and went to sit back down again. He watched in a tight-lipped silence until the boss had finished talking and he'd answered the questions that had been asked of him. Mostly, the questions were about their food supply and the lack thereof, but MacDonald had seen worse at board meetings and he took them all in his stride, bullshitting with all the skill of a master craftsman. By the time they were finished, the crowd was eating out of his hand and it looked like, for a while at least, the survivors were going to stay in line.

After the meeting, when his employees had dispersed and gone about whatever business they'd devised to keep themselves busy, MacDonald called Copeland into his office. He was perched behind his mahogany desk like an angry parrot, and Copeland realised that this was the first time in a long time that he'd seen the boss without one of his flunkies lurking somewhere in the background.

"What the hell was all that about?" MacDonald asked.

"What happened to the plan?"

"Plans can change," Copeland said. "And besides, I had an idea."

"Some idea," MacDonald growled. "And what do we do when the vaccines don't show up, huh? Have you thought about that?"

"Have you?" Copeland asked. He chuckled. "Don't you see, I'm doing you a favour? As long as they're waiting on the vaccines, no one will cross you. They need you. Besides, you're the one who said the only way to keep them in line is to tell a lie. I'm just doing what you told me to."

MacDonald paused for a moment, his brow creasing in concentration as he mulled it over. There was a certain kind of logic there, however twisted.

"Anyway," Copeland said. "If the worst comes to the worst, we can give them water. They don't need to know it's a placebo, and if it makes them feel better then why not?"

MacDonald shook his head. "It wouldn't work," he said. "We don't have enough needles."

"All right," Copeland replied. "In that case, we give them aspirin or an antihistamine. Some sort of tablet. Think they'll buy that?"

MacDonald thought about it again and then nodded his head. "They might," he said. "With a bit of luck, we won't even need to use it. I reckon you might be right. We'll buy ourselves some time by blaming the army and telling them there's been a problem with the vaccine. When we can't hold them off any longer, we'll make up a batch of placebos and show them off to the crowd. But we'll go one better. We'll tell them that it doesn't work as a vaccine. We'll say it has to be used after contact with the animals, and then keep it guarded with the rest of the meds and the food supply. No one will cross me. No one will dare. They'll want to know they can come to me for an injection if they need one."

MacDonald smiled and clapped Copeland on the back. "Well done, Doc," he said. "You did good."

BILL LONG WASN'T LOOKING TOO GOOD.

He'd been taken ill in the early afternoon and had spent several hours in the makeshift latrines, vomiting and shitting and just generally having a bad time of things. There was no running water, and so he couldn't splash his face or wipe the crap from his hands, and he had to do his business into a mop bucket that was placed in the empty toilet bowl. He had a little privacy in the cubicle, which was a godsend, but that didn't change the fact that he had to carry the stinking bucket back out of the bathroom and past a dozen sleeping refugees towards the big bay windows of the second-floor meeting room. They were the only windows in the facility that opened up a full ninety degrees and so they'd also become a vital part of the flushing process. With no running water, the buckets had to be emptied somewhere. Out of the second-floor window and into the bushes at the side of the building seemed like as good a place as any.

Bill Long wasn't the healthiest man to begin with, and he was no stranger to getting the shits at work. This was the first time he'd had to deal with his irritable bowels in such extreme situations though, and it was humiliating to be seen running to and from the bathroom with buckets of his own shit in his hands.

But the humiliation was just humiliation and it would pass. And as the afternoon turned into evening and the sun started to go down again, Bill Long found out just how ill it was possible to feel.

Copeland was summoned to see him at around 10 PM, shortly after the man had crawled into his makeshift bed and passed out. He was talking in his sleep, but it wasn't in a language that Copeland recognised. He suspected that if he took a recording and played it back to the man when he woke up, Bill Long wouldn't recognise it, either.

"What's wrong with him?" O'Rourke asked.

"No idea," Copeland said. He started searching through his bag for a couple of essentials, pulling out a thermometer and a stethoscope, the latter of which he usually used to listen for signs of life in the bellies of the pigs, sheep and cows in their birthing crates. He placed them in his shirt pocket. "Salmonellosis, perhaps?"

"Salmonellwhat?"

"An infection," Copeland said, reaching down to grab Bill Long by the shoulder and shaking him gently. "You can get it from bad meat and eggs. It takes over the intestines and fucks up your digestive system, which would explain why he's been spending so much time in the bathroom. And as it progresses, it can give you a fever and chills and all that sort of stuff. Wouldn't surprise me if that's why he can't stop talking."

"But if it's caused by bad eggs and meat, how'd he get it?" O'Rourke asked. "The rest of us are eating gruel and drinking rainwater."

Copeland shrugged and said, "Beats me." Then he shook Bill Long by the shoulder again, raised his voice a little and said, "Bill, wake up."

But Bill didn't wake up.

"Hmmm," Copeland murmured. He took the thermometer from his breast pocket and put it in the man's mouth, then gestured for O'Rourke to hold the candle a little closer so he could take a measurement. "Easy, now. Don't get the flame too close or it could change the reading."

O'Rourke did as he was told. The reading kept going up and he watched it with mounting concern. He was used to dealing with pigs and not people, but he was pretty sure this wasn't good.

"Jesus Christ," Copeland muttered. "He's at a hundred and three."

"Is that bad?"

"Yeah," Copeland said. "It's bad, all right. We need to cool him down and try to control this thing."

"Is he going to die?"

"Not if I can help it," Copeland said. "Get me some water, we need to keep him hydrated. Get me a flannel for his head as well. We'll let him sleep if we can. His body is fighting something off, and it'll need all the rest it can get. But someone's going to need to keep an eye on him. I'll take the first shift, but I'm going to need a break at some point."

"I'll take care of it," O'Rourke said.

"I'm also going to give him a little medication. Nothing too serious, just a couple of anti-inflammatories. Paracetamol or ibuprofen should do it. They'll help to bring his temperature down."

"And what about the muttering?"

"What about it?" Copeland said. "There's not much we *can* do. Go and get me that water. Other than that, all we can do is wait. I don't know if you're a religious man and I know that I'm not, but if you are then I'd say now's the time to start praying."

***

After Big Jim had turned tail and fled to the south, hugging the wall of the admin building in the hope that it would offer him some shelter, he'd had to think on his feet.

A few of the animals took chase, but those that did were injured or overweight, out of shape and not in their prime, something which almost certainly helped to save the

Scotsman's life. One of them was missing a front leg and another was limping along on a broken ankle, presumably from its escape. Still, the injured animals were more than a match for him. They'd started to gain on him by the time he hit the south-west corner of the building and hit a left, taking him to the east and the sanctuary he was starting to realise was his only chance at salvation.

He took the corner as quickly as he could, knowing all the time that if there were animals on the other side of it, huddled up against the building's perimeter, he was just another hunk of dead meat, another casualty of the great animal uprising. But he was lucky, and even the closest animals to the south-east were further away than the pigs that were bearing down behind him. And there in the middle distance, just over a hundred yards away, was the comforting, familiar shape of Big Bertha.

Big Jim was already running as fast as he could, and he didn't dare try to push himself any further, especially on the uneven ground and the muddy grass that orbited the admin building like a knock-off national park. Instead, he concentrated on keeping his footing while one hand dipped into his pocket and came out with a keyring. There were a dozen different keys on there, but he could recognise the one he was looking for by feel alone, and it fell right into the palm of his hand. By the time the wounded animals rounded the corner behind him, he was thirty yards away and counting. By the time he reached Big Bertha, they were right on his tail and he could smell the reek of their flesh and breath.

The van was still on its side, so Jim reached up and hauled himself on to the tyres and then the roof before slipping his key into the driver-side door, twisting it in the lock and launching himself inside. He slammed the door behind him, and not a moment too soon. The animals slammed right into it, shaking the van where it stood in the dirt and leaving smears of spit and blood on the windows. Big Jim flinched and backed away from the window, then winced as the vehicle's gearstick dug into his lower back. With the van still on its side, he didn't know which way was up and which way was down, and in many ways it didn't matter.

The pigs slammed into Big Bertha again and then again. It rocked some more and Jim banged his head on the ceiling. The vehicle's axles squealed as the animals smashed into it, and this time they caught it at just the right time to add their momentum. For an awful second, it teetered at an angle as though it wasn't sure which direction to fall in. Then it teetered some more and Big Bertha soared through the air and landed on her side, her wheels spinning uselessly in the air, and Big Jim cursed as he tumbled through the air and landed uncomfortably on his shoulders.

The world went still for a moment or two, and there was a shuffling sound as the animals backed away. Jim held his breath and waited. After a couple of minutes had passed, he decided to risk it. He lifted his head like a meerkat on sentry duty and tried to catch a glimpse of the mirror. It had snapped off at some point and was dangling uselessly in the wind, but Jim could see enough to tell that he was in no immediate danger. The animals had backed off, but they were watching Big Bertha lazily in case it showed any further signs of life.

Jim lowered himself back down again and resolved not to give them that sign by wafting his smell towards them or rocking Big Bertha on her axles.

Then he heard a sound, a soft thudding from somewhere near his waist. He looked down and saw the hatch that led to the rear of the van. It was locked from the outside – his side. And Big Jim was still somehow holding the keys.

He rifled through the keyring, allowing the familiar shape of the correct key to jump out at him, and then he inserted it into the keyhole. He twisted it to the left, slid back the security bolt and pulled the door open. His nostrils were immediately assaulted by the smell of sour piss, and he backed away instinctively as the man in the back of Big Bertha drew up to the hatch and stuck his head through it.

Harry Yorke looked like he'd been to hell and back. Last time Big Jim had seen him, the protestor had looked smug. Even though he was being marched off by the security team, he'd acted like a man who was in control of the situation, as though it was all a part of his grand plan, which it probably was. Now, though, he looked terrible, and Jim wasn't surprised. It had only been a day or so, but he'd been locked in the back of Big Bertha without so much as a pot to piss in and with angry animals marauding around the outside of his mobile prison. Big Jim would have pissed himself, too.

"What th–"

That was as far as he got. Big Jim had been expecting this, and he slammed the palm of his hand across the man's mouth before he could make any more noise and bring the pigs running back over towards them.

"Quiet," Jim whispered. Yorke bit his hand and Jim grunted, but he didn't release his grip on the man's mouth. He brought his other hand down to give him a whack across the back of his head. "We've goat tae keep quiet, ye ken. Unless ye want tae be pig food."

Yorke stopped struggling, and Jim lessened his grip on the man, although he didn't trust him enough to let go completely. Still, Harry Yorke had enough space to breathe and to whisper.

"Let me out of here," he hissed. "This is false imprisonment."

"Aye," Jim said. "Tell me about it. Thir's a fucken'

quarantine and wir aww in the shite."

"I don't understand," Yorke said.

"Ah'll bring ye up tae speed," Jim said. "But first, ah'd better climb down tae join ye."

Harry Yorke didn't understand at first, but he shifted out of the way anyway so that Jim could climb into Big Bertha's holding cell. They were safer there, out of sight of the animals and shielded by the thick metal plates that were designed to keep prisoners in but which were instead a tool to keep the animals out.

Jim explained as best as he could what had happened between their citizen's arrest at the communications shed and the point at which he'd fallen from the rope and fled to the relative safety of Big Bertha.

When he finished, Harry Yorke whistled under his breath. Then he said, "Well, it seems to me like we need to meet up with the rest of your team in the admin building."

"Aye," Jim said. "We've goat tae come up with a plan, ye ken, and wait 'til we're sure yon beasties are away fae us."

Harry Yorke wasn't keen on the idea, but he seemed to see the sense in it. It looked like the two of them were going to be spending a lot of time together. Big Jim perked his head up and sniffed at the air. He sniffed again.

"Ah can smell piss," he said.

***

Big Jim and Harry Yorke spent several fruitless days trying to come up with a desperate plan. It had taken that long for the conditions to be just right. The animals could sense them inside Big Bertha, and it took them a long time to tire of the van and the unusual smells that were coming from inside it.

The stench of piss had intensified, but neither of the men had passed a bowel movement. Big Jim liked to joke that the pigs had scared the shit out of them. They just hoped that the smell would somehow help to camouflage them, and perhaps even to cover their eventual escape.

At last, they could wait it out no longer. When they saw a gap in the endless procession of angry animals that looped around the fallen vehicle like policemen on the perimeter of a football pitch, they took their chance.

It was light outside, and the sun was slowly cresting the horizon and casting its light across the complex. Big Jim went first, climbing up into the cabin after checking the mirror. He knew Big Bertha like a pet dog and he'd spent enough time in her to memorise every inch of the cabin, but this was the first time he'd seen it sideways. It was like seeing a familiar face contorted by age to the point at which it was almost unrecognisable. His hands found what he was looking for and he popped the two-way radio out of its harness, then stashed it in the deep pockets of his uniform. It poked out and he couldn't close the zip, but it would have to do. If they made it back to the complex, perhaps he'd even have a chance to use it, but he couldn't risk turning it on out there in Big Bertha, where the snap, crackle and pop of the radio would be more enticing for the animals than any breakfast cereal.

"Awrite," Jim whispered. "It's as good as wir gonnae get. Ye'd best come up here."

Harry Yorke didn't need telling twice, and Jim wasn't surprised. He knew exactly how the man felt. They were sick of Big Bertha, sick of sitting in a pool of their own piss as the animals lowed outside and waited for them to make a mistake. They were dehydrated and they were hungry, and the half bottle of water and the couple of apples that Jim had found in the glove compartment had done little to lift his spirits.

Big Jim and Harry Yorke held their breath as the Scotsman carefully popped the door and swung it open. There were pigs in the distance, and they'd been joined by the cows and the sheep. They were parading the farm like some Orwellian nightmare, occasionally pausing to snap at each other or to chase after one of the few carrion birds that still dared to alight on Sunnyvale soil. Mostly, though, they watched. They waited.

The door swung a little more, opening sideways like the suicide doors on some footballer's Lamborghini, and Jim eased himself out through the gap and dropped to the floor. The grass below helped to soften his landing, but he still winced and looked up instinctively to see whether he'd been noticed. He hadn't.

Jim glanced over to check that Yorke was still doing his part and keeping his eyes trained on the animals. Satisfied, he peered around the edge of Big Bertha and saw what he was looking for. Sunnyvale's only active fire engine, which was actually a converted minibus with a ladder on top, was parked exactly where he thought it was, maybe twenty yards away across the car park. It had been parked haphazardly across a couple of spaces after the fire at the communications shed, which it had arrived too late to help with.

Big Jim flexed the muscles in his legs and then sat off towards the vehicle at a sprint. He was just a couple of yards away when he heard the signal, a poor impression of a hooting owl that Harry Yorke had been instructed to use at the first sign of danger. Jim looked up and sure enough, he'd been spotted, but it didn't matter much now. The next step of the plan was going to make some noise and there was no time for finesse. He pulled the truncheon from his belt and struck the base of it against the corner of the glass.

It cracked, but it didn't shatter.

Big Jim tried again and then again, and the fourth blow finally shattered enough of the glass for him to reach his arm through the gap to unlock the door from the inside. He pulled his arm out quickly, wincing as it brushed against the jagged edges of the glass and sent his blood spilling to the floor. But there were other things on his mind, and while he swore beneath his breath, he didn't slow down. He opened the door and jumped inside, then ran his hands beneath the driver's visor until he felt something. Strictly speaking, leaving a spare key in the vehicle was against regulations, but Jim knew exactly what his staff thought about regulations and he was banking on somebody flouting them. The gamble paid off.

With the key in hand, Jim jammed it into the ignition and twisted it. Nothing happened.

"Shite!" Jim growled.

"What's the problem?"

"Nae fuel," Jim said. "She was on fumes, ye ken."

"And you didn't think to mention it?"

"Ah didnae–"

"Hey!" That voice was unexpected, in part because it came from a woman. It floated on the wind from a couple hundred metres away and belonged to a middle-aged woman who wasn't looking in the best of shape. She was stumbling towards them as though she was drunk.

"Aww shite," Jim said. "Git yon lassie to shut that trap o' hers. Ah've goat tae get some petraw, ye ken."

By the time that Yorke took his first steps towards the woman, Jim was already moving. He'd grabbed a water canister and some other gear and was on his way to another one of the vehicles.

While Big Jim worked at the fuel tanks, syphoning the gas into his improvised petrol can and trying not to swallow too much of the stuff in the process, he watched Harry Yorke as he ran towards the woman. He was waving his arms in the air, but he wasn't dumb enough to call out to her. The woman, whoever she was, seemed to understand what he was getting at and while she continued to run towards them, she did it in silence.

Yorke reached the woman and grabbed her arm, then pulled her with him towards the vehicle. He talked to her as they ran, and while he was doing what he could to keep his voice down, it carried across the eerie silence of the complex and Jim could make out every word of it.

"Who are you?" he asked.

"Diane Hyde," she replied. "I was inspecting this place when the shit went down."

"And you survived?"

"Somehow," she said. "I've been hiding out in the ruins of the generator room. I thought I was the only one alive out here."

Harry Yorke said nothing in reply. They'd just reached the car, and he opened one of the doors and ushered her inside. Big Jim had finished syphoning fuel and was pouring what he had into the vehicle's tank. There wasn't much. They just hoped that there'd be enough.

"We'd better hurry up," Yorke said. He was looking nervously over Jim's shoulder at where a storm of sheep was brewing. There were cows, too, and one or two pigs. There were even a couple of their former patrol dogs. They didn't look like they were being good boys. They looked… hungry.

"Aww, shite," Jim said. He threw caution to the wind and smacked his heavy fist against the horn. The sound echoed out across the grounds. Jim put the vehicle into reverse and pulled off a nifty three-point turn before gunning the engine and driving towards the complex. The animals were getting closer, and more of them were coming, joining the end of the line like the tail of a comet as it streaked past the Earth. Jim swore again as he gunned the engine and raced the vehicle across the grass towards the admin building. They'd only have one shot at it, and they'd have to cut across the cattle at an angle if they wanted to reach the only place he could think of where they might have a chance.

And so they raced to the south-east corner of the complex, where Jim hit the brakes and tore up the grass as the vehicle skidded to a halt. He jumped from the driver's seat and hit the ground running with Harry Yorke just a couple of steps behind him and Diane Hyde hot on their heels. The animals were closer now, too close for comfort.

"We're cutting it fine," Yorke shouted, but Big Jim didn't bother to reply. He'd popped open the back of the modified van and pulled down the steps that led to the roof, where the second ladder was. Jim went first because he was the only one who knew how to extend the damn thing. He was also the only one who knew what they were aiming for.

Something wet and rancid came flying through the air and struck him on the head, but Big Jim had spent two days in the back of Big Bertha and the smell of shit and piss was nothing new to him. Then there was a shout, and he knew they'd been spotted by one of the survivors. They said something about getting help, but Big Jim was having none of it.

"There's nae time," he bellowed. "Ah'm sendin' up the ladder. Grab the end and haud on tae the fucker."

There was a vibration from below as the first of the animals reached the van. It was a sheep and it barely made a dent in the panelling, but Big Jim knew it for what it was: a warning shot. Yorke wobbled unsteadily, but he kept his feet and found enough stability to help Jim to guide the ladder to the window. At his side, Diane Hyde was looking down at the animals and shouting a torrent of panicked curses. There were a couple more faces at the top, and they'd done what they could to help by swinging the window open as wide as it would go. Someone was leaning out of the window while the others held on to their shirt, ready to pull them back if they looked like falling. The ladder teetered precariously in the air for a second and then the man's fingertips closed on the metal bars and pulled it towards the windowsill. The ladder was long enough to reach it, but only just. It wobbled and vibrated as the solitary animal below was joined by a couple more sheep and an angry-looking pig with a deep welt on its hindquarters and an empty eye socket.

"You first," Jim said, grabbing the bottom of the ladder to give the protestor a solid foundation to climb from. Yorke clapped the security guard on the shoulder, all rivalries forgotten as they fought for their lives, and then placed his hands on the rungs and started to climb.

"Hurry up," someone shouted, and the van rocked again as the animals renewed their attack. Something crunched and there was the howling of tortured metal, and then a much louder bang as the first of the cows arrived and started bashing its mighty head against the vehicle. Yorke reached the top, then climbed over the threshold and in through the window.

"Wait for me," shouted Hyde, while Jim stared at her from his heavyset eyes. She put her hands on the ladder and stepped on to the bottom rung. There was another bang from somewhere beneath them, and this time the vehicle itself started to move, inching slowly through the mud as it followed the tyres along their natural path. For a moment, Jim wondered whether he'd forgotten to put the handbrake on, but then he realised that he hadn't. It just wasn't making any difference.

Hyde was still climbing, but there was no time for Jim to

wait for her. He placed his hands on the ladder and started to climb it, one foot after the other, taking it as slowly as he dared so that the ladder didn't slip and send him tumbling to the ground. From above him, there was a cheer as Hyde reached the top and was pulled through the window. Jim wondered whether they'd still be cheering when they found out who she was.

He was halfway up the ladder when there was the biggest jolt yet as it came loose from its dock and started to slide across the roof. It gave him quite the shock, so he threw caution to the wind, scuttling up the rungs in a desperate attempt to win the race against gravity.

"Ah'm nae lettin' this happen agin!" Jim roared, risking a quick glance down to the bottom of the ladder. His brain ran a series of quick calculations and arrived at the inevitable conclusion: he wasn't going to make it.

"Fuck it," he murmured, and then he pushed himself off from the rung he was on and made a jump for it. He was aiming for the outstretched hands of the growing crowd of people on the other side of the window, the scared survivors who were drawn to the source of the noise like moths to a flame. Jim swung his hands through the air in a desperate search for fingertips, but he didn't connect and then he was falling, falling...

...and his hands smashed against the windowsill and some instinct made him brace against the pain and hold on. He thought he felt something break, the pinky or the ring finger of his left hand, and then his momentum took his body into the wall. He grunted as the air was knocked out of him, but he held on. From somewhere below him, there was the sound of breaking glass and the angry lowing of what sounded like half the animals on the complex. The vehicle was carried away in a sea of momentum as the pigs and the sheep and the cows pushed against each other and leapt at the walls of the building, like cats on their hind legs trying to catch pieces of string between their teeth.

But Big Jim was still holding on, and as the noise in his ears rose in volume and intensity until it drowned out everything around him, he steeled himself for the final climb.

He shook his head to try to clear it and then pulled himself through the window and back inside the admin building. He'd never been happier to be there.

BIG JIM WAS THE TALK OF THE COMPLEX, and even Harry Yorke had found himself a place amongst the survivors in their post-apocalyptic society. They were a tiny island nation in a sea of meat, and John MacDonald was the closest thing they had to Churchill. Harry Yorke was like the French. The Sunnyvale staff had hated Harry Yorke, once upon a time. But now that the great animal holocaust was underway, they were teaming up together to form a resistance.

And Diane Hyde, the woman who'd called the quarantine in to begin with, represented the Germans.

MacDonald was asleep when they made their triumphant entrance. He'd passed out right there at his mahogany desk, and no one had the heart to wake him, at least to begin with. But then he'd woken up anyway after the animals had carried the vehicle away. No one could have slept through that.

As soon as he got a handle on things, MacDonald called another war council in his office and gave Big Jim the floor. No one wanted to stand too near to the man because he still reeked of the piss from the back of Big Bertha, but they all wanted to hear what he had to say and he didn't disappoint them, running through what had happened since he fell from the roof.

"So who's this guy?" MacDonald asked, jabbing a finger aggressively towards Harry Yorke.

"Eh's a protestor," Jim replied. "But eh's awrite. Wir aw stuck here, ye ken."

"Shit and piss," MacDonald said, turning to look Harry

Yorke up and down as though he were some potential new employee in an interview room. "A protestor, huh?"

Harry Yorke nodded but didn't say anything, and that was probably for the best.

"All right," MacDonald said. He stroked his beard for a moment or two and then turned back to Big Jim, who was hovering beside Harry Yorke with the thumbs of both his hands tucked into his belt. "Put him under citizen's arrest and we'll deal with him later. Find a room somewhere and stick him in it. Then have one of your men stand guard until we figure out what to do next."

"You're going to keep me here?"

"Of course," MacDonald replied. "Do you think I have a choice? Do you think any of us has a choice? We're all stuck here until help arrives. You'll just be stuck in a smaller room."

"But—"

"Enough!" MacDonald shouted, and Darragh O'Rourke stepped forward. He had his cuffs on his belt and so he took them off and fixed them around Harry Yorke's wrists. Then he led him out of MacDonald's office and deeper into the complex.

Once their backs had retreated away from the room and along the corridor, MacDonald turned his attention to their other guest. "What about her?" he asked. "Who's she?"

"Diane Hyde," she replied, introducing herself before Big Jim stepped in to stop her. "I'm from Environmental Health."

"So you're the enemy."

"You could say that," Hyde said. "But we can't afford to fight amongst ourselves."

"We're not fighting amongst ourselves," MacDonald replied. "It's us against you. Seems pretty clear cut to me."

Several of the survivors murmured their assents, and

there was a bad vibe in the air, a desperate feeling of impending doom. Diane Hyde seemed to be the only one not to notice it, like a sheep sunbathing amongst a pack of wolves.

"That was before the world changed," she said. "You've seen for yourselves what the animals can do. Do you still think I've made the wrong decision?"

"We're all going to die in here because of you!"

"Shut it, Keyes," MacDonald growled, whirling around to face the dissenter before turning back to look at the new arrival. "You're saying it's all of us against the animals?"

"That's exactly what I'm saying," Hyde said. "There's no time to play silly buggers. We have to unite and focus our efforts. We'll succeed together or we'll fail apart."

"Take her away and put her with Yorke," MacDonald said, addressing his head of security. "I'll deal with her later."

Big Jim nodded, first at MacDonald and then at Mike Chase, and the young security guard followed the unspoken order by frogmarching the Environmental Health inspector out of the boss' office.

"Where were we?" MacDonald asked.

"Ah awmost forgot," Jim said, pulling Big Bertha's radio from his pocket and dropping it on John MacDonald's mahogany desk. "Ah grabbed this wee gadget. Thought it might come in handy."

When John MacDonald saw what it was, he shot to his feet and then grabbed Big Jim by the shoulders. He leaned in and kissed the man on his forehead, not even wincing when the ammonia smell hit him.

"You beauty," MacDonald said. "Let's just hope it works."

The early indications weren't looking good. For a start, it wouldn't power up without a couple of 9V batteries, and it took them a while to find some, eventually coming up lucky in one of the drawers in what used to be the finance department. In Big Bertha, the radio ran off the engine, but with no engine to plug into, all they had were the batteries. If those didn't work, they didn't have a backup.

The radio worked as soon as they tried it, and the small congregation in MacDonald's office burst into applause as they heard the familiar static crackle of a short-wave radio. But the applause was short-lived as they cycled through frequencies and tried to pick up a signal. MacDonald worked the radio himself, all thoughts of the meeting forgotten, and the rest of the survivors watched nervously as he tried to make contact with the outside world.

"Come in, come in," he repeated, the words rolling out of his mouth like a prayer or a mantra. It was almost hypnotic. But there was nothing.

MacDonald sighed and tapped the side of the radio as though it was a computer that needed reformatting. "Any ideas?" he asked.

"The roof," Copeland said. "If there's a signal for us to find, we'll find it out there."

For a moment, it looked like the vet would be the next to get a kiss on the forehead. Then MacDonald nodded at him, the nod of one equal to another, before scooping up the radio and leading their party out on to the roof.

It was terrifying out there, like a scene from Dante's Inferno but in the middle of the Chiltern Hills. Big Bertha was somewhere to the south-east and they could only see to the north, but the seething mass of meat and bones and brutality was out here too, nudging each other out of the way to get a little closer to the stench of the humans inside the building.

The survivors tried to put the sight and the sound out of mind. They were in no immediate danger, at least not as far as they could tell, and MacDonald had noticed a slight, subtle change to the quality of the dead air from the radio. He led the way up even higher, to where the food cauldrons sat empty by the light of the early afternoon and an array of bowls, pots and tubs were laid side by side to catch any moisture from the rain and the atmosphere.

Someone started to say something but MacDonald shushed them, gesturing for Big Jim to set the radio up on the raised table where the cooks had been doling out the gruel from the cauldron. Big Jim was happy to oblige, and the rest of the survivors gathered around as he hit the on switch and the static washed over them.

MacDonald lifted up the receiver and clicked the transmission button. "Hello, hello," he said. "Come in, please. This is Sunnyvale. Over."

The static continued to crackle but there was no disturbance in the airwaves, no response from the men outside the gate or from a nearby hobbyist, tinkering in his garden shed in the hope of picking up a signal.

Big Jim bashed a heavy fist against the device and MacDonald winced, but he didn't try to stop him. The static squealed and steadied itself again, and Jim reached over and tweaked the dial to cycle through the different frequencies. MacDonald tried again and again on each of the different channels, but there was nothing. They were beginning to lose hope.

"This is bullshit," he said.

"Aye," Jim replied. "It's them fuckin' hills awright. The signal's shot tae shite as soon as ye pass through the gates."

MacDonald tried again and then again, but there was still no response. After an hour or so spent trying to reach someone – *anyone* – under the watchful eyes of his employees, MacDonald slammed the handset down in frustration and turned his back on it.

"See to it that we have someone manning this thing around the clock," he snapped, an instruction that wasn't meant for anyone in particular and which he'd hold them all responsible for. "Give it ten minutes at a time and then switch it on and cycle through the bandwidths. Do what you can to save the batteries. This might be the only lifeline we have."

A response came later that evening, after the sun had gone back down and the survivors had bedded in for the night. Darragh O'Rourke was working his shift at the radio and trying to stay warm by rubbing his hands together inside his jacket. Winter had arrived, and a cold wind blew in from the south-east while the pressure slowly dropped and the first wispy tendrils of a stormy sky started to settle in.

Darragh O'Rourke had just broadcast his exploratory message for the seventeenth time that evening when the airwaves crackled again and a disembodied voice filtered through the speakers.

"Copy that, Sunnyvale," the voice said. "Reading you loud and clear. Who am I speaking to? Over."

Darragh O'Rourke was so surprised that he dropped the handset to the floor. Then he barked off a quick response and dashed down the gantry to get MacDonald, who was dozing at his desk with his feet up on the mahogany. When O'Rourke shook him by the shoulder, he woke abruptly and almost fell off the chair, but it didn't take him long to gather his thoughts and to follow the deputy head of security to the gantry. Once they were up there, he raced across to the radio and picked up the receiver.

"Come in, come in," he said. "This is John MacDonald, CEO of Sunnyvale. Who are you?"

There was a crackle and then an uncomfortably long pause. MacDonald was about to pick up the handset and try again when the quality of the static changed and a deep, authoritative voice came through the transmitter's shitty speakers.

"Copy that, Sunnyvale," the voice said. "This is Lieutenant Colonel Ben Runciman of the British Army. It's good to hear from you. Request number of survivors and current location. Over."

"We're still alive and kicking over here, Lieutenant Colonel," MacDonald said. "There's a couple dozen of us holed up in the admin building."

"Copy that," Runciman repeated. "Do not, I repeat, do not engage the animals. We've been forced to pull back to your outer perimeter."

"What the fuck are you guys doing?" MacDonald demanded. "We could really use your help in here."

There was a pause for a moment, and the group of survivors held their breath and collectively prayed that the radio connection hadn't been severed.

"Hello?" MacDonald said. "Is anyone there?"

"Sorry about that, Sunnyvale," Runciman replied. There was a shake to his voice, a genuine shake, and they could believe it. He *sounded* sorry. "We've taken multiple casualties and are reassessing the situation."

"I'm sorry to hear that," MacDonald replied. "Any idea what's going on?"

"It's unclear at this time," Runciman said. "Request any relevant information from your end. Over."

"That's a big negative on the information front," MacDonald said. "If we had something for you, we'd share it. Tom Copeland, our vet here, thinks there's something wrong with them, some disease. That's as much as we've got. What's the situation on your end?"

"The quarantine's still holding," Runciman said. "So far, at least. But we've moved people away in the surrounding areas. Just as a precaution, you understand. Honestly, I've never seen anything like this. It's good to hear you guys are still hanging in there."

"We've had our moments," MacDonald admitted, thinking about the employees he'd lost since the outbreak and the faint splash of gore and viscera across the grass below the gantry where the remains of Greg Hamze were still lying out there in the darkness. "What's wrong with the animals?"

"We don't know," Runciman said. "The best I can give you is a guess."

"That's more than we've got," MacDonald replied. "Give me the bad news."

There was a pause for a moment and MacDonald found himself struggling with the troubling thought that they might have lost contact again. The signal was weak at best and the incoming storm was playing havoc with it. But then the voice filtered back through again and MacDonald realised that Lieutenant Colonel Ben Runciman had been stalling for time.

"The disease is *complicated*," Runciman said, eventually. "We're still carrying out analysis in the lab, but we're working on the basis that it's a hybrid of COVID-19 and foot-and-mouth disease. It certainly resembles it in the early stages."

MacDonald's head whirred around on its shoulders like he was Regan McNeil in *The Exorcist* until his eyes alighted on Tom Copeland. He beckoned the man forwards and gave him the handset.

"Tom Copeland here," he said. "Sunnyvale's veterinarian. Did you say foot-and-mouth? *Aphthae epizooticae*? And coronavirus?"

"That's correct, Dr. Copeland," Runciman said. "Only it's a mutation from hell. It has an incubation period of a week or so where no symptoms are present and the beasts pass on the infection. Always a problem where large numbers of animals are gathered in a single place."

"But *aphthae epizooticae* only affects animals with a cloven hoof," Copeland said. "And whatever the hell this is, it's affecting all of them."

"Like I said," Runciman told him, "it's a mutation from hell. After the incubation period, the animals come down with a fever and start to get blisters inside their mouths. Classic foot-and-mouth, to begin with. But then the virus changes, and it's only at this point that we can tell the two apart. The first stage is a coma, unlike any coma we've seen before. The heart and the lungs stop functioning, and the brain goes into a kind of suspended animation. After a couple of days, the virus has wiped out memory, emotion, personality, and all that other stuff that makes an animal unique, until it's left with just the most basic drives. The desire to eat, sleep, drink and reproduce. Sound familiar?"

"It would explain why the animals are on a rampage," Copeland admitted. "But we haven't seen any comas here. Unless…"

"Unless what?"

"We normally check the pens every couple days for dead animals and ship them off to the crematorium," Copeland said. "But what with one thing and another, we missed a check."

"Then there's your answer," Runciman said.

"If what you're saying is true," Copeland reasoned, "an outbreak could have occurred without us knowing. Even if an animal was infected, we'd mistake it for dead and burn the body. But the crematorium has been quiet for a couple of days. The dead were left there for the other animals to feast on. It's a god damn cannibal disease."

"And so the animals rose back up."

"I don't buy it," Copeland said. "You're telling me that we're dealing with what, zombie animals?"

"Not zombies," Runciman said. "They're—"

The signal cut out again, and John MacDonald took the opportunity to rush forward and to grab the handset back from Copeland. They waited for the signal to come back but there was nothing, so MacDonald turned the dials and adjusted the frequency. It took them a while, but they managed to re-establish the connection on a higher frequency, but the signal was bad and they didn't hold up much hope that it would last for long.

"—actually die."

"What was that?" MacDonald asked. "Please repeat. We're losing signal here."

"Roger that, Sunnyvale," Runciman replied. "Then I'll make this quick. You have to understand the nature of the animals. They're not dead or undead, at least in the conventional sense. Your boy's been watching too many movies. Those animals of yours are still alive. They're just behaving like mindless drones. They'll die just as easily as they would have died before the infection, only they don't feel pain. After the coma, the animals wake back up. But by then, they've changed. They've turned into vicious, bloodthirsty killing machines."

A chill seemed to settle over the Sunnyvale Survivors, but perhaps it was just the wind from the storm as it drifted inexorably across the sky towards them.

"How is this disease transmitted?" MacDonald asked.

"I was getting to that," Runciman replied. "As far as we can tell, it's transmitted through the consumption of infected flesh or through a bite from another infected animal. It can be transferred through sexual intercourse as well. The conditions are just right for the disease to spread. But there's worse."

"What?"

"About that," Runciman said. "Understand that we're still investigating and experimenting."

"I understand," MacDonald replied. "But I don't give a damn. Tell me what you know, and if you don't know, tell me what you suspect."

The static crackled again and Runciman's voice faded out for a second. "–lifespan is significantly reduced," he was saying. "But only due to natural accidents and their poor nutrition. Do you copy?"

"Negative," MacDonald said. "Please repeat."

"The virus can be spread through aerosols and through contact with contaminated equipment, vehicles and clothing," Runciman said. "We suspected as much. That's why we were called in to impose an immediate lockdown on the facility in the first place. The disease is too dangerous, too contagious. And it's mutating. Our lab boys are still carrying out tests and we'll update you as soon as we can, but we have reason to believe that the disease could spread to–"

The signal cut out again, and this time they couldn't get it back. The wind was picking up and the first drops of rain were starting to strike against the rooftop. The storm was on its way, and the crippled admin building had no heating or electricity. The air was already whipping through the smashed doors and inside the building, and it was only going to get colder, windier and more unpleasant.

MacDonald scowled and gave the order. "Pack up the radio and take it inside," he said. "We'll try it again tomorrow."

LIEUTENANT COLONEL BEN RUNCIMAN was still mourning the loss of his men on the exploratory foray into Sunnyvale. He was also surprised that he was still in charge of operations, if only nominally.

Since the fatalities, the number of animals had swelled. A lively debate had been held in the Houses of Parliament about whether the army should reclaim the bodies, but neither public opinion nor angry backbench MPs could sway the powers that be. The failed mission had been seen as proof that the quarantine must hold, that it must be made stronger than ever.

And against Runciman's hunch and his first impressions, they'd succeeded in establishing contact. There were people alive in there. The lieutenant colonel wasn't sure whether to be happy that there were survivors or pissed off because his job was becoming more difficult by the minute.

And as if all of that wasn't enough, then the press arrived.

It started innocuously enough, with a couple of reporters travelling to the facility, following the army's directions as they approached it and then pulling up in the temporary camp. To begin with, Runciman had dealt with each of them individually. Then an unflattering article went out in the *Daily Mail,* and attention to the quarantine exploded. Suddenly, journalists were flooding to the site, and so were members of the general public who wanted to stick their noses in to discover the truth behind the headlines.

After that, the days took on a monotony, with Runciman

dividing his time between organising his teams, interpreting the results of experiments and giving guarded interviews to the press. The hope was that they'd lose interest over time, but it was a foolish hope. After the first initial flurry of interest, the number of visitors to the site began to dwindle, but the journalists were soon replaced by protestors, members of the Buckinghamshire Save Group who kept trying to talk to him about someone called Harry Yorke, and the worried families of the employees, who badgered him endlessly for the updates they knew he couldn't give. Runciman was a busy man, and he only had a finite amount of patience. He was also a stickler for the rules, and so any enquiries had to be forwarded through the proper channels.

One day, his men were out in the no man's land between Sunnyvale and the army camp, laying temporary landmines on the ground in case any of the larger livestock tried to make a break for freedom. As they worked, they were supervised by the snipers up in their makeshift towers. Every now and then, a shot rang out over the landscape as one of Sunnyvale's animals managed to escape from the perimeter fence and to saunter on to no man's land.

It was a process that his team was intimately familiar with. So far, nothing had made it more than a third of the way across the no man's land. As far as they knew.

But the gunmen were used to opening fire on the larger animals, the pigs and the sheep. The chickens, despite demonstrating less intelligence, were harder to hit, and while they weren't necessarily the fastest, they were unpredictable. But even then, the snipers usually hit them after a couple of warm-up shots.

The soldiers in no man's land, who were laying the mines and the tripwires, were mostly focussed on the ground right in front of them, which is what caused the first shout to go out. Something small, a squirrel perhaps, was scuttling along the ground and across the minefield. There was another shout, this time an order, and the soldiers started to fall back, just in time to avoid the brunt of the heat from the explosion. The squirrel wasn't heavy enough to set off the pressure traps, but its path took it straight through a tripwire, which did its job perfectly.

The explosion sent a couple of the soldiers tumbling to their hands and knees, though once the shock wore off, they were up and running again on sheer instinct. The squirrel had been liquefied, and droplets of blood and muck came down with the soil in a fine rain. The soldiers were wearing protective gear over their faces and so there was no chance of cross-contamination, but they knew they'd be in for a tough time under quarantine regardless. They had protocols to follow.

"On your feet!" Runciman shouted, but he was in the safe zone and too far away for them to hear him. It didn't matter though, because they'd got the idea. They were up and running again in no time, heading back towards the relative safety of the army encampment.

In the midst of the chaos, as he was hauling himself to his feet after the explosion, one of the soldiers was bitten on the back of the ankle by a rat that had sized him up and seized his opportunity. It was a small bite, and one that he didn't even notice at the time, but it was a bite that would go down in history. Especially if it were to go unnoticed by the decontamination team.

Which it did.

***

The storm hit hard, and the survivors inside the admin building got little sleep as the panes of glass rattled in the windows and the moos and grunts of a thousand angry animals filtered in and echoed around the complex. The reality of their situation had finally started to sink in and the men and women who huddled together for warmth had started to take on the sallow-faced look of refugees after a natural disaster. It wasn't just the hunger. It was the pain and the things they'd seen combined with the amount of time they'd had to let it all stew over.

The rain broke the following day, but the winds were as bad as ever and they couldn't establish contact with the soldiers outside their front gate. Some of the survivors had started to whisper that the army was just going to leave them to die in there. MacDonald privately agreed with them.

Lee Keyes was kicking up a fuss, of course. More and more of the survivors were listening to his divisive murmurings and the atmosphere inside the admin building took on a different tone. A hierarchy had formed, seemingly all by itself, with MacDonald and his most trusted staff at the top, the chefs, the security team and the other volunteers in the middle, and Lee Keyes and everyone else on the bottom. MacDonald was still running things as the resident despot, and he was surprised to find that it required the same set of skills as running a company.

MacDonald planned to busy himself conducting one-to-one "morale check-ups" with each of his employees, where he'd invite them to share their concerns and take notes with a pen and paper with a promise to deal with the main concerns as quickly as he could. He suspected that their diminishing food supply would be towards the top of the list of concerns, and he didn't have a solution to offer them. Another supply run was out of the question. They'd have to focus their energies instead on rationing while hoping for some help from the outside world.

But first, he had Big Jim fetch Diane Hyde from the old supply cupboard, where she'd been secured with Harry

Yorke. That was all he needed – two more mouths to feed.

Big Jim led the woman into the office and thrust her roughly into one of the armchairs, then nodded at MacDonald and left them to it, closing the door behind him. The woman posed no threat, and he had orders to wait outside the door so that he could be summoned if needed. Diane Hyde was feisty, but she was also in a foreign environment with nowhere to go even if she was somehow able to overpower him. Harry Yorke might be crazy enough to try, and Lee Keyes definitely was. But Diane Hyde followed a different kind of playbook.

And besides, even if she were to attack him, he had the size advantage and a small letter opener in the drawers of his mahogany desk.

"This is quite some operation you're running here, Mr. MacDonald," Hyde said, sitting forward in the armchair and looking like an eagle about to take flight. She pulled out a pair of glasses from her shirt pocket and slid them on. The left lens was cracked and the right was missing entirely, and the frame had been warped and bent out of shape and then crudely back into it. "Luckily for me, I can still see a lot without these things."

"Young Mike Chase wears contacts," MacDonald said. "He's been banging on about them ever since we went into lockdown. He can't see shit without them. Doc Copeland says it's only a matter of time until he gets an eye infection."

"You have a doctor here?"

"A vet," MacDonald corrected her. "It's his job to keep the animals alive for long enough to make it to slaughter. Or at least, it was. Just like it was your job to find any reason you could to shut us down."

"I wouldn't say that, Mr. MacDonald," Hyde replied. She was sitting back now, looking a little more at ease, almost as though the conversation was proceeding along the lines that she'd anticipated. "Believe it or not, it's in my best interests to give your facility a pass. We're incentivised to, just like you're incentivised."

"Financially?"

"There are other ways to reward people," Hyde replied. "We have targets and quotas, just like you do. When I called in the quarantine at Sunnyvale, I made an exception. And do you know what, Mr. MacDonald? I'm glad I did."

"But now we're all stuck here," MacDonald said. "And to me, you're just one more mouth to feed. What do you propose that I do with you?"

"Put me to work," she replied, smiling disarmingly at him. For a brief, surreal moment, the scene in the office seemed more like an interview than a post-apocalyptic negotiation. "There must be something for me do."

MacDonald shook his head. "We have no need of an environmental health inspector."

"You have no need of a secretary or a butcher either," Hyde reminded him. "What we used to do is no longer relevant. But perhaps I can help you in some other way."

MacDonald thought about it for a moment as the birds sang their frantic chorus from the other side of his window. The sound, which might have been reassuring in the old world, was a reminder that they weren't alone. And when the pigs and the chickens were out to kill people and dozens of employees were locked down in a former office building, loneliness was something that came at a premium.

"Right now," MacDonald said, "you're a liability. If I let you roam the complex, I can't guarantee your protection. Perhaps you're right and we're all in this together. Perhaps not. Either way, I have no control over how my staff will react to you. There's only one thing that I can do."

"And what's that?" Hyde asked. The colour had drained slightly from her face, and MacDonald observed that her initial air of confidence had been replaced by something else entirely. She hadn't prepared for this.

"I'm going to keep you locked up in the supply cupboard with Harry Yorke," MacDonald said. "At least until I decide what to do with you both."

"Is this a citizen's arrest?"

"Think of it more like police protection," MacDonald replied. "I'll have Big Jim escort you out."

***

It was also the day that Tom Copeland faced one of his toughest tests to date.

Maude Harrison had complained of a toothache a couple of days earlier, and it had only got worse as time ticked by. It all came to a head after she took a drink of water. The second she swallowed it, her face had contorted and she'd sank to the floor like she'd received a shock. In a way, she had. She started to cry out in pain and beat her fists against the floor, then some sort of intuition took her and she reached out to Darragh O'Rourke, who was manning the water line. Strictly speaking, the water was rationed, but she looked like she needed it and so he handed it over.

She took a gulp from it and held the water in her mouth, and a sort of serenity came over her. It soothed her and she swallowed it, and then she immediately regretted it as the pain kicked in again and she started screaming.

"My tooth!" she shouted. "Jesus wept, my tooth!"

"Someone fetch Copeland," O'Rourke growled, leaping over the water table and rushing towards the woman. He clamped his hand over her mouth to try to stifle her screams and shouted, "Now, please! Before those damn animals decide to investigate what the noise is."

Copeland was already on his way. He'd heard the noises

and decided to investigate, but he hadn't been expecting to have to deal with it.

"She needs a dentist," he said, once he'd arrived and taken a look at her.

"She'll have to make do with a vet," O'Rourke replied. "You're all we have. Do you know what's wrong with her?"

"I think so," Copeland said, leaning in closer to the woman to take another look at her mouth. It was hard to make too much of a judgement because she was writhing in agony and still trying to scream, although she was running out of air. O'Rourke squeezed her cheeks in a pincer grip to force her jaws open and Copeland did his best to inspect her teeth, but she wasn't a cow or a pig and so it was at least 20 percent guesswork and 30 percent intuition.

"What's wrong with her?" O'Rourke asked. "We have to do something."

"I'm not sure," Copeland admitted. "But I've got an idea. I think it might be irreversible pulpitis. I've seen it before in the animals. It's a tooth infection, a bad one. It means the infection has reached the pulp where the nerves and the blood supply are. The bacteria grow and get fought by the body until that little space beneath the tooth is filled with dead cells. Then the animal drinks, and the cold water shrinks the nerve and the crap expands to fill the gap. Then when the water wears off, the nerve expands again and presses against all the crap in the pulp. I've heard of people shooting their horses to put them out of their misery only to find out it's a simple tooth infection. But I never thought I'd have to treat a human."

"Can you help her?"

"Yeah," Copeland said. "But it won't be pleasant. We need to remove the tooth. Have someone grab my kit bag. We're out of ketamine, so we're going to have to do this without anaesthetic."

Maude Harrison's screams redoubled when she realised what that meant for her. It was hard to tell what she was saying, though.

"We've got some painkillers," Copeland said. "I'll give her a shot of morphine."

"You'll do no such thing." That came from John MacDonald, who emerged on the scene at the same time that his niece ran in with Copeland's medicine bag. "We need to preserve supplies. I'm not wasting them on a toothache."

"With respect, sir," Copeland said, "this is going to hurt."

MacDonald opened his mouth to argue again, but then he seemed to change his mind and hit upon a compromise. "Give her a smaller dose," he said. "Let's get this over with."

It took a few minutes for the morphine to be administered, but as soon as it kicked in, Maude Harrison visibly relaxed and stopped fighting. That was all Copeland needed to perform the extraction.

He removed the tooth with a scalpel and a pair of pliers, making small incisions into the gum before pulling the tooth from the woman's head. It was pretty obvious which tooth was the infected one. The gum had turned white and inflamed around it, and the tooth itself looked rotten and ready to break, as though it had been left for weeks in a glass of cola as part of a high school science experiment. O'Rourke held her head down while Copeland pulled at the tooth, and it eventually ripped free from her head with a crunching sound like a car driving over a sheet of glass on gravel.

One of the onlookers passed out and hit the floor with a heavy thump, but Harrison herself seemed instantly better. With the tooth removed and the morphine in full effect, she simply lay back and stared up at the ceiling as her breathing started to return to normal. Copeland used the tip of the scalpel to clear the detritus from the infection and then treated the wound with an antiseptic. Then he placed a wad of dressing over the wound and asked Harrison to bite down and to apply pressure to stop the bleeding. She did so.

"She'll be fine," Copeland said. "But she'll need antibiotics. Otherwise the infection could spread."

"Make it happen," MacDonald said.

Then he walked out and left Copeland and O'Rourke to deal with the aftermath of their makeshift operation.

JOHN MACDONALD was overseeing the chefs on the rooftop as they cooked more gruel when he first heard the sound of the helicopter. The sky had turned a miserable grey and the visibility was relatively poor, but not poor enough for the army to call off the mission altogether.

The Chinook approached from the north and came gliding over the lake's turgid water before slowing over the top of the admin building. Its powerful tandem rotors buffeted the roof with strong gusts of air that threatened to carry them off the sides of the rooftop. MacDonald ordered his men to go back inside, but they could barely hear him over the roar of the rotors and nobody moved, except to find a vent to crouch behind.

There was movement from above and a large sack flew through the air and thwacked against the roof of the building. It was followed by another and then another, and then by another which burst on impact and sent packaged rations skidding across the rooftop. Then came a large crate that was lowered by a winch.

MacDonald tried again to hold his team back, but the noise had summoned a crowd and with no one on guard outside his office, a dozen people had made their way on to the roof. It was chaos. From somewhere up above them, two soldiers in chemical warfare gear were still tossing sacks of food down to the survivors. MacDonald tried to smile at the irony, but it didn't come naturally. The army was unable to send men into the complex or to give them any information on what was happening in the outside world, but they wouldn't let them all starve to death, either. It was a quarantine the likes of which had never been seen before, but there was still *some* humanity. Not much, but enough.

There was a shout from behind him, and Hector Fernandez, the cleaner, burst out from the crowd and raced towards the middle of the rooftop. At first, nobody moved. They just watched in silence as his feet pounded the floor and launched him through the air. He landed on top of the winch just as it finished disengaging from the supply crate, wrapping his hands around it.

"Take me with you," he shouted, although his words were almost swallowed by the howling of the wind and the brutal blades of the chopper as it lifted away from the rooftops. "Take me out of this hellhole."

By then, the pilot had realised what was happening. From his vantage point on the rooftop, John MacDonald could see the black shape of the man in the cockpit as he leaned into the tilt of the chopper and twisted the controls. The winch swung around in wide, angry circles, and Hector Fernandez held on for dear life, his will to live somehow holding him there, and then the chopper stopped spinning and lifted higher up into the sky. It hung there for a second as a dozen necks craned up to look at it.

And from over the top of the blades and the engines, there came another sound, the whip-crack of a gunshot. Time stood still for a moment.

Then Hector Fernandez let go of the winch and hurtled towards the ground. He was swallowed up by the darkness before they saw him land. Up in the air, the helicopter abandoned its supply drop and flew back to the north.

And out on the grass around the admin building, the animals watched and waited.

***

It was fight night at Sunnyvale.

It was all Big Jim's idea. MacDonald had spent two days in a row biting his nails to the quick and worrying about the lack of entertainment.

"The devil finds work for idle hands," MacDonald kept saying. "We need to find something to keep people busy. If we don't, they'll lose morale. They might even start listening to the rubbish that Lee Keyes keeps spouting."

"Aye," Jim replied. "Ah've bin thinkin' about that, ye ken. Ah reckon ah might huv an idea."

Big Jim's idea was a bareknuckle boxing match, something that MacDonald had initially been wary of sanctioning. But Jim had continued to plead his case, and he'd roped Will Makon in to argue for the cause, too.

"Eh's gonnae be ma opponent, ye ken," Jim said. "Big Jim versus wee Will Makon. The fight ay tha fucken century."

"I don't know, Jim," MacDonald replied, but that was when Will had jumped to Jim's side and made his voice heard.

"Go on, Boss," Makon said. "What have you got to lose?"

"You're sure about this?" MacDonald asked. "What if someone gets hurt?"

"That's what happens in a fucken bareknuckle boxing match," Jim replied. "It's part ay the fun, ye ken. Ah promise ah won't hurt the wee lad too much."

"If you land a fucking punch in the first place," Makon added. He grinned and jabbed Big Jim half-heartedly in the arm. The security guard just looked at him.

"Okay," MacDonald said eventually, holding his hands up. "Do what you want. I won't stop you."

That was all the two men needed.

Some of their colleagues weren't too impressed with

their plan to box each other, but some of them couldn't help themselves. Lee Keyes even started taking bets. None of them had much cash on them and food was too scarce for them to gamble with, but he promised to keep track and to make sure that all debts were settled when they made it out of the complex. *If* they ever made it out of there.

The fight was fixed for that evening, when the sun was hanging low in the sky. They were to fight on the rooftop in a makeshift ring that had been marked out on the floor with coats, handbags and rucksacks, whatever they could find in the admin building that was easy to move around. Will Makon spent the entire day getting himself in the zone, following a strict warm-up regime that he'd developed with his coach in another life, back before the quarantine. Back before he'd even joined the team at Sunnyvale.

Big Jim spent the day going about his duties, which largely consisted of acting as John MacDonald's bodyguard and making sure that his men kept the peace. But he was hoping that the fight would quell any thoughts of violence that the other survivors might have had. He had nothing against Will Makon, and Will Makon had nothing against him. They were just two men with too much testosterone who needed a scrap to vent some steam.

The fight was well attended; every survivor that was still standing turned out to see it. Big Jim and Will Makon had both stripped down to their shorts, but if they felt the cold, they didn't show it. John MacDonald acted as a reluctant emcee, but he didn't have to do too much. He stepped out in front of the two fighters.

"Ladies and gentlemen," he said. "It's fight night. Big Jim and Will here have been kind enough to supply some entertainment. I want to make it clear that any fights outside the ring won't be tolerated."

"Whatcha gonna do about it?" someone shouted.

MacDonald ignored them.

"Now I want a nice, clean fight," MacDonald said. "Nothing below the belt."

"Aye," Jim said. "Let's git a move on. It's fucken freezing."

"All right," MacDonald said. "Well, we don't have a bell, but you know where the ring is and I want you to keep the fight within it. There are no rounds and no time limits, just come out swinging when I say so and the first man to get knocked out or to throw in the towel will be the loser. Are you ready? On your marks. Get set. Fight."

The two men came together on John MacDonald's mark, and then they broke apart like a wave crashing into the rocks. Makon was fast, much faster than Big Jim, and he managed to connect with a couple of light jabs to the torso before breaking away again. Big Jim shrugged it off and slowly circled his opponent. He was smiling.

They came together again, and this time they stayed there, their heads low and their fists bunched tight in front of their faces. Big Jim caught the youngster with a sucker punch to the shoulder but took another few jabs as a reward for it, including a knuckle to the face that drew first blood. But it was no worse than he'd experienced in a thousand Scottish street fights and if he noticed it, it was only with the passing interest of a stranger.

The survivors huddled closer, forming a circle around the outside of the makeshift ring. Makon snapped off a couple more punches and Big Jim struck out with a hairy palm, catching Makon with a glancing blow to the side of the head that sent him stumbling into the crowd. They caught him and pushed him back towards the centre like a bunch of sweaty rockers in a mosh pit.

Big Jim was starting to tire, and it looked like Makon was getting the upper hand. He landed a couple more jabs to the body and narrowly missed connecting with Jim's chin, but the Scotsman pulled back just in time. They were both flagging, the initial fun of the fight lost somewhere in the adrenaline rush. The sound of the crowd was disorienting and suddenly Big Jim felt like he was back in a supermarket car park again with a bottle of whiskey working its way through his liver.

He forgot where he was for just long enough to snap his head forward in a Glasgow kiss. His forehead connected with the bridge of Makon's nose and smashed his brow in a single stroke. It was against the rules, of course, but they weren't sparring for points or for a shot at the heavyweight title. They were fighting tooth and nail, pacing back and forth across the bitumen on the roof of the admin building, all ideas of a friendly fight forgotten. It wasn't even a case of honour, because honour was a luxury. Both men wanted to win because both men liked winning. But only one of them could come out on top.

Makon was already on the defensive, and blood from his nose was getting in his eyes and mouth. At the same time, Big Jim was applying the pressure. While the Scotsman wasn't about to win any awards for accuracy and finesse, all it would take was one good punch.

And after approximately four and a half minutes of combat, an expanse of time that felt at least five times longer than it actually was, a winner was decided. Those who were watching called it a lucky punch. But Big Jim knew it was more than that.

It was an unexpected left hook when Makon was preparing for a right, and the Scotsman's hairy fist hit him right beneath the eye before he had a chance to turn away. It made a sound like a baseball bat connecting with a tennis ball, a hefty thwack that seemed to hover on the air like a sound effect in a comic strip.

"'Have some o' that, ye fucken scally," Jim said.

Will Makon dropped to the floor like a sack of potatoes. John MacDonald counted to ten, but he didn't get back up.

***

The thing that lurked beneath Sunnyvale was hungry. It was always hungry.

On that particular night, Bob Knowles was the unlucky soul who'd chosen to sleep outside of the group, somewhere on the third floor of the admin building where the servers were stored next to the cleaning supplies. He was in a bad mood and sick of the sight of his colleagues. He'd only started working at Sunnyvale to save up enough cash to record an album. Now the music was a distant memory and he was stuck on the wrong side of the quarantine, and worse – everything smelled dirty, like a used gym kit left out on the side for a couple of days. And his fellow survivors reeked, too.

He'd found himself a corner to lie in away from the rest of the survivors, but that also made him the perfect prey. While Knowles was asleep, he couldn't hear the thing as it moved around the facility inside the walls and through the pipes.

In fact, nobody heard it, even though the building had fallen quiet since the power went out. Somehow, despite the dozens of legs that seemed to pull it in different directions, it moved silently, or at least too silently for a human to hear it. The animals knew it was there, though. They made it known in the way they sounded off at the moon.

Knowles slept on, oblivious of the thing that was burrowing through the floorboards beneath him. It found its way up and out of the wall through an air vent, a vent that had been useless since the power went out, and scuttled out on to the floor of the building. It made its way uncertainly across the room towards where Knowles was lying, meandering back and forth like a drunk on a Friday night bender.

Then the thing crawled on top of him and lay on his stomach as it sniffed his flesh and looked for some sort of opening. It lowered one of its heads and nipped at Knowles' skin, just a tiny little bite on some of the exposed flesh from above his navel, where his matted hair had curled up and around like a question mark. Then it lowered another head, and then another, and the creature flew into a frenzy, nipping and biting and gouging at Knowles' supine body. He woke up with a start and pulled himself to his feet, but the creature still clung to his chest with its myriad teeth and claws and the blood was flowing freely. There was a lot of it, so much so that Knowles slipped and went tumbling to the floor.

But the Rat King refused to let go, and its angry mouths worked in unison as the rats made a meal out of him. Knowles screamed and beat at himself as though he was trying to put a fire out, but the Rat King held on with its vicious claws and its rabid mouths even as he rolled over on the floor to try to crush it.

He'd lost a lot of blood, and he was also losing the will to fight and to live. Still, Bob Knowles screamed again and grabbed at the thing on his chest. The Rat King shifted itself and suddenly his hand was unresponsive and the vein on his wrist was spewing blood with every heartbeat. Knowles went down on to his knees and fell backwards. He opened his mouth to scream once again, but the Rat King had crawled up his torso and on to his neck and face. It sunk its teeth into his throat and started working away at his Adam's apple and then further in until its tiny jaws were clamping down on his vocal cords. The scream died in his throat, and the rest of him died shortly afterwards.

***

He didn't live long enough to hear the patter of feet as Big Jim and his security team burst onto the scene. They lit him up with a couple of torches and the light sent the Rat King into a frenzy. It started to snarl, sounding almost like a dog but with the odd natural harmony of a swarm of bees.

"Holy fucken shitbaws," Big Jim shouted. "Ye've goat tae be yankin' ma fucken chain. What the fuck is that?"

"I don't even want to know," Taylor said. "We should kill it."

"Good call, Phil," Dunlop said. It wasn't Carl Taylor's name, but it *was* his nickname. It just wasn't a nickname that he cared for.

"Call me Phil again and I'll knock your fucking block off," Taylor said, rounding on his colleague and squaring up to him. "You're about ten years old, kid. How do you even know who Phil Taylor is?"

"My dad used to watch the darts," Dunlop said. He grinned sheepishly and reminded them all of how young he was. He was twenty-two, but he looked fifteen.

"Oi, ladies, can this wait until after the fucken thing's deid?"

"Kill it!" O'Rourke shouted, and Jack Dunlop and Carl Taylor raced towards it with their truncheons drawn. It was too late for Bob Knowles, and his skull burst apart like a watermelon under the weight of their truncheons. Taylor caught the Rat King with a glancing blow, and it howled like wind through the eaves of an old building. It raced towards them and pounced at Jack Dunlop, catching a little air time before landing on his leg and sinking its teeth into it. The young man screamed and danced on one foot as he tried to shake it off, and then Taylor's truncheon started smashing into his limb and the Rat King let go and scuttled away into the night.

Jack Dunlop started to scream. Big Jim and Darragh O'Rourke cast their torches around in search of the Rat King, but there was no sign of it. They thought it'd probably be back, though. It had that sort of inevitability that comes from being an immovable object or a natural disaster. Carl Taylor, meanwhile, had raced across to his injured colleague, and the two of them were doing their best to check his wounds. They were significant, but they wouldn't be fatal. At least, not unless they got infected.

PREDICTABLY ENOUGH, an infection set in.

Copeland examined Dunlop as soon as Big Jim summoned him over to the scene of the attack. He gave him a tetanus shot and a dose of antibiotics, then treated the wound with some of the antiseptics that the army had delivered the night that Hector Fernandez fell to his death. There had been no contact since then, but at least there were more supplies to keep the survivors going.

But Dunlop's condition worsened over the next twelve hours, and the flesh around his wounds took on a pallid grey colour. He developed a fever that they treated as best as they could by keeping his forehead cool with a damp cloth, but then his flesh turned black and started to necrotise and Dunlop cried out over and over for his mother. But she was a long way away and in no position to save him.

When Copeland was consulted, he refused to give a public diagnosis but insisted instead on talking to John MacDonald alone.

"It's the disease," Copeland said. "He's infected."

MacDonald swore. "What are we going to do?"

"I have no idea," Copeland replied. "If he was an animal, I'd say we should put him down as a precaution. We can give him what antibiotics we have left, but we gave most of them to Maude Harrison. Hell, even if we had the whole lot, I don't think we could take this thing down. Look at his goddamn leg, John. It's festering."

"So what are we going to do?"

"We need to contact the army and get him some medical attention," MacDonald said.

"We can try," Copeland said. "But we'd better make it quick. The infection is spreading faster than I would have thought possible. If we don't do something, and if we don't do something quickly, we're going to be left with only one alternative."

"Which is?"

"We'll have to operate," Copeland said. "We'll have to amputate his leg and try to contain the infection."

MacDonald winced. He knew what that meant. Copeland had never operated on a human being before, and the conditions were hardly ideal. They didn't have an operating theatre, for one thing. They didn't even have a way to sterilise the equipment other than by plunging it into a fire before they used it.

"We'll try to get him some medical attention from Runciman's boys," MacDonald said. "How long do we have?"

"Honestly? A couple of hours."

"Then we'd better get started now."

"What if we don't hear from the army?" Copeland asked.

"We'll ask Dunlop," MacDonald said. "We'll let him make the call. I can't ask a man to let a vet chop his leg off without giving him a choice."

"But without the amputation, he could die."

"He could die anyway," MacDonald reminded him. "We all could."

Copeland couldn't argue with him. He saw the sense in what he said.

When the two men approached Jack Dunlop and gave him the choice, on the evening of the second day after his clash with the Rat King, he refused to make it. He told them to leave him alone so he could think it over.

Then he slipped into a coma.

***

Lieutenant Colonel Ben Runciman was alone in his trailer at the end of another shift, lying in his bunk and thinking about masturbating, when the klaxons went off.

"Shit the bed," Runciman murmured. That klaxon could only mean one thing. There'd been a breach of the quarantine.

Runciman was one of the lucky ones because he was awake and fully dressed when the klaxon went off. He sacrificed thirty seconds to pull on his boots and to retrieve his pistol, and then he burst out of the door and into the camp, which was in uproar.

The klaxon was even louder outside, and the harsh artificial lighting cast everything in an ethereal glow. Runciman could see plenty of movement and hear the sounds of rounds being discharged, as well as the occasional boom of a grenade. This was no drill. This was something serious, something much more intense than the sole gunshots in the night that the camp was used to whenever a watchman spotted movement. This was a desperate fight against a concentrated attack, and the situation turned out to be even worse than he'd expected when he reached the battle front.

The security fence that his troops had built was the second line of defence, after the facility's own walls and fences. In between, there was a no man's land, and while occasional animals had found their way through weak patches and out into the middle ground, there'd been no real threat of them reaching the main camp.

But something had changed, and Runciman could just about figure it out, though the lights only reached so far and he could only guess at what he couldn't see. Something had gone wrong. The first perimeter had been breached somehow, only instead of a single animal that had blundered its way out by accident, there was a whole damn horde of the things. He saw chickens, sheep, pigs and cows, all congregated like some unholy vision or the wrath of god. There were dozens of them – no, hundreds of them – and they were already most of the way across the no man's land.

On either side of Runciman, soldiers were firing off pot shots with their rifles, and one harsh bang in particular, which hung on the air and gnawed at the brain, reminded Runciman that they had the snipers in their watchtowers. He pulled out his own pistol and started to fire it into the darkness, but he already knew it was useless.

There was a shrill whistle and a bang as someone fired an RPG, a new addition to his team that had been sanctioned after the failed attempt to reach the admin building. It scored a direct hit and lit up the night, sending chunks of roasted bacon flying through the air and gouging deep tufts out of the bloodied earth. But in the light of the explosion, Lieutenant Colonel Ben Runciman realised that even the RPG was just pissing in the wind. There were thousands of them – tens of thousands of them – and there was no way in hell that the fence would hold.

"We need to fall back," he murmured, and then he realised that no one could hear him. He put his hands to his mouth and repeated it, bellowing into the night, but it was drowned out by the further rattle of gunfire and the howling of wounded, angry animals. His hand went to his waist to grab his radio, but he realised too late that he'd left it behind in the trailer.

And then the animals were at the fences, and Runciman's men were throwing everything they had at them, but it wasn't enough. Even amongst the hail of bullets and the explosions from the mines and the RPGs, as meat and gristle and bone flew through the air and showered the soldiers in muck and gunk, the animals kept on coming. They climbed on top of each other, like performers at a circus creating a gory perversion of a human pyramid, and then the fence began to buckle before collapsing beneath the weight of the massing animals.

Runciman turned and ran backwards, not daring to look over his shoulder to see what the chaos was like. He was too busy focussing on the chaos in front of him, behind the lines. Something was wrong.

His own men were attacking each other, staring down the barrels of each other's guns as muzzles flashed in the darkness. It was anarchy, impossible to tell who was siding with who. For a moment or two, Runciman thought there'd been a revolt, some sort of coup d'état. But then he saw what was really happening.

Some of his men were tearing at the others with their hands and their teeth. They were men who'd died, men he'd buried. Men who had clods of earth and splinters of wood in their hair. Men with dried, fetid blood clotting over their dog tags. Men they should have burned instead of buried, but the realisation had come too late.

He knew what he was looking at. He'd seen the movies. He'd also read the early reports that were coming back from the laboratories. He knew that the virus had evolved and mutated. And at the sight of his own men turning on each other as the barricades around the complex fell, he knew something else. He knew that the virus had spread, and that their quarantine had failed.

And then a stray bullet, fired almost at random during the heat of the moment, hit him straight in the middle of the forehead. He didn't have time to think about anything else before his body hit the ground.

***

The survivors talked of little else but the Rat King, and the creature from the depths beneath the complex became a very real threat, as real as hunger and disease. Few people had seen the creature, but it was impossible to miss the fear and the awe with which they talked about it. They were terrified.

"But what the hell is it?" Maude Harrison asked. She'd recovered from her toothache and while she still talked with a lisp, she felt like she'd got off lightly. The worst of it was over.

Lee Keyes, who was sitting across from her in the darkness and sharpening a knife on a paperweight, looked up at her with a glint in his eye. He smirked.

"It's the Rat King," Keyes replied, still scraping the blade across the rock like it was as natural as leaning back in a chair in the middle of a meeting. "A dozen rats, maybe more of them, all Frankensteined together. I've heard of them before, but I've never seen one. Some say it starts when they spend so much time in muck that their tails get twisted in a tangle and caked together. Others say it takes a human being, a cruel one, to tie their tails together like little pieces of string. My money's on the latter. I reckon Big Jim has himself a hobby."

Maude Harrison made a noncommittal noise, but that was hardly surprising. She wasn't exactly friends with Big Jim, but they were on speaking terms. Everyone knew that Sunnyvale's long-term employees had a code of honour of their own, and Jim and Maude were two of John MacDonald's first hires.

"If there was something fishy going on," Maude said, "John MacDonald would have sniffed it out."

Lee Keyes guffawed, then leaned over and spat a great glob of phlegm onto the floor.

"Did I say something funny?"

"No," Keyes said, but he was still grinning. His teeth shone out of the darkness like a score of marble obelisks in a city centre square. "I just don't think old MacDonald could sniff something out if he tried."

"What do you mean?"

"The man has no sense of smell," Keyes said. "It's an open secret. They say that's how he can stand to spend so much time here."

"Was he born like that?"

Keyes shrugged. "Who knows? I heard he had an accident as a kid with his chemistry set. It might all be a load of bollocks, of course. But I can believe it."

"So can I," Maude replied. "But still, I don't think there's much that goes on here that John MacDonald doesn't know about. If Big Jim has been making himself a Rat King, Old MacDonald knows about it."

"Perhaps he does," Keyes said. "Perhaps it was his idea."

It was a long evening in the darkness, with Jack Dunlop slipping in and out of consciousness and screaming deliriously every time he saw the light. But Jack Dunlop wasn't the only one who was under the weather. It seemed like half the complex was coming down with something or another. Flu season was on its way. At least, they hoped it was the flu. If it wasn't the flu, then it was something else.

Meanwhile, the less-than-satisfactory sanitation system was taking its toll, and a half dozen more were suffering from the shits and stomach bugs. And with no running water and rapidly dwindling bleach supplies, it was only going to get worse.

Amidst all that, Maude Harrison's rotten tooth was starting to look like a minor injury.

***

Harry Yorke and Diane Hyde had lost track of time. It had been weeks – *months*, perhaps, or it might as well have been – since they'd seen the sunlight. They'd been down there so long that their eyes had adjusted to it, and they were blinded by the light every time the door swung open and the gruel was pushed in.

But as supplies started to run out, the gruel was delivered with less and less regularity, until eventually it stopped being delivered at all. That was when time became irrelevant. Until then, they'd had the meal drops to focus on, even if they were unpredictable. Once the food stopped coming, the hope faded faster than the light did when the doors swung closed.

To begin with, they passed the time by talking, but the two of them had little in common. Even though they were both devoted to protecting animals, Harry Yorke did it because he felt morally compelled to do so. Diane Hyde did it because she was getting paid to.

They tried playing I-spy, but there was nothing to see and no light to see it by. They tried playing twenty questions, but they ran out of people and besides, it wasn't much fun and did more harm than good when it came to morale. They stopped playing games to while the time away after the first couple of days, and they stopped talking to each other after the first couple of weeks.

But when the food ran out, they started talking again. They had to.

"How are we going to get out of here?" Hyde asked, breaking the silence and eliciting a start from Harry Yorke, who'd been lying on the floor and staring moodily up at the ceiling as though there was something other than blackness to see up there.

Yorke grunted and then said, "We're not. We're stuck here."

"We could try shouting again."

"Who's going to hear us?" Yorke asked. "Only the people who've locked us up in here. Besides, we tried that. The first time we did it, I lost two of my teeth and you got a black eye. And the second time we did it, nobody came."

"We could kick the door down," Hyde suggested.

"And who's going to do that?" Yorke replied. "You? Something tells me we'll be here for a while."

"You could do it, a big, strong man like you."

"That's a little sexist," Yorke said. "I couldn't kick that thing down at the best of times. Something tells me they've barricaded the other side, and I'm so weak, I can barely stand. I need food."

"So do I," Hyde said. "We all do. I don't suppose things are much better outside this room. Here's a thought. What if they're all dead? What if they've starved to death out there and we're stuck starving to death in here? What if–?"

"What if, what if, what fucking if?" Yorke snapped. "I'm sick of being hungry, I'm sick of being tired, and I'm sick of hearing your stupid fucking voice."

"How about a game of–"

Harry Yorke put his hands over his ears and screamed.

IT HAPPENED AT DAWN the following day, kicking in like a sudden explosion that sent aftershocks rolling around the English countryside. The pigs, the cows and the sheep had charged the walls of the chicken shed and broken them apart as easily as a slice of toast piercing the yolk of an egg. Something, some shared consciousness perhaps or else a side effect of the disease, had brought the wild beasts together again for one last strike on the facility. The admin building was built from brick and old stone, and its shattered front doors were the only weak point in the entire building. But the long, thin animal buildings were of a cheaper, flimsier design, mostly wood and aluminium.

And so as the sun rose over the complex, so too did the harsh sound of tortured metal and the buck-buck-buck of the chickens as they emerged into the light and tried to haul themselves into the air on their crippled wings. One or two of them got some air time, but true flight was impossible and they were trapped on the ground just like the other animals and the survivors cooped up in the admin building. The tables had turned.

The escape of the birds didn't pass unnoticed by the people inside the admin building, but it did pass without official comment. Everyone had been expecting it, and the chickens were less of a threat than the heavier animals. It was the pigs above all else that had the survivors cowering in their bolt hole and hoping that they wouldn't meet their maker beneath the hooves of three hundred kilograms of bacon.

Still, the army had experienced at least one success. So

far, their positions around the complex were holding, and the no man's land between the two perimeter fences was yet to be penetrated. Every time one of Sunnyvale's animals got close enough to the interior fence, a shot or two rang out over the hills as one of the army's snipers lined up their sights and pulled a trigger. The corpses of the dead animals were starting to form a stinking line along the perimeter, and so the soldiers had attacked them with flamethrowers, hosing them down with burning fuel until the smell of pork crackling hung thick on the air for miles around. It was a safety precaution, but it had another unanticipated advantage. It seemed to be warding off the other infected animals. For now, at least.

The survivors saw the escape of the birds as a bad omen. It was a horrible, grey day, a day where the rain came down from the clouds and refused to let up, and where the howling winds snuck in through the air vents and around the building. The survivors huddled up for warmth, but John MacDonald was in a buoyant mood.

"Think of all the water," he kept repeating, and he set up a rotating schedule of water gatherers to empty the full buckets into whatever receptacles they could find. Then the empty buckets could be taken back outside to start the lengthy process of refilling them from the rainfall.

There was a break in the rain in the early afternoon, when Jack Dunlop died. The young man didn't stand a chance, and he passed through the pearly gates at around 1:20 PM. Only three people were present when he died, and those three people were Big Jim Benson, John MacDonald and Tom Copeland.

Copeland glanced down at the body and frowned.

"This should never have happened," he said.

"No," MacDonald agreed. "It shouldn't have. But it *did* happen, and now we have to deal with it."

"So what do we do?"

"We feed him to the pigs," Copeland said. "We have to. We can't keep him here. It's unsanitary."

"And he'll start to smell," MacDonald added. He paused for a moment. Then he sighed and gestured towards Dunlop's legs. "You grab his feet. I'll grab his hands. We'll take him out to the roof and throw him down."

"Eh wis jist a kid," Jim murmured. He closed his eyes for a moment or two and shook his head. And by the time he opened them up again, Jack Dunlop was gone.

***

Even with fewer mouths to feed, supplies were scarce. They had plenty of water after the rainfall, but they were running low on the grain they'd seized from the supply depot, and the rations from the army were all but gone. There had been no more contact from the troops on the radio.

No one knew how long they'd been trapped in the admin building. To begin with, they'd counted out the days by marking them off in a tally chart on the whiteboard in MacDonald's office, but that had all gone to shit after a couple of weeks when people got confused about whether a tick had been added. And besides, there were rumours that Lee Keyes had sneaked in when no one was looking and added a few tallies of his own, although his reasons changed on every retelling.

As a general consensus, the survivors estimated they'd been in there for two to three months. But really, it was anyone's guess.

The situation came to a head when Darragh O'Rourke was standing guard over the supplies one night. Carol Rawlings sidled up along the third-floor corridor and said hello to him. O'Rourke was fiending for a smoke, and he had been ever since they'd first found themselves under quarantine. His cigarettes were still lying there in Big Bertha's glovebox, though the vehicle itself was upside down in the grass somewhere along the admin building's south wall.

But apparently Rawlings still had a couple left. She slipped him a smoke and offered a light, and then she engaged him with a little small talk while her accomplice, Neil Gibson, tried to sneak around behind him. If the food supply had been running a little higher, he might have got away with it, but it wasn't just a case of sneaking in, filling his pockets with grain and then slipping back out again. He had to look to find the food, and doing so took longer than he was hoping. Darragh O'Rourke caught his reflection as a dim shape passing across one of the windows and spun around, cigarette smoke still trailing from his mouth.

"Oi," he shouted, "what the fuck are you doing?"

And then Carol Rawlings was on his back, her fingernails tearing at every inch of exposed flesh, gauging at his eyes and getting knocked aside by O'Rourke's thick, hairy arm. He staggered backwards into the wall, knocking the air out of his assailant's lungs and dropping her to the floor. He looked up again and Neil Gibson was coming for him with a chunk of wood that was destined to burn beneath the cauldron on the rooftop. He swung it at O'Rourke and caught him a glancing blow on the shoulder, which the security man shrugged off. He retaliated without thinking, swinging his cigarette hand towards the man's face and putting the stub out just beneath the bridge of his nose. Neil Gibson screamed like a pig in the slaughterhouse and stepped back just far enough for O'Rourke to unhook his truncheon from his utility belt and to swing it in a wide arc into the man's windpipe.

He dropped to the ground like a felled tree in the middle of the rainforest.

***

By the time that Big Jim and John MacDonald arrived on the scene, O'Rourke had the situation under control. Carol Rawlings had her arms cuffed behind her back. While she was technically free to make a run for it, she was just standing there and staring insolently out at the world. After all, there was nowhere to go.

Maude Harrison had arrived, too. She was the facility's resident social butterfly, one of the few employees who got on with almost everyone. She'd held up better than most during the quarantine, and she was still making the effort to wear foundation and eyeliner. Her blonde bangs were a little greasy, perhaps, but while the rest of the survivors looked like refugees who'd been lost at sea for weeks, Maude Harrison looked like a mum at a festival. She looked almost normal, apart from the look of pure horror on her face.

"Stop fighting!" she shouted. "Please, guys! We're all in this together. We need to work as a team."

"Bullshite."

"Jim, think about what you're doing," Harrison begged. "Think about Carol's kids."

"Fuck the wee bampots."

Maude Harrison turned to look at John MacDonald, who had fire in his eyes like a vengeful Greek god. He didn't look like he was in the mood to bargain with her.

"John," Harrison said. "John, please."

But John MacDonald just looked away from her.

Neil Gibson, meanwhile, was on his stomach on the floor with Darragh O'Rourke's knee in the small of his back. "Glad you boys could make it," O'Rourke said, smirking up at them. "It's about time."

"Looks like you've got things under control here," MacDonald said. "So what happened?"

O'Rourke told him, omitting the cigarette, and the boss stormed off to examine the storage room and to take a quick inventory. When he came back, he wasn't exactly satisfied, but at least he knew they hadn't lost anything. The only thing that Rawlings and Gibson got away with was their lives, and even their lives were only temporary. It was just a stay of execution.

MacDonald called a council, bringing all the survivors together in a single room with Carol Rawlings and Neil Gibson at the head of it. They'd been bound and gagged, tied to blue office chairs and paraded in front of their fellow employees like prisoners of war in a concentration camp. Tensions were understandably high.

"People of Sunnyvale," MacDonald said. "We have two traitors in our midst. Carol Rawlings and Neil Gibson were caught trying to steal supplies, breaking the rationing rules and taking food out of *your* mouths. So what should we do with them?"

"Kill them!" someone shouted.

"Why would you say that?" Jill MacDonald replied, glaring around like an over-protective Yorkshire terrier. There was a world of difference between who she was then and who she'd been when she'd first signed up as an intern at her uncle's company.

"The girl has a point," Maude Harrison added. "What are we, savages? Have none of you read *Lord of the Flies*?"

"Still," another voice said. "We should feed them to the pigs."

"They were hungry," Jill shouted. "Give them a break."

"Well, we need to do something!"

"What does the boss man say?" This came from Lee

Keyes, the perpetual dissenter.

John MacDonald sighed and stepped into the middle of the room. "We don't have enough food to spare for people who can't be trusted," he said. "And we have no idea how long we might be in here. No, we can't afford to be lenient. It's time to take a stand."

"Kill them!" someone shouted again, but MacDonald shook his head.

"We can't afford to be lenient," MacDonald repeated. "But that doesn't mean I'll show no mercy. Let's hear them out. Let's give them a chance to explain themselves."

The assembled pairs of eyes all turned to look at Carol Rawlings and Neil Gibson, who were on their knees now with Big Jim's security team standing behind them. It was like a scene from a terrorist cell's execution video. It felt like it, too.

"Carol," MacDonald said. "Please tell me you have a good reason for what you did."

"I'm sorry, John," Carol replied. "What do you want me to tell you? I was hungry. I'm just trying to keep going for long enough to get out of here. I want to see my kids again. I want to see my husband."

"We all have loved ones on the outside."

Neil Gibson laughed, but it was a hollow laugh. There was no humour in it, just anger and irony. MacDonald turned to look at him with his piercing, perceptive eyes.

"What's so funny?"

"I don't believe you've got anyone on the outside," Gibson said. "The only person you've got is your niece, and she's stuck in here with you."

MacDonald glared at the man and then tried to smile at him, but it didn't work. He looked like a crocodile eyeing up its prey in some swamp somewhere.

"Do you have anything else to say for yourself?"

"Fuck you," Gibson replied, twisting his head around to spit at John MacDonald. He managed to get a mouthful of saliva out and into the air, but it landed harmlessly a foot and a half away from its target.

MacDonald's eyes hardened. "Very well," he said. "You can leave with your lives and your limbs intact. From this day forward, the two of you are unwelcome here in the admin building. If you can't follow the rules of our society, you'll no longer be a part of it."

MacDonald clicked his fingers and Big Jim and Darragh O'Rourke stepped forward. He'd already briefed them on what to do.

"I'm not a ruthless man," MacDonald said. "I want you to have the best chance there is to survive out there. Do you understand me?"

The two prisoners just looked at him, their eyes wide and white with pinprick pupils that reflected the fear they felt. They were still bound and gagged, but they had enough freedom of movement to nod their heads, which they did just as soon as they realised it was what MacDonald was waiting for.

"Good," he said. "I'm glad we're eye-to-eye on this. Jim, untie them. We'll let them leave this place with a little dignity."

Big Jim did as he was told, and the first thing that either of them did with their freedom was to pull the gags from their mouths. Neil Gibson just scowled at MacDonald as he tried to massage some life into his arms, but Carol Rawlings did the opposite, begging MacDonald to reconsider and to let her stay. She even dropped down to her knees and clasped her hands together like she was praying to some meaty god up there on the top of the admin building. But that meaty god's name was John MacDonald, and he was having none of it.

"Dignity, Mrs. Rawlings," MacDonald said. "And besides, you might want to be quiet. The animals will hear you."

That did it. Carol Rawlings looked like she'd been slapped in the face, and she closed her mouth so hard it looked like she was trying to bite her tongue off.

"Jim," MacDonald said, "if you could do the honours."

He offered up a smart salute and said, "Yes, sir." Then he grinned at Rawlings and Gibson. "Now, we've put together a new rope for you to use. You'll see it over there. It's made out of twine and parcel string, but don't worry. We've tested it. It'll take your weight."

He leaned in a little closer and leered at them. "You're going to have to lower yourself down, I'm afraid," he said.

Carol Rawlings opened her mouth to protest again, but she didn't seem to see the point in it. Gibson, meanwhile, had accepted his fate and walked over to the edge of the gantry, where the makeshift rope was hanging in the breeze. It looked surprisingly substantial. He lowered himself down a foot or two at a time and reached the ground without incident.

For Rawlings, it was a little more difficult. She refused to go at all until Big Jim threatened to just toss her over the side, and even when she did go, she tried to talk her way out of it right until the last second, when Jim closed his hands around hers and forced her to hold on to the rope. She lowered herself down as slowly and gently as she could, but then gravity took over and she was falling, the rope whizzing through her fingers and bringing out bright red callouses. Then she hit something and the air was knocked out of her.

Neil Gibson, who'd only just got the feeling back in his hands, was already wishing that he hadn't. Rawlings wasn't a heavy woman, but she'd been travelling towards him at quite some speed and he thought he'd heard something snap, a wrist perhaps, before his entire body exploded with a pain so great he almost vomited. But they didn't have time to waste, and he knew that. They were outside and on the ground, a walking, talking meal for any animal that came across them.

He lowered Rawlings to the ground and patted her on the back as she tried to fill her lungs with the shit-tainted air that surrounded the complex.

"Are you okay?" he asked.

"Never better," Rawlings replied, standing up a little straighter but still leaning on the man for some support. "What now?"

"We need to get out of here," Gibson said.

"How? We're under quarantine."

"I know," Gibson replied. "But I've got an idea. Follow me."

Gibson looked cautiously around and then, when he was satisfied that they hadn't been spotted by the animals, he struck off to the north at a steady jog. Rawlings followed closely behind, her breath rasping and coming in short bursts. She was out of shape, not overweight but simply unused to anything more strenuous than pushing a shopping trolley. She was also barefoot because the only shoes that she had were the high heels she'd slipped her feet into on the fateful day of the quarantine. But she was running for her life and she knew it, so she didn't stop to complain.

They made good time, but their journey hadn't gone unnoticed. It was the chickens, of all things. They caught sight of the two fugitives and started clucking, and that set off the cows and their long, malevolent moos. The animals leapt into action like runners coming out of the starting blocks.

"Shit!" Carol screamed.

"Faster," Gibson growled, not even bothering to turn around. They were running to the north, towards the great lake and its promise of freedom. If they could swim across it, which was a pretty big if, then they might find safety on the other side.

When they hit the beach, the two of them stopped dead. There were remains there, human remains, as well as the carcass of a speedboat which had more holes than a colander. Even if they'd been able to get the engine running, which seemed unlikely, there was no chance that it would stay afloat. So they took to their heels again and raced towards the water.

The animals were gaining on them, but it almost didn't matter. Gibson had already reached the muddy shore, and Carol Rawlings wasn't too far behind him. He started to wade into the water.

"What are you doing?" she asked.

"We're going for a swim," Gibson replied. "Come on."

"In there?" Rawlings asked. "You must be joking."

But she didn't stop running, and she took to the water the moment she reached it, and not a second too soon. She was up to her shoulders by the time that the first of the animals, the pigs, reached the shoreline and ploughed into the lake. There were a lot of them, and their momentum pushed a surge of water towards Rawlings and Gibson, who were paddling away as fast as their out-of-practise front crawls could carry them.

"Can pigs swim?" Rawlings shouted.

Gibson barely heard her above the grunts of the animals and the crash of the artificial wave that had surged across the lake. And from somewhere beneath the water, the fish woke up from their slumber.

"I hope not," Gibson replied. "Keep going."

Rawlings risked a backwards glance, and she was relieved to see that the animals were keeping their distance. They were swimming up and down along the shore, but they wouldn't venture deep enough to reach them.

Rawlings looked forward again and Gibson had disappeared. She panicked and paddled on the spot for a second, bobbing around in the water as she looked for him. She shouted his name but there was no response.

And then something bumped against her foot.

She swore and struck out again on the water. They were barely a third of the way across the lake and there was still no sign of Gibson, and then something bumped against her leg and she felt a strange sensation that quickly spread to her waist and then her chest. At first, it felt like a thousand tiny kisses, the kind that a mother might give to a baby, but then the lips turned to sandpaper and the water around her started to turn red. She looked down through the murky water and saw something that she'd remember for the rest of her life.

She was surrounded by a shoal of fish, nothing normally carnivorous but typical freshwater fish from Sunnyvale's production line. Most of them were bottom feeders, more used to nibbling up worms or weeds, but they were making themselves felt on her arms and legs and then something else, something bigger, bashed into her side and dragged her under.

The water was serene and silent for a couple of seconds, and then Carol's head broke the surface and she coughed out some water and screamed. It echoed across the water and out into the countryside. Then she felt a couple more thumps against her legs and a downward force as the massing fish surrounded her in an aquatic cloud, nipping at her with their tiny mouths, pushing against her with their heads and dragging her beneath the water.

She fought against it, but the pull was too strong. One of the last things she saw was the corpse of Neil Gibson, weighted down beneath the water by the fish that were feeding off it. Only his head was exposed.

It was just a hideous, grinning skull. The fish had nibbled it clean in the space of a minute.

Carol Rawlings sank down, and the darkness greeted her with open arms. She knew nothing else after that.

THERE WAS SOME DISSENT amongst the ranks. Unsurprisingly, Lee Keyes was at the head of it.

"We're feeding an extra mouth," he was grumbling. He said it loudly enough to make sure that everyone heard it, but not so loud that it would force a response. It was a shrewd move, cold and calculated, and he pulled it off perfectly. There was a low murmur of agreement from some of the other survivors. Those who'd done the mathematics, and who'd realised that the departure of Neil Gibson and Carol Rawlings had left them with the same number of mouths thanks to the arrival of Harry Yorke and Diane Hyde, said nothing.

They were sitting in one of the empty offices that had once belonged to the marketing team, whose job had been to combat any bad publicity by trying to seed some good news. Their level of success was debatable, but they'd been given a decent-sized office in spite of it because John MacDonald believed that creativity had its own demands, and that a big room to practise in was one of them.

"What's MacDonald planning to do with that guy, anyway?"

Someone took the bait. "What guy?" they asked. It was hard to tell who, but it didn't really matter. All the voices were the same in the darkness.

"I'm talking about fucking whatshisname. Harry Yorke, the protestor. Why are we still feeding him? We barely have enough to feed ourselves."

"Yeah!"

"And what about Diane Hyde?" Keyes said. "They were

the enemies before lockdown and they're our enemies now. They're two extra mouths to feed, and that means less for the rest of us!"

"Fuck 'em!"

There were some more murmurings, louder in volume and spread out around the room, and Lee Keyes knew that he'd got them right where he wanted them. He was just vocalising what the rest of the survivors were thinking.

"I'm telling you, something has to be done," he said. "And if John MacDonald won't do it, we're going to have to do it ourselves."

"What do you mean?" someone asked.

"Here, here," someone else added.

"I'm hungry," Keyes said. "And I'm damn well sure that you guys are hungry, too. When was the last time anyone had a proper meal?"

"Days ago."

"Weeks ago!"

"I, for one, can't remember," Keyes said. His voice was louder now, more confident, and he was standing up in the middle of the room instead of being just a lone voice in the darkness. "And it's all their fault."

"Let's get 'em!"

"Yeah!"

"Yes," Keyes agreed. "Let's go and make our voices heard. Let's go and do what needs to be done."

He'd attracted a few followers by then. While there were only half a dozen of them, that was enough. There weren't many survivors in the first place, and nobody had any fight left. Besides, Harry Yorke's room was unguarded. The door was wedged shut behind some wooden struts, presumably salvaged from someone's desk, which were wedged between the wall and the door. And because the protestor had been stored in the old supply room, they'd also locked him in with the key.

The wooden struts were easy to remove, and Keyes and his men made short work of them. This was no lynching, though, no mob justice. They were silent as they worked, at least until the struts were out of the way. Then they rushed the door, all of them putting their backs into it at once, and the lock broke and the door flew open. It whacked against the wall with a noise that could have woken the dead, a big boom of wood on wood as the door hit the skirting board. It echoed throughout the complex.

"We'd better work quickly," Keyes said. "Old MacDonald will have heard that."

"The animals will have heard it, too," someone grumbled.

Keyes had picked up one of the two-by-fours that had been propping the door shut and was wielding it with two hands like a bastard sword.

"Holy shit," he murmured.

It took a moment for his eyes to adjust, even with the light from their only torch shining through into the darkness. The interior of the store cupboard looked like the production line in the abattoir. It reeked of piss and shit, but there was something else in the air, something stronger. At first, it was just the coppery smell of blood, the blood that was plastered all over the walls like an impressionist painting. Then it resolved itself into the simultaneously sweet and repugnant stench of rotting flesh, something that Sunnyvale's production workers had been used to long before the quarantine kicked in.

Their eyes adjusted further, and they could see Harry Yorke, curled up in one of the corners, his knees pulled up to his chest. His hair had grown long and dishevelled and had matted together with his excrement, like fur on a lazy cat. He was holding something in his hand that looked like a raw chicken drumstick.

"Meat!" one of the rebels said. "Finally! I'm fucking starving."

"Look closer, you cretin," Keyes replied.

To Harry Yorke's right, Diane Hyde's body lay festering in the darkness. It was hard to tell how long she'd been dead, but her skin was crawling with maggots and it was clear it had been some time. Her skin had receded, giving her the impression of having large teeth and vicious fingernails. Chunks of flesh had been torn out of her, and each of her fingers had been sheared to the bone.

Harry Yorke dropped his hunk of meat.

"She wouldn't stop talking," he said, his eyes wild and unseeing, blinded by the light from the torch. "She just wouldn't stop talking."

He was still cowering in the corner, all skin and bones, a shadow of his former self.

"He's gone all Hannibal Lecter," someone moaned, their voice weak and muffled, as though they were holding back a mouthful of vomit.

"He killed her!"

"He did more than that…"

"Let's get him!"

If the impromptu mob had been of a rational mind, they might have noticed that cannibal or not, he wasn't a threat. They might have registered the reek of piss and shit or heard him as he begged for his life. But they weren't of a rational mind, and Yorke's pleas of "My kids! My kids!" fell on deaf ears.

Yorke got an arm up in time to deflect the first blow, but the bone in his arm snapped as soon as the two-by-four made contact. He howled and tried to back away, but then the wood came round again and caught him in the side of the head. This time, he didn't get his arm up in time to deflect it and the plank of wood hit him right in the skull. There was a sickening crunch when the wood made contact. And in the darkness, a splash of blood and gore flew out of Harry Yorke's head and the man went down to the floor.

He was still alive, technically speaking, but he wouldn't be for long without immediate medical attention.

Lee Keyes wanted to make sure that medical attention was out of the question. It was bad enough that the man was stealing the food from their mouths. Worse still that he'd turned to cannibalism, though perhaps he'd done them all a favour. He wasn't going to let the man get away with stealing their medicinal supplies, too. So he drew back his arms and brought the wood down again and again and again, until Harry Yorke's face was just a smear of blood and bone on the floor. Then he threw the plank of wood to the floor, where it bounced once or twice before slowing to a halt in front of the writhing mass of flesh that had once been Diane Hyde's left leg.

He turned around to look at the rapidly gathering crowd. The rest of his vigilante crew had retreated to the doorway, and a few of the other survivors had been summoned by the noise to see what was happening.

Lee Keyes looked like a demon. The dead man's blood had sprayed all over him and it was running down his face and into his eyes and mouth. He licked his lips, cleaning some of the blood away with his tongue. Then he spat on the floor.

He pushed his way through the milling crowd and out into the hallway. He nudged John MacDonald with his shoulder as he pushed past the man. Then he let himself out on to the rooftop through the door in the boss' office.

It was raining outside. The water felt refreshing as it fell from the heavens and soaked through his hair and clothes. He lay down with his arms beneath his head in a makeshift pillow and looked up at the stars.

And as he lay there, the rain splashed his face and rolled down his cheeks. It took the blood with it as it fell, and the claret swirled and floated away until there was nothing left of Harry Yorke but the broken-faced corpse with its bloated stomach full of the rotten meat of former Environmental Health inspector Diane Hyde.

He looked up at the heavens and laughed so hard he made himself vomit.

Later, he dragged the two corpses outside and tossed them off the gantry.

***

Bill Long was the next to die. It came out of nowhere, like a thief in the night. But it wasn't the night, it was the early evening, when the sun had just gone down on Sunnyvale. He'd been waiting in line for that evening's bowl of gruel when he suddenly doubled up and started coughing and wheezing in a horrific paroxysm.

Tom Copeland was a couple of steps behind him, waiting for his own food to be served, when the man collapsed. He rushed over to him and checked his vitals, then barked an order for someone to fetch his kit bag and John MacDonald, and not necessarily in that order. Meanwhile, Bill Long had started to fit, and while Copeland wasn't an expert, he knew enough to roll the man into the recovery position.

"Bill," he kept repeating, "Bill, can you hear me?"

But if Bill could hear him, there was no response.

MacDonald arrived soon afterwards, followed by Darragh O'Rourke, who'd personally brought the veterinarian's kit bag from their supply store.

"What's wrong with him?" MacDonald asked.

"Some sort of fit," Copeland replied. "Problem is, I don't know what it is."

"He used to take medication," Maude Harrison said. She'd been somewhere between Bill Long and Tom Copeland in the food line when it all went down. She was watching the scene with some concern, but she was also holding a steaming hot bowl of gruel in her hands. "He was complaining about it. Said he needed it and he didn't have a supply in here."

"Do you know what he took?" Copeland asked.

But Harrison shook her head, and Copeland cursed and turned his attention back to the man on the floor, who was still convulsing. His face had started to turn purple.

"What's going on?" MacDonald asked.

"He's not getting enough oxygen," Copeland said.

"So what are you going to do?"

Copeland knelt down beside the man to listen to his airways, but it was quickly becoming clear from his great, gasping coughs that there was a blockage. Some sort of fluid, perhaps.

"I've got an idea," Copeland said. "A tracheotomy."

"A what now?"

"We cut a hole in his neck and put a pipe in to help him breathe," Copeland said.

"Will it work?"

Copeland shrugged. "Probably not. I've never done it before. But it's the only thing I can think of."

"No," MacDonald said. "We can't risk it."

"If we don't, he might die."

"He might die if we do," MacDonald said. "And this place isn't exactly a hospital. It's too risky."

"You're the boss," Copeland said. It was clear from the way that his shoulders slumped that it was a relief. In that single second, everyone in the room knew he'd been hoping he wouldn't have to do it, and it looked like he was getting his wish.

But it didn't make much difference. Bill Long never woke up from his seizure, and after a couple of hours he had a second, larger seizure which finished him off. Copeland pronounced him dead at some point in the night. They weren't sure exactly what time it was. All of the clocks had been wiped out by the power surge.

But really, it didn't matter.

***

The rebellion began that night when the boss was asleep. It was Lee Keyes who was the mastermind, but he had no shortage of supporters. Even Bugsy Drew, John MacDonald's formerly reliable operations manager, had turned Judas and joined Keyes and his band of merry rebels.

The plan wasn't exactly well-refined. Big Jim and his security team held most of the power thanks to their heavy batons and their handcuffs, but Keyes and his rebellion had the element of surprise. Word had spread in the dark nights as the cold seeped throughout the complex alongside rumours that the soldiers had forgotten them and left them there to die.

It was Bugsy Drew who made the first move. He'd armed himself with a stolen letter opener, which he'd sharpened at night by filing the sides on a paperweight until the blunt steel was sharp enough to maim, if not to kill. Besides, it had a big old spike on the end of it.

Drew waited until most of MacDonald's men were asleep and then snuck through the hall to where Jill MacDonald was sleeping in one of the booths in the finance department. He pressed his hand against her mouth and then held her down as she woke up and started to struggle.

"Shh," he whispered. "It'll be all right. I don't want to hurt you. We just think it's about time we had a word with your uncle about who's running the show in here."

His words weren't reassuring, and Jill MacDonald kept struggling, biting at the man's sour fingers like a dog chasing a string of sausages. He cursed and pulled his hand away from her and then smashed it against the side of her head. That did the trick, and Jill MacDonald went limp, though not unconscious. Just dazed and docile.

"What do you want?" she whimpered.

"You're coming with me," Drew replied, dragging her to her feet and placing the letter opener against her neck, then pulling her out of the cubicle.

Arnie Lorn from the sheep department was waiting for them, and Lee Keyes was watching from the doorway, where he was simultaneously acting as a lookout. He might have been running the show, but he didn't want to get his hands dirty.

"So what now?"

Keyes frowned at him, his dark eyes staring out at her from under a shock of brown hair. He'd grown a beard during the time they'd spent in quarantine, and it made him look even rougher and more haggard. He looked like a man who'd broken out of a maximum-security prison and spent six months on the run with nothing but his paranoid thoughts to keep him company.

"We wait for the signal," Keyes said.

But the signal didn't come, which meant that Keith Gowan and Kim Roach from the pig team had either failed in their mission or backed out of it completely. Keyes had told them to subdue John MacDonald's security guards, who were stationed outside his office. But who knew what had happened?

"Change of plan," Keyes said. Then he threw his head

back and shouted at the top of his voice. "John MacDonald! Get down here. I want to talk to you."

The result was like a jolt of life in a corpse as lightning struck the roof of a mad scientist's laboratory. There was no light, but there was movement. The Sunnyvale Survivors were congregating on their spot in the breakout room on the second floor. It had been stripped clean of its furniture and the moonlight filtered in through the windows and lit up the empty room.

Keyes and Lorn formed a spearhead with Bugsy Drew behind them, still holding the letter opener to Jill MacDonald's neck. The room started to fill up around them, but they maintained their position with Jill MacDonald tucked away at the back. She'd started to cry, but she wasn't fighting. Drew guessed she had a minor concussion and that the fight had been knocked right out of her.

When John MacDonald entered the room, Drew tightened his grip on the letter opener and waited for Lee Keyes to speak.

"What the fuck is going on here?" MacDonald said.

"It's time for a change of management," Keyes replied. "A few of us aren't happy about the way you've been running things."

"I've been doing my best," MacDonald said, taking a step closer and spreading his hands like the feathers of a peacock.

"Stay where you are," Keyes said.

MacDonald obliged. Even in the near-darkness of the room, there was no mistaking the glint of moonlight off the blade at his niece's neck.

"Here's how it's going to work," Keyes told him. "You're going to let Arnie Lorn here take you away somewhere. From this moment forward, you're under citizen's arrest. Your security team, too. We can't have them running around and causing trouble."

"And what if I refuse?"

Bugsy Drew pushed the letter opener a little closer to Jill's neck and raked it across her skin. She gasped out in pain and MacDonald's face lost its colour.

"Just do as I say," Keyes said.

A tense silence hung over the room and the seconds seemed to stretch into minutes and hours. Big Jim and his security team had arrived by this time, and they were looking at MacDonald for instructions.

Something inside him seemed to die.

"Do what he says," MacDonald said.

And so John MacDonald, Big Jim Benton and the rest of the security team had their hands secured with their own cuffs. Then Bugsy Drew frogmarched them up to the third floor and into one of the stinking, shit-stained supply cupboards. By the time that they closed the door and barricaded it with a couple of desks, there were six of them. John MacDonald, Big Jim Benton, Darragh O'Rourke and Carl Taylor were all in cuffs, but there weren't enough to go around. Mike Chase got off lightly as the most junior security man, and Jill MacDonald was shoved roughly inside without cuffs, too.

It didn't matter too much. Lee Keyes stationed a couple of men outside at all times, and now they had a new resource. They had the security team's heavy batons and the gun that MacDonald had been storing in one of the drawers of his mahogany desk.

By the morning, Lee Keyes and his renegades had been joined by Steve-o Puck and Yvonne Strong from the avian team, as well as Bruce Laing from pigs. Not everyone was happy about the new regime, but not everyone had a voice.

In the space of twelve hours or so, the Sunnyvale Survivors had undergone a revolution. And as the dust started to settle, so did the balance of power. An uneasy peace settled over the facility.

It wouldn't last.

A COUPLE OF DAYS PASSED and life started to get back
to normal, or as normal as it could be with a couple
thousand head of livestock milling around the outskirts of
the stricken admin building.

Lee Keyes had started holding court in John
MacDonald's office, although little had changed under his
leadership. He'd increased the ration allowance, but there
were only so many oats one could eat before the idea of a
refill started to lose its appeal. The stock of grain in the
storage room was running dangerously low, but Keyes
didn't care. He'd been careful to make a smaller, separate
stash of his own.

He also took the opportunity to experiment with some of
their medication. He'd asked Tom Copeland to provide him
with a private supply of ketamine, morphine, "and anything
else that can take the edge off."

At first, Copeland had refused. "Why should I?" he
asked.

But Lee Keyes had just smiled an unsettling smile, the
smile of a man who's losing his touch with reality and who
knows it.

"You'll get me what I ask for," Keyes said. "If you don't,
I'm going to take the gun from MacDonald's desk, I'm going
to walk into that room and I'm going to shoot one of them in
the head. Are we clear?"

Copeland stared him down for an uncomfortable
moment or two and then lowered his eyes.

"Okay," he said. "You win. I'll get you your damn
drugs."

"Good," Keyes said. He smirked. "It's as I thought. It's time for you to pick sides, Doc. Don't choose the wrong one."

"I won't," Copeland murmured, and he meant it.

But the lines between sides were blurred at best. Keyes had decreed that the "prisoners" were to be given no food and just a half cup of water per day, but his rules were being flouted even by his own people. There was no question of them trying to escape. Four of the six were still cuffed and their morale was at an all-time low. They had to piss into a bucket in the corner of the room.

And amongst all the excitement and the facility's unexpected change of leadership, one of their most valuable resources had been overlooked.

No one was manning the radio.

***

It wasn't long before the survivors were rocked by another death. This time, it was Will Makon from the cow team. He was found by Yvonne Strong in what used to be a cubicle in the women's bathroom. Makon had hanged himself from a light fixture with a tie around his neck. No one had noticed he was missing during the change in management, and by the time that he was discovered, he'd started to smell. Rigor mortis was already well underway.

But Yvonne Strong lived up to her surname, so she didn't panic. She didn't scream, although she did shout for Lee Keyes to get over there. Then she calmly tried to loosen the tie and, when that didn't work, she got closer to the body and took the weight of it on her shoulder like the corpse of one of the animals. Then she lifted the body up and over, unhooking the makeshift noose in the process.

She dropped Will Makon's body on to the toilet like a

sack of potatoes and then backed away from it. She leaned against the wall for a little support and breathed the relatively fresh air in deep, heaving gulps.

Lee Keyes entered the bathroom at a run and followed Strong's outstretched fingers to the corpse in the cubicle. He rushed over to it and looked the body up and down.

"He hung himself," Strong supplied, as though Keyes couldn't see the tie around his neck or how his face had swollen up and started to collapse in on itself like an overripe tomato.

Keyes leaned a little closer to the body and gingerly started patting it down and reaching into the pockets.

"What are you doing?" Strong asked.

Keyes ignored her, but it became apparent what he was doing when he hit pay dirt and pulled a folded note from Will Makon's back pocket. He opened it up and shone his torch at it.

"What does it say?" Strong asked.

Keyes looked a little closer at the note and read it aloud as best as he could in the half-light.

"I can't go on any longer," he read. "I'm a fighter, but there are some things you can't fight. We're all going to die in here. Disease. Violence. Murderous animals. Life is violent and death is painful. I refuse to play a part in this game. It's time to be free, at last. Forever."

"What else does it say?"

"That's it," Keyes said. He shrugged. "Game over, I guess."

"So what should we do with him?" Strong asked.

"Get some people to give you a hand," Keyes said. "Drag him down the hallway and chuck him out the window. Feed Makon to the bacon. Let the pigs have him."

And so that's exactly what they did.

***

Life continued much as it had before, and Lee Keyes and his team of rebels had started to settle into a regular routine. They woke with the dawn and waited for help to arrive, whiling away the hours by playing cards or gossiping about who'd be next to die. It was true trench life for the Sunnyvale Survivors.

The next one to go was Kim Roach, the production worker from the pig team. She'd been looking peaky for several weeks, and it had progressed from a cold to the flu to full-blown pneumonia. Copeland treated her as best as he could, but his experience with pneumonia came down to wrapping blankets around animals and giving them more hay during the winter. He gave her a cocktail of drugs from their rapidly dwindling supply, but it could only deal with the symptoms.

When she cried out in pain, Lee Keyes told Copeland to give her paracetamol. They were starting to run out of morphine, and he'd claimed all of that for himself. Copeland had wanted to disobey, but he hadn't.

Kim Roach's condition continued to deteriorate after they treated her, and it didn't take her long to die. She rocketed between being red hot and being ice cold to the touch, and Copeland gave up on using his thermometer because the readings were so unreliable.

When she did die, she died in her sleep without ceremony. They wrapped the body inside a tarpaulin and threw it out of the window in the middle of the night, but if Lee Keyes was hoping that the death would pass unnoticed, he was wrong.

It was Tom Copeland who took the lead, reluctantly, because everyone else just expected him to. They met up in the same room they'd been using since the quarantine first hit, but where there had once been standing room only, they now had plenty of space to sit down and get comfortable.

"This can't go on," Copeland said. "We're dropping like flies."

"So?" Keyes said.

"So bring back John MacDonald," Copeland said. "Let's deal with this together."

"We were dropping like flies when John MacDonald was in charge," Keyes replied. "Or don't you remember that?"

"They're probably safer in that room of theirs than we are out here," Copeland said. "Don't you get it? No help is coming. It's just us against the world. And you've locked up the only trained security guards we have."

"The animals aren't coming in here," Keyes said, "so what the hell do we need with security guards?"

Copeland murmured something under his breath and then added, "So what are we going to do?"

"There's nothing we *can* do."

"There's *always* something we can do," Copeland said. "We can try to make contact with the outside again. Or perhaps we can try to bust out of here."

"If we leave this building, we'll die," Keyes said.

But Copeland wasn't the only dissenter, and the momentum was slowly starting to gather in the gossip that spread whenever the boss wasn't around. It was just the same as it always had been, and the change in management had made no difference.

But Kim Roach's death acted as a catalyst, and tensions were running high amongst the survivors. It didn't take much to start an argument, and the *sujet du jour* was the stench which had settled on each and every one of them. With no running water and no change of clothes above and beyond the rags, towels and curtains that they'd been using as garments, the atmosphere was a little ripe. When they huddled together at night, the smell was so bad that it was hard to breathe, as though they were sitting in the smog of an inner city and not just the fug of a dozen sweaty, scared survivors.

A great debate was held, where the remaining survivors gathered to talk through the arguments. They split into two parties, remain and leave, and they took it in turn to make their cases. The only constant was the fear of uncertainty, and neither side came out on top. They couldn't even agree to disagree, and tensions continued to rise after the debate until they were almost at boiling point.

And then the tensions boiled over and Jerry Jones stabbed Keith Gowan in the leg after losing a game of cards. Lee Keyes stepped in to intervene and Jones reacted on instinct, swiping his bloody knife through the air like a sword instead of like the six-inch steak knife that it was.

"Put that down," Keyes said. "You'll do yourself a mischief."

"I'll do *you* a bloody mischief in a minute," Jones said. "Back off! Give me some space."

"Why?" Keyes asked. "So you can think?"

Jones grunted, and Keyes took the opportunity to take a step forward. He took another and then another, like a cop in some Hollywood action movie who was trying to talk a criminal down from the edge of a precipice.

But real life wasn't like the movies, and Jones took it the wrong way and swung the knife at him. Keyes reacted on instinct, blocking the man's arm with his own before charging at him and driving him against the wall. Jones crumpled as the air was knocked out of him and the knife went clattering to the floor. Keyes drew back a fist and punched him in the stomach, and the man was done. He collapsed to his knees, panting and wheezing like a dehydrated dog in the summer sun.

Keyes raced across the room to where the bloody kitchen knife had clattered to a halt and grabbed at it. His first attempt missed, and it slipped out of his hand and fell back to the carpet. But he got a good grip on his second attempt and then rushed across to Jerry Jones, who was still on all fours. It reminded Keyes of the time he'd helped out in the slaughterhouse when the electricity had gone down, and he did what came naturally.

He walked up behind Jerry Jones, grabbed the man by his hair to yank his head back and then dragged the knife across his throat. It was blunt and it wasn't easy, but he applied a little pressure and the man's skin split apart like a pig being hit with a hatchet.

It took him a long time to die, and Lee Keyes started to come to his senses while Jones was still twitching on the floor. Keyes himself looked like a tribal warrior who'd doused himself in the blood of his enemies. It wasn't a pretty sight.

He looked up and noticed, for the first time, the survivors who were surrounding him. They reminded him of statues or ghosts in a churchyard. They weren't moving. They were just watching him.

"What?" he roared. "What the fuck are you all looking at?"

They faded away into the complex shortly afterwards. Keyes dragged the body to the window and threw it out into the darkness.

***

Time ticked on, and the Sunnyvale Survivors grew closer together as though their interpersonal relationships could somehow save them from the inevitable death of the world.

In the stock room, the jail within a jail was starting to smell pretty fragrant. Their jailors were still giving them food and water, but there wasn't enough water for them to waste it washing. Their piss bucket wasn't being emptied enough, either.

The quarantine had been in effect for long enough that they'd lost track of the days. Some said it was spring and some said it was summer. One or two people thought that the summer had passed and that they were heading into the early autumn. It didn't really seem to matter.

One day, as the sun rose, the bull came out to say hello.

It was a Sunnyvale legend, the biggest of the big, the bovine Prometheus. It was superhuman, super-beefy, at least seven feet tall. Its legs were muscular, sinewy, full of veins and more powerful than a piston machine. And it was full of hatred. It hadn't been fed for a long time.

The bull had been kept under lock and key in the back of the cow shed. It was a cannibal, fed on the flesh and bones of the animals that had fallen in Sunnyvale's slaughterhouse or succumbed to disease when standing shoulder to shoulder with the other animals. His semen was worth hundreds of pounds when measured per millilitre.

But the bull didn't know any of that.

It just knew it was angry.

***

Tom Copeland watched the bull from one of the windows as it made its destructive way across the complex, kicking up great divots of earth with its massive hooves and spearing the smaller animals with its horns. The chickens got it the worst. The beast kept lowering its great head and scooping up a half dozen birds at a time as it made its way through the clucking crowd.

Copeland shook his head and turned away from the window. Things were bad enough as they were, without him torturing himself by watching the bull as it made its inexorable way around the outskirts of the admin building.

"If Sunnyvale is hell," Copeland murmured, "then the bull is Cerberus."

He was just glad that it didn't have three heads. Three heads would mean six horns.

But Copeland couldn't let himself dwell on the outside of the building too much. He was much more worried about what was going on inside.

He found Lee Keyes in John MacDonald's old office. The boss and his security team had been under guard for the best part of two weeks, and that was what Copeland wanted to talk about.

"We need to let them out," he said. "I don't know if you've noticed but we're dropping like flies here. Rationing won't be a problem if there's no one left."

"Let me worry about that," Keyes said.

"I've tried that," Copeland said. "But I can't. It's weighing on my conscience, Lee. You have to let them out."

"I'll think about it."

"At least let me see them. Let me check them over and make sure that they're healthy. It can't be good for them to sit in there, day after day. You've got them shitting in buckets, Lee."

"We're all shitting in buckets," Keyes reminded him. "We have no other choice. Why should I let you see them?"

"If you don't, I won't keep pumping your arm full of morphine."

"Fair point," Keyes said. Copeland had been watching him over the last couple of weeks as the habit took hold. He'd been trying to find a way to work it to his advantage, and it looked like he'd finally hit the jackpot.

Keyes thought for a moment and then nodded at Copeland, whose overalls had started to lose their colour and whose sunken eyes spoke of night after night on little-to-no sleep.

"Okay," Keyes said. "You can go and see them. Check in with them twice a week to see if they're still alive."

"And you're going to let me back out again if I go in there?" Copeland asked. This was something he'd been worrying about. He was surprised that he hadn't already been locked up with them.

But Keyes grinned at him and said, "Of course. You're the only medical help we have around here. And besides, I'll need my shots."

The two discussed terms and came to an agreement, which they sealed with a handshake that brought the two men together.

Copeland paid his first visit to the five men and the one woman in the lockup room later that day. They were holding up surprisingly well, although they were perhaps a little stir crazy, and they were happy to see him. Copeland went around them one by one, checking their vitals and examining them for visible injuries. The men in the cuffs were starting to come out in nasty-looking rashes where the metal was chafing against their skin, but it wasn't too late to head off infection.

They were also free of disease, as far as he could tell, and in remarkably high spirits. John MacDonald had called it "the safest place in the whole facility," and Copeland was inclined to agree. All the same, he didn't like to see them there. They were his closest friends in the complex, if you could call them friends. At Sunnyvale, after the outbreak, it was every man for himself.

The worst of it was seeing little Jill MacDonald, who'd

celebrated her nineteenth birthday within the quarantine. She looked scared but determined and the vet's heart went out to her. Copeland smiled at her as he left, and she tried her best to return it. Then he knocked on the door and was escorted back out again by Keyes' heavies.

"You need to take off their cuffs," he said, as he left the room. "They're starting to chafe. We don't want an infection to set in. We'd have to use antibiotics to treat it."

Lee Keyes himself escorted Copeland away from the makeshift jail cell. He smiled at the vet and said, "I guess you'd better go and prepare my shot."

THE MORPHINE was enough to keep Keyes busy for a couple of hours or so, but as the sun went down, everything changed. Perhaps it was the Rat King, sowing chaos as it roamed beneath the complex, or perhaps it was just something in the air. Some of the survivors would later say that they could smell and hear it, some sort of evil out there in the darkness.

And then John MacDonald and Big Jim Benton lit the fuse.

Against his better judgement, Lee Keyes had given the order to free them from their cuffs. Within half a day, the prisoners had risen up and tried to fight their way out when his heavies opened up the door to give them their daily half cup of water. They were all thinner than they'd been when they'd first gone in there, but they were also all more desperate. Even Jill MacDonald had joined the fight, scratching and clawing for her freedom as more heavies arrived with batons and started to lay into them.

Keyes himself was late to the party, and all six of the prisoners had been subdued again, re-cuffed and dragged back inside the room. Big Jim had taken the worst of the beatings, and he was lying there semi-conscious on the floor. There was blood coming out of one of his ears. John MacDonald was looking a little better, but he had an angry welt on his forehead and his eyes had a desperate, hunted look.

"What the fuck's going on?" Keyes asked.

Keith Gowan, who was shaking with adrenaline and who'd been responsible for knocking Big Jim out, was the one who told him.

Keyes marched off without a word, and a heavy, expectant silence descended upon the group. They'd had enough, all of them, and something had to give. The door lay open between them but nobody made any attempt to move. The fight was over.

And then Lee Keyes came back with something in his hand. The five men and one woman looked up at him and saw the murder in his eyes. Keyes hesitated for only a second. Then he raised his right arm and pointed the pistol at John MacDonald.

"Any last words?" Keyes asked.

"Put the gun down, Lee," MacDonald said. "It doesn't have to be like this. We're human beings, not animals. We're all in this together."

Lee Keyes shrugged and said, "You're wrong."

Then he squeezed the trigger and put a bullet in the middle of John MacDonald's forehead.

***

After the echoes died away, there was a moment of silence. A thin wisp of smoke aired its way out of the barrel of the gun and floated away.

Then Jill MacDonald screamed and the spell was broken.

Her uncle had fallen to the floor after the bullet hit, and something lumpy and grey had started to leak from the hole in his skull. He wasn't moving, and he would never move again. Copeland ran over and knelt beside him, the gore and the murk seeping into his clothes, and checked John MacDonald's injury. But the bullet had gone in one side and out the other, taking a chunk of his skull with it. The exit wound was larger than the entry wound.

"You bastard!" Jill shouted. She started towards Lee

Keyes, but she was pulled back by a newly-conscious Big Jim and his hairy arms. He pulled her away from her uncle's body and back into the corner of the room.

"Eh's oaf his fuckin heid," Jim growled, pushing Jill MacDonald behind him to protect her. Carl Taylor, Darragh O'Rourke and Mike Chase stood on either side of him, forming a human wall in front of her. Not that they could do much against a gun.

"There's only one top dog in here," Keyes said. "And there's no law. I'm the law. This gun is the law."

"Until you run out of ammo," someone murmured.

Keyes pointed the gun at the ceiling and fired a round into it. A thin rain of plaster trickled down and settled on the floor.

"Copeland," he barked, "bring me my shot."

"It's the last one," the veterinarian said through gritted teeth.

"Then we'd better make it count."

And with that, he turned his back on the survivors and marched out of the room.

***

Everything changed after that. Some of the survivors thought that Lee Keyes had lost his mind, while others thought he was perfectly sane. Perhaps the truth lay somewhere in the middle. It didn't really matter.

Jill MacDonald was hysterical, so hysterical that Copeland gave her a little of the dwindling dope supply just to keep her quiet. He was worried that if she didn't calm down, she'd do herself a mischief. It was a reasonable thing to worry about. But with the dope in her system, she simply slumped down and sat on the floor with her back to the wall. She watched events unfold in front of her with a vacant expression on her troubled face.

Keyes hadn't given his men any orders, and no one had the heart to lock the door and to leave the prisoners in there with John MacDonald's body. It didn't seem right, and besides – it was MacDonald himself who Keyes had seen as the biggest threat. Now that MacDonald was dead, there didn't seem to be much point in locking up the rest of them. Darragh O'Rourke and Big Jim Benton picked MacDonald up by the arms and the legs and carried his body out on to the gantry, which they tossed it off. His niece hadn't been too keen on the idea, but they had no choice. They couldn't go outside to bury him, and if they kept him inside, he'd start to smell.

It was all so surreal, and the admin building felt somehow emptier without John MacDonald inside it. Those who were keeping track noted that they were down to just sixteen survivors. They'd started the siege in the admin building with close to thirty. The strangest thing of all was that the people were calm, almost serene. They'd accepted their position and knew death like an old friend, and all they could do was wait for it. There was no point fighting any more. John MacDonald had tried to fight it and look at what happened to him.

If Keyes cared that his prisoners were no longer prisoners, he didn't show it. He didn't show much at all. In fact, he locked himself in John MacDonald's office with the old mahogany desk pushed in front of the door. He refused to move it for anyone except Tom Copeland, but not even the vet wanted to go inside. For all they cared, he could rot in there.

It was Copeland himself who took action. The rest of the survivors were sitting around in a daze, as though they'd forgotten who they were and what they were doing there. But Copeland was one of the few people who'd actually liked John MacDonald, at least on a professional level. He thought he'd finally figured the man out, and now it was all for nothing.

Lee Keyes is a fucking animal, he thought. And it was thoughts like those that led him to do what he ended up doing.

When Copeland prepared the shot, he didn't have to cook heroin on a needle and suck it into a syringe. He doubted he could have done that even if he'd wanted to. Instead, he usually followed the same process. He'd take a syringe from their dwindling supply, the supply that people had died to liberate from the supply shed. Then he'd fill it with a little water and a little morphine, and he'd shake up the syringe until the substances mixed together. While he was doing this, Keyes would usually be tying his belt around a bicep and pulling it tight to expose a vein. Then Copeland would find the vein, jab it with the sharp tip of the syringe and hit the plunger.

But this time was different. This time, Copeland didn't cut the shot with water. He'd kept a little morphine back just in case, and he filled the syringe with the last of it. There was three times the regular dose in there, and Copeland substituted water for ketamine to give it a little extra kick. It was a potent shot, a shot that was designed with one purpose only.

It was a murder weapon.

But Copeland wasn't a killer, or at least not a cold-blooded killer like Lee Keyes with his trigger-happy fingers. He'd spent his professional life following the Hippocratic oath of "do no harm," but at the same time he knew that doing nothing could be the most damaging decision of all.

Still, he had no desire to kill anyone, so he thought of it as euthanasia. And for the first time since Keyes had started taking the shots when he became the facility's despot-in-chief, Copeland didn't inject him. He simply gave Keyes the syringe when he pulled the mahogany desk aside to open the office door. Then he walked away and left him to it.

***

By the time that the sun rose on Sunnyvale, Lee Keyes was dead. But his body wasn't discovered until the early evening, when some brave soul tried to take him a bowl of gruel. Even after everything he'd done, for better or worse, they were all in it together.

There was no answer when Bugsy Drew, the former operations manager, knocked on the door to MacDonald's office. He almost left it at that, but there was a nagging feeling of doubt that he couldn't shake off and so he put his fear of the gun aside and pushed his shoulder against the door, slowly at first before applying a little more force. He could hear the heavy desk groaning as it slid across the floor, taking the carpet with it.

When he saw Lee Keyes, he dropped the bowl of gruel to the floor without thinking. Then he raced over to the man's side, but it was clear he was dead just from looking at him. He had vomit down his shirt, and at some point he'd swallowed his tongue. His face had turned blue and the needle was sticking out of his arm like a flagpole. His eyes had rolled back in his head as though he was trying to see through the ceiling. His right hand was still gripped around the syringe and the rigor mortis was well and truly underway.

Drew shouted to raise the alarm and was working at pushing the desk out of the way when Big Jim arrived with Copeland and Jill MacDonald a couple of steps behind him.

"Shite," Jim said. "Ah wis hopin tae settle up with yon bawbag."

Jill MacDonald wasn't listening to him. She'd rushed over to Lee Keyes' prostrate body and had started to kick it in the head, trying to beat it to a pulp like a circus clown swinging a sledgehammer at a watermelon. Big Jim ran after her and wrapped her in a bear hug, then dragged her away from the body.

Copeland just stood in the doorway. He didn't want to go in there. He didn't want to see what his fatal shot had done to Lee Keyes. It put him in mind of the lethal injections they had at American prisons, but with less of the finesse. He still wasn't sure if he'd done the right thing, but life was cheap amongst the survivors.

Death was cheap too, and the reaper's work was far from finished at Sunnyvale. The smell of death hung heavy on the inside of the facility until Big Jim and Darragh O'Rourke scooped up Keyes' body and carried it out through the fire escape and on to the gantry before swinging it over the edge and letting it fall to the ground with a crunch.

Jill MacDonald and Tom Copeland spent most of the night out on the gantry, wrapped up in their makeshift blankets to ward off the cold. They were watching the animals as they approached the facility and started to devour the survivors' latest offering.

They felt no sympathy for the dead man. They didn't even flinch at the cracking of bones that came when one of the pigs started to chow down on his spine.

***

There were fifteen survivors left.

From the admin team, there was Jill MacDonald, the trainee receptionist and niece of the former CEO, as well as operations manager Bugsy Drew and Maude Harrison from reception, who was still acting as their head chef when they cooked their meals on the roof. Tom Copeland technically belonged to no department, but he'd been adopted as an honorary member of the admin team alongside his new role as advisor to Big Jim Benton, the unofficial leader that they'd been left with after the deaths of Lee Keyes and John MacDonald.

From the avian team, production workers Steve-o Puck and Yvonne Strong were still standing, while Janet Peston and Keith Gowan represented the pigs. Bruce Laing and Arnie Lorn remained from the sheep shed. There was no one left from the cow team.

Perhaps unsurprisingly, it was the security team that was faring best. True, Greg Hamze and Jack Dunlop had gone the way of the dodo, but Carl Taylor, Darragh O'Rourke, Mike Chase and Big Jim were still going strong.

The fifteen of them had gathered around in the empty supply room to take stock of the situation and to have an emergency discussion about what to do next.

"What happened to the supplies?" Taylor asked. He'd lost a lot of weight since being locked inside the makeshift jail cell, and his thick, bushy beard was threatening to take over his face completely.

"What supplies?" Darragh O'Rourke replied. "Lee Keyes frittered them the fuck away. We had a rationing system for a reason."

"So what are we going to do?"

"Feck knows."

There was a silence, and it wasn't comfortable. Maude Harrison had spent the time indexing what they had, and it wasn't good news.

"We've got enough food for a couple more days, maybe three if we stretch it," she said. "As for water, maybe a week or so. We'll die of thirst before we starve together, but either way, it'll be a slow death unless something changes. We need to do something."

"Agreed," Copeland said. "But what?"

"We can't wait here any longer," O'Rourke said. "If we don't make a move, we're as good as dead."

"What about the army?" someone said.

"What about them?" O'Rourke replied.

"The radio," Copeland said. "What happened to the radio?"

The last time anyone had seen it was back when MacDonald was in charge, but they had a pretty good guess of where he might have stashed it. He'd been keeping it in one of the drawers of that mahogany desk of his.

"Ah'll huv someone take a look at it," Big Jim said. "In the meantime, O'Rourke is right, ye ken. We've goat tae come up with some other plan."

The other plan consisted of getting the hell out of there, but that was easier said than done. Each of the survivors had a different idea of how to go about it, and not everyone was on board with the idea in the first place. But it was all they had.

The Sunnyvale Survivors held a second ballot, a second referendum, and this time the leave campaign came out on top. Their campaign promise was simple enough. At least if they made it out, they'd have a chance.

"If the army is still out there," O'Rourke had argued, "we'll have to take our chances against the guns. Better to die by the bullet than to starve to death."

"Tell that to my uncle," Jill MacDonald said. "Lee Keyes didn't give him the choice."

An awkward silence descended upon them, but only for a moment. Jill MacDonald was by far the youngest of the remaining survivors, and she was also the most naïve. But over the last couple of weeks, ever since the ill-fated coup and her subsequent lockup, she'd hardened. She wanted to live. The rest of them just didn't want to die.

"Why would the army shoot at us, anyway?" O'Rourke asked.

"Because we're under quarantine," Copeland replied, as though it were the most natural thing in the world and not a living nightmare. "They might think we have whatever the animals have."

"So what?"

"So what if it's contagious?" Copeland said. "What if they're licenced to terminate with extreme prejudice?"

"Ah, that's just fae the movies ye ken."

"We could try the radio?"

"We've tried the fucking radio," O'Rourke snarled. "Don't you get it? We're all alone here. For all we know, we're the only ones left. Whatever this thing is, whatever this disease or plague means and wherever the hell it came from, we can't stop it. But that doesn't mean they're not going to try. Maybe they're still holding the line out there and they're maintaining radio silence because they know that we have to die in here. Call me crazy, but I don't want to become target practise for some trigger-happy grunt with a god complex."

"Ah've made up ma mind," Big Jim said. "And unless any fucker says otherwise, ah'm also in charge, ye ken. We've goat nae choice. We'll huv tae try to reach those army bastards and if we cannae get em on the walkie talkies, we're just gonnae huv tae make a run for it. They cannae shoot us aw."

"I'm not so sure about that," Jill MacDonald said, but it was just a parting blow and a little food for thought. The decision had already been made. It was time for them to plan their escape.

THEY TRIED TO HAIL the soldiers three times that day, but they were greeted by a stifling wave of snowy static that made them feel more alone on the roof of the admin building than ever.

The animal population outside the building had thinned out, and it was anyone's guess as to where they'd ended up. Some people thought they'd escaped and broken free of the quarantine. Others thought they'd simply dropped down dead, consumed by the disease that was running through them, or that they were sating their hunger by eating each other. Most people thought that the truth was a mixture of the three.

The cold winter was over, which seemed like a good sign to the Sunnyvale Survivors. As the ground started to thaw and spring settled in, it felt like the complex was coming back to life again. Everything looked better in the sunlight, even if it still smelled like shit and death and desperation.

On the morning after the vote, eleven of the fifteen survivors were on the roof, crowding around the radio or waiting for the remaining food supplies to be cooked up in the big cauldron. They had their ears to the radio and their noses to the gruel, but none of them had turned their eyes to the sky. After all, why would they? The silence that surrounded them was a clue, but they were thinking with their stomachs and not their heads. The more perceptive amongst them might have sensed a change in the air pressure, but the suspicions were never vocalised.

So by the time they heard the rushing wings of the birds,

they were almost surrounded. They'd flown in from the north like some nightmarish migratory geese, but without the caw-cawing. It was the wings that gave them away, like a thousand leather jackets flapping in the breeze. Someone looked up and shouted "birds!", but by the time the others had followed the outstretched finger towards the sky, the birds were already upon them.

They weren't even *big* birds, but there were hundreds of them, thousands perhaps, birds of a dozen different species all flocking together into something resembling a mosquito swarm. There were robins and doves, tits and goldfinches, pigeons and blackbirds, crows and sparrows and magpies. Individually, they weren't too dangerous. Bruce Laing even swatted one out of the air like a batsman at a baseball game. But all together, they were a deadly swarm of tiny creatures with razor-sharp teeth and only one thing on their mind.

The people on the roof had no chance. Former operations manager Bugsy Drew was the first one to go down after making a break for the fire escape and the inside of the admin building. The birds swarmed him and sent him crashing to the floor, and then they pecked and pecked until his flesh was rent and he wasn't moving.

The birds around Drew formed a barrier which cut off the only escape route, and after that it was just a matter of time. The swarm worked like a single organism, as cruel as a house fire but with more intent. Maude Harrison, the former receptionist turned chef, tried to cower behind the cauldron, swiping at the birds with her spatula. Then they crashed into the cauldron and sent the boiling hot gruel-water all over her. Harrison screamed and grabbed at her clothes to try to wrench them off, but the birds attacked when her shirt was over her head and they took her down easily. She died when the birds broke through her ribcage and teased out a long line of intestine like a juicy worm.

Keith Gowan, the former pig production worker, was next. He went down swinging, armed with nothing but his fists and his anger. He swatted a half dozen birds out of the air before they swarmed him, pecking at every orifice until his eyes were gone and they'd made their way to his brain through the empty sockets. When he went down, he went back up again. They carried him away with them to the south, his body blotting the skies like a tiny aeroplane.

Next up were Bruce Laing and Arnie Lorn. In their former lives, Laing had been a production worker and Lorn had been the supervisor. There, on the roof of the admin building, there was no such hierarchy. They both died together, borne to the ground under the weight of a thousand angry birds. They were both screaming, at least until the birds broke through their throats and started pecking at their vocal chords like a flamenco guitarist moving his hands across the strings. They died slowly and in a lot of pain.

Then it was time for Carl Taylor and Mike Chase, the two youngsters from the security team. They went down standing back to back, swinging their heavy truncheons through the air and trying to bat the birds away from them. Taylor had his shirt off and his lion tattoo was poking out from his shoulder blade. He fought like one, too. They put up a good fight, but they were overwhelmed like a single survivor in a city full of crazies. There were too many of them, and every successful nip spiked their blood with a little more of the virus, the deadly cow-pig-sheep-bird-flu. Taylor died first. Mike Chase went out with his mother's name on his lips and tears running down the sockets where his eyes used to be.

Perhaps it was fitting that the birds left the former avian team until last. Steve-o Puck and Yvonne Strong had been led towards the centre of the rooftop like protestors being kettled by riot cops. The birds were circling the building like some flapping hurricane and slowly closing in on the remaining three survivors. They closed off the air above them and then came down from above, wrapping themselves in hair and pecking at faces.

The last thing they heard was the rush of thousands of tiny wings and the horrific sound of beaks clicking mechanically together.

***

Tom Copeland, Jill MacDonald, Darragh O'Rourke and Big Jim Benton were sitting in MacDonald's old office when the attack began.

Luckily, O'Rourke was standing by the door when the first shout went up and when he stepped out onto the gantry and looked up, he had just enough time to take in what had happened to Bugsy Drew before slamming the door shut.

"What's gaein on?" Jim asked.

"Feck knows," O'Rourke replied. He'd crouched down with his hands on his thighs and looked like he'd finished a marathon. "Birds. It's a battlefield out there."

"Should we help them?" That came from Jill MacDonald, whose face had a lot more colour. But she hadn't seen the birds.

O'Rourke shook his head. "We can't," he said. "We need to save ourselves. We need to cover the windows."

"What with?"

"Whatever we've got," O'Rourke said.

"We'd better do it quickly," Copeland said. He looked doubtfully around the room. MacDonald had played a role in the design of the place, and he'd insisted on putting in big bay windows, which were great for keeping an eye on the facility but far from ideal when defending oneself against an army of rabid birds.

"We've goat tae get back," Jim shouted. "The wee laddies' room, ye ken."

"The what?" Jill asked.

"The men's bathroom," Copeland said, understanding creeping in on top of the chaos. "The only place with no windows."

"Aye," Jim said. "And two sets of doors tae get in there. Grab what ye can carry."

And so the final four survivors fled deeper into the admin building, grabbing the last of their food supplies and as much of the water as they could carry.

They heard the first smash of glass when they were having one final sweep for their essentials. That was followed by the unmistakable sound of wildlife in a human habitat, the crashing and banging of John MacDonald's office getting trashed as the birds breached the facility from the air.

"Faster!" Jim shouted, but it was hardly necessary.

There was another crash, this time from somewhere a little closer, and then Jim was racing along the corridor to the defunct men's bathroom and the noise was getting closer, and then suddenly the birds were in the corridor, too. Big Jim heard them there, but he didn't dare to turn around. Instead, he lowered his head and charged at the double doors that led to the bathroom, hoping to high hell that the others were already inside. He hit the doors at a run and burst into the bathroom, then immediately turned and ran back at the door. He hit it with a thump that snapped it closed like the lid of a box, and not a moment too soon.

The cloud of birds hit the door with all the force of a rugby player, but Big Jim had been a prop for Glasgow Hawks RFC and he was no stranger to the sensation. He dug his feet into the tiled floor and pushed back at it, and then he felt movement behind him and Darragh O'Rourke was there too, and so were Tom Copeland and Jill MacDonald. They'd made it, then.

"Goddamn fucken birds!" Jim shouted. "Ave that, ya cunts."

The feathery onslaught continued for several hours. By the time that the siege was over, their muscles were so tired that they could barely move them. They were eventually able to break down the doors of the cubicles and to use them to create wooden struts that wedged the door shut. Shortly afterwards, when even Big Jim couldn't push against the door any longer and he let go, the struts held.

That left them with another problem. They could still hear wings flapping in the corridor that connected the toilets with the rest of the building, and they could hear more birds beyond those, a distant but fuller sound like a freight train gliding across the rails.

"Ah hate tae say it, ye ken," Big Jim said, "but ah reckon wir in fae a long night."

***

It turned out that they were in for a long two days. Throughout those two days, the noise of the birds inside the building never let up, and the remaining four survivors passed the time by telling stories about their old world, the real world, which they'd left behind half a lifetime ago when they'd clocked in for what they'd thought was just another shift.

By the time that the echoes of the flapping wings had died down, they were out of food and almost out of water. They'd waited a little longer than they would have liked, just to make sure that there weren't any stragglers, and then they cautiously removed the struts, snapping them in half to turn them into rudimentary baseball bats, and peered out into the connecting corridor.

They had to fight their way through a carpet of corpses, hundreds upon hundreds of birds that lined the floor like a second carpet. When they first opened the door to the bathroom, the bodies spilled in through the gap. And when they walked across the carpet of birds, they shifted and snapped beneath their feet. One of the birds, a crow, was still moving, but then Darragh O'Rourke kicked it in the beak and its neck snapped.

"Careful now," he murmured, but it wasn't clear who it was addressed to.

The rest of the complex told a similar story. There were dead birds everywhere, and every now and then they'd find one with a little life left in it and reduce it to a bloody smear with some swift justice from their two-by-fours. Broken glass was everywhere, and the entire building was under a carpet of shit that reeked of ammonia. Most of the windows were smashed, but so was almost everything else. The admin building had reeked before the birds, but now it was inhospitable. They had to hold their hands over their mouths and fight their way around the complex by going from broken window to broken window, breathing in the outside air and wincing at the taste of it. It tasted like death and disease, but at least it didn't taste like bird shit.

The four survivors made their way to the top floor and into John MacDonald's office. The big bay windows had been obliterated and his mahogany desk had somehow been pushed across the room and out of the gap in the wall, where it had tumbled down to the ground below and landed on top of the skeleton that had once been Greg Hamze, the former security officer.

They walked out onto the gantry and up on to the roof, scanning the sky for any tell-tale signal that might herald the return of the birds. But it was ominously quiet, with no sign of life above or below. The clouds had cleared, and the sun was making its presence known. It was warm up there, and the warmth crept into their bones and gave them new life. It was comforting like a hot bath, but they couldn't relax too much. Not with what they were looking at.

The roof of the admin building looked like a Halloween display at a village fayre. Copeland counted eight skeletons to begin with, and then he saw a ninth. Worse, he could recognise them by the rags that were still flapping in the wind. He saw young Mike Chase, the junior security guard who'd started at Sunnyvale at the same time he had. His skeleton was only recognisable because it was wearing a leather belt with a truncheon on it. Maude Harrison's corpse was still wearing her prim black shoes. A couple of millimetres of flesh was sticking out of the leather and holding on to her ankle bone, but the rest of her clothes had disappeared, torn away with her skin by the birds.

Everything that the birds hadn't taken had been exposed to the wind and the rain, and the entire roof had been blanketed in guano. The four survivors walked through the carnage in a daze. Big Jim spotted something glittering amongst the bird shit and bent down to pick it up. He held it up to the light and examined it. It was Carl Taylor's ID badge.

Jim swore and put the badge into his pocket. Over to his right, Jill MacDonald was throwing up into the food cauldron. Copeland bent down and rubbed her back. And Darragh O'Rourke was standing on the gantry, watching them all from a distance, ready to run back inside at the first sign of any trouble.

"What the hell happened?" O'Rourke asked, demanding it of the group as though they owed him an answer.

"Ah huv nae idea."

"Those birds weren't raised at Sunnyvale," Copeland said. "If they were infected, the disease has spread even farther than I thought was possible."

"They had the disease," O'Rourke said. "They must have done. That's why they were trying to kill us."

"But why attack now?"

"Why not?"

"Whae cares?" Jim said, spitting on the guano and scowling at the others. "We've goat tae get outta here."

***

Meanwhile, in the burrows and the tunnels beneath the facility, the Rat King was moving through the shadows. The death and destruction seemed to have given it a new energy, and it scampered along in the darkness killing everything in its sight, from little worms and snails to rats and mice and even a mole that was disturbed in its sleep by the pitter-pattering of the Rat King's tiny claws.

Each kill strengthened him, each drop of blood helped to replenish it as though each of the rats drew its strength from the others. The Rat King made no logical, biological sense, but it would never be dissected inside a laboratory or studied from behind glass in a public zoo. It just *was*.

And as the weather grew warmer above ground, the Rat King retreated further beneath the soil, navigating by instinct as its tails tightened around each other and it tried to pull itself apart.

And when it found the right spot, the Rat King laid its many heads down. It shifted slightly, its wriggling mass dancing nightmarishly beneath the surface of the earth.

It closed its many eyes.

And it prepared to sleep.

***

It was raining, but with the admin building trashed and the complex surrounded by the meaty fug of decaying flesh and covered with more guano than Crab Key, the rain was a relief.

Tom Copeland, Jill MacDonald, Darragh O'Rourke and Big Jim Benton were sitting in the remains of MacDonald's old office and looking out through the remains of the bay window to the north of the complex. They told themselves they were scanning the ground to figure out how many animals were left, but they spent most of their time with their eyes on the skies in case the birds came back.

"Ah reckon it's time," Jim said. The others turned to look at him and nodded. He looked tired and battle-worn, but he also looked ready.

"Let's do it," Jill whispered.

Jim led the way down to the first-floor stairwell, which they'd barricaded many moons ago when the quarantine first hit. Perhaps ironically, it was the deepest part of the admin building and had been the least hit by the birds. There were just a half dozen corpses dotted across the room, and much of the dust was still undisturbed. As per their new, unspoken protocol, Big Jim and Darragh O'Rourke went round with their truncheons and gave each of the corpses a couple of swipes. Little love taps to make sure they weren't going to move again.

It took them several hours to clear the rubble away, partly because they were trying to be quiet. They had no visibility to the front of the building and no way of knowing what they'd find on the other side, and it had been a hell of a lot easier to fill the gap with broken desks and computers than it was to drag them back out. But by sundown, they'd cleared enough room to crawl through, and Darragh

O'Rourke had made a couple of trips outside to check the lay of the land.

"It's now or never," he said. "Looks like they're all to the north. Lining the banks of the lake. I guess it's their only access to water."

"It'll be our only access to water too, if we don't get out of here," Copeland said.

"Then let's git gaein," Jim said.

Big Jim himself went first, barely squeezing through the narrow tunnel that they'd created without popping an eye out on some low-hanging strip of metal. Copeland went next, closely followed by Jill MacDonald. O'Rourke brought up the rear and walked backwards so he could keep his eyes on the animals.

But the night was quiet. As they walked across the no man's land, it quickly became apparent why that was. Most of the animals were dead, and many of them had been dead for some time. As they made their way south to the facility's perimeter, they found themselves constantly picking their way through carcasses or involuntarily jumping aside after a corpse moved. But it always turned out to be just the maggots in a festering wound, dancing on the dead skin as they sheared it away from the bone.

Big Jim killed a dying sheep with a blow to the head when it dared to raise it to look at them, and Darragh O'Rourke smashed a chicken's skull to pieces. Other than that, they were mostly left alone as they ran towards the car park. The main threat was getting further and further behind them and the skies were mercifully clear of birds.

But perhaps the birds weren't the biggest problem. They still had a perimeter to break through, and there was no telling what was waiting for them on the outside. There had been no contact from the army, but what did that prove?

"When we get tae ma car," Big Jim had said, "you're

gonnae want tae strap yeself in. Thir might be bullets, ye ken. Ah might huvtae make defensive manoeuvres."

If the gods existed then they were smiling on them, and the survivors made it to Big Jim's car without incident. It was the same Vauxhall Corsa that Copeland had been in when he'd first entered the complex.

Jim still had his key and the central locking still worked, so when he popped it in the lock and twisted it, the doors opened. They got into the car with Big Jim in the driver's seat and Darragh O'Rourke riding shotgun. Jill MacDonald and Tom Copeland were in the back.

In the driver's seat, Jim slid the key into the ignition and twisted it. The engine whined and tried to sputter into life, but it wouldn't catch. He tried again but no dice. He had no luck on the third or fourth attempt, either.

"Shite!" Jim shouted, hammering his fist into the steering wheel. It set the horn off, and the unnatural sound echoed out across the facility, breaking the silence and scaring the crap out of Copeland and Jill MacDonald in the back seat.

"What's wrong with it?" O'Rourke asked.

Jim glanced down at the array of dials on the dashboard in front of him. "Ah dunno," he admitted. "Ah've goat a tank full aw petrol, ye ken."

"Must be the battery."

"Aye," Jim said. "Auld Greg Hamze drove a Corsa an aww."

Big Jim was about to say something else, but he was interrupted by a shout from the back seat. Copeland and Jill MacDonald were still sitting side by side and staring out of the window, but they weren't just looking at nothing. There was something out there, something hungry that was watching them.

"What is it?" Jim shouted.

Jill MacDonald tried to say something, but the fear had taken her words away. Tom Copeland had turned a deathly pale, but enough of his nerve remained for him to make his voice heard. It shook as he spoke.

"It's the bull," Copeland said. "And it's heading straight for us."

THE ESCAPE

THE BULL WAS WATCHING THEM.

Jim turned the key in the ignition again, but the car wouldn't whine into life and he cursed it out.

"What the fuck are we gonna do?"

"We need a distraction," O'Rourke said.

"What kind of distraction?"

"I have no idea."

Jim tried the engine again and it ticked over but still didn't catch. "Mebbe it's just cold, ye ken."

"Maybe."

"Try it again."

Jim tried again. For a second, it seemed like it was going to work, but then the car died and it took their hope with it.

"It's moving," Copeland said, and Big Jim glanced in the mirror and saw that the vet was telling the truth. The bull had inched a little closer and now stood maybe thirty or forty yards away from them.

It was a hellish creature, and it seemed taller and bulkier than ever. Perhaps it had been feeding on the smaller animals and growing uninhibited with the Sunnyvale virus coursing through its veins and forcing it to fly or fight. But the bull didn't fly.

It was a huge, heavy beast, at least as tall as a man, with wide, muscular shoulders and horns so long that they looked like rapiers and swooshed through the air when it swung its great head from side to side. It had red eyes. When it looked at the car, it seemed to see straight through it and to alight on the people inside it. When it breathed, its great stomach gulped in and out and flashed glimpses of its massive ribcage. When it exhaled, its breath steamed out of its nostrils in a cloud of vapour that made it look like it was on fire.

"Hurry up," Copeland said. "Do something."

"Ah'm fucken tryin," Jim growled. He twisted the key in the ignition again, and the engine spluttered and coughed into life. It petered out again. "Goddammit!"

The bull was running now, its sinewy legs picking up momentum as it ploughed towards them like a runaway freight train. Jim twisted the key again and this time the engine kept running.

"Ya fuckin beauty!"

But the bull was barely ten yards away, and even though Jim slammed the vehicle into reverse, there just wasn't enough time. The bull ploughed into the passenger side door and caved it in towards Darragh O'Rourke's face, and then Jill MacDonald started screaming, Jim yanked hard at the steering wheel and the car started to spin out of control.

There was a horrible wrenching as Jim shifted gears and the car started to accelerate.

"Hold on tae ye hats!" Jim shouted.

He tugged on the steering wheel again and the battered car swung to its left. The tyres couldn't get much grip on the mud and the grass and for a brief, horrible moment, they couldn't find any purchase. But then the tyres bit and the car lurched forwards and raced at the bull. The bull turned to look at them and tried to charge, but it didn't have time.

The Corsa clipped the bull on one of its shoulders and sent it crashing to the ground, where it rolled over a couple of times before trying to pull itself upright again. The bonnet of the car was torn off as one of the beast's horns punctured the metal and pulled away with it. It left the engine exposed, but it didn't block Big Jim's view as he spun the wounded

Corsa around. The bull was behind them, momentarily stunned but not mortally wounded, and it was already starting to drag itself to its feet.

"Floor it!" someone shouted.

Jim didn't need telling twice. He hit the accelerator and pushed the vehicle as hard as he dared, knowing that if the engine cut out then it'd spell the end for all of them.

Jim drove to the south, out into no man's land, expecting a hail of bullets or some sort of incendiary device from the soldiers behind the checkpoint. He was clenching his teeth so hard that one of his fillings popped out, but he didn't notice. He had more important things on his mind than dental hygiene.

Behind them, the bull had climbed to its feet, but they had a head start and even as it started to run, they pulled further away from it. Jim had got the vehicle up to forty, but they were going cross country and he didn't dare to push it any harder. He glanced into the rear-view at the bull, which was picking up speed and kicking up big clods of earth.

"Think we can leave it behind?" Copeland asked.

"No," Jim replied.

The second checkpoint was ahead of them, and Jim turned the car to point towards it. There were still no bullets, and now they were a little closer, they could also see that there was no sign of life. It didn't surprise them.

"Haud on to yer heids!" Jim shouted. Then he tugged the steering wheel to the right and the Corsa drifted on to the road. As soon as the tyres gripped the asphalt, Jim changed gear and pushed the engine harder. They raced towards the checkpoint like a jousting knight in a tournament, and then they hit the wooden barrier, tore it off and crashed through the chain-link fence on the other side. Something hit the windscreen and shattered it on the passenger's side, sending a shower of glass over Darragh

O'Rourke as he flung his hands up to cover his eyes. Then the air bag deployed and hit Jim in the stomach, crushing the air out of him and cutting off the stream of expletives that were falling from his mouth like rotten apples from a tree.

They were on the other side of the barrier at last, finally free of the quarantine that had confined them to the complex. But they were also sitting in a totalled Vauxhall Corsa. And the bull was racing across no man's land towards them.

***

Big Jim was the first one out of the car. Darragh O'Rourke got out second and busied himself with helping Tom Copeland and Jill MacDonald out of the back. Copeland had seen the bull coming and panicked, and the door on Jill's side was buckled and impossible to open. By the time he'd dragged them out of the vehicle and on to the grass, a lick of flame was visible from the Corsa's engine and Big Jim was nowhere to be seen.

The bull, meanwhile, was a quarter mile away and closing.

Darragh O'Rourke looked around in a panic and then pointed a little further along the dirt road out of Sunnyvale towards the army vehicles and their blockade. "That way," he shouted.

And so the three of them started to run, their feet pounding the dirt as they raced further south with the bull to their backs. But the bull was faster than them and it was getting closer. They could hear the thumping sound of its hooves beating the floor. They sounded like the sandworms of Arrakis or some gargantuan monster from a Wellsian sci-fi novel.

And then suddenly Big Jim was running towards them

with a machine gun in his hands. He was shouting something that they couldn't hear, but they got the message all right. The three of them forked slightly to the right to get out of his line of fire, and Big Jim dropped to the ground with his shiny machinegun. It was mounted on a tripod, which Jim jammed into the ground before swinging the barrel around and pointing it towards the bull. It was barely 150 yards away, well within the weapon's range.

Big Jim thought back to his days in their makeshift firing range on an abandoned plot of land in Paisley. Those had been during his dangerous younger days, when he'd found himself rubbing shoulders with Irish dissidents in some of the sketchier bars along the coast. He'd spent a couple of nights in the hills with their heavy weaponry. Most of those guys were in jail now, but Big Jim wasn't. He was free, or as free as he could be when he was breaking out of a quarantine, and he wasn't about to let the bull take that newfound freedom away.

He clicked the safety off and began to fire, not in a random rain of bullets but in the short, sharp bursts he'd been told to use if he ever needed to. Big bloody blooms exploded out of the bull's right shoulder. It was close enough that Jim could see the steam coming out of the wound. But it didn't slow down on its approach and it was only fifty yards or so away and closing.

"Ave that ya fucken bastard!"

Jim fired again, and this time he hit the beast in the neck and tore away part of the throat, but the bull still kept coming and then from their right there was a huge bang and then a strip of fire flew out of the downed Vauxhall Corsa. The windows blew out and then the broken rear door flew off and hit the bull in the side of the head. Part of the lining fell off and attached itself to its back, still burning like embers in a fireplace. But the bull kept coming.

It was twenty yards away. Fifteen. Ten.

A bead of sweat rolled down Big Jim's forehead and into his eye, but he didn't have time to wipe it away. The bull was in his sights and he squeezed the trigger again. This time, he hit his mark.

The bullets hit the bull square in the face and tore half of its skull out. The light died behind its eyes at the same moment that they were torn from the back of its skull. But still its momentum carried it forwards, and Jim realised it was too late to get out of the way. Instead, he curled up in a ball on the floor and tried to protect his head as the beast continued to thunder forwards.

He held his breath.

And the bull passed over him.

It caught Big Jim in the shoulder and a hoof hit him in the lower back, but he came out okay. He pulled himself up to his feet and turned around. The bull was dead at last, its head ploughed onto the ground like some sort of meaty plant.

The Scotsman raised both of his arms in the air and threw his head back. He looked up at the sky and laughed. Then he pulled his utility knife from his pocket and flipped it over. He hobbled over towards the bull just as fast as his legs could manage, which wasn't too fast considering he was barely standing upright. But he made it to the bull's side and examined the carcass.

"Fucken wee beastie's still breathin," he murmured.

Then he approached it from behind. In one swift movement, he grabbed the remnants of the thing's head and wrenched it back before slicing the blade through its jugular. Foul blood spilled out of it, smelling like offal or diseased meat as it did so. The beast shook and Jim backed away from it, but it was just the final death throes of the bull, the biggest animal on the complex.

"Halal, motherfucker," Jim said.

Then he ran off to join the others.

**

By the time Big Jim caught up with them, they were standing in the middle of the army barricade and surveying the scene with horror. It didn't take him long to figure out what they were looking at.

"Shite," he said. "Nae wonder they didnae answer the radio."

The four survivors were standing in the middle of a crimson patch in the cola-brown soil. There were no bodies around, or none that they could see, but some sort of viscera – perhaps a liver or a small intestine – lay curled on the floor like a punctuation mark. It had rotted in the sunlight and been nibbled at by some sort of rodent.

Jim had seen the worst of the damage already, of course. That was where he'd found the machine gun, which he'd left lying in the mud after emptying it of ammo. Now that he was back in the encampment, he started to look around again for something, some weapon he could use.

"Where is everyone?" Copeland asked.

"Where d'ya think?" O'Rourke replied.

"Ah'm more worried about maself, ye ken," Big Jim said. "Am ah gonnae git tha fucken mad animals disease now ah've goat up close an personal wi' yon beasties?"

"I have no idea, Jim," Copeland said, pinching the bridge of his nose and looking like a stressed-out schoolteacher. "None of us have shown any symptoms."

"Yeah," O'Rourke murmured, "but none of us have gone toe to toe with the bull before."

"We have no idea how this virus works," Copeland said. "Let's hope that casual contact isn't enough to spread it."

"Ah fuck it aww," Big Jim said, spitting a little blood to the floor. "Ah'm goan f'ra lookabout."

The three survivors stuck closely to Jim's back as he wound his way through the abandoned vehicles and in and out of the temporary tents. It looked like they'd left in a hurry. They found some standard-issue rations in the second tent and immediately opened the packs and started to pass them around. They were dry and tasteless, but to the four Sunnyvale survivors they tasted like cakes and cookies. They even found some bottled water to wash it down with.

"So what's the plan?"

The question was posed by Jill MacDonald, but it had been weighing heavily on all of their minds. They all knew that they didn't have one.

"We need another vehicle," O'Rourke said.

"Aye," Jim replied. "Ah saw a couple o' those big jeeps outside, ye ken. Ah'm lookin' fae the keys."

"We could hotwire it," Copeland suggested.

"Oh aye, and whae's gonnae do it? You?"

"I thought–"

"Aye, ah ken what ye thought," Jim said. "Ah cannae jimmy an army truck, mind. Thir designed fae security. Wir gonnae need the key."

"And where are we going to find that?"

Big Jim shrugged. "Fuck knows," he said.

Jill MacDonald had been quiet throughout most of the discussion, but then she raised her head and asked the obvious question.

"Where is everyone?" she asked. "It's creeping me out."

"If there was anyone here, we'd all be dead," O'Rourke said. "We broke the quarantine. We're better off without them."

"Yeah," Copeland said. "But what if we're not the first to break the quarantine? What if the animals broke out?"

"Could explain why no one's here," O'Rourke said. "This place is like a ghost town. Maybe they were overrun."

"So what are we going to do?"

"Wir gonnae keep searchin'," Big Jim said. "Wir gonnae turn this place over until we find somethin'."

And so they hunted around the checkpoint for whatever they could find. But they'd learned from the past, and so they grouped together instead of splitting up, using the back of an empty lorry as their base of operations. It wouldn't offer them much protection in the event of another bird attack, but it was better than being caught out in the open.

It was Copeland who found the body. There wasn't much left of it, just bones and clothes and some foul-smelling murk that coated it all with a sticky residue. He was so distracted by the sight of the thing that he forgot to warn the others until it was too late and he'd been jerked out of his reverie by the retching sound of someone vomiting. He turned around, expecting it to be Jill MacDonald, but the young girl had seen enough by now to hold her lunch in. The vomit belonged to Darragh O'Rourke, and the Irishman made no effort to hide it. He spewed again, the foul-smelling stomach acid splashing on his shoes and looking like the murk inside the army uniform.

"You all right, buddy?" Copeland asked.

Darragh O'Rourke didn't reply, but Big Jim braved the stench and leaned a little closer to inspect the uniform. There was a name on it, which he read aloud.

"Runciman," he said. "Huh. It figures. Guess their quarantine didn't hold after all."

"But if the quarantine didn't hold," Copeland said, "then what happened to the animals?"

"Ah dinnae fucken care," Big Jim said. "Leave Runciman be. Eh's nae gonnae help us now, ye ken."

"Should we bury him?"

"We dinnae have time."

But they *did* have time to keep searching.

The next tent that they looked into was empty, but the one after that was a medical tent. They found a heap of bones wrapped around the tattered shreds of a medic's uniform, but there was surprisingly little stench. Most of the flesh had been torn off and carried away before it had chance to rot. Jill MacDonald stood outside with Big Jim beside her, even though the air outside was almost as bad. But Copeland took some time to bustle around the room, checking packs and crates and grabbing everything he thought would come in handy. There were fewer provisions than there had been back at Sunnyvale, but these were for people and not animals.

In the end, he filled his bag with hypodermics, gauze, antibiotics and opiates, as well as sanitiser, antihistamines and everything else he could get his hands on. He nodded at O'Rourke, who was watching his back with one hand on his truncheon. He looked tired, tired enough to fall asleep on his feet and to collapse in the dust. Copeland thought about slipping him some amphetamines and decided against it. They might need them later.

The rest of the tents had little to offer them, although they found some food and water and in one of the crates there was a change of clothes. They were standard issue army outfits and not the most comfortable of items, but they were clean and that was a luxury. They changed inside the tent, all of them too jaded and tired to worry about privacy, and Jill MacDonald packed a second set of clothes and wore a third shirt around her waist.

Then they found some weaponry inside one of the armoured cars. Judging from the amount of blood inside the vehicles, the armour hadn't done them much good. It reminded Copeland of Sunnyvale's abattoir. But inside one of the things, Big Jim had found a couple of shotguns, three handguns and even a taser, although he wasn't convinced it would have much of an effect.

"Ah dunnae ken if ye've fired a gun before," he said. "But we've no goat the ammo to waste, ye ken. Ah'll teach ye what ah can and make sure ye've all goat a weapon. But ah don't want tae hear any shots unless it's life or death. An' if ye do have tae shoot, shoot for tha heid."

There were no arguments. Even Darragh O'Rourke, a working-class kid from the outskirts of Belfast, had no prior experience of firearms. As for Tom Copeland and Jill MacDonald, holding the weaponry felt as alien as a convict nursing a baby.

"As fae the taser," Jim said, "wir up against a half tonne of cow, ye ken. Ye might as well hit it with a shoe."

They were two vehicles away from the end of their search when they hit the jackpot. It was the locker room, but the lockers were weak and no match for a skilled Scotsman. Big Jim worked his way along the locks, popping the things with his pocket knife, and Darragh O'Rourke followed behind him, rifling through their contents for anything that might be of use.

He whistled softly and pulled two fruit-shaped objects from behind a stack of porn magazines. He held them up to the light, which was currently being provided by Big Jim's torch.

"Holy fucken shite," Jim said. "Grenades. Nice."

"Know how to use 'em?" O'Rourke asked.

"Pssht. Accourse. Pull the pin and chuck it at the fucken animaws."

"That's what I thought," O'Rourke said. "All right, I'll take one, you take the other."

"Ah just hope tae shite they fucken work."

The rest of the lockers were disappointingly empty

except for the last one, which contained four hundred cigarettes and a half dozen boxes of matches.

"Jackpot," O'Rourke murmured, slitting the cellophane and helping himself to a smoke.

"They're bad for you, you know," Copeland said.

The rest of the encampment was conspicuously quiet, as devoid of life as a morgue. There were corpses all over the place, mostly of animals, but even the flies were staying away. In the distance, from the direction of the compound, they heard the occasional lowing or the clucking of disturbed birds, but here, through the gap in the perimeter, there was nothing.

They met up by the empty lorry. Copeland and Jill MacDonald perched themselves on the end of the vehicle itself, while Big Jim and Darragh O'Rourke stayed standing, constantly surveying the horizon for whatever the next threat would be.

"What do we do next?" Copeland asked. "We could use a vehicle."

"Aye, we could," Jim said. "But fae the vehicles tae move, we need the keys, ye ken."

"We've looked everywhere," Jill MacDonald said. "If the keys were here, we would've found them."

"Maybe we didn't look hard enough," O'Rourke said, and he was about to say something else when he was shushed by Big Jim, who was holding one of his hairy palms in the air for silence.

"Quiet," he whispered. His voice was hoarse and the sound was harsh, but it did the job. They all turned to see what he was looking at. "Somethin's moving."

AT FIRST, they could only hear it.

It was an unnatural sound, recognisable as movement but not as the movement of anything that any of them had previously come across. It was a shuffling, lurching, meaty sound, like the sound of carcasses smacking against each other on the production line. It was a sound from hell.

All four of them drew their weapons, even Jill MacDonald. Copeland noticed that her hand was steadier than his own, although both of them had the contracted pupils and the tell-tale sweat of a salty fear, the kind that comes from a nightmare and stays long after the lights are on.

"What the fuck?"

"Ah've goat nae fuckin clue."

Tom Copeland and Jill MacDonald hopped down from the back of the lorry and the four of them stepped around to the side of it. They stood with their backs to it, scanning their field of vision for whatever hellish creature the noise was coming from.

"Ah cain't see shit," Jim whispered.

The noise was closer now, the meaty *thwap-thwap-thwap* sound merging with the rustling of the long grass. It got closer still, and the four of them pressed their backs even tighter against the vehicle. Copeland was scanning the skies just in case, but there was no sign of the birds that had rained death on the admin building.

Then Jill shrieked and fell to the ground, and the three men reacted on instinct.

Big Jim was the first to drop down beside her, and he

was the first to see the wizened hand that was wrapped around her ankle, digging its muck-ridden fingernails deep into her flesh. The arm was connected to a shoulder, the shoulder was connected to a body, and the body was wearing a British Army uniform. But it was the teeth that stood out, and it was the teeth that had been making the noise they'd been hearing. The man was catatonic, only the whites of his eyes showing, and he was gnashing at the air like an old man without dentures trying to swallow down a gallon of ice cream. His features were stretched across his face in a demonic leer, and it was Copeland, who was third to the ground, who voiced the unspoken thought.

"He's dead," he said.

Big Jim grunted, his hand stretching to his waist and pulling out the baton. O'Rourke was down too, and he saved Jill MacDonald's life by sweeping a hand across and knocking Copeland's arm away a split second before he pulled the trigger.

"You'll hit the girl!" O'Rourke shouted. His voice echoed out eerily across the grassland, but they didn't spare a thought for what might have been listening in. They didn't have time.

Big Jim swung his baton down and it connected with the outstretched arm in a sickening crunch. He brought it down again and something snapped. The arm fell loose and Jill scrambled away from it. Jim swung the baton again, this time at the dead thing's face. It exploded in a shower of blood and bone.

"Ah should be in Georgia playin' basebaw," Jim said.

There was silence for a second. Then they all started talking at once.

"What the fuck is going on?"

"Did ya see tha' fucken swing?"

"We should get out of here."

"His heid exploded!"

"Quiet!"

They all went silent.

It was Darragh O'Rourke who'd called for silence, but he was calling for it on behalf of Jill MacDonald. She'd slumped to the ground once more amidst the hubbub. She'd gone pale and her skin was clammy to the touch.

"Are you all right, Jill?" Copeland asked. He knelt in to take her vitals.

"He grabbed hold of me," she kept repeating. "He grabbed hold of me."

"But he was dead," Copeland said. "He had to be."

"Unless maybe he wasn't," O'Rourke said. "Maybe he was infected. Like the animals."

Another silence descended upon them as they considered it. The idea of the infection spreading wasn't the issue. The bigger question was what it would mean if it turned out to be the truth.

"We'll have tae figure it out as we go along," Jim said. Then he got down on his knees and leaned a little closer to the body. He patted it down and checked its pockets, then came up grinning with something shiny in his hands. "Well lookie here. Ah've found a set o' keys. Now ah just need tae see which of yon motors it fits."

***

The key belonged to a Range Rover with a camo job, but it took them the best part of an hour to figure that out. When they tried it on one of the cars, it set the alarm off. Big Jim had to reach inside the bonnet and cut cables at random with his pocket knife until the sound died out and the echoes faded away. But eventually they tried the Range Rover. When Jim slipped the key into the door and twisted the lock, the door popped open.

"Success!" he said. "At fucken last."

"We're not out of trouble yet," O'Rourke said. "Check the engine."

Big Jim grunted, hitched himself up into the driver's seat and slid the key into the ignition. He twisted it and the engine whirred, but it wouldn't catch. He tried again, but still no dice.

Jim cursed and popped the bonnet, then hopped back out on to the floor. He ran round to the front of the vehicle and looked inside. He didn't know a lot about cars, but he knew enough to check the basics. The oil needed topping up and the fuel was low, but he couldn't see anything that was obviously wrong or out of place.

"Gimme a hand," he said, gesturing to Copeland. O'Rourke was hanging back with Jill MacDonald, who was sitting in the back of the lorry and refusing to put her feet anywhere near the ground.

So Copeland gave him a hand, and between the two of them, they managed to syphon fuel from the lorry and into a water bottle. It was a long, laborious task, or at least that was how it felt, but they managed to half-fill the tank in twenty minutes or so.

"If we get her running, we'd better fill the rest of the tank as soon as we get out of here," Copeland said.

Big Jim nodded and said nothing, already preoccupied with the next task. They didn't have the equipment they'd need to drain the oil from one vehicle to put it in another, and anyway, Copeland reasoned, that risked polluting the engine with dirty oil. In the end, they took the brute force approach, breaking the windows of vehicles at random until they found a half-empty bottle of motor oil in a glove compartment.

They had the engine running like a charm barely five

minutes after that, and once it turned over a couple of times it settled back down into a steady thrum.

"It's a good job the battery still had some juice in it," Copeland said. "Are we moving?"

"Aye," Jim said. "All aboard."

O'Rourke called shotgun and Copeland helped Jill into the back before hoisting himself in beside her. Jim was about to gun the engine again when O'Rourke grabbed his shoulder and whispered, "Do you hear that?"

There was a pause as all four of them strained their ears and tried to listen. The noise was getting louder, a little closer now, close enough for them to tell what it was. It was the thundering of thousands of feet hitting the floor, the rattling of meat and bones as forelegs bit into the turf and sent big chunks of mud and grass flying through the air. It was the sound of a stampede and it was heading towards them.

"Shite," Jim said, slamming the car door and twisting the key in the ignition. "We've goat tae get out of here."

They couldn't see the animals, but they didn't need to. It was enough just to know they were there and that they were moving a little closer with every second that passed.

Jim gunned the engine and swung the car around, executing a messy three-point turn until its nose was pointing south. Then he eased into the accelerator and they took off across the country.

Copeland caught a glimpse of the animals in the driver-side mirror. He could see the dust now, and he could also see the shapes of a couple of the larger animals.

They'd passed through the gap in the first perimeter and were swarming their way across no man's land.

***

Big Jim drove south.

It wasn't really a road that they were on. It was more like a narrow dirt path leading away from the complex. The dust flew up in the air around them as the car thundered along the ground, but the larger dust cloud was behind them and somehow still gaining, even though Jim was pushing the needle.

They hit fifty and then sixty, but Jim didn't dare to push it any further. Their vehicle was designed to go off-road, but Jim was intimately familiar with the potholes on the route out of Sunnyvale. He was worried that he'd have to put the machine to a real test, cutting across a field and through a hedgerow.

Slowly but surely, the animals in the rear-view mirror started to drop away, but then Big Jim swore and adjusted course and all four of them turned their heads to look to the vehicle's left. There were more animals, a whole army of sheep and pigs and cows who were running at full pelt across the countryside.

"Shite!" Jim repeated. "They're fucken aww ower the place."

"Those are from Sunnyvale," Copeland said. "They must have broken their way out while we were under siege in the admin building."

"Doesn't matter where they're from," Jill said. "They'll kill us all the same if we don't get out of here."

"Ah'm oan it," Jim said, but then he swore again. There were more animals to the right of them. They were funnelling through the trees and spreading back out again. "Thir fucken everywhir."

"We can't outrun them," Copeland said. "They're going to cut us off."

"Between a rock and a hard place," O'Rourke murmured.

"What are we going to do?"

"Stop the car," O'Rourke said. Big Jim glanced across at him from the driver's seat with a look of disbelief plastered across his face like propaganda on the wall of a Second World War tube station. "I said stop the car!"

"You crazy?" Jim shouted. But he did as O'Rourke asked, hitting the brakes so hard that Tom Copeland flew forward and bashed his chin against the back of the driver's seat.

"Get out of the car," O'Rourke shouted. His hands flew to his side and he unbuckled his seatbelt and drew his gun before any of them knew what was happening. "I don't have time to explain. Get out of the car and keep running."

"Darragh," Jill whispered, her voice hoarse and raspy from long-term dehydration. She sounded thirty years older than she actually was. "What is this?"

"Go!" he shouted. Then he pointed his gun towards the ceiling and fired off a warning shot. In the close quarters of the car, it sounded like an old naval ship had just been hit by a pirate's cannonball, and the acrid stench of the gunpowder smelled like hell itself. It was somehow worse than the reek of shit from the pigs and sheep back at Sunnyvale.

The other three survivors scuttled out of the car, Jill MacDonald pausing for a moment to help Copeland with his seatbelt. The discharge had brought back memories of John MacDonald being shot in the face by Lee Keyes, both men now dead and feeding the pigs and the chickens. O'Rourke shifted himself into the driver's seat and then put the vehicle into gear.

"What's he doing?" Jill shouted.

"Shite knows," Jim replied. "Fuck him. We've goat tae get outta here."

And so they fled on foot, with Big Jim leading the way and Tom Copeland and Jill MacDonald a half step behind

him while in the distance, Darragh O'Rourke turned the car
around and drove it back towards the north.

***

Darragh O'Rourke reached over and turned the radio
dial, but there was only static. He cursed and reached into
the glovebox, looking for some tunes to go out on, but all he
could find was an unmarked CD. It would have to do.

He put the CD into the dashboard and skipped through
a couple of the tracks. He settled on Erasure and turned his
attention back to the task at hand.

O'Rourke had slowed the vehicle to a stop in the middle
of the field, but he hadn't bothered to engage the handbrake.
He reached into his pocket and pulled out a pack of
cigarettes. Then he unwrapped the foil, put a cigarette
between his lips and lit it with one of his matches.

He looked out of the window and then glanced in the
rear view. The animals were closer now, stampeding
towards the vehicle from three directions. To the south, the
other three survivors had struck off at an angle through the
fields. Their route looked free, for now at least.

O'Rourke took a drag from the cigarette and then turned
the volume up. He kept twisting the knob to the right until it
would twist no more. Then he flicked a switch on the
steering wheel and wound down the sunroof.

He climbed up until he was standing with one foot on
each of the front seats. Then he poked his head and his
shoulders out of the hole in the roof.

The animals were much closer now, still racing towards
him from all three sides. It wasn't like a cavalry attack,
though. This was open warfare with all sorts of animals in
weird combinations gathering together against a common
enemy. He saw shrews, woodpeckers, sheep, cows, pigs,

hedgehogs, badgers, chickens, chaffinches and everything else, all racing towards him as fast as their little legs or wings could carry them.

O'Rourke pulled the rucksack through after him and unzipped it on the roof. There wasn't much in there, but there was enough. He grabbed the handgun and removed the safety, then lined up the sight with a pig that was at the front of one of the stampedes. He pulled the trigger and the gun went off, and then the pig fell down and flipped over before being swallowed beneath the feet of its compatriots.

That was one pig down, but there were a couple hundred more, and that wasn't counting the sheep and the cows and the chickens. O'Rourke checked his weapon, but he didn't know much about the things. At best, he could guess it was a 9mm. As for how much ammunition the clip carried, it could have been empty already. Either way, there wouldn't be enough to fight off the onslaught. He fired a couple more times and another pig went down, but the animals were closer now, fifty yards at best and counting.

O'Rourke fired another round from the weapon as smoke blew from his mouth and he spat the cigarette away. Then he reached back into the rucksack and pulled out the hand grenade that Big Jim had given him. He'd told him not to use it unless he had to. O'Rourke spat on the roof of the vehicle, removed the pin from the grenade and squeezed the trigger.

Darragh O'Rourke tossed the hand grenade in front of the vehicle and then raised his weapon again. The animals were twenty yards away now, and then ten, and then five, and he squeezed off round after round until the gun wouldn't fire anymore. Then he hurled the thing at the animals as they crossed the final few yards towards the vehicle.

Then it exploded.

BIG JIM, JILL MACDONALD and Tom Copeland had reached the trees by the time that they heard the gunshots. Jill turned around and almost doubled back, but Copeland grabbed her arm and continued to steer her towards the south. Their feet hit the floor like pistons on a production line, mechanical, unthinking, their legs leading the way as their brains shut down and fought for their survival.

The explosion was bigger, louder, and the sound vibrated in the air and threatened to bowl them over. Even Big Jim stumbled as he ran, but he was way out in front of the pack with the other two lagging behind him. They caught up with him and clapped him on the back, but there was no time to talk. There was only one thing for it. They kept on running.

In between breaths, Jill MacDonald managed, "He's dead, isn't he?" But they didn't answer her. From somewhere to the north there was a dreadful chorus of howls and clucks and animalistic outrage, and then the cavalry arrived and the cows broke through the boundary and out into the field.

"Shite!" Jim shouted.

"The trees!"

"What?"

"Run for the trees!" Copeland repeated. "We have to climb them. It's our only shot."

"Some shot," Jim grumbled. "What if we end up stuck in the fucken foliage?"

"It's our only chance!"

"What about the birds?" Jill asked. "What if there are

birds in the trees?"

"What do you want from me?" Copeland asked. "We don't have time for this. You got a better idea?"

"Point taken."

They were near the tree line, now; they just had to vault a small fence and shimmy up the things. They were old English oaks with low-hanging branches, but Copeland hadn't climbed a tree since he was sixteen years old, unless you counted the time old Mrs. Pemblebrooke had lost her cat and she'd called his surgery instead of the fire brigade.

Copeland reached the trees first, but he hung back at the bottom until Jill and Jim arrived and the Scotsman boosted her up into the branches. As soon as he knew she was safe, Copeland ran across to a neighbouring tree and slowly pulled himself up into the canopy. Jim was the last to climb, but he vaulted his way up like a much younger man with a skill he'd acquired from a misspent childhood. And not a moment too soon.

Big Jim was still in the lower branches when the stampede arrived, barely six feet above the ground with four-foot cows thundering past him. He reached up and put his foot on another branch, but then it snapped and fell to the ground to be crushed into dust beneath the hooves. He had to pull himself around to the other side of the trunk and then haul himself up on to a smaller, thinner branch which wobbled but didn't break. And then he was up amongst the canopy, while Tom Copeland and Jill MacDonald were up amongst theirs.

***

They stayed in the treetops for eleven hours.

The stampede stopped after five or ten minutes, but that wasn't the problem. They'd dodged the main force of the animals. The problem was that every stampede left stragglers, and the Sunnyvale stragglers sat beneath the trees like they were studying gravity.

It didn't help that Tom Copeland kept talking. He'd shout across from his spot in the trees, asking questions like, "What the fuck are we doing?"

Big Jim, for his part, shouted back about bawheids and fannybaws while Jill MacDonald just waited it out in silence. She had her pack with her, and her pack had some rations and enough water to keep her going. For Jill MacDonald, the biggest problem was how she'd go to the toilet.

In the evening, a thick mist descended and soaked them through, simultaneously cutting off any chance they had of watching the ground. When night fell, it brought a total darkness with a bite to it, the kind that came with a taste and a smell. It was so cold that they could see their breath in front of them, and they slept in a sort of fever dream as they clung to their spots in the branches.

But the mist lifted, and they were cold but alive and still breathing. Big Jim made the call. He put his fingers to his mouth and whistled, imitating some sort of owl but sounding more like a cat whose tail had been stepped on.

"Oi," he shouted. "Ah reckon we're good tae get outta here."

"Oh yeah?" Copeland replied. His voice was muffled with a head cold perhaps, or maybe he was just too depressed to keep fighting. "You first."

"With pleasure, ye fucken southern fairy."

Big Jim dropped to the ground and landed on his feet like a Scottish cat. Then he pulled himself up to his full height and raised his hand to his brow. He scanned the horizon.

"Aye," he shouted. "It's all clear."

The other two survivors were trusting, but they weren't

that trusting. It took the best part of twenty minutes for them to give in and to lower themselves down, like militants calling an end to their hunger strike and tucking into whatever food they had available. It didn't matter anymore. They couldn't have stayed up in the trees any longer.

"What happened?" Jill asked.

"Ah've nae fucken clue," Jim said. "Ah guess our old pal Darragh saved our lives with his wee distraction."

"So now what do we do?"

"We run," Jim said. "Ah'll gie ye five minutes tae stretch ye legs and get ye shit together. Then we move out. We'll huv tae go on foot."

***

Tom Copeland and Jill MacDonald hadn't stretched their legs for the best part of a day, but they were still ready to move in under three minutes. They continued to walk south, to follow the path they were already treading when the stampede struck.

"Do you think it's a good idea to go in the same direction as the animals?" Jill asked.

Big Jim just shrugged, and Copeland said simply, "What other choice do we have?"

Nobody had a better plan, so they continued to walk. Any worries they had about the animals were quickly dispelled as they started to cross the terrain. Even in the Chilterns, they were never further than eight miles away from the nearest town, and the army's half-arsed quarantine was just a distant memory. But the fields were dead, devoid of life, and the flowers had died as though the water they drank had been spiked with arsenic.

"I don't understand," Jill said. "What the hell happened?"

"Ever seen *28 Days Later*?" Jim murmured.

"What?"

"Nothin'."

"What about you, Tom?"

"What about me?" he asked.

"What do you think happened?"

Tom Copeland shrugged. "The best I've got is a guess," he said.

"Then give me your guess," Jill insisted.

Copeland sighed and acquiesced. He was too tired to argue, too tired to do anything except to keep on walking through the countryside towards civilisation, if civilisation still existed.

"Sunnyvale was a factory farm," he said. "Based on the American model. We pumped the animals full of antibiotics, fed them each other's shit and then slit their throats and threw them into scalding tanks. Disease is always a problem when you get enough animals in a single place. That's why the Black Death killed half of Europe."

"But that was back before–"

"Before what?" Copeland interrupted. "Before MRSA? Bird flu? Ebola? Coronavirus? The warning signs were always there. We just ignored them."

"But this isn't Ebola," Jill said.

"Aye," Jim said. "Ebola doesnae bring men back from the dead."

"That was one guy," Copeland said. "Look, what happened back at the checkpoint–"

"He grabbed my leg, Tom," Jill said.

"I checked his pulse," Copeland snapped. "It was weak, but it was there. He wasn't dead. He was dying."

"Ah know what ah saw," Jim said. "And ah saw a fucken zombie."

"You didn't see a fucking zombie," Copeland shouted.

The other two cringed back for a moment, and then all three of them looked guiltily around as though the animals might return at any time, although the field was still dead and derelict. "No, I'm sorry, I'm not buying it. If there *are* zombies, and that's a pretty big if, then how come we've only seen one of them?"

"Because the animals got all the others before they had a chance to turn," Jill murmured.

A silence descended and they continued to walk. They finally reached the end of the long dirt path that led towards the complex and found themselves in the English countryside. A road wound its way away from them in two different directions, and a couple of empty beer bottles were tangled up in the thicket, a reminder that civilization meant more than just a cup of tea. The road felt empty, almost haunted, and while they were standing right there in the open on the kind of lazy day where the wind settled and carried sound on its wings like the echo inside a cathedral, they couldn't hear even the hint of a motor. And there was still no wildlife, either. There was nothing.

"Which way?" Jill asked.

Copeland shrugged, his bearings gone, but Jim remembered the route and pointed to the right. They followed his outstretched finger.

"Ah reckon it's about five miles that way tae Great Missenden," he said. "It's the closest place. If wir lookin fae civilisation, that's the place. Roald Dahl used tae write stories fae wee bampots in a shed there, ye ken."

"Oh, *well*," Copeland replied. "If it's good enough for Dahl, it's good enough for us. And what do we do after that?"

"Wull ah dunnae fucken ken," Jim growled. "Ah'm no in charge, ye fucken radge. Ah'm jist a fucken observer. All's ah can do is try tae survive."

"Tom," Jill whispered. "Let's just get there and see what happens, okay?"

The vet grunted and said nothing. Then he threw his head back to look at the sky. He squinted as the sun hit his eyes.

"What is it?" Jill asked.

"I don't mean to be the bearer of bad news," he said. "But I think it's snowing. We should probably get a move on."

***

The fields around Sunnyvale were wetter than normal thanks to the mist, but they were also cold and barren and so when the snow started to come down, it really came down. Within the hour, they'd been blanketed by the white stuff and it showed no sign of slowing. If anything, it was coming down faster than ever before, and before long the mud turned to slush. A cold wind was blowing in from the Baltics and the temperatures dropped so rapidly that it took them by surprise. Even wrapped up in their coats and their extra layers, the cold still bit at every exposed surface.

Jill MacDonald had never experienced anything like it, while Tom Copeland was reminded of a sudden snowstorm in the Alps on a skiing holiday he'd gone on in his twenties. Big Jim said it was just like the Scottish summertime, but that didn't stop him from shivering.

"I'm not a doctor–"

"Aye, I think ye've made that pretty clear."

"–but if we don't find somewhere to shelter soon, we're in trouble," Copeland continued. "If the animals don't get us, we're at risk of hypothermia. We were better off back in the admin building."

"Don't say that!" Jill shouted.

"I didn't mean it like that," Copeland said, thinking back to the trail of destruction they'd left behind and feeling a moment of guilt for the dead. "All I'm saying is that we need to get inside, pronto."

"How much further to go?"

"It's goat tae be half a mile," Jim said. He had to raise his voice to be heard, and they noticed that a chill wind had crept up to keep the snow company and that it was starting to howl around them in a tiny cyclone. Out there on the country roads, they were too exposed.

And Big Jim turned out to be right because they reached the first houses barely ten minutes later. They were the larger houses which backed out into the countryside, the old farmhouses which had been made redundant by the same forces that had built Sunnyvale and started churning out cutthroat meat at cutthroat prices. They were houses that had once been built for a purpose and which had since been adapted by middle-class creative types who'd earned a fortune in the city and retreated to the countryside for a simpler life. Copeland knew the type well because they'd made up the bulk of his work at the old practice before he'd been forced to pack his bags and move to Sunnyvale.

"I bet they've turned the cattle shed into a games room," he said. "They always have."

It was getting dark by the time they arrived, the kind of darkness that comes without streetlights when only the moon and the stars are lighting the way. The lack of light was the first thing they noticed as they approached.

"Perhaps there's no power," Copeland said, doubtfully. "They cut the power at Sunnyvale. Maybe they cut the power out here, too."

"That wee shite Harry Yorke killed the power at Sunnyvale," Jim reminded them.

"So what do we do?" Jill asked. "Do we just go up and

knock on the door?"

"She's right," Copeland said. "What if the quarantine didn't hold?"

"It didnae fucken hold," Jim said. "We got out, and so did a couple thousand tonnes of Old MacDonald's prime pork. Sorry, Jill," he added, when she glared at him like a parent with an unruly child.

Copeland shuffled forwards and grabbed their arms, one in each hand. He leaned towards them and whispered.

"Listen," he said. "We don't know what this thing is, but if I'm right, and I think I am, we're dealing with something serious. I'm talking about a global pandemic on an epic scale. And if these guys haven't got their lights on then that can mean only one of two things."

"What's that?"

"Well, the first is that they're not at home and we're going to have to let ourselves in," Copeland said. Then he frowned and paused for a moment.

"Go on," Jill said.

Copeland swallowed and looked up at her. He looked like a man who'd just seen his mother burnt at the stake for witchcraft, as though he'd seen something that he could never un-see.

"There's only one other option," he said. "And that's that Sunnyvale was just ground zero. I'm worried we might be the only ones alive out here."

A tense silence descended, not even broken by the birds in the trees because there wasn't any wildlife. There was nothing.

And then the silence was broken by a noise from behind them. It was the noise of a twig snapping beneath a boot.

THEY SPUN AROUND and found themselves face to face with one of Big Jim's zombies.

Up close and personal, it was hard to tell. Perhaps it was dead and perhaps it wasn't, but when it reached for them with its transparent hands and they saw the bones poking out of the flesh, it didn't really matter. Copeland moved to push Jill aside, ever the gentleman, but she reacted faster and was using him like a human shield. Big Jim, meanwhile, had reached for his pistol and fumbled it, sending the firearm scattering to the ground where it landed in the snow.

"Shite."

"Kill it!"

"Ah'm fucken tryin, ye dickheid!"

The man – because it *was* a man, a big fat man with a long beard like some sort of skeletal Santa – reached out, and Big Jim brought his head down in a Glasgow kiss, butting the thing's arm with such force that it snapped something. Zombie or not, it showed no sign that it had noticed the injury, and it reached forward again with its other arm. Jim was off balance, skidding in the snow, and he went rolling to the ground just as Copeland reached his side and grabbed for his belt. He missed the belt but came out with his hand wrapped around the truncheon, Big Jim's backup weapon, and the vet had just enough time to think about how every neuron in the brain needs to strike at the right time in the right way for critical thinking to be possible before the truncheon smashed the corpse in the forehead and sent it crumpling to the ground. There'd been a bit of give when the wood connected with the skull, and the shock of the impact had sent pain flaring up Copeland's arm and into his shoulder. He dropped the truncheon and turned around, then quickly vomited a steaming pile of bile and acid into the pristine snow beside him.

Big Jim pulled himself to his feet and wasted no time running over to his discarded weapon and picking it back up. Then he ambled back over to their assailant and brought it down once, twice, three times on the back of its head until the brains had sprayed out and landed on the ground by Copeland's vomit. It looked like some chef's idea of avant-garde cuisine.

Whatever it was, it was dead now. But Jim hit it again anyway, for good measure. Then he wiped the blood and gore off the baton in the snow. It left a slimy trail as though a giant snail had gate-crashed a winter wonderland.

Ho, ho, ho, Copeland thought.

"Let's check the house," Jill said, and before either of the other two could say anything, she stalked off towards the front door of the nearest cottage. Copeland followed her just as soon as he was able to compose himself, and Big Jim came last after scrabbling around in the snow to reclaim his firearm.

The front door of the farmhouse was locked, but Big Jim caught up with them and made short work of it by smashing the glass with the end of his truncheon and then reaching in to unlock the door from the inside. When it swung open, it squeaked on its hinges. The hallway inside was covered in a light layer of dust.

"Looks like no one's been in here for a while," Copeland murmured.

"Spread out," Jim said.

"Hell no," Copeland said. "Jim, lock the door. We'll go from room to room. You first. Keep your gun out."

The inside of the house was exactly what Copeland had been expecting. It reeked of middle-class semi-opulence, from the mahogany dining table to the massive TV that took up most of one wall in the living room. Copeland tried the light switch, but no dice. It was as dead as the man out on the driveway with his skull smashed in.

The kitchen was empty too, but they didn't spend too long in there despite its huge bay windows and the sliding doors which led outside into the back garden. It was a big, open expanse and they couldn't see the ends of it. It was creepy, unnerving, and even with the curtains pulled over the glass, there was something about the darkness which seemed to beckon to them. After the great siege of the admin building, the thin pane of glass seemed unlikely to protect them from anything.

Big Jim scanned the surfaces and reached into a bread bin, then rapidly withdrew his hand when he saw what he was reaching for. The bread wasn't just mouldy, it was an almost neon blue with big spider webs of white across the surface. It hadn't been fresh for a long time.

"Anything?" Copeland asked.

"Nothin'."

"There's nothing here, either," Jill said. "Come on, guys, we're—"

But what they were would have to wait because Jill was interrupted by a click and then a bang from back in the hallway. All three of them looked up at the sound, which didn't seem natural in the oppressive silence of the dead civilisation. Copeland reached for a knife from the cutlery draw and succeeded in drawing his own blood when his fingers slipped down the handle and gripped the blade. Jill shrank back and hid herself behind the not insignificant bulk of the Scottish security guard. For his part, Big Jim picked up one of the dining room chairs and smacked it against the floor, sending splinters of wood flying everywhere like a cloud of angry midges.

"Ah'm fucken glad ah've nae goat tae clean up eftir meself," Jim said, investigating the remnants of the chair and picking up a hefty wooden leg that had all the weight of a police truncheon. He wielded it casually, like a badminton player waiting for a tournament to start, but he wasn't waiting to hit a shuttlecock. He was waiting to hit a cock without a shuttle. He was waiting to hit anything made out of flesh and virus.

There was another bang from the hallway, followed by a sound like air leaking out of a punctured tyre, a breathy, mucus-filled gasp like those made by ventilator patients on pandemic wards. It wasn't a healthy sound, but it cut through the air like a car alarm on a quiet night in lockdown. It was a warning.

"Ah, shite," Jim growled. "We've goat company, ye ken."

"But you locked the door!" Jill replied.

"Aye," Jim said. "But maybe yon beasties've goat tha fucken keys."

There was another sound from the hallway, a sound like a sack of sand falling through a wooden beam and shearing it in two on its way to the ground. That was followed by a couple of seconds of silence, and then a gurgling death rattle that sounded like a man with a hole in his throat trying to drink and whistle at the same time.

A gnarled hand appeared on the doorframe.

"It's a person, Jim," Jill whispered.

"It's nae person," the Scotsman replied. "Eh's fucken deid."

The rest of the man's body followed. He was young, probably in his early twenties, although it was hard to tell through the dirt and the viscera on his face. It looked as though he'd been chowing down on the other dead man in the dirt outside. Height-wise, he stood at around five foot ten, but it was difficult to tell with his posture. A large chunk of his skull was missing, as though it had been blown away by a shotgun or crushed beneath steel-capped boots, revealing the pulsating brain within. The skin had turned green and it was floating in a layer of pus.

The dead man's movements were slow, but they were also threatening. He was moving at little more than a shuffle, but as soon as he came into the room he made a beeline for Jill MacDonald, who shrieked and threw a pestle and mortar at him. They connected with the intact side of the man's head and drove him backwards, but only momentarily. Then he surged forwards at Jill MacDonald again.

Copeland came in from the side and thrust the knife into the dead man's back, but he connected with bone and the blade snapped, whirring off across the kitchen like an elastic band. The man turned round to look at Copeland, his opaque eyes focussing on the vet for a moment or two, and then he stepped towards him. Copeland looked down at the knife in his hands and then back up at the dead man in front of him.

"Oh, shi–"

"Ya fucken doss cunt!"

Big Jim's battle cry was straight from the stands at Celtic Park, and Copeland only just had time to fall backwards on to his hands and feet before the Scot's chair leg curved through the air like a scimitar and connected with the oozing skull, which exploded. Blood and gore and spattered the walls and showered the three Sunnyvale survivors like powdered paint at a Holi festival.

"Ah fucken yeah right!"

"Again?" Copeland exclaimed.

"Now I *really* need to wash myself," Jill murmured.

Big Jim hit the corpse a couple more times for good measure, then he wiped the chair leg off on the dead man's trousers and turned to look at his fellow survivors.

"How'd he get in?" Jill asked.

"He must have done what we did," Copeland said. "Reached in through the glass and let himself in. Interesting. Some former memory remains. Some glimmer of intelligence."

"Ah'd better block yon door."

"It's just like being back at Sunnyvale," Copeland said.

***

After the melee, the three Sunnyvale survivors took a breather before continuing their search of the building. Before the outbreak, the horrors of the last ten minutes would have been enough to guarantee each of them a lifetime of psychotherapy, but they'd seen so much death that they'd grown desensitised, like a horror movie critic picking apart the VFX and the story line instead of having heart palpitations after every jump scare.

The brutal truth was that the outbreak had hardened them, and their emotions were untroubled. No, it was the adrenaline that was a problem, along with the aching of their muscles. Mentally and emotionally, they were unaffected. Physically, they were exhausted.

When they were ready to finish their sweep, they climbed the stairs and checked the bathroom and then the two bedrooms. The first was a small box room, but the second was the master bedroom and despite a flat, musty smell, it had held up pretty well. It even had a full-length mirror, which they quickly turned to face the wall. They didn't want to have to see themselves. They weren't a pretty sight.

"Okay," Jim said, "Ah'll huv the first watch. We'll aww kip in here tonight, ye ken."

"You want me to share a room with two men?"

"We've been locked up together for months," Copeland reminded her. "It's not like we're strangers. What's the problem?"

"Before, we didn't have a choice," Jill said. "Now, we're in a proper house. There are separate bedrooms and everything."

"It's safer to spend the night together," Copeland replied.

"Aye," Jim added. "And ye've seen worse. Just be grateful ye've goat a fucken bed. We huvnae seen one of those for a long time. Ye can pretty yeself up wi' yon perfume an aww."

"Are you trying to tell me I smell?"

"We aw fucken smell," Jim said. "Wir aww covered in blood an shit. An before ye start wi' yer feminist shite, ah'm no sayin ye huvtae be a pretty wee wildflower in the middle of aw this. Ah'm just sayin' ah'd fucken kill for a bevvy or a bottle o' scotch an ah wouldnae hold it against ye if ye wanted to feel like a woman. Ah wantae feel like a man, ye ken."

"You just caved someone's skull in," Jill said.

"Twice."

"Exactly," Jill replied. "You should feel man enough. And besides, I saw a bottle of scotch in the kitchen."

"Where?"

"It's tucked behind the microwave."

"Sounds like our man had a drinking problem," Jim said. "That's where ma dad used to hide his. Until my ma started drinking an aww." He grinned. "Ah'll be right back," he said. Then he left them to it.

***

It was a triumphant return to civilisation, or at least it felt like one. The atmosphere became almost jubilant and celebratory.

Jill MacDonald was in her element. She raided the master bedroom and came out with a makeup kit and a half dozen changes of underwear, as well as some jeans and some T-shirts. True, the makeup was stale and the clothes made her look a little frumpy, but it was still better than the stuff she'd been wearing.

The bras weren't the right size. They were too big, but she found some toilet paper to stuff them with. She also found a bunch of carrier bags, all of them stashed inside a more durable canvas bag. She emptied the bag and took it with her as she started to scout around for supplies. She went back upstairs and got Copeland to stand guard at the door while she washed her face and her armpits. The water was off, of course, but there was plenty of the stuff in the cistern. It smelled slightly stale, but that was okay. She didn't want to drink it. She just wanted to splash it beneath her armpits and to use a little of the soap. She cleaned her face as well, this time with the wet wipes she found in the medicine cabinet, and then she used some shaving foam from an overnight bag in the master bedroom and a disposable razor from the shelf above the sink to attack the thatch of hair on her legs and under her armpits. It didn't have to be perfect. It just had to be good enough to feel almost normal again, almost human. She cleaned her teeth with someone else's toothbrush, all oral hygiene warnings forgotten as the old-familiar spearmint of the paste washed over her taste buds. Her mouth felt clean for the first time in months. She even found some roll-on deodorant and a little bottle of perfume. It wasn't the kind of smell that she would normally have gone for, but she wore the stuff anyway, just to feel human again, like a woman and not a sexless refugee.

She looked at herself in the mirror and almost recoiled from what she found there. Her mousy brown hair had grown long and matted, and it looked more like shit and mud than like the beautiful brown of fallen leaves in the autumn. Her blue eyes were dark and hollow, more grey now than anything, and her teeth had gone from brilliant white to a pus-stained yellow. She tried to smile but it looked more like a grimace.

She did the best that she could with the makeup kit. After she'd finished washing herself and changing into the new clothes, she went to sit with Copeland in the master bedroom. He watched as she slowly applied layer after layer on to her face, checking her reflection periodically and shifting position every now and then to get a little more light. There was no electricity, but Copeland had rustled up a torch and a stash of batteries from somewhere and they'd put it on top of the dressing table so that it bathed the entire room in a soft glow. It wasn't perfect, but it was better than sitting around in the darkness.

***

Jim found a bottle all right, but it wasn't scotch. Still, he also found some bin bags beneath the sink and managed to load one up with a veritable feast, from vodka and gin to a half dozen cans of lager, a bottle of white wine and even a couple of energy drinks. The food in the fridge and the freezer had been reclaimed by time, and Jim wouldn't have touched it if he'd been paid to do it. But in one of the cupboards beneath the sink, he found a stash of crisps and biscuits which had somehow survived. They were out of date, but only just. And he'd trust them a hell of a lot more than the yoghurts he'd found in the powered-down refrigerator. They'd grown a disconcerting green moss across the label.

He took his bag and hiked back up the stairs and into the master bedroom. The booze wasn't great, but it was better than no booze at all. They drank it in the darkness, too afraid to risk finding and lighting a candle in case it brought the creepy crawlies out. They didn't know how deep the infection went. What if they made some light and it attracted a horde of moths who were intent on stripping the skin from their bones before incinerating themselves on the flame?

So they just sat in the darkness as they waited for the booze to hit. Jim took the first watch, continuing to tap the bottle as the early morning rolled around. At around 3:30 AM – it was hard to tell without a watch or a clock – Big Jim nudged Tom Copeland awake and they switched over.

In the morning, by the dull light of day, everything seemed clearer. It was almost normal, except for the fact that Jill MacDonald was taking the final watch while Big Jim and Tom Copeland spooned each other in the bed like a couple of newlyweds. Jill was running a comb through her hair, trying to get rid of some of the knots and tangles. It was the first time she'd had access to one of the things since the quarantine. It was hard work, and painful at times, but it kept her occupied and stopped her mind from wandering.

Once the three of them had woken up, they took turns in the bathroom to wash themselves with the water that was left in the cistern. Then they wandered downstairs and regrouped in the empty kitchen. They opened the curtains and looked out into the garden, but there was no sign of any trouble.

"Ah think we should keep our eyes open," Jim said.

But they'd been keeping a stricter watch ever since the bird attack, and they couldn't open their eyes any wider than they already were. So many people had died along the way that there was no real way to relax. That was why they worked slowly and methodically around the kitchen, taking advantage of the natural lighting to search every cupboard and surface. Most of the food had gone rotten, but there were still some snacks and some tins amongst the mouldy perishables

Before they left, they stuffed themselves full of junk food and washed it all down with tins of peaches in syrup. Their texture was disgusting, all gloopy and sugary and lumpy, but they tasted like a little slice of heaven. It was the first fruit any of them had touched for months, and it was exactly what they needed. Scurvy was a real threat, and the four tins of peaches they'd found were the only weapon they had against it.

They gobbled the last of them down and then dropped the empty cans in the bin, even though it seemed like a futile gesture in a world that had gone to shit. It seemed unlikely that anyone would come along and empty the bins after they moved out. It seemed unlikely that there was anyone around at all.

"We'd better get a move on," Copeland said. "While we've still got some light."

"Agreed," Jim said. "Let's move."

Back outside, the snow had thinned out but it was still there, blanketing the country roads with white and keeping the temperature down. It had been warm inside the house, barricaded in the tiny room on the first floor, but it was cold outside in the snow and they didn't want to stay in it any longer than they had to.

"We need to find a car," Copeland said. "Another one."

"Aye," Jim said. "We don't have much luck wi' 'em."

"Let's look round the back," the vet suggested. The house that they'd stayed in was the first of three farmhouses on a narrow dirt road, and it opened up at the rear into a large yard with a big storage shed. The door was padlocked, but the wood itself had rotted through and all it took was a couple of kicks and it disintegrated completely. Then they took the chain away from the wood and opened up the door.

For a second or two, they thought they'd hit the jackpot. It was a beautiful black Mercedes C Class, just sitting there gathering dust inside the storage shed. But then they saw what was sitting inside it.

"Ah guess we found the rest ay the family."

The corpses inside the car were so disfigured that they were barely recognisable as human beings. There were three of them in there, one in the driver's seat and two smaller ones in the back. One of them had been strapped into a baby pink child seat in front of mounted DVD player, but the electricity was as dead as the occupants. The car's windows were sealed but not airtight, and so whatever had been inside with them had leaked out into the shed. But the inside of the car was still a mostly sealed environment, and the corpses had started to rot. All three of them knew what the ghastly scene represented. They'd taken the easy way out.

"This is bad," Jill said. "This is really bad."

"Tell me about it," Copeland replied. "This isn't your typical rural suicide. That's a mother and her children. Mothers usually fight. How come this one didn't?"

"Maybe it wasn't a fight she could win."

They backed away from the vehicle, not because of the stench of flesh but because the sight of the two smaller bodies was too awful to think about. And so they retreated instead to the front of the property and then walked on down the street to the next one.

"Jackpot, baby," Copeland shouted, before immediately covering his mouth with a hand and looking guiltily around. But there was no sign of any wildlife, not even there in the middle of the countryside. But there *was* another vehicle, a much more modest 1998 Mini Cooper.

"Oh, ye've goat tae be fucken kiddin'," Jim said. "Ah'm fucken six four."

"Can you get it running?"

"Ah can try," Jim replied. "Here, hold this."

Copeland frowned and took what Jim was offering. It turned out to be his firearm, and Copeland held it as though he was lifting a hot potato out of an oven with his bare hands.

"What the hell, Jim? How do you even fire this thing?"

"Ye'll figure it out," he said. "If ye have tae. Let's hope ye don't."

Jim made short work of the lock on the door and got inside the vehicle within a couple of minutes, but popping the lock was the easy bit. As a lad, he'd done that a couple dozen times per day, cracking open the doors of the cars on the estate and then rifling through the glove compartment, stealing the radio and making a quick getaway. The designs had changed since he'd been a kid, but the basic principles were the same. Where skill and technique didn't work, brute force took its place.

Getting the engine running was harder, and it wasn't a specialty of his. That was what the other kids did, but Jim had always stopped short of full-blown grand theft auto. Still, he'd learned a thing or two and after fiddling about with the cables beneath the dashboard and messing around beneath the hood, he brought the car to life somehow. It roared like a lion on the savannah before settling down into a low purr.

"All aboard!" Jim shouted.

"I could have sworn you said you didn't know how to hotwire one of these things," Copeland said.

"Aye," Jim replied. "That ah did. But mebbe ah wasnae

bein truthful, ye ken. Thir's a time and a place fae it."

"Where are we going?" Jill asked.

"Shite knows," Jim said. "Wir offtae London I guess. We needtae find out what's going on."

"And what if we're right?" Copeland said. "What if the quarantine didn't hold? What if the whole country was compromised? What if the whole damn world is gone?"

"We'll find out when we get closer to the city," Jill said, and so it was agreed. Jim eased himself into the driver's seat, fiddling with the settings until it was scooched back as far as it would go, but he still felt like he was sitting in a clown car beneath the bright lights of some surreal circus. Copeland got in second, tilting the passenger seat forward and climbing into the back. Jill passed their rucksacks to him, and they piled up the seat beside him with their supplies. Then Jill climbed into the passenger seat and slammed the door.

"Let's go," she said.

"Aye," Jim replied, easing the clutch and putting the car in gear. "Strap yeself in."

They did as he said and Jim pulled the car out of the driveway and on to the roads.

"There's just one thing I'm not sure about," Copeland said.

"Oh aye?" Jim replied. "Ah can think of a few things."

"Who put the padlock around the door?" Copeland asked. "After they started running the engine?"

"Aye," Jim said. "And which wee fucker took out the catalytic converter? Hard to kill yeself wi carbon monoxide fae a new car, ye ken. Ma Uncle Bobby learned that the hard way. And fae that matter, who rolled up the windows after the job was done?"

"It must have been the husband," Jill said.

"But *why*?"

"He did it for love," she said. "It was a kindness. Think about it. The infection started at Sunnyvale and spread out to the nearby villages. We're close enough that this would be one of the first places to get hit. My guess is that the guy with his brains in the snow was the husband. We found the wife and the kids out in the storage shed. They must have figured out they were infected. Perhaps they didn't want to find out what would happen if they waited it out."

"Aye," Jim said, reaching down to the dashboard and flicking through the different frequencies in search of a signal on the radio. "Or perhaps before it aw went to shite. Those bawbag politicians made a statement, ye ken. All fire and brimstone."

"And so they took the easy way out," Jill said. "And you can hardly blame them. After the job was done, the husband closed up the windows and locked the shed. And then he went back to the house and waited to die."

"It's a good theory," Copeland said.

"Aye," Jim said. "And then I hit him in the face with ma truncheon."

THE ROADS WERE DESERTED. Well, mostly deserted.

They kept away from the town centres but drove through the outskirts of a half dozen little villages as they wound their way towards the motorway. They expected to see wild rabbits running across the roads, birds singing in the skies, people walking along the streets pushing pushchairs or walking dogs. But there was nothing, it was just a dead zone.

Then they pulled on to the motorway. If there'd been any doubt beforehand, it vanished from their minds as soon as they saw the roads. There were cars everywhere, abandoned at the side of the road or even just spun around higgledy-piggledy on the tarmac. They had to drive slowly to pick their way amongst the wreckage, and every time the sun glinted off a window or the wheels of the car scraped against some detritus, all three of them jumped and looked nervously around. They were painfully aware that they were stuck on a narrow, thin lane with no way to exit unless they reached a junction, and even though the Mini was nimble enough to nip around the abandoned cars, there was no chance of them picking up a decent lick of speed. It was starting to look like it would be quicker to walk, but the vehicle was their only protection.

"What's that noise?" Jill asked.

"What noise?"

"Turn the radio off," she ordered. "And wind the window down."

"The radio's dead, ye ken," Jim said. "Wiv goat a fucken CD oan."

"Whatever," Jill snapped. "Just turn the damn thing off."

Jim did as he was told, but he didn't dare to cut the engine. He wasn't sure if he could have got it running again.

"You hear that?"

They listened out and they heard it, all right. It was a horrifying sound, but a sound that somehow seemed familiar. It was a percussive, meaty sound, the sound of thousands of tiny little legs all pounding the floor at the same time. They knew that sound.

"Animals!" Copeland shouted.

"What kind?" Jim asked.

"Does it matter?"

"Ah guess not," he conceded, and then he did the only thing he could think of. He wound up the windows, wrapped his hand around the steering wheel and steered through the wrecks.

The noise was getting louder now, closer, but the road was also clearing up a little bit, enough to follow straight lines for twenty yards or so before navigating the next abandoned vehicle. They passed a couple more cars before they saw what was coming, like a moving blanket of flesh and bone.

"Rats!" Jim shouted. "Rats and fucken mice!"

"Thousands of them," Copeland murmured. "Tens of thousands of them."

Jim kept driving, and the Mini reached the blanket of rodents as it was leaning into a bend. The wheels chewed up their tiny corpses and sprayed a film of blood and viscera into the air. While some of the creatures fled around the sides of the vehicle, still others tried to tackle it head on. Rats were finding their way onto the hood and trying to chew at the windscreen wipers or bashing their skulls against the glass. Jim turned the wipers on but continued to drive as normal, wrenching the wheel to the right to bring the car straight again. The rats stretched back as far as the eye could see, but Jim kept his shit together and pushed the Mini forwards. The bones broke beneath them and made it sound as though the road was made from Rice Krispies.

They kept driving, edging through the traffic and along the clogged motorway as the mice and the rats kept charging at the car like Kamikaze warriors. The three survivors sat there in silence, awed by the waste of life and the sheer volume of meat and blood that was rushing towards them. And they all knew it would only take one rat on the inside of the car and it would be game over.

Just when it seemed as though every rat in the world was running towards them, they saw an end to it all. They carried on driving until the last of the rats had passed by, and then they drove some more to shake the stragglers from the bonnet and the windscreen. Then the vehicle puttered to a stop again.

"What is it?" Jill asked.

"It's not gonnae work," Jim said, shaking his massive head and drumming his fingers on the steering wheel. "We've goat tae get oaf the motorway."

"How long until we hit a junction?"

"Five miles?" Jim said. "Ten, mebbe. It's gonnae take us a good few hours, mind."

"Then we'd better get going."

Big Jim grunted and put the car back in gear.

***

It took them longer than they expected to get off the motorway, and it was almost dark by the time they reached the junction and turned off. It wasn't helped by the fact that there had been an eight-car pile-up by the exit ramp and that Big Jim had been forced to shunt one of the cars aside with the nose of the Mini.

They came off at Junction 1A near Fulmer. They were well out of the Chilterns by then and the rolling hills were long gone. They were back in civilisation and less than thirty miles away from the capital city. But there was still no sign of movement.

The junction near Fulmer brought them out in the middle of nowhere, far enough away from the town that if the worst came to the worst and the dead were walking the earth, at least they'd be walking the earth a couple of miles away. And besides, it would only get worse as they continued the journey to London.

Tom Copeland suggested sleeping in the car, but Big Jim pooh-poohed the idea by pointing out that he could barely sit in the thing, let alone lie in it. So they scouted around instead for a suitable location and found the perfect place on the outskirts of an industrial estate, where four caravans had been parked haphazardly in a car park beside some bottle banks.

"Ah never thought I'd be glad to see a fucken caravan," Jim said.

"There are cars, too," Copeland observed. "Perhaps we can refuel the tank."

"Aye," Jim said. "If ah can even get this thing goin' agin. Ah say we nick that Citroen C8. My auld man got one o' those beauties to carry gear around when eh's playin golf or giggin' wi' eh's buddies. Plenty o' room to stretch out, ye ken."

"First thing's first," Copeland said. "Let's check out the caravans."

"Aye," Jim said. "Ma legs are killin' me. Wir gonnae huvtae sleep in the same van, though. Ah'm no havin' us splittin' up now, not after we've goat this far."

"Whatever you say," Copeland said. "You first. You

might want to hold your weapon, just in case–"

But he didn't get a chance to finish the thought because the door of one of the caravans opened and someone walked out. Big Jim whipped his gun from its holster and pointed it towards the movement, reacting more on instinct than anything. He felt his fingers closing automatically around the trigger as though they had a will of their own. As though they wanted blood.

"Jim!" Jill shouted, grabbing his arm from her perch on the seat beside him and pulling him off balance. "It's just a kid!"

"Ah don' care if it's a fucken leprechaun," Jim roared. "Ah'm nae gonnae die today."

"But what if–"

The kid was closer now, close enough for Copeland to make out her face and to guess her age at maybe six or seven years old. She was covered in dirt, grimy from head to toe. Her movements were slow and jerky, as though she was a wind-up toy or just a piston on an assembly line.

"Get oaf ma fucken arm," Jim growled. "Ah'm gonnae fucken shoot her."

"Maybe she's right," Copeland said. While the two of them were arguing, he'd been watching the child, and something worried him. Perhaps it was that she'd subconsciously raised her hand to her mouth and stuck a thumb between her lips.

But in the front seat, Big Jim had finally worked his arm free. He had his weapon in his hand and it was pointing at the child. He went to pull the trigger and then cursed, stopping himself. He wound down the window and leaned out of it, aiming the weapon at the little girl's head.

And then just as he was about to pull the trigger, she spoke to him.

"Help me."

It was just two words, but they were powerful words and they were strong enough to force Big Jim to lower the weapon.

"Excuse me?" he said.

"Help me," the girl repeated. "I'm so hungry, mister. Do you have anything to eat?"

In the back, Copeland rummaged through the rucksacks and pulled out a chocolate bar that they'd taken from the house in Great Missenden.

"Here," he said. "Give her this."

Big Jim took the chocolate bar and then held it out of the window. The little girl kept her distance, but she leaned in and reached out just enough to grab it, as though they were running some sort of post-apocalyptic relay race.

"What happened to your parents?" Jim asked.

"They're dead," the girl said, simply. "I'm here all by myself."

"Can we come into your caravan, little girl?" Jill asked. She'd unbuckled her seatbelt and was opening up the car door. Big Jim was quick to follow, not because he trusted the kid but because he wanted to keep a close eye on her.

"Sure, okay," the kid said.

And so in they went, although Jim kept his hand on his weapon, just in case. But the girl seemed more scared than they were, and inside the caravan, the closeness was almost unbearable. Jill MacDonald and Tom Copeland went in first and sat down on the sofa, which presumably doubled up as the little girl's bed. Jim sat on the end of the sofa, while the little girl backed up into the bathroom and peeked out from behind the door at them.

"What's your name?" Jill asked.

"Suzie," the kid said. "What's yours?"

"I'm Jill," she replied. "This is Tom and, uh, Big Jim."

"Nice name!"

"Ah like this kid," Jim said, begrudgingly.

"How come you're here all alone?" Jill asked.

"I don't know," Suzie said. She sniffed a little and then started to cry. "All the people were feeling sick. They said we were going to get out of here. They said we were going to go on holiday. Then Mummy got sick and Daddy got sick and then they went away and they left me here and I've been all alone here ever since."

"Well, don't worry, you're going to be safe with us. Is it okay if we sleep in your caravan tonight?"

The little girl shook her head and stared at Big Jim, who excused himself and said he was going for a breath of air.

"It's okay," Jill said. "We'll look after you, I promise."

The girl shook her head again, but this time with a little less enthusiasm. Jill smiled at her and reached a hand out.

"Come on," she said. "We'll cook you a good meal and keep watch at night to make sure that nothing happens."

"What about the big man?"

"Big Jim?" Jill laughed. "Don't worry, he's a sweetheart when you get to know him. Trust me, everything's going to be okay."

***

"Everything's fucked," Jim was saying. Copeland had followed him outside and was watching him as he walked back over to the Mini and kicked the vehicle's tyres. The vet held back, halfway between the vehicle and the caravan.

"How so?"

"Wir gonnae end up stayin' here wi' the wee girl," Jim said. "You mark ma words. We'll end up getting too comfortable, ye ken."

"So what if we do?" Copeland asked. He sighed. "Jim, I'm tired of all this. And besides, we might be the only chance that the girl has."

"Don't you get it?" Jim growled. He kicked the tyre again. "We cannae survive this. No one can. Ah'm no bein' funny, pal, but everythin's gone tae shite. Thir's nothin' left fae us in London. Ah reckon the whole fucken city burned down or got overrun by the fucken foxes an shit."

"But if that's the case," Copeland said, "then why shouldn't we stay here? We're close enough to the middle of nowhere that we can be pretty sure no one's going to find us."

"You mean like how yon little girl thought she was safe and no one would find her?"

"Yeah," Copeland said. "Exactly like that."

"Listen," Jim said. "Ah'm no sayin' stayin' here's a bad thing, ye ken. Thir's no point gaein tae London. Ah reckon it's obvious we're on our own out here."

"So what's the problem?"

"The problem's the girl," Jim growled. "Ah'm nae lookin' fae another mouth tae feed, ye ken. We've goat nae room for dead weight."

Copeland frowned at him, but Jim didn't see. He had his back to the vet and while he'd stopped kicking the tyres of the vehicle, he was still staring at them ferociously as though he was trying to set them on fire with the power of his mind.

"We'll take any ally we can find," Copeland said. "If we leave her here, we're leaving her here to die. We'd be no better than the animals."

"Aye," Jim said. "Ah'm no' a bad man, ye ken. Ah have a heart. It's jist…"

"Just what?"

"It's jist what if yon lass is infected?" he said. "Like her parents, ye ken. How does this disease even spread itself?"

"I have no idea," Copeland replied. He paused for a moment to mull it over. He thought about the animals and the way they'd been forced to eat each other's shit and live in such cramped quarters that they couldn't even move a wing. And he thought about the trail of the dead that they'd left along the way.

That was when he was hit with the insight. It was in the blood. You could see the difference if you looked closely enough. When Big Jim had caved in the face of the man outside the farmhouse, the blood had been wrong, more grey and transparent than it should have been. In some places, where the remains of the man's skull lay spread across the snow, it had been hard to tell the difference between the blood and the brain matter. It just didn't look right.

"We need a blood sample," Copeland murmured. "It's the only way."

"How're we gonnae get a blood sample?" Jim asked.

Copeland paused and thought about it for a moment. Then he smiled, a bleak, grim smile that felt like it had a life of its own. It felt like a Dorian Gray smile on an old painting in someone's attic somewhere.

"You leave that to me," he said.

SUZIE CALMED DOWN in the end, thanks mostly to the soporific effect that Jill MacDonald could have when she put her mind to it. She could make a room feel more at ease just by being there, and when she started asking probing little questions, the kid started opening up to her.

That evening, Big Jim managed to get the stove going by stealing a bottle of Calor gas from one of the neighbouring caravans. He also raided their pantries and cupboards and finally found himself a bottle of scotch. He also found a little food, and some of it was still in good shape. Two of the caravans had battery-powered fridge-freezers and one of them was still running. The fridge was mostly empty and what was left had shrivelled up and died, but the freezer was packed full of frozen meat and chips. It was a proper feast, and it cooked up well on the hob.

Copeland passed on it and ate a couple of bags of crisps instead. He said he'd gone off meat, and they couldn't blame him.

The vet found a folded-up newspaper on the table inside the caravan, and he picked it up and scanned the pages for information. It was dated a couple of months after the outbreak, and while Copeland's grasp of time was a little hazy by now, he suspected at least six months had passed since its date of publication.

But it wasn't the date that had caught his attention. It was the headline, *The Dead Rise in New York City and Tokyo*, and the photos that ran with it. It was also the implications.

"I guess the quarantine didn't hold," Copeland said.

"Aye," Jim replied. "Ah suspected as much. Ah thought

it was awfay quiet roond here."

"Do you think it's just a coincidence?"

"Aye," Jim scoffed. "An' it's jist a coincidence that Sunnyvale exported to the US and Japan an aw."

"You make a good point," Copeland said.

"What else does it say?"

"I'll take a look," the vet said, and the group spent the next half an hour or so reading through the tabloid rag with increasing discomfort. Even though it wasn't exactly a linear narrative, the information was there, enough for them to piece it together at least.

Livestock imports and exports had been suspended across the globe, but not until it was too late and the animal population was infected. From there, the animals had escaped en masse, Sunnyvale style, from their prisons all over the world. The pattern was almost unanimous: the local wildlife became infected, then the infection spread to humans and before anyone knew it, the dead were walking. The story was the same all over the world. No country was safe, especially once the infection spread to the birds.

The pundits in the newspaper predicted that every human being on the planet would be dead within twelve weeks, a figure which Copeland also put roughly three to six months earlier.

"So it's bad news then," said Jill MacDonald, who so far had listened to the conversation with growing unease but who hadn't added anything.

"Pretty much," Copeland said.

"Aye," Jim added. "Wir fucked, awrite."

"Language," Jill scolded, nodding at the little girl who was watching the huge Scotsman with a look of rapt fascination.

That night, when it was time for bed, Tom Copeland made hot chocolate by mixing powder with hot water from an old-fashioned kettle on the stove. He mixed a little something in with Suzie's hot chocolate to help her sleep, but she didn't need it. The poor kid was exhausted. She passed out in Jill's arms on the sofa bed and the young woman followed suit shortly afterwards.

Then Big Jim nodded at him, and the vet reached into his pockets and pulled out a syringe that he'd stashed from their medical supplies. He moved slowly, calmly, trying to steady his shaking hands as he searched for a spot to aim for. He found it in the crook of the sleeping girl's elbow, a tiny little vein like a stream meandering through the countryside. He pushed the needle into her skin and then pulled back on the plunger until the chamber filled up. The girl stirred in her sleep and shuffled on to her side, and for a horrifying moment it looked like Jill would wake up and start asking questions, but then she started snoring and the two men relaxed. Copeland withdrew the needle and backed away from the girl, then took the blood sample over to his makeshift laboratory in the bathroom.

He worked by the candlelight which filtered in through from the main room. He was flying by the seat of his pants, making up the science he needed to come to some sort of deduction, knowing full well that if he got it wrong, it could kill them all.

But before he'd even started, he had a hypothesis. When he examined the blood and saw its consistency, his theory was confirmed. It just didn't *look* right, as though it had been watered down and mixed with flour. His suspicions grew when he ran it through a piece of kit he'd picked up back at the army barricade, which was designed to identify a person's blood type in emergency situations. It only took a couple of minutes to give a result, but the result was void. According to the chemical test, it wasn't blood at all.

He wondered whether it was the test itself, and so while

Jim stood guard outside the door in case the girls woke up, he took a sample of his own blood with a fresh needle and ran it through the kit. It gave him a result in just a couple of minutes. O negative. It was correct.

Jim gestured for Copeland to follow him and led the way out of the caravan and into the cool air outside. The snow had melted, but it felt as though it was an imminent threat and that it could come down again at any time. The two men stood a couple of feet away from the van and talked in hushed voices so that they wouldn't be overheard, but they didn't want to go too far. There was safety of a sort inside.

"So what's the deal?"

"She's compromised," Copeland said. "I ran the blood and it's not normal."

"But she can walk and talk."

"So could Stephen Hawking, for a while," the vet replied. "If you want my guess, she's infected somehow and it can only be a matter of time."

"Until what?"

"I don't know," Copeland admitted. "But I wouldn't want to be around her to find out. My guess is that she'll turn into something like that chap you hit with your truncheon. What are we going to do?"

"We'll huvtae get rid of her."

"We can't," Copeland protested. "She's just a child. Besides, for all I know, you're infected too."

Jim paused for a moment and scratched his chin. Then he turned around to look at him. "Ah hadnae thought o' that," he admitted. "Can ye test us?"

"I'm going to have to," he said. "But what if we're infected? What do we do then?"

"Ah huv no idea," Jim said. His eyes looked dark and sunken into his face, and his beard had grown long and wiry. For the first time since Copeland had met him, the man looked defeated. "Ah guess we'll huvtae deal wi' that if it happens."

***

"You did what?"

Copeland flinched and took an involuntary step backwards, bashing against the stove. With four of them inside what looked like a two-man caravan, there wasn't much room to manoeuvre.

"I took a blood sample," Copeland repeated. "I had to. Look, if I hadn't taken the sample, we wouldn't have known."

"You could have just asked," Jill growled.

"She would have said no."

Suzie was sitting in the corner of the van, chewing on the frayed ends of her hair and watching the grownups argue. "I'm here, you know," she said.

Jill rushed over to her and swept the hair out of her mouth. "I know, sweetie," she said. "I know. We're worried that you might not be very well."

The little girl's eyes shot open until they hung in the middle of her face like flying saucers in the night sky. "Am I going to die?" she asked. "Like Mummy and Daddy?"

"No, sweetheart, you're not going to die."

"Well ah dunnae think ye should be makin' any promises," Jim murmured.

"We need to test the rest of us," Copeland said. "We need to know where we stand."

"You're not sticking that thing in me," Jill growled. "And don't get any ideas about jabbing me when I'm asleep, either."

"Ah'll go first," Jim said.

"Go ahead," Jill replied. "I'm not doing it."

Jim opened his mouth to argue, but Copeland interrupted him before he could get any words out. "Fine," he said. "I'm just trying to help. Jim, get over here."

If it was an attempt to bring her round to his way of thinking, it was unsuccessful. Even after Copeland retested himself, in front of her this time so she could see how it worked, she refused to allow him anywhere near her. He shrugged, grabbed a fresh needle and found a spot in Jim's arm. Then he took the sample and ran the test.

"Well?" Jim growled. "Ah'm ready, let's hear it."

"Let me take another sample," Copeland said.

"No!" Jim growled. "Ah wanna hear it."

Copeland sighed, and it was at this point that both Big Jim and Jill MacDonald rushed over to him to take a look.

"It's not good news, Jim," Copeland said. He showed them the blood sample in its little plastic tray in front of them. Then he pointed out the consistency and the colour and the little X in the box that meant "no match".

"I don't understand," Jill said.

"According to the test," Copeland said. "Big Jim doesn't have a blood type."

"How long have ah goat?"

"No idea," Copeland said. "Jim, this doesn't have to be a death sentence."

"Ah'm no safe tae be around," he said. "Shite, ah'm as bad as the girl."

Then he looked across at her. "We've goat tae get away from you," he said. "We'll take the car and head tae London. See if we can find a cure."

"We'll come with you," Jill said, but Copeland grabbed her by the arm and pulled her towards him.

"Nae chance," Jim said. "Ah've no brought you this far to end up killin' ye. No. The girl comes wi' me. We'll see what happens. If nothin' changes, we'll come back."

"I don't want to go with you," Suzie said.

"Ah doan fucken care," Jim replied. "Ah'm no doin' this for you. Ah'm doin' this for them."

Then the girl started crying, and Jill MacDonald shot a fierce look in the direction of the security man before scooping her up in her arms. She felt pitifully thin, malnourished, and she was lucky to be alive in the first place. Then Jill started crying, too.

But it had already been decided, and as much as the two girls hated it, they also had to admit that there was wisdom in the plan. It was for the best.

It just felt like it was for the worst.

***

Jill wanted them to stay there for another night and to set out in the morning, but Jim argued that delays begat delays and that if they stayed for the night, they'd stay for a day and then another day. They spent an hour or so unloading the Mini and splitting up the supplies, and then Suzie gave Jill one last hug before Jim led her out into the street and into the back of the Citroen C8. He'd found the keys for it hanging up on the wall in one of the caravans. It only had half a tank in it, but the engine worked a charm. It'd do the job all right.

All four of them were crying by the time that Jim put the car in gear and drove off towards the south, and Jill kept crying for the rest of the afternoon and late into the evening, until Copeland finally took her mind off things with their last bottle of wine and a slap-up meal on the stove. She finished off the rest of the sausages while he heated up a couple of tins of macaroni and cheese and drowned the stuff in pepper. He still didn't feel like eating any meat.

The conversation was tense that night as they sat at the tiny table in the caravan and talked about the future, or whatever was left of it. It was filled with awkward silences and long pauses, and none of their easy companionship was left. It had gone with the trust when Copeland had held his tests in the dead of night, and look where that had left them.

"So what do we do next?" Jill asked.

Copeland shrugged and just continued to eat the macaroni. She'd had a couple of dollops of it with her sausages, not because the flavours were complimentary but because times were dire and it was hard to tell where the next meal might come from.

"I think we should stay here," Jill said. "In case Jim comes back."

"Jim isn't going to come back," Copeland said. "But if that's what you want to tell yourself, I won't argue with you."

"He *will* come back," she said, suddenly. In that moment, Copeland was reminded of just how young she was. She sounded almost petulant. "If you don't think he's coming back, why on earth do you want to stay here?"

"Where else would we go?" Copeland asked. "There's nothing left that we *can* do. All we can do is wait it out."

"What if there's no end to it?"

Copeland didn't have an answer.

***

The silence was overwhelming, at least to begin with. Left alone to their own devices, Tom Copeland and Jill MacDonald didn't have much to say to each other. Everything that they could have said had already been said. And so they whiled away the time playing card games and waiting for something to happen. They felt robbed of their own initiative. If civilisation had fallen, what else was left? They had no hope of rebuilding it, not on their own.

Or did they?

It was Jill MacDonald who broached the subject first. She was no longer the shy little girl that she'd been when she'd first interned for her uncle's meat production facility. The violence around her had taken its toll, and any innocence that she'd had was long gone, a victim of the blood and the gore.

"Tom," she said, matter-of-factly, as they sat together on the stained old sofa that stretched across the caravan's wall. "Do you think we should have sex?"

The veterinarian sat up suddenly and almost choked on his own saliva. He gave her a look that suggested he'd smelled something deeply unusual – not unpleasant, perhaps, but more like something from his youth that he'd half-forgotten and never expected to smell again.

"What do you mean?" he asked, carefully.

"Well, I mean, we could be the last two surviving members of the human race," Jill said. "And if that's the case, we have a duty to repopulate. And besides, I don't want to die a virgin."

Copeland laughed a bitter laugh and shook his head. "I should have known," he said. "For all we know, sexual contact could spread the disease."

"But you're not infected, are you?"

"I don't think so," Copeland admitted. "But that's not the point. I'm old enough to be your father."

"So?"

"It's the end of the damn world," Copeland said. "This is no time to be thinking about children. That's no basis for a relationship."

"Who said anything about a relationship?"

"I'm confused."

"Me too."

Another silence descended, but the quality of it had changed somehow. Before, it had been a calm, amiable silence, the kind that two friends could maintain, but now it was the silence of a formal meeting when someone's running ten minutes late and a group of people who've never met before are forced to wait for them.

"Tom," she said, trying again, "if we don't have children, there'll be nothing left. Humanity could die with us."

"But think about it," he said, stifling a sigh as he was forced to take on the role of bearer of bad news. It was a role he'd had to play before, but never at this scale and with stakes so high. "Even if we did have kids, what then? In twenty years' time, when they reach adulthood, would you expect them to have sex with each other? And even if they did, incest is no joke. It causes genetic defects and all sorts of other problems."

"I hadn't thought of that," Jill admitted. She thought for a moment, a look of perplexity drifting across her expressive young face. Then she shook her head. "There must be something we can do. I don't want us to die alone."

"We won't be alone," Copeland said. "We have each other."

"But no children."

"No children," Copeland repeated. "Even if we wanted them, we couldn't have them."

"What do you mean?" Jill asked. "You're not... I mean, you're not gay, are you?"

"Of course not," Copeland replied. "I had a wife and kids."

"So?" Jill said. "I wouldn't judge you."

"And I'd tell you if I was."

"So what's the problem?"

And so Copeland told her, and a single word told her everything she needed to know. And in that one word lay the fate of humanity, decided in a single decision made long before the outbreak began. Copeland had no way of knowing its full implications at the time.

"I had a vasectomy," Copeland said. "That's one of the reasons why my wife and I parted ways. She wanted more kids and I didn't, so I went ahead and made the decision for both of us."

He paused for a moment to take a sip of stale water from one of the gnarly plastic cups that he'd found in one of the cupboards. Across the table, Jill MacDonald met his eyes. There were tears in them, in both of their eyes.

"I'm sorry, Jill," Copeland said. "We have no choice. I guess this is the end of the line."

A COUPLE OF DAYS PASSED, mostly without incident. The weather got a little warmer and the snow started to seem like a distant memory. Jill found a notepad and some paper inside the box for an old board game and spent most of her time drawing, although she wasn't much good. She just needed something to keep her hands busy. Copeland spent his time sorting through the caravans and taking an inventory. He started moving all the stuff that they didn't need into one of the other caravans so that there'd be more space for them to move around in.

Life was almost back to normal. And then Jill started to get sick.

To begin with, it was barely noticeable. She wasn't eating as much as she had been, but she'd blamed it on a poorly stomach and he'd fallen for it. But pretty soon he caught her vomiting in the caravan's tiny bathroom and then she took to the sofa with her pens and paper and started drawing increasingly erratic sketches.

"You don't look so good," Copeland said.

"I don't *feel* so good," she admitted.

"Let me check your vitals." She acquiesced, and so he took her pulse and checked her temperature with an old meat thermometer. They weren't normal, but neither were they unheard of. She was also having some trouble breathing, which was more concerning. He had nothing to give to her.

"You should get some rest," he said.

"Yeah." She paused for a moment and then added, "Tom?"

"Yeah?"

"Can you run your blood test on me?" she asked. "You know, just to be sure?"

Copeland smiled, but it wasn't a happy smile. "Of course," he said.

She winced as he pushed the needle through her skin and into a vein before drawing back the plunger. She refused to look at him while he did it. The sight of her own blood had always made her a little queasy. It was strange how the sight of other people's blood hadn't bothered her.

It didn't take long for the results to come back, and Copeland made a preliminary diagnosis while the blood was still in the chamber.

It was the wrong colour, whiter and more translucent, and when he ran it through the last of the army issue blood tests it came back without a match.

She was infected.

***

Copeland smashed his fist against the tiny table inside the caravan. He hit it so hard that the entire vehicle wobbled on its axles.

"Damn it," he shouted. "It's not fair!"

"Life isn't fair," Jill said. She smiled sadly at him, nineteen years old and already resigned to whatever was coming. "I'm going to die in here."

"But I can't keep going without you," Copeland said. He felt a thrill of selfishness as he realised what it was that scared him. "You can't leave me alone here."

"I don't plan on quitting any time soon."

"You'd better not," Copeland said. "Shit! If only we knew how this damn thing spread."

"It's a virus, Tom," she said. "It's everywhere. In the air, perhaps. In the water. The food."

"The food?" He thought on it for a moment. "The sausages?"

Jill shrugged. "I don't know, Tom," she said. "Perhaps it was just my time. I just want to know what we're going to do next."

"I have no idea," Copeland said. "You think I know what I'm doing but I'm telling you, I'm flying by the seat of my pants here. I can't protect you."

"But you can promise to help me."

"I can't!"

"You can promise to *try*."

Copeland was crying now, although he had no idea when it started. He thought he'd seen too much to ever tear up again, but he was wrong. He shuddered and then used a dirty sleeve to wipe his eyes clean. He looked across at her and tried his best to smile.

"I promise I'll try," he said.

And so he tried. The caravan turned into a makeshift hospital room and Copeland spent his time making sure that his patient was comfortable, whether he was fluffing her pillows or pouring water down her throat. After the first night, in which she barely slept and kept on tossing and turning with nightmares and prophetic visions, she settled down and stopped moving. She just lay there, staring at the ceiling, occasionally asking for more water or eating a bowl of soup from the hob in the little kitchen.

It was then that Copeland felt at his loneliest. Jill wasn't company, she was just *there*, like a decoration. Outside, the wind was howling even though the sun was shining and he spent most of his time listening out in case he heard the distant murmuring that heralded the arrival of the rats, the birds, the pigs or the chickens. When he closed his eyes, he could still see the animals at Sunnyvale as they ripped apart his co-workers and fought against each other in a misguided bid for freedom.

By the end of the following night, Jill MacDonald was hardly there. Her fever was running high and her eyes were closed but flickering as though she was looking out upon another world. She was murmuring something, but Copeland couldn't make it out. He wasn't even sure she was talking in English. All he could do was keep her forehead as moist and as cool as possible.

It was about three o'clock in the morning when Tom Copeland was woken from his slumber by a noise outside. He'd told himself he'd keep watch all night, that he'd keep watch as long as he needed to until Jill got better... or until the worst happened. But try as he might, he couldn't force himself to keep his eyes open, and he'd passed out sitting upright at the foot of the bed with one eye closed. The noise from outside was a single, simple noise, but there was no mistaking what it was. Even in his semi-conscious state, he could recognise the sound of a twig snapping beneath some creature's heavy foot.

And then came the voice, and there was no mistaking that, either. It came with a thick, heavy accent and kept using words like "shite" and "fuckbaws."

It was Big Jim Benton. He'd come back. And he didn't sound too happy.

***

When Big Jim hammered against the door of the caravan, it shook the thing on its unstable foundations and made a horrific banging sound like mortar fire on a battlefield. Copeland was amazed that Jill slept through it, even with her fever and the infection that was coursing through her veins.

"Tom Copeland!" Jim shouted. "Come outside and play, ye wee shite."

Copeland shivered and felt himself backing away from the door. He steeled himself, grabbed the axe he'd been keeping beneath his pillow and then swung it up to rest it on his shoulder. Then he opened the door of the caravan and stepped out into the night.

Big Jim didn't look so good. He'd never had much colour about him except for the fiery ginger in his beard, but what little colour there was had drained away and been replaced by a waxy pallor that made him look more like a robot than a person.

"Ah," Jim said. "There ye are, ye wee shite."

"Why the hostility, Jim?"

"I'm here to kill ye," he said.

"Why?" Copeland asked. But he had a pretty good idea. "And where's the girl?"

"Wee Suzie didnae make it," Jim said. He smiled, but it was more like a hellish leer than a genuine grin. It was terrifying, somehow inhuman. "But ah'm feelin a loat better, ye ken."

"No, Jim," Copeland said. "I don't believe you. Show me your hands."

"Why?" he asked. "So ye can see if ah'm holding a fucken weapon?"

The Scotsman held his hands up in the air to show that they were empty.

"Let me into the fucken caravan, Tom. Ah survived this thing. Mebbe thir's hope after all."

Copeland hefted the axe on his shoulder and stared across at Big Jim. The Scotsman was nearly a foot taller than him and built like a brick shithouse, but his system was also teeming with whatever the hell had originated in the depths of Sunnyvale's factory sheds. He wasn't human – not anymore, not really. Sure, he could talk like a human and think like a human, but he wouldn't act like a human. Copeland could see it in his eyes. He'd act like an animal.

"You're not coming in," Copeland said. "I'm sorry. You've had a wasted journey."

Something changed in Jim's head, and he roared like a wounded bull before running through the darkness at Copeland, who was at a disadvantage because his eyes were still adjusting. A little light was filtering out from the caravan, but not enough to track him through the darkness. The Scotsman grabbed him around the ankles and bore him down to the ground, and then the two of them were fighting in the dirt, gouging at each other's eyes or lashing out with closed fists at whatever flesh they could connect with. Copeland was a lover and not a fighter, but he was like a dog that's been backed up into a corner. It was the only thing he could do.

"You've changed, Jim," Copeland shouted, as the two men grappled out there in the dirt.

Jim grunted but said nothing. He was the stronger man and he made short work of the veterinarian, pinning him to the ground first with his arms and then his knees after he shifted position. He reared up like a bear on its hind legs, his massive head blocking out the moon, and then he drew a slab-like hand back ready to deliver the killing blow.

And then something passed over his features, and he wobbled to and fro like a Friday night drunk in Glasgow. Copeland pressed home the advantage and threw his weight to the side, sending Big Jim toppling away from him and freeing himself from the man's weight. He shuffled across the ground towards his fallen axe, grasped it with one hand and then rolled himself over, convinced Big Jim would be racing towards him to finish him off.

But no. The Scotsman was on his knees with his head

facing the sky. Some sanity had returned to his eyes.

"Ah'm fucked," Jim shouted. "Tom, ye've goat tae kill me."

"What?"

"Kill me!" Jim roared. "Kill me now afore I kill ye first, ye ken."

Then Jim stiffened again and the madness was back in his eyes. He pulled himself up to his feet as Copeland hefted the axe in his hands. He hesitated for a moment.

And then he swung.

The axe hit Big Jim in the middle of the forehead, cleaving a wedge of bone from his skull. Blood sprayed through the air on impact and started pulsing out with each of Big Jim's final heartbeats. It was infected blood, and Copeland jerked back to avoid it before wrenching the axe out of the gore like he was yanking Excalibur from a stone.

Big Jim was gurgling something and Copeland approached him cautiously, but he couldn't make out what it was. He rolled the big man over with his foot until he was lying on his back and facing the stars. He had a smile on his broken face.

Then he took one last deep, shuddering breath and his body shut down. Copeland wiped the axe off on the long grass to the side of the caravan and then walked back inside.

And then there were two, he thought.

***

Jill's condition continued to deteriorate, and by the morning she was barely breathing. She hadn't woken up during the drama outside the caravan, and he hadn't the heart to wake her when he walked inside.

Copeland caught a couple of hours of sleep at best, and the dreams he had swam before his eyes and kept waking him every couple of minutes. When he finally gave in and stopped trying to sleep, he felt worse than he had before he started.

He woke up at around 4 AM, although his watch had stopped months ago and so he'd learned to guesstimate the time from the quality of the light. It had helped when he'd kept watch back at the admin building. There was something about staying up all night that taught a man to measure time without even meaning to. It was a habit, one that kicked in automatically. And even if he'd got the time wrong, he could be pretty sure about how long it would be until sunrise.

There was a noise coming from the darkness, and it took him a few seconds to pull himself together and to figure out what it was. It was Jill MacDonald.

"Tom," she was whispering. "Tom..."

He moved quickly, lowering his head to her mouth so he could hear her. "What is it?" he asked.

"I don't feel well," she whispered. Her voice was dry and cracked, so he gave her a little water.

"I'm here," Copeland said. It felt useless and a little redundant, but it was all he could say. It was all he could think of. "Everything's going to be all right."

"You really think so, Tom?"

"I really think so," he lied.

Jill was silent for a few minutes, and Copeland took her pulse and her temperature. Neither of them looked too good. He took a length of cloth from his kit and soaked it in water, then used the rag to mop her sweaty brow. He said a silent prayer as he did it, though he wasn't religious. He just didn't want to be alone there. He didn't want to be the last man standing. The last man on Earth.

Then Jill spoke again.

"Do you think it's really going to happen, Tom?" she

asked. "Do you think I could really be a vet?"

In spite of himself, Copeland laughed. It was her old dream, the goal she'd told him about when he'd first joined the facility. Back then, he'd promised to take her under his wing. They just hadn't been expecting things to turn out like this.

"Sure," he said. "I mean, the loan's a bitch and it takes a few years, but you're a bright girl. You can do anything you put your mind to."

"Like Eminem," she whispered, ethereally. She was silent for a moment or two before adding, "I don't want to be a vet anymore."

"You don't?"

"No," she continued. "I want to be a doctor. I want to help people."

"What about the animals?"

"Fuck the animals," she whispered.

And then she fell asleep. But for Copeland, sleep was like a long lost relative that he'd never see again. And he didn't much want to see it, either.

When the sun rose, it rose on a scene of horror in the grass outside the campervan. Copeland spent a couple of hours watching Jill, but once he was convinced that she wasn't going to change, he hopped out of the van and raided one of the others for supplies. He found a snow shovel out there, and he took that shovel and walked around in the grass, digging it in at random until he found a likely spot. He found it twenty yards away from the van in the shade of a large hedge. The soil was a little softer there, and the deep roots and tendrils from the hedge didn't spread out too far outside of its borders.

He dug most of the grave in a single go as the sun was at its highest in the sky. It was dirty, depressing work, but it felt good to give his muscles a workout and to feel the light on his arms while he did it. But Big Jim was a big man, and a big man needed a big grave. It was the least he could give him. He'd got them this far, after all. For better or for worse.

Copeland meant to take a break and to resume work in the afternoon, but any chance of that went rapidly out the window when he re-entered the caravan. Jill had deteriorated still further, he could tell it from the way she breathed. The long, ragged gasps, like a drowning man coming up for air, were a thing of the past. They'd been replaced by short inhalations that sounded like someone puffing on an electronic cigarette. She wasn't getting enough air and he didn't know what to do about it.

Her temperature dropped shortly afterwards, and the speed of it was what scared him the most. She'd gone from burning up to shivering in her sleep within just a couple of minutes. Copeland flicked through his kitbag for something to treat her with, but there was nothing obvious, nothing he could do except maybe ease her suffering, and he wasn't ready to give up the fight just yet.

The battle was lost just before midnight, when Jill took one last deep breath, shuddered and then breathed no more. Copeland had been expecting it, he'd seen all the signs, but his heart hadn't known it and when he checked her pulse and there was nothing, it finally broke.

"Fuck!"

He shouted the word as though it could offer some sort of salvation, but it was just cathartic. He didn't know what else he could have done, but he still felt guilty, as though if he'd watched over her during her final hours, he could have stopped her from falling into the big sleep.

It was starting to get dark outside, but Copeland didn't care. He managed to find a couple of outdoor candles, the kind designed to ward away the moths and midges, and while they didn't give off much light, it was enough to dig a grave by. The hole had almost been big enough for Big Jim to fit inside, but now Jill needed to slide in beside him. It wasn't the perfect burial, but he had to give her something. He couldn't just leave her there.

Tom Copeland wiped the sweat from his brow on his dirty T-shirt and then dug the shovel into the dirt again. It was going to be a long night.

COPELAND FINISHED THE GRAVE at 2 AM, and it was 3:30 AM by the time that he'd dragged the two bodies out into the hole in the ground and covered them up with the excess sod. He patted it down in the candlelight and smoothed it over as best as he could. Then he tossed the shovel to the ground and walked back towards the caravan. He didn't care about the noise he was making. The way he saw it, if the animals found him, they found him. But there was no wildlife around, and the night remained eerily quiet except for the sounds he made himself. It seemed like he was the only living creature for miles around.

When he entered the caravan, he slid the clumsy lock on the door across and then flopped into Jill MacDonald's deathbed. It still smelled of her, not the perfumed smell of the pre-quarantine world but the earthy, gone-off milk smell that was cultivated by a lack of running water.

He settled down at the table with a battered old notebook and a couple of pencils and began to write.

***

What makes the animals act the way they do? Is it a virus? Something that can be passed between species? And what happens when it spreads to homo sapiens?

I have a theory, though it's impossible to verify. I think it started at Sunnyvale and that it began to evolve with each subsequent species that it spread to. The great siege of Sunnyvale was only the beginning. Somehow, the quarantine didn't hold and the virus continued to spread. And then the virus spread to people. God knows why it didn't kill us all in the admin building, maybe because we didn't come into contact with it. It can't be airborne. It must be transmitted through the blood or the consumption of infected flesh. Christ, and Sunnyvale supplied half the supermarkets in the country.

But why did the animals act the way they did? I'd guess that the pathogen flows through the blood and takes over the brain, focusing it on the most primal urges of all. The urges to kill, to eat and to reproduce. Perhaps some part of the core personality remains, in both animals and people, and maybe there's even a cure. If there's anyone left to work on it.

And then there's the Rat King. That unholy thing must have come about for a reason. Maybe the rumours are true and Big Jim created it by tying rats' tails together. Maybe it somehow came about organically. For my part, I believe it's a symptom or perhaps even the cause of the disease. And I believe that it's my job to kill it.

I have to go back to Sunnyvale. I have to face off against the Rat King.

***

He fell asleep almost immediately, before he even took his boots off.

He spent the following day just lying there, too demoralised to take a bite to eat from his dwindling supplies. Besides, his muscles had seized up from the digging and he was coming down with something. He felt like a lone man on a desert island, just waiting hopelessly on the beach for a rescue that might never come. He almost hoped that the animals would find him there in his aluminium tomb and smash the thing apart while he was still in it. But no such luck.

He was so worn out that he slept for eighteen of the next twenty-four hours, but when he finally woke up, a little sanity had returned. Not much, but a little.

It was enough to restore a sense of self-preservation, and so Copeland spent the day cataloguing the last of the supplies and packing the essentials into plastic bags. There were three vehicles out front if you included the Mini they'd arrived in. The plan was to get one of them to work, but he didn't want to start fiddling with the vehicles until it was time to go. If he packed the stuff and couldn't get a car going, he'd have to think of something else. But in the meantime, packing the bags and cataloguing the supplies with the notepad that Jill had been drawing on gave him something to do with his time, something to distract his mind. It was all he had.

As for the destination... well, he had a little something in mind. There was only one place he *could* go. He was going to go back to Sunnyvale. He was going to go back to where it all began.

Copeland finished his packing in the early evening and then turned his attention to the vehicles. The Mini was totalled thanks to Big Jim's handiwork with the wiring, and another of the vehicles was shot to begin with. It was propped up on bricks and missing its front wheels, a piece of gypsy art that could have cost a life when the outbreak began.

That left a little red Peugeot. Copeland hadn't learned a thing from Big Jim and so he had no idea how to hotwire it, but he didn't need to. He simply smashed the window with the butt of his axe and unlocked the door from the inside. Then he searched the vehicle, lucking out by discovering a key taped to the back of one of the visors. He did the same thing himself, and he always had done. It was an old habit from back in the days when no one thought twice about leaving their doors unlocked. It was an outdated way of thinking in this day and age, but he was thankful for the small mercy nonetheless. It even had a quarter tank of fuel – not much in the grand scheme of things, perhaps, but enough to get him to his destination.

Copeland opened the boot, then carried his supplies from the caravan two bags at a time with the axe tucked into his belt. He wished he had a different weapon instead of the one he'd used to put Big Jim out of his misery, but beggars couldn't be choosers. It was all he had.

With the boot full, Copeland slammed it shut and started loading the last few bags into the back seat. It was mostly dried foods like crisps and instant noodles that hadn't expired and which, while not exactly healthy, would at least keep his body going. For a while, at least.

He left the caravan door open as though to show that there had once been some life there, and then he climbed back into the driver's seat and shut the door. He strapped himself in.

Then he saw something in the rear-view mirror that almost gave him a coronary.

It was Jill MacDonald, back from the grave and with hair that looked like a rat's nest. She was covered with dirt and even from inside the car, Copeland could see her eyes. There was something wrong, but it took him a moment to figure out what it was. The pupils filled the whiteness like a single punctuation mark on a piece of paper. They were blacker than the blackest black. It was like she had two black holes in the middle of her face.

She had her mouth open as though she was trying to talk, but Copeland couldn't hear anything. He'd thought it was the roar of the engine that he heard in his ears, but perhaps it was just his blood as it pounded its way through his system.

Jill held a hand up, but Copeland knew it wasn't Jill anymore. She was dead, he knew she was dead, and that made what came next a little easier. He put the vehicle in reverse and drove it straight towards her. He couldn't pick up enough speed to do any real damage, but he hit her at about twenty and knocked her back down. Copeland swerved the car around and then hit the accelerator, bouncing up and down in his seat as the car rolled over the body. Then he put the car into neutral and applied the handbrake before unbuckling his seatbelt, grabbing his hatchet from the passenger seat and exiting the vehicle.

He walked over to where Jill MacDonald – or the shell of Jill MacDonald – was pulling itself to its feet. It was bleeding heavily from one side of its face, and even from a distance, Copeland could see that it wasn't the right colour. It was the colour of the dead, the same colour he'd seen when he'd finished Big Jim off with the axe to the head, and in what felt like a perverse déjà vu he found himself covering the same ground again, swinging the axe in the same way, his arm shuddering at the moment of impact as something worked its way loose inside him. He didn't aim for the head this time, but only because he couldn't bear to do it. Instead, he swung for the heart, and there was a viscous *schlop* as the axe connected. Jill's chest caved in from the impact and part of her ribcage flew out into the air and hit him in the face. He closed his eyes just in time to avoid losing one.

The force of the impact drove Jill back down to the floor, but it didn't stop her from moving. Her chest stayed flat because she wasn't breathing, but her arms and legs twitched as the virus flooded her system and tried to take over. But it was too late. She was dying again, this time for good.

Copeland hit her with the axe again and then again until there was nothing left of her ribcage and nothing left of her heart. The eyes were still open, but she wasn't moving. He grabbed the corpse by its legs and dragged it back over to where Big Jim was buried. The earth he'd scattered across the top was in disarray from where Jill had dug herself out of the ground. He dumped the body unceremoniously back where it belonged.

Then he returned to the car and cut the engine before getting down to the task in hand. Burial alone hadn't been enough. He'd have to try a cremation.

***

Tom Copeland spent one last night in the caravan, but he had a lot of work to do before he could lay his head down. He started by gathering wood, books and other flammable materials from both the caravans and the field they were parked in.

He had no idea how to build a pyre and he couldn't exactly Google it with no mobile phone, no network coverage and no electricity. So instead he did his best, building the thing like he was getting ready to burn a guy in November. He started with a thin layer of kindling at the bottom, which he'd light to start the thing, before layering up on top of that. It was maybe four feet high and as many across, more like a dome of jelly than a funeral pyre, but it would have to do. Jill MacDonald's body was heavy, even though it didn't look it, and he grunted as he heaved it onto his shoulder and from there to the top of the pyre. The woodpile shook slightly but somehow held up.

Copeland lit the kindling at the bottom of the pile using the mechanical oven lighter that hung from the wall beside the gas stove in the caravan. The fire started slowly to begin with, but it spread rapidly and before long the lower half of the pyre was on fire. It went up faster after he poured a little gasoline on. He didn't use much, because he didn't have much of the stuff going spare, but there was enough to get a pretty good blaze going and then the wood did the rest.

He stayed out there for a while, for long enough to make sure that Jill wasn't about to get back up again any time soon, but the smell of cooking flesh was disconcerting and started clinging to his nostrils. Even when he went back into the caravan, he could still smell it. He slept feverishly, the sweat pouring down his brow and into his eyes. He remembered waking up at one point and praying that he wasn't infected himself.

When he woke up properly, the pyre was still smouldering, although the majority of the flames had gone out. Jill MacDonald hadn't risen from the grave, but she hadn't been cremated either, not fully. The skin had burned and bubbled away, mixing with the ash of the wood, but the bones were still there and her skull grinned up at him from its precarious place on the remnants of the woodpile. For a moment, his mind flashed back to an earlier time when he'd seen David Tennant play Hamlet, holding up a similar skull and delivering the immortal line.

He shook his head to clear it and then climbed back into his stolen car. He guessed it didn't matter anymore. He slipped the key into the ignition and gunned the engine. Then he drove away from the pyre and the caravan, watching them shrink in his rear-view mirror as the vehicle started out on the drive back to Sunnyvale.

***

It wasn't an easy drive.

Copeland was out of practise. He'd had to drive a lot back in the day, but he hadn't sat behind the wheel of a car since first starting at Sunnyvale all those months – or was it years? – ago. The feel of the machine was alien and unfamiliar, and he was just glad that he'd found an automatic instead of a manual. He'd supposed that learning to drive a car was like learning to ride a bike. But right then, he wouldn't have fancied his chances on a bicycle, either.

Copeland didn't have a plan, and he was pretty sure that he didn't have a hope either. Truth be told, he didn't have a clue what he was doing or why he was doing it, but he had to do *something*. Everyone else was dead and he was all alone out there in an apocalyptic wasteland, if an abandoned rest stop in the Home Counties could count. And now it was time for him to go back to where it all began. He didn't know what he'd find there. Some sort of closure, perhaps.

Throughout the drive, he let his mind relax as much as he could. He just watched the world as it rolled by in front of his windscreen. He hummed to himself as he steered his vehicle through burnt-out cars and abandoned motorbikes, winding his way through the back roads and the quintessential sleepy villages as he circled back towards the complex. He thought about the old admin building, still waiting for him out there like an infected tooth sticking out of the earth's gaping jaw. The bird shit and the blood and the guts and whatever else he'd left behind there was just so much plaque on a tongue that needed washing.

The thought of the birds should have scared the shit out of him, but it didn't. He was past that now, and his fear had stayed behind in the ashes of the funeral pyre. He knew it was only a matter of time. Death had always been a certainty, ever since he'd first crawled out of his mother's womb and into the world, but now it was closer than ever. It stalked him as he wound through the backstreets towards the complex. But its presence was almost comforting. When death finally came for him, he'd welcome it.

Until then, he had no way to defend himself, not really. The metal frame of the car might offer some protection and he still had his trusty hatchet, but that wouldn't be much use if the heavens opened and the birds came down again. Privately, Copeland thought that was unlikely. The world smelled of death and despair. He felt like he was alone. Not a creature was stirring, not even a mouse.

It was the silence and the lack of life that was most overwhelming. Everything was just too still. There were no birds flying in and out and pecking at the branches or rodents digging at the roots. There was only Tom Copeland, sitting behind the wheel and staring out at the road in front of him with his bloodshot eyes. His knuckles gripped the wheel so tightly that they shone white.

After a little while, he tried the radio, but it was just as dead as his former colleagues. Copeland wasn't surprised. He guessed he was less than ten miles away, a twenty-minute drive at most on a regular day, but it took him closer to an hour to reach the end of the long and winding road back towards the complex, which nestled amongst the hills like a tumour on the countryside.

It had been a long, long time since he'd first found himself on that road as Big Jim himself had escorted him onto the complex for his first day. A lot had happened in the days in between, and yet except for the subtle lack of life, very little felt different.

Copeland hummed to himself as he cruised the car along the narrow dirt path. In one of the fields off to the right, a large crater in the dirt and a trail of twisted metal marked where Darragh O'Rourke had made his final stand. Judging from the bones that were scattered across the field, he'd taken a good few of the animals with him. But surely not all of them. Either way, Copeland was still alone there.

He continued down the path for another half mile or so, inching his way closer and closer to the facility. The first of the two checkpoints was finally in sight when the vehicle puttered to a slow but inevitable stop. Judging from the dials, he was out of fuel, but he was close to his destination by now, and he didn't fancy picking through the abandoned army vehicles even if he took the time to refill the tank.

Tom Copeland got out of the car and slung his backpack over his shoulders before setting off on the rest of his journey on foot.

THE SUN WAS HIGH in the sky, and Copeland guessed it was the early afternoon. The snow was a distant memory and the sun felt good on his bare arms as he wandered around the checkpoint. He wasn't sure what he'd been expecting, but he hadn't been expecting it to be exactly the same as they'd left it.

"I don't get it," he murmured, knowing full well that there was no one around to reply to him. "Everyone's dead. They stayed dead. Or at least, I think they did."

It *looked* like they had. The corpses that had been left behind at the army checkpoint had broken down, their flesh decomposing over time until the maggots stripped their bones clean and left them lying there in the dirt to be bleached by the sunlight. Some of the corpses were still in their uniforms, but all of their meat was gone. Perhaps that was why they were staying dead. There was nothing left to hold them together.

He was still holding his axe, and he swung it idly as he walked through the detritus. He wasn't afraid. He just wanted to hit something.

In one of the tents, Copeland found the corpse of a soldier that hadn't been there before, but it wasn't a threat. It was little more than a soupy stew of bones and mucus in an army uniform. Copeland held his nose as he approached it and nudged it with his foot, and then his eyes lit upon something attached to the back of it. It was a firearm, a 9mm handgun by the looks of it, although Copeland wasn't exactly an expert. Whatever it was, it was tucked into a little holster that was attached to the rest of the uniform by a belt.

Copeland picked up the gun and the holster, gingerly at
first, and then he took it outside. He wiped it off on the grass
and then attached it to his own belt.

On his way out into no man's land, he caught a glimpse
of himself in the door mirror of one of the abandoned army
cars. His hair had grown long and dishevelled and his eyes
were so bloodshot that the little arteries traced lines across
the surface like a treasure map. He also had a thin but
noticeable beard, and when he opened his mouth to check
his teeth out, he saw they were stained a dirty yellow and
covered with plaque and other build-up. The face itself had
lost a lot of weight, and so had the rest of his body. The gun
at his waist made him look like a junk-addicted gunslinger.

But it was the walk that he noticed the most. He walked
like a man with nothing left to lose, which is exactly what he
was. He was the loneliest man in the universe.

He put one foot in front of the other and kept on
walking.

***

The no man's land between the first and the second
checkpoint was a killing field. Copeland couldn't walk in a
straight line because his route kept being intercepted by the
carcasses of Sunnyvale's livestock. It was the cows that were
the worst. Their ribcages stuck out of the ground like the
jaws of some giant Venus flytrap.

His route into the complex was unopposed again, and it
was in sharp contrast to when he'd fled it with the other
survivors, with a thousand head of cattle chasing them away
from there. Without all that life, Sunnyvale felt like the
remnants of a concentration camp after the liberators had
arrived, freed the prisoners and burned the thing to the
ground. Something crunched from near his feet and for a

second, he thought it was some other life. Then he realised that he'd stepped on a chicken's skull and that it had imploded beneath the weight of his boot.

Copeland continued to put one foot in front of another, sidestepping the corpses whenever he needed to. He kept one eye on the horizon and another on the floor in front of him. He had no desire to fall over.

The second checkpoint, the one that marked the entrance to the facility proper, was getting closer and closer, and before he knew it, he was passing through the ineffective barriers – the barriers that even the army had been forced to pull back from – and into the car park on the other side.

"It feels good to be back in Sunnyvale," he murmured, though he didn't know who he was saying it to or why. He certainly didn't believe it.

The vehicles in the car park had started to gather a coat of grime as the winds worked their way across the Chilterns and scooped up the dirt from the floor. The grass was supposed to be dead and buried beneath the gravel, but it had been a long time since the car park had been resurfaced and little shoots of green had already started to poke their way out from between the stones and the gravel.

Copeland walked on, out of the car park and towards the south-eastern corner of the complex. He still found himself picking through the occasional carcasses, including those of his former colleagues. He couldn't tell who was who, though. Their flesh had long since been stripped away and so all that was left were skulls and bones and little scraps of fabric from their uniforms. It reminded Copeland of unknown soldiers and mass graves. There was something dehumanising about it all.

The emotion – which had been building up inside him since he'd buried Jill MacDonald and then put her back down again after she'd risen from the grave – overwhelmed

him. It broke down the barriers of his mental aqueducts and
flowed through his body, sweeping everything away with it
as it went. It was like the banks of a great river breaking in
the middle of a tropical thunderstorm. The grief washed
over and overwhelmed him.

He dropped to his knees in despair, surrounded by
death and destruction. Then he threw back his head and he
howled.

***

Time passed, but Copeland had no idea how much.
He'd lost track, but it wasn't important. Time was something
that had happened before the quarantine, when there were
things to do and people to meet. It stretched out in front of
him like the track of a rollercoaster, and the big, long dip at
the end was looming.

Copeland looked around, but all he could see was death
and destruction. It was the end of days, not through
biochemical terrorism or nuclear warfare but through a
global pandemic. It was a man-made disease, a threat that
humanity had brought upon itself. And for all he knew, he
was the final representative of the human race. It was a job
that he was unprepared for, a herculean task that had been
thrust upon him without consultation.

He could feel the pressure weighing down on him like a
rucksack full of bricks. It was an enormous pressure,
something physical that threatened to swallow him whole
and drag him down into the ground, like Jill MacDonald in
her improvised grave.

Copeland sank down to his knees and felt the water
from the mud seeping through his dirty trousers and onto
his skin. It was cold and unpleasant, but it made him feel
alive again, at least for a moment. He curled himself up into

a ball and lay there in the moisture, waiting for the end to come.

But the end didn't come. Something else did.

It was a many-tailed, many-mouthed, ill-smelling fiend of a creature, a creature of legend and a favourite tale to be passed between the lips of the survivors during the quarantine. There were dozens – no, *hundreds* – of rats inside the writhing mass of living anger, and some of them had died and started to rot while others had grown larger and more powerful than they could ever have been by themselves. The Rat King had grown during the initial outbreak, but with most of the animals scattered to the four winds and nothing left for it to eat, it was starting to starve. It was feeling the pinch of the winter weather, as billions upon billions of animals had done before it.

But those billions upon billions of animals hadn't been the Rat King. And the Rat King was hungry.

Copeland was lucky. He heard it coming as it shuffled through the grass. He'd stood up, and he could see the movement in the long grass that had grown since Hector Fernandez had last mowed the stuff. He felt no fear, but he still reacted on instinct. He retreated to the asphalt path that circled the complex and hefted his axe.

The Rat King burst out of the grass twenty feet away and scuttled towards him at a remarkable speed. Copeland saw it and swung the axe before he had a chance to process what he was looking at. He took it in with the impassioned glance of a veterinarian examining a patient, but it could have been an alien for all he cared. It wasn't about his own academic interest anymore, and nor was it about the self-preservation that pushed him to save his own life. He just wanted to hit something with his hatchet, and the Rat King had volunteered itself by charging towards him.

It was a strange fight and an unusual showdown. The

Rat King was fast when its constituents were working together, but as soon as the first blow of the hatchet landed, it was every rat for itself. They pulled against each other and scrabbled for purchase while Copeland pounded down at them, each impact sending rat brains spraying through the air. Some of the rats, half-starved already and crazy with the panic, turned upon their brethren and started to eat the brains from each other's fur. And Copeland swung again and again and again.

The Rat King tried to run, but its own diversity worked against it. Thousands of tiny legs ran in different directions, and then the axe swung through the air and smashed into it, this time scoring a blow that ripped through flesh and tore the Rat King in half.

And then there were two of them, and then three and then four, and with every axe blow they were torn apart and multiplied like some sort of self-replicating amoeba. Copeland backed away from them, still swinging, and then he was off the path and in the grass. He couldn't see them, just their movement amongst the greenery, and he swung the axe through the air in big swathes, flattening the grass as the rat corpses surrounded him.

They began to pile up, and there was a turning point in the fight as they scattered to the winds, fighting and scrapping until there were a dozen Rat Kings, all battling for the crown like the Targaryens, gnashing away with their little teeth. Copeland kept swinging the axe in front of him, but the Rat King was now just a dozen rat princes, and they were retreating from him at the same time as they fought each other tooth and nail.

Copeland swung the axe again, his arms getting tired, and there was a nightmarish *splotch* sound as the hatchet hit them. There were eight rat princes left, then six, then three. They were wiping themselves out without his help, although he hefted the axe again anyway for good measure.

He made short work of the final three rat princes until all that was left was a single rat with a half dozen of its dead brothers entangled with it in a web of filth and gore and blood. The rat looked at Copeland and for a split second, it was as though the two of them were communicating. They shared the same unspoken thought.

Then the hatchet came down through the air one last time and obliterated the rat in a shower of blood and bone. Copeland hit it again and dimly registered the pain as it shot up his arm and into his shoulder. He thought he'd felt it pop out of his socket, but there'd be time to deal with that later. He hit the rat again. It was still twitching, as though its little whiskers were searching through the air for one last meal. He spat on it and then kicked it with a heavy boot.

Copeland picked himself up and walked back out of the grass and onto the asphalt. He started to walk along it towards the admin building. He made it a couple of dozen steps, the pain flaring up every time his feet hit the ground and sent little shockwaves through his body, and then he collapsed, spent and emotionally exhausted, to the ground.

Above him, the heavens opened. The first drops of rain started to fall as a lick of thunder rumbled across the hills. A storm was coming.

***

Copeland was dreaming of a time before the quarantine. It was a time before he'd even started to work at Sunnyvale, back when he ran his own practice in a sleepy little village. Before he'd been caught stealing ketamine from his own supply cupboards. Before he'd had a vasectomy and his wife had left him.

He was dreaming of a time when he used to cycle to

work through the English countryside, saluting the magpies as he saw them and whistling out-of-key pop songs. The birds used to sing with him, and it wasn't uncommon to see a badger or a fox running skittishly across the path, often forcing him to slam on the brakes and occasionally sending him headfirst over his own handlebars.

It was a vivid dream, a dream in technicolour, so close that he could smell freshly mown grass in the air and taste the faint tang in his saliva which reminded him it was pollen season and that he hadn't had a tablet. It was the kind of dream that he used to have as a kid, when he'd wake up at eight on a Saturday morning swearing blind that the weekend had already happened and he was due at school to hand a paper in. It was the kind of dream that he never wanted to leave, a painless, cotton wool type of dream where everything was fine and no one and nothing came to harm.

It was a nice, relaxing dream, a defence mechanism that his tired mind had thrown up to distract him from where he really was and what was going on around him. He wanted to grab hold of it and to grip it so tight that it couldn't escape from him. He wanted to stay in the dream and to never wake back up again. But nothing lasted forever, and he swam back to consciousness with all the grace of a toddler trying to stay above the waterline by flailing its arms in a windmill.

When he woke up, he was soaked right through to the bone, lying there on the asphalt in half an inch of water while the heavens continued to pour down on him. In any other circumstances, the rain might have been refreshing. Then and there, as he bumbled reluctantly to full consciousness, it was an unwelcome guest, like Jehovah's Witnesses at the door on a Sunday morning, back before the shit had hit the fan and the world had ended.

Copeland pulled himself up to his feet and wrapped his arms around his shoulders. He was starting to shiver, and he was pretty sure from the acrid smell that was following him around that he'd pissed himself, either when he was asleep or when he was swinging the axe at the Rat King. His shoulder still ached and throbbed something rotten, hanging loosely from its socket. He groaned, gripped the bad arm with the good one and popped his shoulder back into place with a resounding click that echoed out across the complex like a fart in a church.

The pain was so bad that he blacked out from it.

When he returned to consciousness, his arm looked much better and the pain was mostly gone. He dragged himself to his feet again and took a moment or two to check himself over for bite marks. He worried that he'd been out so hard and so long that something could have started nibbling on him without him noticing. For all he knew, a bite from an infected ant or a sting from an infected wasp could be enough to turn him over to the dark side. He'd seen what happened to Jill MacDonald and he didn't want that to happen to him.

He seemed to be clean, but that didn't mean he'd stay that way. And as much as the animals posed a threat, they couldn't hurt him if there were none of them left. Right then, the weather was his biggest enemy, and the dark, grey clouds that were blowing in on the wind signalled that the worst was yet to come.

Copeland retreated for cover to the most logical place. He retreated towards the admin building.

THE RAIN STARTED COMING DOWN harder, and
Copeland was dismayed to see that the admin building was
no longer waterproof. In the weeks since he'd fled the place
with Big Jim, Jill MacDonald and Darragh O'Rourke, part of
the roof had collapsed, many of the windows had been
smashed and the elements had taken their toll. The guano on
the walls had started to grow mould. There were few signs
that the admin building had ever been fit for purpose.

Copeland meandered through the building, not really
sure what he was looking for. A memory, perhaps. Some
sign that life had once been normal, or normal enough that
he could order a pizza from a smartphone app or stop by the
butchery in a supermarket to pick up some sausages. But the
sausages had fought back, and the pigs he'd helped the
Sunnyvale machine to grow had run amok and broken loose.
Now they ruled the roost, wherever the hell they were.

The former veterinarian wandered around the empty
building, casting his eyes around the rooms he used to work
in. It was dark and dirty. The death still hung on the air and
the shit from the birds had started to congeal and to meld
with the wallpaper and the carpets. When he looked out of
some of the windows, he could see skeletons at the bottom
where they'd been tossed out of the complex. He could
recognise a few of them.

There was nothing there for him, but he hadn't been
expecting to find anything. He'd been expecting to find
himself back in the darkness at Sunnyvale and to let it wash
over him. He hadn't been expecting to kill the Rat King. He
hadn't been expecting the wind and the rain to whip at his

face even on the inside of the building thanks to the broken windows and the crumbling walls. And he hadn't been expecting it to still stink of shit even though it was remarkably well ventilated.

The storm got worse, and Tom Copeland found himself huddling beneath the remains of Old MacDonald's mahogany desk as he tried to protect himself from the elements. The wind and the rain soaked through his flesh and chilled him to the bone. He started shivering, and he knew that once he started shivering, he wasn't going to be able to stop.

He looked down at the gun in his lap, then pulled it out of its holster and fiddled around with the safety. He had no idea what he was doing, but he figured it out as he went and managed to first check it was loaded before he overrode the safety catch.

Then he lifted the gun up and held it against the side of his head. The metal of the barrel felt unnaturally cold against his skin, even when he was already shivering from the wind and rain. It felt artificial, too. He'd never held a gun before, and he'd never thought he'd be holding one for real, especially not up against his temple with his finger upon the trigger. He paused there for a moment, feeling ridiculous, and then he was lit up as a bolt of lightning touched down in the grounds somewhere. The thunderclap hit shortly afterwards and ripped through the building like an earthquake.

Copeland lowered the gun and tried to wait it out, but the night got darker and darker and his mind turned to what he'd had before the outbreak, his cosy little house with his cosy little family and his cosy little veterinary practice. He'd had it all, and now it was gone. And as the rains kept pouring and the winds kept blowing, the despair grew worse and worse and worse until there was nothing left but the emptiness that Jill MacDonald had left when he'd burned her corpse and found himself all alone in the apocalypse.

He picked up the gun again and put the muzzle against his head. Then he pulled the trigger.

***

Somehow, Tom Copeland survived the night.

It started with the gun, which jammed and didn't bang. When Copeland pulled the trigger, something *did* happen, but the bullet remained inside the weapon and his brains stayed inside his head. Confused, he pointed the weapon at the ceiling and pulled the trigger again. This time, it did go off, and when the second bullet hit the first one, the two of them combined into a wall of lead which ripped half the barrel off. It wouldn't fire after that. Copeland wasn't sure whether it was the gun itself or whether it was out of ammunition. It didn't really matter.

His hand was bleeding freely and he was temporarily deaf, and he was also shaking from the shock and the adrenaline. Still, the veterinarian took the misfired firearm as a sign from above. He didn't believe in God, especially after what he'd seen since the start of the quarantine, but he did think of himself as a fate agnostic. Clearly, the gun wasn't meant to be.

"I'll have to think of something else," he murmured, and then he jumped at the sound of his own voice. He hadn't realised until just then how lonely he was. He was potentially the last man on Earth. It was a sobering thought, and it pushed the thoughts of suicide to the back of his mind, at least for a while. It wouldn't be fair on the rest of his race. He had to fight, to survive. He *had* to. He had to do it for everyone else who'd died along the way.

The storm got worse before it got better. By the end of the night, Copeland was so cold that he worried about pneumonia and hypothermia. He knew what the symptoms were in animals and could make a pretty good guess as to what they'd look like if they manifested in his own system. By the time that the rains stopped and the winds slowed down, his skin had taken on a blueish tinge and his limbs were shaking so badly that they stopped him from sleeping, although his mind wasn't helping him there, either. He kept himself busy by counting sheep, but it didn't take him to sleep. Each of his imaginary animals wanted to kill him, so they kept him on his toes.

When the sun rose the following morning, it was the most beautiful sunrise Copeland had ever seen. It was a bloody sunrise, a screaming, claret salute to the new day. For Copeland, it was worth more than just the warmth. It gave him hope, the rarest commodity of all. He couldn't remember the last time he'd had some. He even felt good enough to dip into his supplies, treating himself to a slap-up meal of stale crackers. It wasn't much, but in comparison to some of the other meals he'd had since the outbreak it was a positive treat.

He ate his meal on the rooftop by exiting through the gantry in MacDonald's old office. The roof was in even worse condition than the interior of the building, and he could see the skeletons of several of the former survivors where they'd fallen in the battle of the admin building. Once upon a time, he would have found the sight disconcerting. Now, after everything he'd seen and everything he'd done, it didn't bother him. He let his eyes wander lazily across the scene while he ate the crackers. He devoured every last crumb.

By the time he'd finished eating, his clothes had dried out in the sunshine and a little colour had returned to his cheeks. He sat down on the gantry and swung his legs out into the open air. He had nothing to do, nowhere to go, but he had hope again. And there was something else. He could hear something.

It was a sound that he hadn't heard for what felt like half an eternity. It was an alien sound, one that he hadn't even heard at Sunnyvale before the quarantine.

It was the sound of birds in song, carried peacefully on the breeze from the trees that lined the facility's perimeter. He couldn't see them, but he didn't need to see them. Just hearing them was enough.

Then he noticed something else that felt different somehow. It was written across his face and stretched from his lips to his eyes.

It was a smile.

Copeland reached back into his pack and pulled out some more of the crackers, which he crushed into little crumbs and scattered to the wind. He was patient and happy to wait, and the birds seemed scared and timid, as though they were tired of the blood and the death. But he continued to scatter the crumbs from the rooftop until they picked up the courage to approach. It started with a magpie, which he saluted, and then it was followed by another.

Two for joy, he thought.

The magpies were followed by a starling and then a couple of blackbirds. Copeland watched, mesmerised, continuing to throw the crumbs. The birds hopped a little closer and he threw the last of his crumbled supplies in their direction. He held out his hand, more out of instinct and a vague, uncertain hope than anything else. And to his surprise, a tiny little robin flew down from somewhere behind him and landed on it. He could have crushed the thing's skull if he'd wanted to, or at least if he'd been able to close his hand fast enough to catch the bird before it flew away. But he didn't want to kill it. There'd been enough death, enough destruction, enough blood and broken bone.

It was time to try something a little different.

***

Out in the grounds and over in no man's land, a peace had descended. There was no sign of humanity, but the animals seemed like they were their old selves again, as though the virus had run its course or as though those who'd remained uninfected had been able to develop an immunity. An owl was asleep in one of the trees, and a hornet's nest in another was alive with activity. In one of the ditches, a family of voles huddled up for warmth and groomed each other.

The animals came from everywhere and nowhere. Some were former Sunnyvale residents, marked out by their concentration camp style tattoos and the electronic tags in the ears of the larger, more valuable animals. Others were new arrivals, attracted to ground zero by some sixth sense. Here and there, a symptom of the great plague would manifest itself and one of the animals would attack another, but it could also have been their natural instincts reasserting their dominance. For the most part, the horror seemed to be over. The disease had burned itself out, the infected animals had finally succumbed to it, and the only ones left were those with some sort of natural immunity.

A cow meandered lazily eastwards, chewing at the grass and pausing to take a gargantuan shit in a patch its mouth had just mown down. Its udders were distended from years of captivity and intense milking, but the look on its face was one of beatific happiness, like a blind man who was somehow able to see again.

A pig was heading west, trotting along on its little

hooves and digging up huge chunks of earth. It was a big beast, much bigger than Sunnyvale's pigs were usually allowed to grow.

From the south, a sheep walked north, its overgrown wool looking like ovine dreadlocks. It was matted with shit and mud, the white wool dyed brown. It was bleating as it went, a horrible, almost artificial sound that broke through the silence like a fire alarm at a burning warehouse.

And from the north, a chicken walked south, strutting as it went and pausing every now and then to peck at an invisible morsel amongst the grass, a bug perhaps or a speck of grain that had been carried away from the complex by the winds. The chicken hopped along with a carefree surety that was a remnant of a simpler time, some moment in its evolutionary ancestry in which its brethren had been kept in fields instead of under metal roofs and artificial lights.

The animals met up in the middle of the field and stood side by side as though they were posing for a calendar. Life was almost back to normal, or as normal as it had ever been for the animals. They grouped together as though they were huddling for warmth, but they paid little attention to each other. The cow, the biggest of the animals, had its head down and was ruminating on the long grass. The pig was lying down, the roots of its docked tail twitching as it tried to swish it to the left and right. The chicken was still pecking at the grass, and it twitched its head backwards and flicked a worm up into the air. It caught it as it fell back down again. And over to one side, the sheep simply stood there and stared at nothing.

Forty feet away, the two hundred and six bones of an adult human's body were exposed to the elements, all of the skin long since nibbled and pecked away. But the skull and the ribcage poked out of the dirt, and it was the ribcage that poked out the highest. It had been savaged by something, some large animal which had smashed apart the bones until they stuck out of the mud like the crow's nest of a sinking pirate ship.

A raven flew down and landed on the ribs, driving them a little deeper into the ground. It stretched its wings and flapped them twice before tucking them away. It cawed, and the sound echoed out across the wilderness. The chicken turned to look at it, but the other three animals all ignored it. It was no threat to them, and they were no threat to it. They could coexist in peace, at last.

The raven hopped off the rib and on to the grass, where it pecked at the mud like the chickens for a couple of beats before something startled it and it took to the air again, unfurling its wings like some feudal banner and flapping them in the breeze. Within seconds, it was two hundred feet high and still climbing.

Sunnyvale was stretched out beneath it, a cancerous blight on the British countryside. But as the crow flew higher and higher, the blight shrank from the size of a large tumour to the size of a beauty mark, and then a mole, and then just the tip of a needle or a tiny pencil mark on an otherwise pristine piece of paper. And then the crow flew higher still and Sunnyvale disappeared beneath it.

Up there, in the sky, it was peaceful at last. The crow spread its wings and flew to the east, towards the still-rising sun. It was the beginning of a new day, a new tomorrow. The rape of the planet was over. It was time for a new species to rise to the top of the food chain.

THE END

APPENDIX I: LIST OF SUNNYVALE EMPLOYEES

WHILE JOHN MCDONALD is the only person who knows how many employees are officially on the company's payroll, most estimates put it at around three to four hundred full-time employees and part-time contractors. Many of them played no part in the events of the novel and so for the sake of brevity and usefulness, they're not included here.

The major characters are shown below and listed alphabetically by department. The euphemistic title of "production worker" is given by Sunnyvale to any minimum wage employee who works on the production line, regardless of their actual role or the type of animal that they work with.

ADMIN

Bugsy Drew: Operations Manager
Maude Harrison: Receptionist
Jill MacDonald: Trainee Receptionist
John MacDonald: Chief Executive Officer (CEO)
Carol Rawlings: Secretary/Personal Assistant

AVIAN

Hamish Gray: Production Worker
Jerry Jones: Production Worker
Robert "Bob" Knowles: Production Worker
Steve "Steve-o" Puck: Production Worker
Yvonne Strong: Production Worker

COWS

Will Makon: Production Worker

OTHER

Tom Copeland: Veterinarian-in-Chief
Hector Fernandez: Cleaner

PIGS

Pete Fields: Section Manager
Keith Gowan: Production Worker
Janet Peston: Production Worker
Kim Roach: Production Worker

SECURITY

James "Big Jim" Benton: Head of Security
Mike Chase: Junior Security Officer
Jack Dunlop: Junior Security Officer
Greg Hamze: Security Officer
Darragh O'Rourke: Deputy Head of Security
Carl "Phil" Taylor: Security Officer

SHEEP

Lee Keyes: Production Worker
Bruce Laing: Production Worker
Arnie Lorn: Supervisor

SLAUGHTERHOUSE

Neil Gibson: Production Worker
Bill Long: Production Worker

ANIMALS

Broiler chickens: 90,000
Dairy cows: 9,000
Egg chickens: 70,000
Fish: 480,000
Geese: 18,000
Meat cows: 9,000
Pigs: 18,000
Sheep: 9,000
Turkeys: 24,000
Veal cows: 2,000

NON-EMPLOYEES

Diane Hyde: Environmental Health Inspector
Dena Lymbery: Environmental Health Supervisor
Rob Roland: Deputy Head Protestor from Buckinghamshire Save
Ben Runciman: Lieutenant Colonel in the British Army

Alisha Yorke: Young Protestor from Buckinghamshire Save
Harry Yorke: Head Protestor from Buckinghamshire Save
Jack Yorke: Young Protestor from Buckinghamshire Save
Janet Yorke: Protestor from Buckinghamshire Save

APPENDIX II: FURTHER READING AND RESOURCES

IF YOU'D LIKE to learn more about the subjects that are covered in this book, I recommend the following:

BOOKS

Animal Factory (2011)
by **David Kirby**

Eating Animals (2011)
by **Jonathan Safran Foer**

Factory Farming (1991)
by **Andrew Johnson**

Farmageddon: The True Cost of Cheap Meat (2015)
by **Philip Lymbery** and **Isabel Oakeshott**

Farmageddon in Pictures (2017)
by **Philip Lymbery**

Gristle: From Factory Farms to Food Safety (2010)
edited by **Moby** with **Miyun Park**

DOCUMENTARIES

Cowspiracy (2014)
by **Kip Anderson** and **Keegan Kuhn**

Earthlings (2005)
by **Shaun Monson**

Farm to Fridge (2011)
by **Lee Iovino**

iAnimal: Through the Eyes of a Pig (2016)
by **Shad Clark** and **Jose Valle**

Meat the Truth (2007)
by **Gertjan Zwanikken**

Our Daily Bread (2005)
by **Nikolaus Geyrhalter**

PlantPure Nation (2015)
by **Nelson Campbell**

Speciesism: The Movie (2013)
by **Mark Devries**

The Animals Film (1981)
by **Victor Schonfeld** and **Myriam Alaux**

The Game Changers (2018)
by **Louie Psihoyos**

The Ghosts in Our Machine (2013)
by **Liz Marshall**

VEGUCATED (2011)
by **Marisa Miller Wolfson**

What the Health (2017)
by **Kip Anderson** and **Keegan Kuhn**

What You Eat Matters (2018)
by **Nina Messinger**

CHARITIES

Compassion in World Farming:
http://www.ciwf.org.uk

Compassion Over Killing:
http://www.cok.net

Mercy for Animals
http://www.mercyforanimals.org

APPENDIX III: INTERVIEWS WITH THE EXPERTS

WHILE I WAS WORKING ON THIS BOOK, I was able to interview a number of experts to pick up some tips, tricks and advice to help make the virus – and the setting itself – more realistic. Here are the highlights.

Pembroke Sinclair

Pembroke Sinclair is the pseudonym of author Jessica Robinson, a zombie expert. As well as writing *Life After the Undead* and *Death to the Undead*, two post-apocalyptic zombie novels, she's also the author of non-fiction book *Undead Obsessed: Finding Meaning in Zombies*, which tracks her obsession with zombies and documents her research.

What are some of the best/most high-profile uses of zombie animals (and particularly zombie livestock) in books and other media?

The only zombie animals I can think of off the top of my head come from *Resident Evil*. If you recall, they had some zombie dogs, and I think as the films go on, a few other animals mutate. There's also the film *Zombeavers*, which I highly recommend. It was hilarious! There was also this horrible zombie film about a fried chicken place that's built on an Indian burial ground that turned people into zombies. I can't remember what it was called, but it was one of the only zombie movies I turned off because it was awful.

In *28 Days Later*, infected chimps turned people into zombies, although they weren't zombies themselves. There was also a film called *Forest of the Dead* where science genetically alters trees so that they grow faster and the sap turns people into zombies. Not the best film, but I didn't turn it off.

Other than that, I can't really think of any zombie animal films or stories. There may be an occasional animal here or there that has turned, but nothing where they're the main cause.

Can you recommend any good non-fiction books about zombies?

There are a lot of books that look at film criticism when it comes to zombies, but none that really explore what makes a zombie a zombie.

Where did you do your research about zombies?

My research on zombies took me to a lot of different places. The main goal for my non-fiction book was to look at how our environment could potentially lead to the creation of zombies. I looked at viruses, biological weapons and genetically modified organisms (a practice that science has been doing to our food for a while) among other things.

For your case, you'll want to look into bovine spongiform encephalopathy, more commonly known as mad cow disease. It actually started in England, and it involves cows consuming other cows that have been infected with the disease. It affects prions (misfolded proteins) in the spinal column and brain. It can also be spread to humans through consumption.

I'd guarantee there are professors and scientists all over England who are looking into the problem. Here in Wyoming, we have a state vet lab, and I know there's a scientist/professor there who's working on this disease, but I never had the chance to interview him for my book. It's both fascinating and scary.

Have you got any other advice/pointers that are relevant?

Please remember that zombies are fictional, which means that you can make them be and do anything you want. While it's fun and intriguing to base the story in reality (and by all means, do it), don't forget to have fun!

Lindsay Wolf

Lindsay Wolf is the Vice President of Investigations at Mercy for Animals, an international non-profit organisation that's all about preventing cruelty to animals on factory farms and encouraging people to adopt a vegan diet. Headquartered in Los Angeles, the organisation has also carried out a number of undercover operations since being established in 1999.

Please provide a top-line overview of how factory farmed animals are often mistreated.

This is a very broad question, but some of the standard practices that take place in the animal agriculture industry include suffocating or grinding up male chicks in the egg industry, confining hens to cruel battery cages, pigs to gestation/farrowing crates and baby calves in veal crates, castrating piglets and tail docking animals without painkillers, forcefully impregnating cows in the dairy industry and taking their babies from them shortly after birth, overcrowding, animals suffering from injuries and illnesses, and overall disgusting and disease-ridden environments.

Are multiple species often grouped at the same facility?

It depends on the facility, but farms are typically focussed on individual animals: egg laying hens, broiler chickens, dairy cows, etc.

What kind of illnesses and diseases do the animals suffer from?

These industries are disgusting and a breeding ground for bacteria and diseases. There are a plethora of illnesses that farmed animals are forced to endure. If you Google "farmed animal illnesses," "injuries," etc., you'll find a bunch of information.

What governing bodies are in place to ensure compliance? What sort of infringements do factory farms make? And are there any practices that are within the law but probably shouldn't be?

There are many practices that have been listed as exceptions within the animal agriculture industry, such as castration and tail docking without painkillers, extreme confinement, overcrowding, etc. If even one dog or cat were treated in the ways that farmed animals are treated, there could be felony level cruelty to animals charges. We also see routine animal abuse; animals punched, kicked, hit and thrown.

What are the animals fed? And how do they get water? Is the system usually manual or automated?

Much of this depends on the facility and the type of animal. But in general, automated feeding/watering systems are used.

Philip Lymbery

Philip Lymbery is the CEO of Compassion in World Farming (CIWF) and the author of *Farmageddon: The True Cost of Cheap Meat* and *Dead Zone: Where the Wild Things Were*. A keen birdwatcher, he's been active in the field of animal rights for over twenty-five years.

In all of your time working at CIWF, what's the worst case of cruelty that you've come across?

I was most shaken by the plight of pigs in China. I talk about this in my "Ethos" video[1] and also in the short video I filmed in China at the time[2].

What is it that first made you aware of cruelty to animals in factory farms/CAFOs (concentrated animal feeding operations)?

I was ignorant of factory farming until my teens. The moment that opened my eyes to the realities was when a speaker from Compassion in World Farming came to my school to do a talk. I remember being horrified at the pictures of pigs and calves in factory farms. The hens in battery cages and how they couldn't flap their wings (never mind fly!) particularly upset me. I thought about the wild birds that mesmerised me. The hens in cages seemed a crime. I was outraged, and I vowed to do something about it.

As a keen birdwatcher, what can you tell us about factory farming's effect on local ecologies/bird populations/etc.?

In my lifetime, Britain has lost forty-four million birds. That's a breeding pair every minute. Turtle doves, skylarks, barn owls and other once common farmland birds have gone into steep decline.

It's not just the birds and farm animals that have

---

[1] See: http://bit.ly/ethosfilm.
[2] See: http://bit.ly/farminginchina.

disappeared from the land, but also other animals and insects. In the last forty years, the total number of wild mammals, birds, reptiles, amphibians and fish worldwide has halved. It's a shocking statistic and even more shocking to realise that it's the food on our plate that's responsible for two thirds of wildlife loss.

And much of this decline is down to the two sides of factory farming.

The first side is where the animals are kept. Chickens taken from bushes and rangelands to be kept in cages. Mother pigs, who prefer to raise their piglets in woodland edges, kept in crates so narrow they can't turn around. Cattle taken from pastures to be confined in mega-dairies or feedlots where they're fed grain instead of grass.

What looks like a space-saving idea actually isn't. By keeping them caged, crammed and confined, we then have to grow their feed elsewhere, on scarce arable land, using chemical pesticides and fertilisers. Factory farming's second side.

As crop fields expand in the wake of industrialisation, so the trees, the bushes and the hedges disappear, along with wildflowers. And when they disappear, so too do the insects, and the seeds, and the birds, the bats, the bees that depend on them. Even the worms disappear, along with soil fertility, leaving little else but the crop.

Then we take this crop and feed it to factory farmed animals, losing most of the food value of that crop, be it in terms of calories or protein, as it's converted to factory farmed meat, milk and eggs.

What's the biggest threat from the meat industry in your eyes? Pollution? Diseases? Decreased antibiotic resistance?

It's hard to choose between these! We've been campaigning very hard on so many fronts for over fifty years. We need to cut consumption and production of animal products for so many reasons as explained in my books, *Farmageddon: The True Cost of Cheap Meat* and *Dead Zone: Where the Wild Things Were*. The campaign to end factory farming, transform food systems and redefine the role of livestock is being fought on grounds of animal welfare, public health, environment, biodiversity and more. For the sake of us all, we need fundamental change.

Food production is the biggest use for that most finite of resources: land. It already occupies nearly half of the Earth's useable land surface, and that proportion is growing by the day at the expense of forests. At the same time, the number of mammals, birds, reptiles, amphibians and fish has halved in the last forty years. Agriculture and the way we farm animals is at the heart of the problem for over 70 percent of globally threatened bird species.

Yet the global livestock population is set to near double by 2050, intensifying pressure still further on a natural world in steep decline.

Profiteers shout about a coming global food crisis and the need to double food production by mid-century. What they don't acknowledge is that the system already produces enough to feed everybody – and plenty more. Enough for sixteen billion people, in fact, if only we didn't waste it, not least through feeding factory farms instead of people. Industrial farming makes up a third of global production and is responsible for the greatest damage and the greatest inefficiency. The biggest single area of food waste comes not from what we throw in the bin, but from feeding human-edible crops to industrially reared animals, losing much of its calorific value in the process.

Why do you think more people aren't taking action against intensive factory farming and the meat industry? Is it just a case of people not knowing what they don't know?

I think that one of the problems is that consumers are deliberately kept in the dark about the reality of their food. Labels on meat, egg and dairy products are often the only clue we have into the life of the animal they came from and yet, all too often, they're extremely confusing. Labels on intensively reared products often display images of rolling landscapes, cosy family farms and happy animals when in reality the livestock are crammed into barren cages or kept in such close confinement with one another that they're unable to express their natural behaviours. Generic, meaningless phrases are brandished across a lot of factory farmed food packaging, such as "farm fresh" and "natural", when in fact more appropriate slogans would be "raised in confinement" or "grown quickly, without access to the outdoors".

In 2004, mandatory "method of production" labelling for all eggs sold in the European Union was introduced, allowing customers to easily see the system used to produce them, whether it be caged, barn, free-range, or organic. Since then, the proportion of hens in cage-free systems has more than doubled. When consumers know which farm system has been used to produce their eggs, many opt for higher welfare. In turn, this increases demand for higher welfare eggs, helping to drive welfare improvements for millions of egg-laying hens. This is an excellent example of how effective and honest labelling can re-shape the market.

Compassion in World Farming is campaigning for honest labelling. We believe that all meat and dairy products should be labelled by method of production, to show the conditions in which each animal was reared. Clear labelling would create confidence for producers wishing to invest in higher welfare farm systems.

What's one thing that everyone can do that will help to advance animal welfare and the goals of CIWF?

As consumers, we can also take action on our plate. We all have the power to reduce an awful lot of farm animal suffering and to save wildlife three times a day through our food choices, by choosing to eat more plants and less and better meat and dairy from animals kept pasture-fed, free range or organic.

What will happen if we continue with established factory farming practices? Can humanity even survive? What happens if China adopts the American approach to factory farming?

The way forward for healing our planet is to get animals out of cruel intensive systems and back on the land where they belong, in living landscapes. Mixed, rotational farming which works in partnership with nature and the wildlife that lives there is the ultimate key to preserving biodiversity.

Beyond political action, to enable more compassionate and wildlife-friendly farming to develop, the Western world needs to reduce consumption of meat and dairy, eating only from non-factory farmed foods.

We can't meet our Paris targets[3] unless we move to humane and sustainable food systems. The future of humankind really does depend on transforming food systems for the sake of our health, animals and the environment.

What's next for you? Will you be writing any more books or working on any documentary films? And what's the next big campaign that you want to focus on?

For me, bringing about a solution requires a global agreement to replace factory farming with common-sense farming before it's too late. I'm working on developing a campaign for a new global agreement, something akin to the framework UN convention on climate change, that would transform food systems, end factory farming and bring about humane and sustainable agriculture. I'll also be starting to write another book next year focusing on these issues.

---

[3] A legally binding global climate change agreement adopted at the Paris climate conference in December 2015. The aim is to limit global warming to below 2°C. For the agreement to be adopted, at least 55 countries representing at least 55 percent of global emissions had to provide their approval.

AFTERWORD

IT'S HARD TO WRITE the acknowledgements for a project that's been so long in the making. Still, the usual shout outs are due to Donna Woodings, Carl Woodings, Alan Woodings and Heather and Dave Clarke. Thanks are also due, as always, to my editor and partner in crime, Pam Elise Harris, as well as my cover designer, Larch Gallagher. It was a lot of fun to work with Steve Woodcock again for the illustrations, too.

I'd also like to say a big thank you to the Wycombe Arts Centre team and the extended community around it for the inspiration and support throughout the years. A surprising number of us are vegan (myself, Ruth Gunstone and Tabitha Gunstone-Pollock) or vegetarian (Dave Ford, Clive Whitelock and Amanda de Grey, amongst others). And thanks are also due to Amanda and Dr. Caroline Eliot from the Arts Centre for being my beta readers. Dr. Cedric Laize provided some additional military and firearms expertise, as well as beta reading part three.

When you write a book like *Meat*, you have to take certain liberties when it comes to the story line. Big factory farms on the scale of Sunnyvale are only really found outside of the UK, but in a period of political uncertainty, who knows what might happen? Now that Britain has left the EU – and therefore the remit of EU legislation – it's unclear at the time of writing what the future will look like.

Regardless, facilities like Sunnyvale tend to specialise in a particular animal, but I took some poetic licence for the sake of the story. Likewise, the virus that affects the animals (and the people!) in the novel isn't a thing… yet. That said, it's not as implausible as you might think. Approximately 80 percent of all antibiotics in use in the United States are given to farm animals. As viruses continue to build up a resistance to different strains of antibiotics, we may be left with no effective antibiotics with which to treat ourselves. On top of that, factory farms are a hotbed for propagation and mutation – so when the end times come, it could well start in a facility like Sunnyvale.

This book mostly focusses on the appalling conditions that factory farmed animals are exposed to, but factory farming also has a huge environmental cost that not many people are aware of. It destroys land, pollutes the water and takes up a huge amount of energy. Converting wheat into meat is a wasteful process – and it's certainly not the answer to global famine considering you end up with less food than you started with.

And unfortunately, it's not just the meat industry that's responsible. Eggs, milk and cheese are also produced in inhumane conditions, and even bees are mistreated to farm honey. If there's one thing that I've learned during the creation of this book, it's that human beings show no lack of imagination when it comes to making a profit. People (rightly) criticise the Yulin Dog Meat Festival because 10,000 dogs are killed there every year. But in comparison to some of the atrocities that happen across the globe every day just to fill people's dinner plates, the Yulin Dog Meat Festival is nothing.

I was a vegetarian when I started writing this book, but I was a vegan before it went through its first round of edits.

I'd been a vegetarian for twelve years, but after learning what I learned during the research phase, I realised it was no longer enough. And besides, I'd feel like a hypocrite if I released a book like this and still had eggs and cheese and milk.

After changing my diet, I felt a lot better. At the same time, it revitalised my love for food. Before I became vegan, I had stomach problems and no real appetite. Eating became a chore, something I had to do just to stay alive. After becoming vegan, I started to look forward to every meal, and it gave me a great excuse to branch out and to try new foods that I hadn't tried before.

The food that you eat is a personal choice, and I'm not here to tell you to become a vegan or a vegetarian. Just remember that the choice of what you put in your mouth is one of the few things that you have 100 percent control over. Too many people just blindly eat whatever's put in front of them without stopping to think about it. So while I'm not saying you should cut meat from your diet or eat less dairy, I do think you should be aware of what you're eating and where it's coming from. I guess that's the point of this book.

It's up to you what you eat and where you source it. I just hope that next time you're tucking into a juicy steak or a fast food burger, you think of Sunnyvale. Likewise, the goal of this book is to entertain first and to educate second. I just hope that it's made you see animals as something more than just cogs in a factory farm.

As human beings, we're the only species that can choose whether to be herbivores, omnivores or carnivores. Exercise that choice.

Now, who's hungry?

JOIN THE CONVERSATION

CONGRATULATIONS! YOU SURVIVED SUNNYVALE.

Whether you loved the book or you hated it, I want to hear your thoughts. Please do leave a short review on Amazon and/or Goodreads – and be sure to share it with me on your social networking site of choice! I love to learn from my readers' feedback, and I share my favourite reviews with my social media followers.

While you're at it, why not give me a follow to hear the latest book news as and when it happens? I'll see you sometime soon!

http://www.danecobain.com
http://www.twitter.com/danecobain
http://www.facebook.com/danecobainmusic
http://www.youtube.com/danecobain
http://www.instagram.com/danecobain

MORE GREAT READS
FROM DANE COBAIN

No Rest for the Wicked (Supernatural Thriller) When the Angels attack, there's *No Rest for the Wicked*. Cobain's debut novella, a supernatural thriller, follows the story of the elderly Father Montgomery as he tries to save the world, or at least, his parishioners, from mysterious, spectral assailants.

Former.ly: The Rise and Fall of a Social Network (Literary Fiction) When Dan Roberts starts his new job at Former.ly, he has no idea what he's getting into. The site deals in death. Its users share their innermost thoughts, which are stored privately until they die. Then, their posts are shared with the world, often with unexpected consequences.

Come On Up to the House (Horror) This horror novella and screenplay tells the story of Darran Jersey, a troubled teenager who moves into a house that's inhabited by the malevolent spirit of his predecessor. As tragedy after tragedy threatens to destroy the family, Darran's mother decides to leave the house and start afresh. But is it too late?

Driven (Detective/Mystery) Meet private detective James Leipfold and computer whizz kid Maile O'Hara in the first book of the Leipfold series. A car strikes in the middle of the night and a young actress lies dead in the road. Putting their differences aside, and brought together by a shared love of crosswords and busting bad guys, Maile and Leipfold investigate. But not all is as it seems...

Printed in Poland
by Amazon Fulfillment
Poland Sp. z o.o., Wrocław

63029036R00253